FOREVER Yours

BOOK 1
THE TEMPTATION SERIES

ANNIE CHARME

First Published in 2021 by Chambre Rose Publishing

Forever Yours. The Temptation Series.

ISBN: 978-1-7399906-0-2

Cover Designed by: Annie Charme

Formatted by: Lunaria Press, Inc.

This book is written by a British author. Therefore all spellings and grammar are British English.

Annie Charme on Spotify

cw: Infidelity. Mature themes. One discussion on a previous pregnancy loss and stillbirth that happened off page in the past.

*To all the women who are only known as the funny one,
the talented one, the intelligent one, the caring one...*

But never the sexy one...

*Embrace your beautiful body and be the sexy one as well...
Love yourself, whatever your shape or size...*

PROLOGUE

"You're my best friend, Steph."

"You're mine too, Cal." A lump forms in the back of my throat.

"There's nothing I want more than for us to be together." He pauses and sighs, leaning back against the headboard on his bed. "But if we broke up, our friendship would never be the same."

"I know you're right, but what if we never broke up? Who's to say we'll break up?" I pick at the baby blue nail varnish on my thumb while I swivel from side to side on Cal's desk chair.

"I care about our friendship too much." He tucks his unruly black hair behind his ears.

"I feel the same, but I'm willing to take the risk. Last night was one of the most amazing nights of my life. I don't think we can go back to just being friends after that, do you?"

"You felt it too?" He gazes into my eyes, fiddling with his eyebrow ring.

The stirring returns in my stomach. My body trembles while my mind scrambles to form the right words. His mesmerising dark brown eyes have me at his mercy. "Yes, it was incredible. I want us to be so much more than friends."

"Come here." He holds his arms out, beckoning me over to the bed.

I join him, and he hugs me tight. His warm breath in my hair sends a tingle through my core.

"I just don't want to lose you as a friend." He caresses my cheek with his large hand.

"You won't." My eyes plead with him, hoping he will kiss me again. I lick my dry lips and inch closer.

He tilts his head towards me. "I will, I know I will."

"I promise—if we break up—I'll always be your friend."

He kisses my forehead. "I hope you will. I couldn't bear to not have you in my life."

"Me neither." I sigh and hug him tighter.

"Did you have a good day at work?" He strokes my arm, swathing my skin in a flurry of goosebumps.

"Yes, I actually did." I spent all day reliving the memory of Cal making love to me the night before, our first time together, my best friend. It just sort of happened as we lay on his bed in the attic bedroom of our student accommodation. I look up at him and I want to relive it again. He licks his lips and inches closer, the tips of our noses' gently kiss and our tongues engage in a slow dance once more.

"Morning. You must be the new girl."

That voice is familiar.

I drop my warm Danish pastry on my desk like a hot stone and swivel my chair around. He's the last person I expected to see. My mouth falls open, letting the buttery flakes tumble from my lips. The boy I loved is now a man, more delicious than my orange swirl. My taste buds pop like there's exploding candy on my tongue. I could ravish his lips surrounded by the dark scruff on his face. He's smoking hot, but not as hot as my cheeks right now.

His eyes grow wide. "Steph. It's you."

My hand frantically wipes the drool and marmalade from my lips. I close my mouth. My tongue runs along my teeth, removing any remnants of food, while I brush the crumbs from my clothes. My heart does a hop, skip, and jump. *What's he doing here?*

There's an awkward moment where I don't know whether to shake his hand, hug, or ignore him. After all, we haven't spoken in twenty years. He pinches his eyebrow where his piercing used to be. He would always twist the ring when he was nervous.

The erratic rhythm in my chest rings loud in my ears. "Do you work here?"

"Err, no. I thought I would just come and steal some breakfast."

He still has that sarcastic humour, then?

He smiles, running his fingers through his raven hair. "Of course I work here. I'm one of the marketing consultants."

"Oh." I cover my gaping mouth with my hand. This means we'll be working together.

He clears his throat and tucks his wavy hair behind his ear. "I had no idea it was you. I knew a girl was starting today but never imagined..." He pauses.

I've turned into a blob of jelly; it's a good thing I'm sitting down, as I don't think my legs could hold me right now. He continues to gaze upon me, and I gulp the air down my dry throat. There's a jumble of gymnasts cartwheeling in my stomach. After a long silence, I ask, "Where's your desk?"

"It's just here." He gestures to the desk, staggered opposite mine.

"You've got to be kidding me." Did I say that out loud?

"Is that a problem?" He smirks.

"No, no, not at all. I'm surprised to see you, that's all." *Breathe, just keep breathing.*

Finally, a few other people walk in and dissipate the tension. Including my boss, "Ah, Steph. I see you've already met Callum." He waves his hand towards Cal.

"Yes." I don't mention that we already know each other. Cal doesn't mention it either. I let out a breath and relax my shoulders. I'm not ready to get into all that right now.

"Let me introduce you to the team." My boss turns around and gestures to the few people who have just walked in. "This is Chris. He's the marketing specialist."

"Hi." Chris stretches out his hand and greets me with a

firm grip. His short hair is going grey on the sides, but it looks good on him.

"And Kelly is our analyst."

She smiles, showing her perfect white teeth, and bobs her head, swishing her silver-blonde hair. I wave my hand at her and mouth the word 'Hi'. She's pretty and looks younger than me, or maybe she doesn't have kids—they certainly age you.

My boss continues to go through the rest of the group. "And James is the promotions manager."

"Hello, Stephanie." James is very dapper in a royal blue suit. Looking much younger than me and fashions the colour well.

"Hello, nice to meet you all." I glance around at everyone and wave my hand in a rainbow.

"There are a few others who will arrive shortly. I'm sure you'll get to know everyone as the weeks' progress."

"Thank you, Sir."

"Call me Jerry." A smile forms under his full grey beard. He's a big fellow with an air of authority about him, but he seems friendly enough—plus, he was more than generous with my salary—I can't ask for more than that. I've been desperate to get another marketing job for a while. My last boss didn't appreciate me, and constantly asked me to work extra hours. I wouldn't mind, but I hadn't had a pay rise in years.

Everyone disperses to the selection of croissants and swirly marmalade things laid out on the table next to the coffee machine. This job is going to do nothing for my waistline. I've never been slim and attend a weekly slimming group just to maintain my current figure; large breasts, curvy hips, chunky thighs, but I can't resist a Danish pastry. I exhale a long breath, relaxing into my chair as I take in my new modern surroundings; an open-plan space with about ten workstations. A smile plays on my lips and I'm filled with a sense of belonging, regardless of Cal's presence.

"Meeting in thirty minutes, folks." Jerry marches through our workspace before disappearing to his private office.

Cal sits down at his desk, which faces mine. Kelly sits next to me on the right. I try not to look over at Cal, but curiosity gets the better of me. Resting my elbows on my desk, I tilt my head in a daze and place my chin in the palm of my hand. He's smarter than I remember. His hand strokes his stubbly jaw and I hear the scratching of a week's growth beneath his fingertips.

My gaze meets with his deep brown eyes and I look away, pressing my mouth together and chewing on my bottom lip. My eyes flit back to his white shirt, a hint of his inked torso peers through the fabric. I try to make out the design on his chest; he didn't have his pecs tattooed when I knew him. I noticed his smart black shoes aren't the usual black boots with large silver buckles he used to wear.

He always wore black. I don't think I ever saw him in anything else. The way those ripped black jeans hugged his toned arse and his black leather jacket hung on his broad shoulders over his Mötley Crüe t-shirt—that's how I remember him. Not that I ever thought of him... much. To survive, I scrubbed away the memory of him until he was nothing but a ghost—now he's back to torment me. My shoulders slump and a wistful smile forms on my face. I'm happy to have a familiar face, but why him? I need to push past this; this job is too good an opportunity to let him mess it up. He already ruined my last year at uni. I'm not letting him ruin any more of my life. For frig's sake, I'm a forty-year-old woman. I need to get a grip.

Cal catches me scrutinising him again and his lips turn upwards in the corner of his mouth, sending a tingle from my head to my toes. I look away, feeling betrayed by my body. How can I react to him this way after all this time?

"Are you ready for the meeting, Steph?" Kelly asks.

I glance at the clock. "Is it that time already?" I've been sitting here staring, not necessarily at him, just staring into space while transported back in time for the last thirty minutes. "Err, yes, what do I need?" Everyone gathers their folders, books and tablets.

"Just a notepad and pen. There are stacks of notebooks in the stationery cupboard if you need one." She points to the cupboard near the breakfast table, but before I can move, Cal jumps up and grabs a book.

"Here you go." He hands me a notepad. "Do you have a pen?"

"Yes, thank you. Do you?" I smile, remembering how he never carried a pen.

He flashes me an endearing look. "I'm good."

"You can hang your belongings over here." Kelly points to a coat stand behind Cal's seat. "And there's a drawer with a lock and key under your desk if you want to put your bag in there."

"Thanks." I put my things away and follow her to the conference room. We walk past a row of filing cabinets that line the wall to the right. Cal walks to the side of me. I make small talk, not wanting any more awkward silences, but I overdo it with all my questions. "How long have you worked here?"

"About ten years. I had some pretty shitty jobs before that." He lets out a small laugh. "One was working in a sock factory."

"What, making socks?" We studied marketing together, why would he be in a sock factory? We corner the cabinets, and large glass doors come into view, exhibiting a contemporary conference room.

"Nah, it was marketing, but the role was more about creating designs for the socks. You know, those cheesy socks that my mum and Gran would always buy at Christmas."

I let out a laugh that's more of a snort. "Oh those, I remember." I look away. My face flushes, and my hands are clammy. "So, do you live locally?" I ask, trying to recover my mortification.

"Yeah, I live about ten minutes down the road." He opens the door to the conference room and gestures for me to enter. "You?"

"I still live in our hometown." I've always lived there, apart from the years spent at uni. Cal grew up there also—we went to school together—until his mum moved them to the city when we were doing our A-levels. "How did you end up back here, well, in the next town?"

I manoeuvre around the large oval conference table. Cal pulls a chair out for me and takes the next seat. "Long story. I'll tell you about it another time."

"Okay." I want to know more about his life after me. He observes me for a moment, tilting his head as his lips turn upwards. His eyes are the same kind eyes that I remember, crinkling up in the corners as his smile widens.

I smile back, unable to control my reactions around him.

His eyes glance towards my hand that rests on the mahogany table. "You're married." He takes hold of my fingers and touches my wedding band with his thumb. His hand feels rough but warm.

Gazing into his eyes, the gymnasts in my stomach are no longer doing cartwheels; they're somersaulting. How can he still have this effect on me after all this time? I slap myself away from his gaze and look around the room. How dare I let myself feel this way? I hate this boy or man. He broke me; I can't forget that. The room fills and our conversation is no longer private.

"Yes, so." I pull my hand away from his grasp. He was the one I wanted to marry all those years ago. I would have done or gone anywhere with him until he left me stripped of his love. I search his hand for a ring but don't see one.

Jerry walks in to chair the meeting. He starts by discussing a new client; a chain of artisan chocolate stores that want to re-market themselves. This should be good. I can see the diet is definitely out the window now as Sarah walks in with two boxes of chocolates from said company. Everyone dives in, including me, of course. An orange flavour with a crunchy texture makes my mouth water. Next, a zesty lemon with a sugary coating, that tastes just like a lemon meringue. It's clear the packaging and logo are not branded correctly for how luxurious they are.

"Steph, have one of these, they're your favourite." Cal picks a round chocolate from the box and places it in front of my mouth. I automatically bite into it. My body betrays me again, reacting to his as it always would. The caramel centre envelops my tongue and excites my tastebuds, along with the closeness of Callum, my pulse races. The gooey middle drips down my lip. Cal wipes my mouth with his thumb and licks the caramel from his pad. My breathing quickens. I'm high on him and sugar. He slides the box towards me, offering me another, which I can't resist.

Jerry continues to discuss the brand. I re-focus, listen and take notes, expressing my ideas. Everyone seems impressed, including Cal. I've come a long way since we dated, although he helped me a lot through my studies.

We all get assigned our own tasks and I go to my desk to come up with a new corporate identity for the artisan chocolates. I love my job; this is very similar to what I was doing before. I've worked in marketing since leaving university.

Before I know it, it's lunchtime. Kelly asks, "Are you joining us for lunch, Steph? We usually go to the pub across the road."

I had brought my lunch in my bag, but it seems pretty lame to sit here on my own with a salad. "Yes, I'll join you." I grab my jacket off the coat rack and pull out my bag from the drawer, minus the salad.

Cal hangs back for me, holding the door open. I stumble over the threshold; he steadies me, taking hold of my arm, and my face is once again on fire. I'm desperate to make a good impression. Why should I care? I have a wonderful husband at home and two amazing kids—most of the time.

"So, who's the lucky fella?" Cal asks.

"What?" I watch where my other colleagues are walking.

Cal lets go of my arm. "Your husband?"

"Oh, his name is Justin." Everyone crosses the road and I notice a pub on the other side. A large metal swing sign hangs on the wall, displaying the words 'The Black Swan' with an illustration of the same.

"What does Justin do?"

"He's a builder. He runs his family's construction business. Are you married?" I think I already know the answer to this.

"Nah."

After we parted, I realised he would never settle down. As much as I tried, he had commitment issues. Most likely caused by his parents' failed marriage and his dad leaving when he was young.

We cross the busy road at the pedestrian crossing. "Any kids?" he asks.

"I have one of each, you?"

"Yeah, two daughters."

"Oh." I draw my head back. He obviously stayed with someone long enough to reproduce not one, but two kids. "So, you have a partner?"

"It's complicated, but I'm no longer with the girls' mother."

That isn't a surprise. "I'm sorry."

Cal pulls the door open to the traditional pub and gestures for me to enter. The bar is bustling with people from the industrial estate. Our group commandeers a long wooden table.

"Don't be sorry. She was never the love of my life. Things just happened, and I stayed for my daughter. Then we had Bethy. I stayed as long as I could, but it just didn't work out."

"You still see the kids, though, right?" I ask with bated breath, hoping he hasn't turned into his father after all the conversations he would have with me about rejection.

"Yeah, of course. I get them a few days a week and alternate weekends. They're everything to me."

I smile at him and nod. I can't imagine what it must be like to not live with your children. The thought triggers old memories of loss, stirring up a hollow sensation in my chest that once consumed me. I would no doubt enjoy a break, but not every week. It would kill me not to tuck them in every night. I'm sure I would even miss the constant fighting and bickering.

As I sit at the table, Cal shrugs his coat off and drapes it on the back of a chair opposite me. "What would you like to eat and drink?"

"Can I have fizzy water with a splash of lime, please?" I search for a menu, but can't find one. "Get me whatever you're having." I grab a tenner from my purse, but Cal doesn't take it and walks to the bar.

"Are you all right there, Steph?" Kelly asks.

"Yes, thank you."

"Do you want me to order you anything, I'm going to the bar?"

"Cal is ordering my food, but thank you."

"Is he now?" She glances at Chris and back to me with a smile. "He knows you're married, right? I can't believe he's hitting on you already."

"He isn't hitting on me. Trust me, I would know."

Kelly walks to the bar as Cal returns with my drink and sits down opposite me. "I've ordered you a Brie and cranberry baguette with chips."

"Thank you. How much do I owe you?"

"Nothing, it's fine." He waves his hand in the air to gesture for me to put my money away.

"Cal, you can't go paying for my lunch."

"You get mine tomorrow, then we're even."

"All right, thank you."

Cal picks at the old oak table. "I still can't believe it's you."

"I know, it seems like another life when we last saw each other."

"Yeah, it does. I'm a different person now, Steph."

"Well, you look the same, maybe your clothes are smarter though." A small laugh escapes me.

"Yeah." He titters, looking down at his attire. "I still have my Rob Zombie t-shirts though."

I sip my drink and smile at the memory of me wearing his tops. "So, tell me all about what you've been up to."

"This and that. I lived in Australia for a few years."

"What?" He always talked about travelling, but I always

thought he meant for a holiday. I can't believe he actually lived there.

"Yeah, I just packed my bags one day, bought a plane ticket and went travelling. I was only planning on staying till my money ran out, but I ended up getting a job in a bar and staying for several years."

"That's wonderful." My eyes go wide. I sip my drink, trying to quench my unbelievably dry throat. He actually followed his dream of travelling.

"I got a job in marketing out there, eventually."

"What made you come home?"

"My mum was poorly, she had cancer." His tone changes, his eyes gloss over as he talks of his mum. He stares at the table where he's been scratching at a groove in the wood.

"I'm so sorry, Cal." I place my hand on top of his, knowing how much his mum meant to him and what a lovely woman she was. He turns his hand over and his thumb caresses my skin; the feel of him sends my entire body into mush. Gazing into his sad eyes, I stay silent, not wanting to bring up any more hurtful memories.

After holding my hand for what seems like an eternity, he clears his throat. "She beat it though, eventually. She's a fighter, my mum." A wave of relief washes over me and I let out a breath I didn't realise I was holding.

"I'm so glad, Cal." Tears threaten my eyes.

Kelly returns to her seat next to me and her gaze hovers on Cal, stroking the back of my hand with his thumb. I pull away. She looks at me with her mouth open and then frowns at Cal. My face heats. I tuck my hands under the table, clasp them together, twiddle my thumbs, and chew on the inside of my mouth.

"What did you get up to after uni?" Cal asks, cutting

through the thick atmosphere. Kelly turns to talk to Chris and I relax a little.

"Nothing as exciting as travelling. I went home, had a few crappy jobs, dated Justin, and that's about it, really. Quite boring, isn't it?"

"It's not boring. I expected as much. I knew… I hoped you would find someone to make you happy. Are you happy, Steph?" He peers into my eyes. I swallow. Nobody has ever really asked me that before. I mean, really asked am I happy. What more could I ask for? I have a new job, a husband and two children; our family is complete. But after seeing him again, I can't help but feel that something is missing in my life. The hole I've filled since he left me is starting to sag. A black void creeps in where his love once resided.

"Yes, I'm happy."

"I'm glad."

Our food arrives. Cal's burger with chips and my baguette looks delicious.

"Is it all right?" Cal points to my plate.

"Yes, thank you, I can't believe you remembered what I like after all this time."

He smiles before taking a bite of his burger.

Kelly turns to me. She must have cottoned on to our conversation. "Do you two already know each other?"

"Yes," we both reply in unison and tell her we went to school together, nothing more. The situation is bizarre enough without everyone in the office knowing that I loved this boy more than life itself, my best friend, my lover, my man. Except he is none of those things now and he hasn't been for a long time. After getting over the shock of seeing him, spending a morning with him and having lunch together, it's almost like we've never been apart.

My phone buzzes. Oh no, I forgot to text Justin.

"Hi," I say into my handset.

"Hi, how's it going?"

"Everything is going well." I look at Cal and feel awkward talking to my husband in front of him, so I excuse myself from the group and head outside. I've finished my food now, anyhow. "Everyone is really friendly. I had a pub lunch."

"What about the salad I made you?"

I tut. "Well, I wasn't going to sit and eat a salad when everyone else was going to the pub."

"You need to watch what you eat, Steph. Pub lunches won't help with your diet."

My eyes flick upwards, and I grind my teeth. "I'll have a light tea to make up for it."

"Fine, I'll see what's on offer in the supermarket."

"See you later, then."

"See ya."

As I hang up the phone, everyone is making their way outside; it's time to get back to work. The rest of the day goes by quickly. I'm ready for a large glass of wine after the shock of today. I say my goodbyes and wave at Cal as he gets into his black Audi.

BY THE TIME I get home, Justin has already started on tea; the smell of chilli fills the entire house. "Did you have a good day?" Justin shouts while I take my jacket and shoes off.

"Yes, it was good." I walk into the kitchen and go straight for the drinks cabinet. "Do you want a glass of wine, Justin?"

He stirs the rice. "Go on then. I'll have the red. There's some low-calorie wine in the pantry for you."

Ugh, I hate that stuff. I sigh and walk into the pantry to get my bottle.

"Are we celebrating your first day?"

"Yes, something like that." I laugh, not telling him the actual truth, that I need something to take the edge off, after being tense all day sat across from my ex-boyfriend. The low-cal white wine tastes refreshing on my tongue at least, but I would have preferred Justin's red. I imagine the rich velvet liquid sliding down my throat.

Just as I sit and relax at the dining room table watching Justin plate up, the kids come running in. "Mum, Cassie called me a stupid idiot," Cairen cries.

Then Cassie follows. "Mum, he was in my room and messing with my dolls." And so it begins. I roll my eyes and take another drink; I have my own problems right now.

"Cairen, stay out of her room, and Cassie, stop calling people names," Justin shouts, seeing my frustration. He places our plates on the table. Cassie has a bigger portion than me.

"Where's the rest of my tea?"

"I've just given you a small amount. You don't want to overdo it after your pub lunch."

I clench my jaw. "Thanks."

"It's made with turkey mince and I've made the sauce myself, so it is slimming for you."

I scowl at him. "So why can't I have a bigger portion?"

"Steph, you know it's not just about what you eat, but also how much. Plus, if you're still hungry after, you can have that salad I made you for lunch."

Even though I'm starving, he's right. He always helps keep me on track.

"So, have you been working on anything exciting?"

"Yes, we're rebranding a chocolate company that makes

artisan chocolates." I tell him about the abundance of Danish pastries in the office this morning, my Brie and cranberry baguette at lunch, and the two boxes of chocolates at the meeting that somehow made their way back to our desks. He doesn't seem impressed and rolls his eyes with each new revelation. "The diet has well and truly gone to pot this week." I laugh. "Hence the wine. I figure I may as well go all in, even if it is only Monday." *Liar,* my subconscious jumps in. *You need the wine to settle your nerves and take your mind off the love of your life.* I sigh. He was the love of my life, but not anymore. *Keep telling yourself that.*

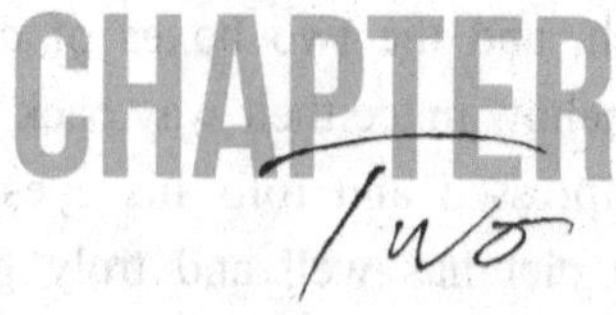

CHAPTER Two

I style my long, warm auburn hair into big waves. Thoughts of Callum swirl around my head. A smile plays on my lips as I picture how he used to be with me, naked in bed. Does he still have that same insatiable sex drive he had in his teens? Is he thinking of me right now? *Doubt it.* The tinkling of metal against glass interrupts my musings as the aroma of coffee wafts up the stairway. Justin brings me a strong hot cup of caffeine, placing it on the dresser, shouting, "Kids get up, time for school."

"You look smart today." He even has a tie on. I'm not used to seeing him like this. Usually, he wears old jeans and a t-shirt on the building site.

"I'm visiting a potential client today who has some land that they want to build on."

"You should wear your blue tie, it matches your eyes."

"I'm going to work, Steph. Not a soddin' beauty pageant." He leaves the room, heading back downstairs.

I sift through my wardrobe for my sexy work attire. Settling on an outfit that I hope still fits. I tuck the cream silk blouse into my black pencil skirt, which actually feels loose since the last time I wore it. After losing a little weight, I admire how my tummy looks flatter than usual, standing sideways in the mirror. I'm not slim by any means, but the older I get, the more accepting I am of my body shape, even if it is getting saggy and softer with every passing year. After walking downstairs and slipping on my black patent leather shoes with a small wedge heel, I'm ready to start the day.

Cassie and Cairen are eating their breakfast. I walk into the kitchen, wrap my arm around my daughter's shoulder and give her a squeeze while I kiss her cheek, which she instantly wipes off.

"Mum, can you do my hair before you go to work?"

"I have to go, sweetheart. Dad will brush it and pop it in a ponytail."

"No, I want a French plait today," she says in her Veruca Salt tone. "Dad can't do plaits."

I glance at my watch, and the optimist in me thinks I can spare five minutes.

"Pass me the brush." I always give in. She hands it to me with a smile, knowing she can wrap Justin and me around her little finger, then turns to eat the rest of her cereal.

I brush her long blonde locks and gather the tendrils at the top of her head.

"I want two French plaits," she demands.

"It's one or nothing." Even though she can get around me, I don't have the time this morning.

"Fine." She huffs and munches down more cheerios, sounding just like her dad when she doesn't get her own way, a right grumpy sod. Although, Justin says she takes after me with the spoiled brat attitude.

"Do you have your leotard for gymnastics after school?"

"Mmm," she mumbles, with a mouthful of food. The milk drips from her chin as she shovels too much in her gob, then wipes it away with the sleeve of her school jumper. *Nice.*

"Cairen, do you have your football boots packed? You have your training today."

"I've sorted it. You don't need to get involved. I've done everything as I always do, including their packed lunches."

Justin's a great dad. He always takes the children to school in the morning and sorts everything out. Running his own business means he can choose his own hours which helps. He stands in the kitchen with a coffee in his hand. His short blonde hair is neater today. I'm not used to seeing his hair styled with gel for work.

I tie off the bottom of the plait with a pink bobble and slide a matching bow clip into the top of her hair, then go to give Cairen a kiss goodbye who is much more loving than his sister and he gives me a big hug and a kiss back on the cheek.

"Love you, have a good day at school."

"Will you be home late again, Mum?" Cassie asks.

"Same as last night. I have a different job now."

"I missed you." My boy melts my heart.

"It's only half an hour later." I kiss the top of his head. They ignore me most of the time. I didn't think they would notice I had a longer commute, but it's nice to be missed. "Okay, I have to go now." I walk down the hallway towards the door.

Justin shouts from the kitchen, "See ya. Low-carb lunch, remember."

Oh, piss off. "Yeah, yeah. Bye." I shout, unlocking the door to my old faithful Suzuki. After starting the engine, I turn on the car stereo to focus on something else other than my tight chest and the lump in my throat. I'm more nervous today than I was yesterday. *I wonder why?* My subconscious hums. Thinking back to my interview for the Marketing Coordinator role at Browns Media and Co—walking through the offices to a small meeting room—how could I have missed Callum? He must've been with a client. Would I have still taken the job if I'd known he worked here? *Of course you would. Who wouldn't want to sit across from that fine specimen of a man?* Finally, something my subconscious and I can agree on.

As I get closer, my hands go clammy. I take in deep breaths and sing along to 'Ironic' by Alanis Morissette—my favourite artist since university—which only reminds me of him again.

Rows of trees line the parking area, and there are plenty of spaces. I find one not too far from the entrance, take in one more deep breath, check my lipstick and grab my bag. A pile of burnt amber leaves skitter across the car park and rustle as they chase me. The building is large and modern, with a glass-fronted reception area.

The young receptionist, Sarah, smiles as I get blown in; she's petite, with long glossy hair and designer framed glasses that make her look sophisticated. "Morning, Mrs Bailey, you're here early again."

"Morning. I wasn't sure about traffic and wanted to leave myself enough time. Call me Steph."

I walk through reception and open the double glass doors that lead to my workstation. The smell of sweet sickly pastries fills the open-plan office. I help myself to a croissant and pour a coffee from the machine. Another good thing about being early is that I won't seem like a total pig in front of Cal, devouring an all too tempting second croissant.

The other desks are covered in papers, books and magazines. I'm sure my desk will be the same once I'm settled in. My desk at home has papers everywhere, but I like it that way. I know where everything is until my daughter rifles through, looking for a sheet of paper to draw on. Many times, I've found a document I'm reading with a beautiful coloured-in unicorn adorning the back of it.

The office fills with the bustling sound of natters and clinking mugs. Cal takes his seat. The familiar lines around his eyes are visible as he beams at me with his beautiful smile. I can't help but smile back.

Throughout the morning, I find it hard to focus with him watching me. Each time I look up, our eyes meet. His gaze burns into me as I walk to the coffee machine. I should ask if he wants a re-fill. The hairs prick up on the back of my neck when his warm breath rests there. Turning to find him close, I suck in the air. The fresh smell of aftershave fills my senses, and I drink in the combination of a salty sea breeze with a hint of mint. My sight draws upwards to meet his alluring eyes framed by dark lashes. Gold and brown flecks spiral in a hypnotic vortex. Time stands still, everything around me blurs, all I can hear is the sound of my accelerated breathing, and I feel the blood coursing through my veins as my heart races, breaking into a sprint.

"Are you going to pour that drink or just hold it?" He's close enough that I get a faint trace of coffee on his breath.

I glance down at the filtered jug in one hand and my mug in the other. "Oh, yes." I pour my drink, trying my best to keep steady.

Cal holds his mug out for me and my hand vibrates further until his fingers wrap around mine over the handle, causing every cell in my body to stand to attention. His gentle grip around my fingers stops my trembling. He takes the jug from me and places it back on the machine.

I don't speak, barely able to breathe, let alone form a coherent sentence. The encounter has me in a dizzy haze. The room is whirling around me, matching the stirring in my stomach as if I'm on a waltzer ride. Swallowing the air down my dry throat, I scoot back to my seat before my legs falter.

THE REST of the week goes the same way; only I get to know the rest of the team better. I like Kelly; it's nice to work alongside another female. I can't decide if she makes me feel young or old listening to all her dating stories, the handsome, the hopeful, and the hideous. She and Callum seem to have a wonderful friendship. She's worked here as long as he has.

At lunch, I've purposely sat away from Cal. I've avoided him all week, which has helped me get to know everyone else much better. Each time I catch him looking at me, I get a flicker in my stomach and it takes my breath. He catches me looking at him, too. I can't keep my eyes off him, and I wonder if he feels the same stirring as me. I'm so glad it's Friday and I may get him out of my head for a few days at least. "Have a nice weekend." I wave as I leave the office.

"You too," Cal replies and gives me a wink.

What was that for? I shake my head and sit in my car, checking my phone before setting off; there's a text from my friend.

It reads, 'How's the new job going?' Instead of texting back, I decide to call; I said I would let her know how my job was, and I totally forgot to call her this week.

"Hello," she answers.

"Hi Claire, how are you?"

"I'm good. How's your new job?"

"You won't believe it."

"What?"

"I'm only working opposite my friggin' ex from uni."

"Which one was he, the one with the piercings and tattoos, when you went through your grunge phase?"

"Yes, that's the one, and I didn't go through a grunge

phase." Cal walks to his car; I can't help but ogle his arse in his tight jeans.

"You got your nipple pierced, didn't you?"

"I was in love with the guy." As I say the words, he looks at me and starts his engine, giving me a nod as he backs out of his parking bay.

"What are you going to do? Does Justin know?"

"No, he doesn't, and I want it to stay that way."

"Yes, that could be awkward." She sings the word 'awkward' like this is fun.

"It brought up so many memories, Claire. I feel like I'm losing my mind."

"Where are you now?"

"I'm sitting in my car, about to leave work."

"Call round on your way home, or better still, get Justin to drop you off tomorrow and we will open a bottle of wine."

"Sounds good. I'll come over at about 7pm tomorrow."

"Great, see you then."

I drive home and pour a gin and tonic; I think I've earned another alcoholic beverage this week.

SATURDAY NIGHT, Justin drops me off at Claire's. "I'll get a taxi home; save you dragging the kids out later."

"No probs. Have fun." I wave him and the kids off as he spins the car around. Claire's house isn't too far from mine, only a ten-minute drive.

"White or red?" Claire asks as she opens the door.

"Red please." She pours us both a large glass. I sit on her oversized cream couch and make myself comfortable. Claire hands me a deep burgundy drink and I smell the sweet richness before I taste it. She joins me on the couch with her legs crossed, wearing yoga pants and a baggy jumper.

"So, tell me everything." She is a professional shrink and I don't mean that metaphorically. She is a trained psychiatrist and right now I feel like one of her clients. This is what she does. She plies me with alcohol so I spill out all my emotions while she listens and says occasionally, 'And how do you feel about that?'

"I was sitting at my desk on Monday and he just walked in. It was like a dream or a nightmare—I can't decide." I sip my wine between sentences. "Ever since I saw him, I can't stop thinking about him, and I stare at him when I should be working."

She nods along, listening intently.

"And I have to admit, I still find him attractive, more attractive now than I did before. Then I get angry with myself for having these feelings."

"Because of Justin?" She swallows a big gulp of wine.

"Well, yes, but no, not really. I'm angry because he hurt me, and here I am still thinking about him when I want to hate his pissin' guts. Claire, I'm so messed up. Help me." My eyes plead with her, hoping she can offer some advice. Although I don't know why I've come to her for relationship advice. She is a forever singleton; but she chooses to be. She loves her independence and I admire her for that. Although she doesn't have a problem finding dates; she's stunning, not to mention highly intelligent. Her ash-brown straight hair falls just above her shoulders and her silvery-blue eyes are piercing into my soul right now, trying to extract every ounce of truth.

"Maybe you need closure. Did you ever get closure?"

"No, not really. He started dating someone else while I was still living in the same student house."

"That must have been awful." She reaches over to squeeze my hand and her lips turn downward with pity.

"Yes, it was." I take another drink of wine, hoping that with each gulp my head will clear of its confusion.

"Like twisting the knife, huh?" She swills the red liquid before taking another sip.

"I moved universities because of him."

"Because he broke up with you?"

"I didn't want to see him again. It was too painful seeing him with someone else. I regret it now. He ruined my last year at a university that I loved. I won't let him ruin this job." Finally, I take a breath. "It feels good to get everything off my chest."

"Honey, that's what I'm here for." A sympathetic smile forms on her face. "If it feels good to say it all out loud, why don't you write everything down?"

"Like a diary?"

"Maybe. A diary, a journal, or notes on your laptop of how you feel each day. Writing is very therapeutic. It helps with your thought processing and helps you deal with locked up emotion."

"What would I write?"

"You can write anything and nobody will ever have to see it unless you want to show them. If you want to keep it more private, you may be better off using your laptop or phone. You can write about your past, your present and even future hopes, dreams, fears, and anxieties. Basically any-thing, just spill it all out on paper. It may help you manage your feelings towards him and help you move on."

"Thank you, but I don't know. I'm not much of a writer."

"You don't have to be, Hun, to just get it all out. Anyway, you know you always have me to talk to, so don't worry about the writing if it's not your thing."

"Thanks, I'm feeling better already… although I'm not sure if it's your company or your wine." We both giggle.

"It's definitely the wine." She pours another glass.

ONE AND A HALF wine bottles later and my taxi arrives. I say my goodbyes and thank Claire as always for listening to all my problems, feeling like I should pay her for the service. The taxi ride is quiet after exchanging the standard pleasantries and talking about the weather. The strong wind rocks the car as we travel through the open stretch of countryside and the trees sway back and forth.

After walking into the hall, I close the front door as softly as I can against the raging wind, hoping not to wake the house. Judging by the quietness and the late hour, I assume the kids are asleep—I hope. Justin is sparked out on the sofa; empty beer cans line the windowsill. Shaking his shoulder, I whisper, "Justin." He stirs, but only enough to roll over, burying his face in the cushion. "Justin, the kids are asleep." I shake him more vigorously, knowing he's like a sloth after a drinking binge. "Justin."

"Hmm, what?" His head jerks up, opening his eyes. "What time is it?" His hand rubs over his face, and he breathes in a yawn before stretching his arms.

"Just past midnight. The kids are asleep," I say again. The alcohol in my veins has made me aroused.

He raises an eyebrow and gives me a knowing nod. We both tiptoe upstairs so as not to wake the kids. Once in our bedroom, we gingerly close the door, leaving the light off, and undress in haste. I lie on the bed; Justin climbs on top, our usual routine. I run my hand along his length, and he quietly groans before kissing my lips. Traces of beer on his breath mix with the hint of sweet wine left on my tongue. We don't speak during sex. We're as quiet as possible, hoping we don't wake the kids.

His hand moves to the apex of my thighs and finds my opening, drawing the moisture from there. Soft moans escape my lips as his fingers stroke and press into me while planting gentle kisses along my jaw. He squeezes my breast with his other hand and wraps his lips around my nipple. Parting my legs with his knees, he rubs himself against me before sliding inside. Rocking my hips against his, we find our own rhythm. I close my eyes, focusing on the pressure building between my thighs.

The dog scratches at the bedroom door. If it's not the kids, it's the friggin' dog; I can't get a moment of peace. I ignore the dog's whines and clawing against the wood, knowing our time is limited before he wakes the rest of the house. My mind drifts; *I hope Justin put the dishwasher on... Did I lock the front door?* Justin continues to thrust into me. The soft moonlight peering through the window highlights a growing struggle on his face as he tries his best not to come before I'm done. I'm close. "Don't stop," I whisper, wrapping my legs tightly around him.

Too late. He releases with one final thrust. Gasping for breath, he collapses on top of me, crushing my breasts for a moment before climbing off.

"Did you...?" he asks.

"Yes," I lie. I can't be bothered now. The dog put me off and I'm still intoxicated by the wine—I just want to go to sleep.

Justin opens the door and heads to the bathroom. Teddy the dog comes bounding in, sniffing at the air. He runs to my side of the bed, then back to Justin's, resting his nose on the edge, as if to say, 'Busted. I know what you've been doing.' I giggle. He must sense when Justin and I get close.

Justin climbs back into bed. "Night."

"Night."

We both go to sleep on opposite sides. We got so used to sleeping this way when our son slept in our bed when he was young. He would starfish in the middle while Justin and I were at each end fighting with the duvet for whatever scraps were left. There's no wonder we had no more kids.

I reach my arm over to give Justin a gentle stroke—turning my body more to reach him—but he's already asleep. I can't even get a cuddle. Rolling onto my back, I stare at a small crack in the ceiling and my thoughts drift to Callum. We would snuggle up in his single bed every night. He would wrap his arms tightly around me like swaddling a baby. The hypnotic pulsing from his chest would rock me to sleep. My eyes close thinking of those times and how I'd love to cuddle him in that attic again.

CHAPTER *Three*

I'm not usually a morning person, but today, I spring into action, looking forward to getting back to work, excited to get the artisan chocolate branding and new packaging designs underway. I love getting stuck into an interesting project. *You love tucking into those chocolates you mean.* Walking out the front door, I sing my goodbyes. My legs skip down the driveway before I hop into my car for my morning commute.

As shocked as I was about seeing Cal last week, it has been nice to have a friendly face and I'm hopeful we can be friends, the forever optimist. I'm willing to put everything that happened in the past behind me and hopefully rekindle the friendship we shared before we dated. He was always fun and never failed to make me laugh. If I was struggling with my studies—or didn't quite understand something—he seemed to explain it effortlessly. We'd hang out in our small group at the shopping centre, cinema, bowling, ice-skating, all the usual stuff you do in high school. I hope we can be *just* friends again.

Of course, all that friendship nonsense goes out of the window by the afternoon, when I find myself staring at him from across our desks. His thick, black, wavy hair looks shorter, falling against the white collar of his shirt. He must have had it trimmed over the weekend. I catch his eye and he smiles with a cheeky grin like he can read my mind. Maybe I should write things down as Claire suggested, get it all out of my system.

———————

I GO STRAIGHT to my slimming group after work. It's time to face the scales. Beads of moisture gather above my top lip as I patiently wait in line. Pictures of all the things that have passed my lips recently enter my head. I didn't come here last week. After the shock of seeing Callum, I couldn't face another shock on the scales. It seemed much easier to go home and comfort eat while drinking my problems away. But right now, I would do anything to lose a few pounds. *Except eat healthy and exercise,* my annoying subconscious tells me. I tell her to piss off as I step on the scales and hope for the best, but know I'm doomed. I can't look.

"Four pounds on," Laura, the group leader, whispers.

I take in a deep breath and exhale; I only have myself to blame. Taking a seat in the group, I chat to Lindsey, another trier. She makes me feel better when she tells me she's put on half a stone after two weeks in Benidorm. At least she has a good excuse. I haven't friggin' been anywhere.

Laura stands at the front of the hall, ready to give us our weekly motivational speech. She is a petite, slender woman who's a walking encyclopaedia on slimming. She bounces as she talks, like a hyperactive pogo stick. I often wonder if she is on something, having lost five stone herself. Surely, it wasn't all achieved with good old-fashioned willpower. Whatever it is, I definitely need some. I imagine her being a bouncing space hopper before she lost the weight, annoyingly exuberant, fun and jolly. She makes her way around the group, and I know my turn is coming.

"Stephanie's had a little gain this week."

Little? It's friggin' astronomical. My face heats, and I nod.

"Do you know where that little gain's come from, Stephanie?" Her voice is condescending.

Forgive me, Laura, for I have sinned. "It all started with a Danish pastry and went downhill from there." I sigh. My subconscious pipes up… *Not to mention the chocolates, the chips, and the wine. You're lucky you only put on four pounds, you greedy cow…* I tell her to piss off again.

"Are you back on plan now?" Laura asks.

"Yes, I am," I reply.

"Do you need any help?"

Yes, I need help; I need a new job, a new body, a life coach and a holiday wouldn't go amiss. "No, I'll be fine," I say and thank the lord when she moves on to someone else.

I GLANCE up as Cal walks past my desk wearing torn black jeans and a black t-shirt, his leather coat draped in his arm, looking more like the Cal I fell in love with. Has he dressed like this on purpose to remind me of how I felt about him? If only he knew, I don't need reminding.

"Morning, Steph."

"Morning." I sip my coffee, staring at his black inked sleeve. A collage of images wraps the length of his arm, including an angel, sun, cherub, and skull all woven together to make one continuous design. He corners the desk and hangs up his jacket. Sitting in his swivel chair, he tucks his thick, black, wavy hair behind his ear on one side.

The room fills, and I focus back on my work. I'm always the first one here as I don't want to be late, and I'm unable to gauge the right travel time.

As the morning progresses, I can't help but get distracted by Cal. His casual look reminds me of when we dated and my mind wanders back to our first time. They say you always remember your first. However, Callum wasn't my first—I tried to erase that one from my memory—a quickie in the back of my friend's older brother's van. He wasn't even my second, which was a much more pleasant experience. He wasn't even my third or fourth. In fact, I've forgotten what number he was. The others roll into one; drunken one-night stands mainly.

But I remember him as my first. He was the first boy I truly loved. Growing up together, I'd never thought we could be anything more than friends. While I was out partying and getting laid by random's, he was always there, looking out for me like a brother, helping me with my schoolwork, and hanging out in our group. I'd always had a secret crush on him, but when we ended up at the same university a few years later, I realised I was in love with him.

We finished our A-levels in June and I didn't see him again until September. He'd been dating a girl for a few months; she was short and curvy with long, black straight hair, dark eye makeup, and black lipstick. She was pretty, but her dark makeup concealed her natural beauty. Her clothes were dark too; at least different to anything I wore. I was more of a baby pink fluffy jumper type of girl. Seeing him with her made me realise just how much I wanted him.

After a few months at university, a few of us on the marketing course rented a house together, Callum, three others and myself. He broke up with his girlfriend for reasons I don't know or can't remember. After that, we were inseparable, and finally got together in February the following year.

My trip down memory lane comes to a halt when everyone stands for lunch. I quickly finish my email and grab my belongings. Cal is behind me, walking out the door, but he turns in the opposite direction.

"Aren't you coming for lunch with us?"

"Nah, I have to nip into town today." He continues to walk down the street. The town centre is a ten-minute walk away. It's easier to walk than go in the car and find a parking space.

"Oh, see you later, then." My shoulders slump, disappointed that he won't be at lunch. I'm used to him just being there now, catching my eye, and silently flirting. It's comforting and familiar even though I want to hate him, but he makes it hard for me to hate him. He only has to smile at me, and all is forgiven. I'm such a pathetic idiot.

I catch up to Kelly and the others. "Isn't Cal with you?" Kelly asks.

"He went into town."

We sit at our usual table. I order myself a tuna and cheese panini, chips with a diet lemonade. At least my drink is slimming, right?

Kelly sits sideways, facing me. "Steph, can I ask you something?"

Oh no. "What's up?" I say nonchalantly, hoping it won't be what I think it is.

"Were you and Cal, you know?" Oh, it is what I thought she was going to say.

"What makes you say that?"

She smiles. "The way I see him looking at you sometimes. Plus, you knew each other in school."

I spit my drink back into my glass. "We dated," I blurt out without thinking.

"I thought so." She looks rather pleased with herself for picking up on our chemistry. "Since you started work here, he's seemed different."

"Really, how?"

"He dresses neater for a start." She covers her mouth as she giggles. "He would always make the minimal effort unless he had a client meeting lined up, and he just seems happier."

My mouth gapes. Could he really be happier because of me? I dismiss it, shaking my head, and take a sip of the cool lemonade. "It won't have anything to do with me, I can assure you."

"Why not?" She asks with a quizzical look on her face.

"Because he dumped me. He hated me by the end of our relationship. We didn't speak for months and we haven't seen each other in twenty years." I sigh.

Our food arrives quickly, and Kelly keeps trying to find out more about our relationship. I tell her the outlines, but don't go into detail. Just as I finish my panini, Cal walks in and sits across from me. My eyes go wide, and I can't stop the smile from spreading across my face.

"What have I missed?" He glances between Kelly and me.

"Nothing." A giggle is ready to burst from her mouth. I've no doubt he can sense we were talking about him. He smirks, reaching over the table to steal a handful of chips from my plate.

"Have you not had any food?" I ask.

"Nah, I didn't get time."

"What did you go into town for?"

"You're nosey, aren't you?" The corner of his mouth turns upwards as he fights back a grin. "It's my mum's birthday today. I'm going straight from work to get the girls and then to hers for tea." My heart melts at how he smiles when he talks about his mum.

"Here, have the rest of my chips." I slide my plate towards him. I could do with not eating them anyway, too many carbs. He tucks in and pours some ketchup on the side. Kelly gives me a look, raising her eyebrow, and I'm unsure what she is implying.

I look back at Cal. "So what did you get your mum?"

"Just some book she asked for, flowers and a bottle of gin. I put them in my car." He was always good at buying gifts. I remember he bought me a ring for my 19th birthday; it was a silver ring with amethyst stones in a flower pattern, not expensive, but it was beautiful, and it meant more to me than any overpriced piece of jewellery ever would.

Occasionally, he would come home from town with a book or CD for me. If he saw something I would like, he would always buy it. He may not have grown up with a steady two-parent family like me, but his mum, being a single parent, had at least one advantage that allowed him to claim a government grant. His tuition fees and living expenses were covered, combined with a student loan, meant his student days were very comfortable. He would often spoil all of us with booze, weed, and pizza.

I loved this boy with all my heart, thinking of how the two of us were; it's hard to comprehend how a year later it all went horribly wrong. That poor girl didn't have a clue of the sorrow that lay ahead. She was all sunshine and rainbows. How could she know? Who would have known that her beautiful knight was actually a dark prince stealing away her soul… although, he never actually stole it—I gave it to him freely.

I come around to Callum waving at me, "What are you thinking about?"

"What?" I blink for a moment before focusing on his gaze.

"You were dreaming again." He grins, knowing that's my thing. I often go into a daze; my daughter has inherited my trait. I get many school reports saying she goes off into her fluffy world. I couldn't be prouder.

"I was just thinking about work," I lie.

"Come on, we best get back to the office." We stand to leave the pub. "Are you all right, Steph?" Cal's voice is soft and caring.

"Yes, why?"

"You just seem distant today." He holds the door open as I step onto the street. The bright daylight is a contrast to the dark traditional bar, and I blink again to adjust my eyes. "If you need to talk about anything, you can talk to me, you know." He's totally oblivious to what's going on with me.

"I'm fine." I can't exactly tell him the truth. *Oh, you know, I just can't stop thinking about you and all the moments we shared, good and bad, and reliving our life is tearing me apart all over again.*

"Are you sure?"

"Yes, thanks, I'm fine." I smile to reassure him, but I'm not sure he's convinced. He knows me too well.

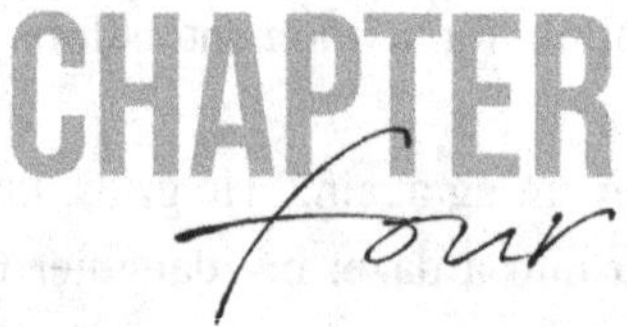

The rest of the day is a blur and before I know it, I'm walking to my car to go home. Cal parks next to me whenever the space is free now. "I hope your mum has a nice birthday." I unlock my car.

"Thanks, I'll tell her you said that," he replies.

I get into my Suzuki and smile as he pulls away. I wonder what his mum will make of me here in her son's life again. Well, working with him at least. She was always kind to me, and I stayed over at her home many times. Although I'll never forget several weeks after we broke up, she came to York to visit for the day, to take her son to lunch. She saw me at the student house and asked how I was doing, sounding like she cared, but said, "Maybe it's for the best." Her words cut deep at what pieces of my heart I had left. How could my heartbreak be for the best? Best for her son, not me; I was fragmented and incomplete. I was no longer myself. He had destroyed the happy, fluffy, and glittery part of my personality and left me with darkness. Sick and twisted thoughts haunted me at night. I wanted to end the pain and suffering I was going through.

A tear rolls down my cheek. I stare at the traffic lights. A car horn beeps repeatedly, making me jump. The light's turned green. I wipe my face. I've already gone through this sorrow once. Why do I keep reliving it? Stepping on the accelerator, I turn onto the main road. Taking slow, deep breaths, I wrack my brain for something other than Cal. My thoughts go to the new book I started yesterday about a girl who moves to London; she's just met a hot guy in a bar. Luckily, he's blonde, with short hair and blue eyes. The way she describes him reminds me of Justin, so I'm not picturing Cal when I read it, which is a bonus.

As I walk into the house, Justin is making a cappuccino. "Drink?"

"Yes, please."

"I picked up some of those skinny cappuccino pods for you."

"Thanks." I flop on the chair at the kitchen table.

"Long day?" he asks.

"Meh, it's been okay." Work is great, but I'm just mentally exhausted. He hands me my hot cup of froth, one of my treats for the day, even though I know I blew all my treat allowance on my panini at lunch, but I'm a trier. Justin tells me about his day. I at least look like I'm listening, but really couldn't give a shit about some window that was ordered wrong and was the wrong shape for the brickwork. I just nod along until he talks about something a little more interesting, like what to cook for tea. "What've we got in?" I ask. He opens the fridge door and suggests a chicken curry or gammon steak.

"Shall we have gammon?"

"Sure. You can have the butternut squash chips, fewer carbs for you."

Ugh, I just want a big fat greasy chip, but whatever. I

should try to cut back since my earlier meal. "Sounds good." I'm grateful that he helps me watch my weight, even if it is annoying sometimes. Plus, I'm glad that he cooks. He wouldn't let me cook even if I offered, *even if you could cook, you mean*. He enjoys it, listening to his 'I love 80s' radio station while preparing the veg and chopping the potatoes. The kids emerge from their bedrooms, running into the kitchen, and notice I'm home.

"Mum, Chloe isn't my friend anymore, and she was being mean to me in class today." Her bottom lip quivers and I can see she is reliving the drama from her school day.

"Why, what was she saying?"

"She said I couldn't play with her and Hollie, and they didn't want to be friends with me anymore."

"I've told you to stay away from those girls. You're always falling out. Why don't you play with your other friends?"

"Because none of my other friends want to do gymnastics and I want to do cartwheels with Hollie, but Chloe said I wasn't doing them right."

"Take no notice of her; she's jealous."

"She thinks she is the best at everything, Mum, you don't know what she is like."

"Oh, I do, if she is anything like her bitch of a mother." I cover my mouth with my hand after realising I said that out loud. "Don't you go repeating that." I point my finger at Cassie. But it has made her smile at least. I went to school with Chloe's mother and she always thought she was something special. She was always jealous of my friendship with Cal too, but he never gave her any attention, knowing that she was horrible to me.

"How was your day, Cairen?"

"Good." A boy of few words. These two kids are polar

opposites. He strokes Teddy, our cocker spaniel, who loves a good ruffle behind the ears.

"How did football practice go?"

"Good." He doesn't look at me and continues to play with the dog while I fold the laundry, flick around with the duster and give the house a good hoover—my usual chores—while Justin stands in the kitchen cooking and watching the game on his tablet.

"Can I go now?" Cassie asks after finishing her meal. I nod. Cassie and Cairen leave the table.

"That meal was delicious, Justin. Thank you." I didn't even mind the butternut squash instead of fries.

"I'll leave you to do the pots." He stands and walks to the fridge, pulling out a beer. I clear the table and open the dishwasher to find it full of dirty pots from yesterday.

"Didn't you turn the dishwasher on last night?"

Justin shrugs. "Not my job."

"I asked you to turn it on when I got distracted by the kids. It was all loaded, you just needed to flick the switch."

"Like I say, not my job."

Ugh, I close the full dishwasher and press the button to start the cycle. I'll have to wash all these pots by hand now. I look at the grill pan full of grease from the gammon. "Justin, could you put foil on this next time? It would save me having to scrub it." He may cook a nice meal, but he certainly makes me pay for it with the amount of soddin' pots and pans he uses.

"If you're not happy with how I cook, do it yourself."

"I would, but you always take over."

"Because I like to taste my food." He laughs. "And the

kids need to have some nutritional meals. If I left it to you, they would have fries and nuggets every day."

"No, they wouldn't."

"Can't cook, won't cook, Steph, that's you."

"Whatever."

He walks off with his beer. I spend the next thirty minutes cleaning up the mess in the kitchen, then I help the kids with their homework, just spellings and reciting the ten times table. Luckily, we're not learning Pythagoras just yet. Being in junior school means the homework is still quite light. I tuck the kids in bed and read them a story. They look so peaceful when they're in their beds, like little angels. I can't help thinking how lucky I am to have my babies.

By the time I settle down on the sofa, it's almost time for bed. I pick up my book. The main character has just found out the guy from the bar is dying and I get all teary. I don't know what's up with me this week; I must be due on my period or something. It must be four or five weeks since my last show. I make a mental note to pack some tampons in my workbag tomorrow, just in case. I never keep track as I'm never on time like every twenty-eight days or whatever it is meant to be.

I WALK into the kitchen to say my goodbyes to find Cairen eating dry cereal. "Why haven't you got any milk in your bowl?"

"Because Cassie drank it all." He spits out the words and scowls at his sister, then sticks his tongue out at her.

She sticks her tongue out. "Stop being a mardy-bum."

"I'm not, you're the mardy-bum. You're a stupid, ugly mardy-bum." She squints her eyes and throws a Cheerio at him. Cairen retaliates, grabbing a handful from his milkless bowl and throws them at her.

I stand in the middle of their chairs. "Hey, stop that. Now." Cassie picks them from her hair. "You can pick those up off the floor. There was no need for that." As I turn back to Cassie, she's goading him, laughing and pulling more faces his way. "Cassie, leave him alone." I sigh. "I have to go. Clear this up before your dad sees it." I kiss them both on the forehead. "No more fighting, please. I must leave or I'll be late. Love you." They don't respond; too busy staring each other out.

Justin passes me in the hall and bobs his head. "See-ya."

"Bye." I open the front door then hear him shout, "What's happened?" I smile, knowing he's seen the mess on the kitchen floor. I leave them to it and jump in my car.

Cal is standing by the coffee machine when I walk into the office. "Morning, Steph. Do you want a drink?"

"I would love a coffee, please." I corner his desk to where the coat stand is, hang up my coat, and drop my bag under my desk before making my way over to him.

Cal turns to face me while we wait for the percolator. "Hey." He smiles, bringing his hand to my cheek.

I suck in a breath, fighting the urge to press my lips against the palm of his hand.

"What's this?" His long fingers run through my hair, gently brushing against my skin.

"What?" The word comes out in a breathy whisper and his eyes study me. I could lose myself in the depths of his gaze, surrounded by those dark lashes on his perfect face, exquisitely framed by his raven hair that I tug in my fantasies. His hand is still near my cheek and I inhale his fresh scent while his fingers entwine in my curls. Heavy breaths escape his lungs as his thumb caresses my skin, sending a rush of goosebumps along every surface of my body like a Mexican wave, reaching as far as my toes. He clears his throat before speaking in a gruff voice. "Have you been rolling around the breakfast table, Steph?"

"What, no, what do you mean?" He pulls a Cheerio from my hair with a smirk forming on his lips.

"Oh." I giggle and cover my mouth, then smooth my hair with my hand to check for any more remnants of cereal. "The kids were fighting this morning."

Cal tosses the Cheerio in the air, then catches it with his mouth. "Hmm, my favourite." He fights back a smile, crunching the dry hoop.

"Cal, you didn't just eat that cheerio from my hair?"

"I've eaten better things off your body, but if a cheerio's all I get nowadays, I'll take it."

I suck in a breath and swat at his chest. "Cal."

He grabs my wrist, pulling me into him. A herd of goosebumps race up my arm and my eyes widen. He inches closer. His ragged breath reaches my lips, making the hairs prick up on the back of my neck. The coffee machine splutters. Aware of my surroundings, I pull away. Cal's lip turns upwards in the corner of his mouth. He lets go of my wrist, turning his attention to the coffee machine to fill up my cup.

"Here you go." He hands me my drink.

"Thank you."

I walk back to my desk, placing my mug on my coaster, and he wraps his arm around my waist, making me lose all control. My heart skips a beat, I can't breathe and the organ between my thighs goes into overdrive.

"There's another one."

"Hmm?" I can't form a word and the sound I make is

more like a purr. He pulls it from the back of my hair and I relish having him so close before he lets me go. "Thanks."

"No problem. I'll bring some milk tomorrow, if you want to bring the cereal again." He laughs and I can't help but smile, thinking of him nibbling food from my breasts. I wonder if he's thinking the same as his eyes rest on my cleavage for a beat too long and I place my hand over my chest, aware of him looking down my V-neck top.

He's so friggin' cocky and adorable. I'm left breathless and unable to focus. Sitting at my desk, I think about him licking cereal off my naked body. I'll never look at a Cheerio the same way again. Not as sexy as the cream he smeared on me once, but definitely less messy. The whipped cream made its way to the carpet, and even after cleaning, the attic room smelt sour for weeks.

I open my emails and get to work, going through the motions, but my mind is elsewhere. Letting out a long dreamy hum as I reminisce. That attic bedroom has a lot to answer for. Some of my best memories are tucked away in that attic, and some of my worst. I've forgotten most of the good times; it was easier to get over him if I hated him, but I could never forget our first time.

We were just friends, chatting, laying in his single bed. The lights were off. As we'd talked, daylight had turned to darkness, and the moonlight shone through the small attic window. He had the best room by far, secluded and spacious.

We faced each other in his small bed, our lips only inches away; I could feel his warm breath on my cheek, my heart beating faster. I was desperate for his touch; it's all I had thought about for weeks, months. I'd never acted on my feelings before, not wanting to ruin our friendship. I think he felt the same, but the electricity that had been building up had finally reached its peak and neither of us could deny it any longer. Slowly inching closer, both of us still unsure—hesitant but longing—he must have been able to feel how my body reacted to his as my breathing sped up and my body trembled.

The touch of his gentle lips awoke my soul. His hand caressed my face. The intensity in the pit of my stomach multiplied, along with the tingling between my thighs. Our tongues entwined into a slow dance. He tasted like strawberries from the sweets we'd shared earlier. The metal in his tongue was different and added a new sensation that I hadn't experienced before.

Our kiss lingered. The feel of his soft stubbly jaw against my skin set me alight, and I felt an ache in me that needed to be filled. Slowly, we undressed each other, taking off one item at a time in between long, sensual kisses. We never spoke—we didn't need to—our bodies spoke in a language of their own.

There was little foreplay, but once we were naked and our skin pressed against each other; I was on fire. He climbed on top of me, caressing my body as if worshipping me, kissing every inch of my face, shoulder, and breasts. Parting my legs he slid inside me with no effort at all. He filled every inch of me and I'd never felt so good, overcome with pure tantric bliss, our souls connected at that moment, everything else faded away as I relaxed into our deepest intimacy. Closing my eyes to blinding lights and ever-changing swirls of colour, as if I was in a trance.

I ran my fingers through his long, thick, wavy hair that fell in front of his face. He continued to brush against my lips. Our tongues danced with each thrust of his hips, slow and deep. We were lost in the sacred space we'd created until we were both completely satisfied, finding our release simultaneously. Sparks of inter-sexual-magic filled the room.

He lay on top of me for some time after, fused together in wondrous completeness while our lips continued to brush and our tongues flickered against each other.

We held each other in the small bed for the rest of the night. He asked me if I was all right. I nodded my head. Elation coursed through me; I was more than all right. We closed our eyes, drifting into a deep sleep. This wasn't my first sexual experience, but it was the first time I had made love. He was the first person I had truly loved. It's true what they say when you love someone; it is so much better. We connected on another level, a spiritual plane. A piece of each other was now locked in our hearts forever. We didn't use a condom, but he came with me to get the morning-after pill a few days later.

The following morning was a Saturday. I crept out of bed early for work, leaving Cal sleeping in the attic while I showered. Taking one last look at him before I left for my shift, I imprinted the picture on my brain. He looked so friggin' sexy, naked in bed, laying on his stomach, the duvet draped over half of his body revealing the black ink near his shoulder; a rose with a trail of thorns almost strangling the skull tattoo at the top of his arm. My eyes wandered down his body to see his toned arse peeking out from under the cover as his knee bent to the side. I'd never seen him like this before and in that moment I felt like the luckiest girl alive, knowing it was my body he was worshipping the night before. How could this perfect boy want me when he could have practically anyone? Most girls would flirt with him and he lapped it up.

The whole day I relived the moment in my head and would feel a slight sensation between my legs stirring from the night before. Each time I thought about him, I would smile from ear to ear. My colleagues must have thought I was delirious. I couldn't wait to go home, to climb up the small attic staircase into his room to see him again, but I was also anxious. Would he still feel the same? Would he still want me as he had last night?

After a full shift of flipping burgers and serving customers, I finally got to go home. I went straight to his room, still in my uniform and name badge with my five shiny stars, my hair in a bun. He was sitting on his bed and beamed at me as I walked in. I sat at his desk in his swivel chair and gazed at him, waiting for him to speak. There were no words for the night before; he obviously felt the same as neither of us spoke.

Several minutes and several smiles later, I said, "So what happens now?"

I waited for him to speak, holding my breath, hoping he would say the words I longed to hear, but he said, "I don't want to ruin our friendship."

How could I know back then at eighteen just how true those words were? But I was willing to take the risk—a hopeless romantic. We agreed to just be friends, but within an hour of agreeing to this; we were back in his bed for round two. Clearly, we couldn't keep our hands off each other.

A week later, on Valentine's Day, he came home from town with the most beautiful bouquet of red roses. I was shocked they were for me—I hadn't even thought about Valentine's—I never got him anything. We were trying to *not* be a thing, so why would I? I burst into tears at the sight of them; gushing that nobody had ever bought me flowers before. I'd never even had a Valentine's card before. Well, I'd had a few over the years, but never actually knew whom they were from, and surmised they were just sent as a joke.

Valentine's was never my favourite holiday until that

day. Cal made up for all the empty letterboxes in previous years. I would smile and get excited when my friends were spoilt by their boyfriends. Finally, it was my turn. He hugged me tight. I'm sure the fact that I was a sobbing mess made him fall for me even more, and he stated he wanted us to be boyfriend and girlfriend; another first for me. All my past relationships had either been casual, friends with benefits or one-night-stands, never anything serious, romantic or loving. He made me feel safe, secure, and sexy.

"Morning. Did you have a good weekend?" Kelly practically sings as she walks into the office.

"Yes, I did." Although, other than getting my period, it's been uneventful. I'm irritable, moody and wanting to eat everything in sight. *No change there then.* "You?" I ask, but I already know the answer. She looks bright-eyed and bushy-tailed this morning.

"I met someone Friday night while I was out with my friends. He took me out for lunch yesterday and we spent the entire day together."

"Wow, Kelly, that's great. Tell me all about him." I wait eagerly for all the juicy details. I'm surprised Kelly is still single. Her petite body is flawless, and she always looks stylish, wearing the latest fashion and oozes confidence with her bubbly, fun personality. She tells me all about how she met him in a restaurant. He kept glancing over at her, and when she got up to go to the bar, he did the same and started talking to her.

I relish her excitement; it's been a long time since I had the flutters you get when you date someone new. Although I don't think they ever went away with Cal, he could still give me goosebumps and butterflies even a year into our relationship. All he had to do was hold my hand or stroke my skin, brush his lips against mine, and that was it.

I look across the desk at my ex. His black shirt hints at the shape of his chest where the fabric clings. A loose hair falls in front of his face as he bites into his bagel. I want to tuck it back into the elastic hair tie, or better still, pull the bobble out completely and run my fingers through his waves. In my mind, I've already pressed my lips to his. My tongue swirls around his mouth as I straddle him in the office chair. My breasts smash against his chest, and I'm grinding myself against his swelling erection. "Hmm."

Kelly interrupts my fantasy just as I was about to rip his shirt off. "I almost forgot, Steph, I finished my book." She pulls a book out of her bag and hands it to me. "I think you'll like it."

"Thanks, what's it about again?" I don't think I was listening the first time she told me about it.

"It's a young adult romance. If you like this book, I have the rest of the series, so I can give you the next part once I've finished. I started the second book last night and I'm really enjoying it." She's still giggly from her date.

"Okay, I'll give it a read." Her teeth gleam, and she claps her hands lightly.

"I can't tell you much more about it without giving away the plot, but it's about a bad boy."

My ears prick up at the words bad boy. "I'm a sucker for a bad boy romance." Cal glances over as I say the words. Not that he was a bad boy; he looked worse than he acted. He treated me well while we were together—in the beginning, that is—but he looked badass with his piercings, tattoos, and long black hair and I loved it. We looked like an odd couple, though, him in his black leather jacket and me in my pink fluffy jumper, but I didn't care what anyone thought of us. "I finished my book too." I rummage through my bag for the book. "Here, let me know how you get on."

"Ooh, I will, thank you," Kelly says.

"I think you'll fall for him as I did."

"Wait till you read mine. I think you'll fall even harder."

"What the fuck are you two going on about?" Cal gripes, tossing the wrapper from his bagel into the bin.

Kelly giggles. "There's nothing more satisfying than sharing your book boyfriend with someone else so you can both discuss how you feel about him."

He laughs. "Your lives must be so fucking boring that you need a book boyfriend."

"Maybe, but not as boring as yours." I narrow my eyes and give him a wry smile. He gives me a sarcastic grin and has no more to say on the matter. I breathe in and puff out my chest, holding back the smirk about to play on my lips.

We've slipped back into the friendly, playful mode from our teens where we try to get a rise out of each other. Sometimes he teases me, other times he's in full-on flirt mode and will say rude or cheeky innuendos, and then there's the overly nice Cal who will compliment me. All of his moods seem to want to engage with me and I'm getting used to seeing him every day now. In fact, I look forward to it.

CHAPTER five

It's lunchtime, and I need to finish penning an email before I go. Cal offers to order my lunch. "What do you fancy?"

"What do I fancy?" *Besides Cal,* my subconscious pipes up. I try to get her out of my head or him, rather. Hmm, I need to choose something slimming; I put four-pound on last week. My excuse was my period, but I know it's all the crap I put in my mouth. "I'll have a jacket potato with tuna and salad please."

"All right, see you over there." He grabs his coat, then leaves with the rest of the team.

Ten minutes later, I'm done and make my way over to the pub. Cal has saved me a seat on the end of the table next to him and got me a flavoured sparkling water. "Hi."

"Hey."

Kelly, Chris and the others smile and wave as I sit down next to Cal.

"Thank you for ordering my food and drink."

"It's fine. Did you do anything this weekend?"

"I have a boring life, remember," I tease.

He lets out a huff as his lip turns upward in one corner. "Yeah, same as me then."

"We went to visit Justin's parents. They live on the East Coast, Sutton on Sea. It was his Dad's birthday."

"I took my girls camping there this summer."

"I love camping."

He nearly spits out his drink. "You go camping?"

I chuckle at his reaction. "Yes."

He has a confused expression on his face. "In a tent?"

"Yes. Why are you so shocked?"

He smiles, letting out a small laugh with his breath. "I can't imagine you doing that. I thought you'd just be into your five-star hotels and shit."

"Well, I do like a fancy hotel, but the kids love camping in a tent."

"I can't help but picture you in some sort of 'Carry on Camping' scenario." He's really laughing now, and I can't help but join in, thinking of Barbara Windsor in that film. "Perhaps next summer we could all go away together."

I shake my head and scrunch up my nose at the thought of Cal sitting with Justin having a beer.

"No? Too weird?"

"Yes." I chuckle. "That's definitely not happening."

He nods, then leans over the table to whisper, "Maybe just me and you then, in a nice hotel?" I catch his warm breath on my neck. A lump forms in my throat. My eyes are wide and my pulse is racing. He raises an eyebrow and smiles. I can't tell if he's joking or if there's seriousness behind it.

"Cal," is the only syllable I can muster. He just laughs. Luckily, the food arrives and I swiftly change the subject. "Did you see your girlfriend this weekend?" I want to know more about his girlfriend, he never talks about her.

"Err, no, I don't have a girlfriend."

"Oh, I thought you did. I'm sure you said something to that effect." I dig into my tuna jacket potato.

"I'm seeing someone casually, but I don't have a girlfriend." Cal takes a bite of his pizza. The melted cheese hangs from the slice like pieces of string. I'm practically drooling but not sure if it's at him or his pizza or both. He's so lucky he can eat whatever he likes and still have an impressive body.

"Oh, okay." I should have known. I wonder if the girl he's seeing knows she is casual, that's so typical of him.

He changes the subject quickly. "How come you had a baked potato today anyway, it doesn't look very appetising."

"It's fine. I need to lose some weight."

"You're not still on a diet, are you?"

"Of course I am." I've been on a diet since I was about ten years old.

"You don't need to diet, Steph; you're perfect just as you are." His words drip from his luscious mouth like melted chocolate. He used to say the same thing when we were together and I loved him for that.

"If I didn't watch what I eat, I wouldn't fit in this chair." I laugh but he doesn't find my jokes about myself funny. "Anyway, I like a tuna jacket potato."

"Suit yourself. Looks fucking horrible if you ask me."

"Well, nobody asked you." I fight a smile and we continue to eat our food. "Thank you, Cal."

"You've already thanked me, it's fine, you can buy lunch tomorrow."

"No, I'm not saying thank you for lunch. Well, I am, but thank you for just being you and being nice to me." I thought working with him would be awkward, but he's made every effort to make me feel at ease.

"Don't go all mushy on me or I'll have to start being a dick."

"Okay." He stares into my eyes with a hint of a smile, like

he's thinking about something. "What are you thinking about?"

"Just..." He pauses. "Just us, we were so young."

"Yes, we were. It's strange, isn't it? I didn't feel young and immature, but looking back, we definitely were."

"Hey speak for yourself, I wasn't immature." I give him a look to say, really? "All right, maybe a little." He uses his finger and thumb to display just how little.

Chris stands. "Best get back to work." And that's my cue to finish up and head back. It was good chatting with Cal today. The more we talk, the more I can see us getting on as friends. I also hope I'll stop wanting to sleep with him as the weeks' progress as this is torture.

ON THE WAY HOME, I stop at Claire's for a catch-up. We sit in her modern townhouse kitchen. Her chrome dining room chairs with leather seats and tall backrest are just as comfortable as her large soft cream sofa.

"So how're things going?" She flicks the button on the red Nespresso machine that ties in well with all her other red kitchen accessories.

"Good actually. I'm getting a handle on things. I'm actually enjoying spending time with him as friends, which I didn't think I could do."

"That's great." She hands me my drink.

I tap my nails against her smoky glass dining table. "I still want him to take me into the copy room, bend me over the scanner, and shag my brains out. But other than having a throbbing vagina on a daily basis, it's all good," I joke, even though everything I just said is true.

Claire spits out her coffee in laughter. "So, progress then."

"I just need to get it all out of my system. I started writing it down as you said, so hopefully, that's going to help me."

"Hun, that's great, I'm sure it will help tremendously."

"How're things with you, anyway?"

"I've been really busy with work."

"Bless you, it must be hard, especially with me and all your other friends offloading on you all the time."

"You know I don't mind listening to your problems. I've started a mindfulness class to help manage stress. You should join. It's fantastic. Similar to yoga but without all the different yoga postures."

"I'll give it a miss and stick with the backward dog type of yoga." Never having done a yoga class in my entire life, or a mindful class for that matter.

She rolls her eyes. "It's the downward dog."

"Whatever, I like the backward dog position better." I chuckle to myself.

"You're so bad."

"I know. I'd best go home soon. Justin will have tea on."

"He's a good 'en, isn't he?"

"Yes he is, don't make me feel worse than I already do."

"What, you've done nothing to feel guilty about, Hun." She always tries to make me feel better.

"I know I haven't physically done anything, but even having thoughts about Cal makes me feel like I'm betraying Justin."

"Pish, most married women have fantasies about movie stars and singers."

"Is that normal?"

"Yes, of course, it's normal. I know it's different because he's your ex and now a colleague, but as long as you don't act on anything and you're actively trying to move on, I wouldn't beat yourself up about it."

"Thanks, Claire." I finish my drink and say my goodbyes.

JUSTIN HAS a wonderful curry ready by the time I get home. The spicy aroma makes my tummy growl as I walk into the kitchen. "This smells delicious."

"It's been simmering ages. Where have you been?"

"Sorry, I called at Claire's for a quick coffee."

"Kids… Dinner," Justin shouts.

We all take our seats and Justin places my plate on the placemat. I'm delighted I have a good portion and draw in the coconut scent. Justin brings out three portions of naan bread.

"Where's the other naan bread, there are four of us?"

"I didn't think you'd want one." He sits down and takes a poppadom from the centre of the table.

"Are you kidding? I'm starving."

"What have you had for lunch?"

"I only had a tuna jacket potato."

"Well done, just think of the weight you'll lose this week."

I stand up, walk into the kitchen, and rummage through the bread bin for the last naan bread, knowing they come in packs of four. I warm it under the grill, two minutes on each side, then return to my seat. Glaring at Justin, I tear off a piece of the bread, imagining it's his head, and stuff it in my mouth. He rolls his eyes and shakes his head.

"I'm only trying to help you."

"Well, sometimes it's just friggin' annoying. You expect me to sit here and watch you all eat naan bread, poppadoms and sauces and not have any myself?"

"Jeez, what's got into you?"

I ignore him. I don't like arguing in front of the kids.

Turning my head away from his stare, I ask in a more cheery tone, "How was your day, Cassie?"

"I got a special mention at school for a poem I wrote."

"That's fantastic, sweetheart." She recites it to us and I'm bursting with pride.

I reach over and grab a poppadom, using it to scoop up a large piece of mango chutney. The sweet sauce on my tongue seems to soften me and I relish the different flavours of the Indian meal.

"What about you, Cairen?"

"School was boring." He rips his naan bread up into small pieces and dips it into the curry.

"What about football?"

"Tell Mum about that goal you scored," Justin says.

"Wow, did you score a goal?"

"Yes, but then Oscar kicked the ball, and it hit me in the face."

I instantly reach over to stroke his cheek and inspect for bruising.

"He's fine, you don't need to mother him," Justin says.

I lift Cairen's chin. "Are you okay?"

"He cried," Cassie says.

"Sweetheart." I kiss his cheek and hug him.

"He is fine. He needs to man up if he's going to play with the big boys."

"Justin, he's seven." I scowl at him. Just when I was forgetting about the previous situation, he pisses me off again. I inspect Cairen one more time and I'm satisfied that there are no marks or bruises.

A FEW DAYS pass and the weather has turned awful. I flick the car wipers on the fastest setting on my morning commute as the rain hammers against the windshield. As I step out of the car, my umbrella is at the ready and I pop it open, but the wind blows it inside out. *Great.* Walking from the car to the office, the nippy blasts lift my long curls, blowing them in every direction possible.

I walk to the coat stand, which is behind Cal's desk.

"Morning." He looks up at me from his swivel chair.

"Morning, Cal."

He grins with his pen in his hand, tapping it against his bottom lip. "You look like you've just been fucked."

"If only." I titter.

"That can be arranged." He raises an eyebrow and grips the pen between his teeth. His words flutter between my legs, and my stomach tightens.

"Cal, stop," I say with a breathy voice that only he can conjure.

Kelly walks into the office. Her short bob doesn't have a hair out of place. "Steph, you look like you've been dragged through a hedge backwards."

"Ok, I get it. I look bad. Although your analogy is better than Cal's."

"Why, what did he say?"

"You don't want to know."

I go to the toilets to sort out my mop, passing Chris on the way. He pulls his head back to look at me.

"Don't say anything."

He smiles and continues walking.

Looking at my reflection in the ladies' room, I looked better when I got out of bed this morning. I needn't have bothered curling my hair. Luckily, I always carry a bit of smoothing balm in my handbag.

Returning to my desk, more composed, I turn to Kelly, noticing Cal looking over at me. "Is that better?" I ask her, referring to my less unruly hair.

"Perfect," Kelly says.

Callum gets up and walks around to my desk with his coffee mug and leans over, whispering in my ear, "I preferred the freshly fucked look." My face flushes and the heat also travels to my centre. I squirm in my seat, unravelling at his words, and the flicker returns in my panties.

At lunch, Cal and Kelly have a business meeting with Jerry and a client. I'm not sure where the other guys went, but I'm happy to grab a sandwich from the little shop on the corner. I brave the weather once again; it has stopped raining, but the wind is pure evil and nips at my face. Finally, back at my desk and thawed, I eat my chicken salad on brown bread while reading the book that Kelly gave me. The main character reminds me of Cal, with piercings and tattoos. Callum had a ring in his eyebrow and a bar in his tongue. Neither is present now. The character listens to heavy metal too, just like Cal. I try to not picture him while reading, but it's hard. I'm enjoying the book though. The drinking and partying reminds me of my uni days.

Towards the end of lunch, Cal returns from his business meeting. "Hey."

I look up from my book. "Hi, how did it go?"

"Good, yeah." He takes off his coat.

I look around for Kelly. "Is Kelly not back yet?"

"Nah, she nipped to the shop after the meeting."

I nod and carry on with my chapter. It's just the two of us in the office. Everyone else is still out at lunch. Cal fidgets in his chair, looking bored. I know he won't want to start work while it's still officially lunchtime. He stays silent while I continue with my book. The main character is about to go down on his girlfriend. I don't know if it's my facial expression or if I let out a sound, but Cal leans forward. "Are you enjoying that book over there?"

My cheeks immediately flush, and I can't help but giggle.

"Yes." I press my lips together, trying not to give away too much information.

He smirks. "What's your book boyfriend doing, Steph?" He raises an eyebrow.

"Wouldn't you like to know?"

"Yeah, I would. Tell me." His elbows press against the desk and his chin rests on his clasped hands.

I bite my lip and twirl the locket around my neck, clearing my throat. "'He slides a finger inside me and it is an incredible combination with his tongue.'" I say the words in my husky voice.

His mouth opens, and he licks his bottom lip before pulling it under his teeth.

"Go on."

I continue to read it aloud. Watching his reaction has all my organs pulsing. "'His finger keeps entering me and drawing out slowly. I moan again as he licks and sucks—'"

He clears his throat, cutting me off. "That'll do now, or you're gonna make me hard." He has a slight twinkle in his eyes as the corners crease. I'm sure I'm bright red by now, though I don't know why? We used to read to each other all the time, sharing more sexual experiences than what's in this book.

"It won't be the first time." I try to sound confident, but my voice wavers slightly.

"True." He pulls his bottom lip between his teeth and strokes his eyebrow with his middle finger. "What's your book about anyway, besides porn?"

"It's a young romance. The guy is from London."

"Is he a Cockney?" He laughs under his breath. Why that's funny to him, I don't know.

"No, I hate that Cockney accent" He knows I do too; maybe that's why he is laughing.

"If he's from London, he must have a Cockney accent."

"Stop tarnishing my imagination with visions of Delboy and Rodney Trotter."

He is laughing out loud now. Knowing how to wind me up and I bite every time. "How do you know what his accent is, anyway? It's a fucking book."

"It's my fucking book, and I can give him whatever accent I want." I run my fingers along the cardboard bookmark. "And by the way, just so we are clear... he talks like Jon-friggin'-Snow okay."

"You like Jon Snow?" He smiles.

"Yes, so, I bet you like fucking Daenerys Targaryen."

"I wouldn't mind fucking Daenerys Targaryen."

"Ha-Ha."

"I prefer Margaery Tyrell." He licks his lips, most likely thinking about Margaery's breasts.

"Oh, really. I'm surprised. I thought you'd like the dragon girl."

"Margaery Tyrell reminds me of you." I suck in a breath and gulp. I can't believe he just said that.

"If only I looked like Margaery Tyrell. It must be the long hair as I can't see any other resemblance."

"All right, you're more like Ros," he mocks and I throw my bookmark at him, which is the only thing I had in my hand other than my book.

"Piss off." I try my best to stop the smile from playing on my lips. "You wish I was like Ros." I smirk, knowing full well her character is a prostitute, very attractive though with auburn curly hair.

"Yeah, I do, that would be fun." He has a cheeky smile. "Did you read the books?"

"I read the first few, but when the series came out, I didn't bother with the rest. Did you?"

"Yeah, still waiting for the next instalment," he gripes.

"What other books do you like?"

"You know me, I read anything. I still like Tolkien though." He was always a geek for Tolkien. I'm sure he could speak the language in full. He even had a map of middle earth. I laugh to myself, remembering his little geeky quirks.

"I saw the movies at the cinema with Justin. When the films came out, I thought about you, remembering you liked all those books."

"You were thinking about me while watching the movies with your husband?" He raises an eyebrow.

"No, that's not what I meant," I lie, but he smiles like he knows otherwise.

"The films were all right. Not as good as the books."

"They never are. I had a thing for Legolas." I cover my face with the palms of my hands after my embarrassing confession.

He howls. "What was it that did it for you? His long blonde hair or his elvish ears?"

"I don't know what it was." I join in his laughter. "What about you? You always liked Liv Tyler. Did she do it for you with her Elvish ears?"

"Yep, she was hot as fuck in that movie." He simpers, most likely thinking of Liv. "I thought Aragorn would be more your type."

"Yes, of course, I fancied him, too. You remind me of him, especially now you're older." I gasp and realise I just said that out loud.

"Are you saying you fancy me?" The way he looks at me has my walls clenching and I squeeze my thighs together.

"Piss off." He must know I fancy him. I fancied him back then, and he's sexier now.

The office fills with everyone back from lunch. Cal chucks me my bookmark back. What are we doing? I can't decide if this is flirting or just friendly banter. It's been so long since I did any actual flirting and it's the last thing I want to encourage, but I do like him playful like this.

I get back to my work and pop my earpods in and listen to my playlist. I've started a new playlist lately, and I've been adding random songs I like over the last few weeks. Listening back, I've realised that all the songs remind me of Callum.

Currently playing is, 'I would like' by Zara Larsson. All I can picture listening to this song is Cal on top of me, maybe not the best choice of song. Nothing beat falling asleep in his arms watching TV, although my favourite pastime was listening to him read aloud while I lay on his chest. All he had to do was stroke the bare skin on my arm and I would feel it somehow between my thighs. We made love in every position possible. Having several other boys and men to compare, he ranked above average. He was tall and slender—only slightly muscular—which made his package look even bigger against the rest of his body. His nimble fingers and tongue knew exactly what to do to make me ready for him, and even more so to make me orgasm. I don't recall a time when I had to fake one, ever.

The next song plays, 'Why should I Care' by Toni Braxton. I'm sure her lyrics are written for me and not just for this song, but practically every song she's ever written. Silently singing along in my head, I think why should I care for him after all these years? I used to cry myself to sleep listening to her album after we broke up; she sings so many sad songs of loss and heartache. Twenty songs later and I'm emotionally drained, I've gone through every feeling from hating his guts, to wanting him back, to sleeping with him. I should call this Cal's playlist. I wonder what he's listening to. Most likely Marilyn Manson or some shit. Does he still listen to that crap? I have no idea.

ANOTHER BRIEFING ON MONDAY MORNING, and some of the team, including Cal, have been marketing a new bar in the city. The owners are having a VIP launch party on Thursday night before their official opening on Friday. The client has invited us all as a thank you for the hard work the company has put in. Jerry announces he will put taxis on for all of us to get to the city at 8pm Thursday night. I get the jitters in my tummy and my legs become restless as I anticipate the event.

Back at our desks, Kelly asks, "What are you wearing on Thursday?" Cal looks up like he's trying to listen to our conversation.

"I'm not sure. What are you wearing?"

"I don't know. I might buy something new. Do you want to go shopping after work?"

"Yes, good idea."

I call Justin at lunch and tell him about the VIP event coming up on Thursday.

"I'm going shopping with Kelly tonight too."

"Oh?"

"I'll get tea out with her, so don't bother making me anything."

"Why, what time are you planning on coming home?"

"I don't know. When I've found something for the event."

"Fine." He sounds pissed off.

"Is there a problem?"

"Yes, I was going to have a drink with the lads tonight after work."

"You never said."

"I'm saying now."

"Okay, I won't go shopping then."

"Go if you need to, just don't be all bloody night. The kids miss you when you're not home."

"I know. I'll make it up to them and you."

"Good, I'll see you later and look forward to my reward." He sounds better knowing he may get a blowjob tonight.

I put my phone down. Cal is staring, and I realise he just heard my entire conversation, well, my part at least. I hope he is jealous, but I doubt it.

"Everything okay for tonight, Steph?" Kelly asks.

"Yes, fine."

"Does he not like you going out?" Cal asks.

"It's not like that. He had plans of his own, that's all." I don't want Cal to know my husband is a grumpy sod.

He stands, shrugging on his coat, then unhooking mine from the rack and bringing it to me. "I get it. If you were mine, I wouldn't want you going out either."

I take my coat from him and stand still with my mouth open. My stomach clenches. I find it hard to breathe. I want to say something, shout, scream but I remain frozen. He walks ahead, leaving me alone in the office. How can he say that? I'd been his before. Even after he finished with me, I'd thrown myself at him daily—doing anything to have him just one more time. Snapping out of my statue-like state, I remind myself that he dumped me, he's playing with me, and that he isn't interested in me one bit. Even though his words and eyes tell me differently. But is it just wishful thinking on my part? I'm so confused.

CHAPTER Six

The workday is over, and I follow Kelly's car to the shopping centre. This is just what I needed. We look around several shops for something to wear on Thursday night. She is younger and slimmer than me and can get away with wearing whatever she likes. She tries on several outfits, including a short gold dress; the shimmering lightweight fabric drapes at the back. She stands sideways in the full-length changing room mirror.

"What do you think of this one?" she asks.

"I think that looks amazing on you. It would look even better if I couldn't see your blue bra fastening at the back."

She giggles, turning her head to look in the mirror, then unclips the bra and pulls it off underneath the dress. You wouldn't know she was braless. Her breasts haven't moved—still in the same perked position—lucky sod.

"You don't think it's too low at the back, do you? I don't want something too revealing for a work event. You can't see my arse-crack, can you?"

"Kelly, it's fine. I can't see your arse-crack, don't worry."

She giggles again. "I'm going to buy it." Phew, thank goodness, my feet are killing me, and I haven't even got anything for myself yet.

"Great, shall we grab a sandwich, and then you can help

me find something?" The shops Kelly dragged me in offered nothing in my size. I couldn't get one leg in most of the skimpy items in those young designer stores.

Finally, we come to a shop that's more me, one of my favourite high street brands where I get most of my clothes. Kelly picks up several outfits in my size and I grab some I like, too. We head to the changing rooms; between us, we must have about ten dresses. I try them on, one after the other. I take a royal blue dress from the hanger, unzip the side, and pull over my head. *Shit, this is tight.* My breasts squash under the fabric; it's so tight and I can't get the zip up. The size label is wrong, surely. I pull the hem to lift it back over my head, but it won't go past my breasts.

"Oh, for frig's sake." I exhale all my breath, hoping it will allow the dress to move, but it won't budge.

"What's wrong?" Kelly opens the curtain. My eyes plead with her for help as my chest tightens, and not because of the cotton fabric restricting my lungs.

"I'm stuck."

She bursts out laughing. Clearly, she's never known this fear.

"Help."

Still chuckling away to herself, she helps me pull the blue linen upwards.

"I'm scared I'm going to tear the fabric," I whisper. My arse is sweating now. I fight the urge to fill my lungs in fear the dress will burst at the seams.

"Let's get it over one boob at a time," she suggests. Taking small shallow breaths, I manipulate the dress over one hump as she suggested, which allows me to wrestle my arm free and pull it over my head.

"Thank goodness for that." I exhale deeply; lean my head

back against the cubicle partition, close my eyes, and silently thank the Lord for his small mercies.

"I take it you won't be choosing this one." Kelly titters as she places the dress back on the hanger for me.

"Definitely not."

"What others have you got?" She looks through the remaining few dresses and I wonder if I'll find anything at all. I'm losing the will to live—I can't face another store—I'm knackered. "Try this one on." She hands me a black dress that she picked out for me. I take it from her and she steps back out of the cubicle, fiddling with the curtain.

I pull it on slowly and breathe out when it fits comfortably. "Kelly, I like this one; you chose well." Black makes you look slimmer after all. The fabric around the middle section gathers, hiding my flabby stomach. It has a cowl neckline with slim straps, and falls just above my knee, covering my dimply thighs.

Kelly pulls the curtain back. "Yes, Steph, that's the one. You have to get that. It's sexy enough for a club, but also formal enough for work."

"I will, thanks for your help."

We head to the checkout before making our way to the car park.

"I'm so glad we came shopping," she says.

"Me too."

"We should go shopping again sometime."

I smile at her and we say our goodbyes. I think she's enjoyed this more than me; my feet are throbbing and my legs ache.

JUSTIN HAS SETTLED the kids in bed and is sitting watching re-runs of Baywatch. I flop onto the sofa, lifting my tired feet up onto the footstool.

"Did you get anything?" Justin asks, still fixated on the TV.

"Yes, I got a black dress."

"What's up with all your other black dresses?" he groans.

"I just wanted something new. None of my old dresses are really suitable." *Not sexy enough.* "Do you want to see?"

"Whatever." He barely looks up. CJ does her usual run across the beach. I lift my dress out of the bag and hold it against my body. The brunette on the show has joined in with the running now. I stand in front of the TV to get his full attention.

"Well?" I shout.

He yawns. "Same as all your others." Waving his hand at me to step aside so he can focus on the running. I roll my eyes and huff, deciding I need to put it on so he can get the full effect. I slip into the downstairs bathroom and change; it feels silky against my skin. The straps are just wide enough to hide my white bra; obviously, I'll wear a black one to match on Thursday.

Stepping back into the lounge, I stand in the middle of the room. "What do you think?"

He looks over this time, nodding. "It's fine."

Fine? Just fine? Although to be fair, I could wear a bin bag and Justin would say I look fine. He's never been my go-to for fashion advice. That role belongs to my sister.

"It doesn't make my bum look big, does it?" I turn around and try to get a look at my behind in the mirror above the fireplace, which is just too high for me to get a good look.

"Your bum looks big in everything, Steph, there's no getting away from that." He laughs. "But it will do." Well, at least he's honest. You'd think after years of marriage he would learn when to keep some things to himself, but he's never been one with words.

"What about my belly?" I turn sideways, trying to suck in my gut. "I have some Spanx that I can wear on the night." He turns the TV off and stands up, stroking his chin, assessing my middle area.

"You should have kept up that gym subscription I bought you, then you wouldn't have this problem." I let out my stomach and slump. I know he's right, but it wouldn't hurt him to lie and tell me I look good for once. The bridge of my nose burns as I fight back my emotion. One more word and I'll either explode or burst into tears. I already feel anxious about this event. I just want to look the best I can.

"Why are you so bothered? You're not usually this worried about your appearance."

"I just want to look good with all the twenty-something's that I work alongside, that's all." *And you want Cal to see what he's been missing all these years.*

"You can't compete with all the twenty-year-olds." He chuckles. Talk about knowing how to make me feel good about myself. I can always rely on him to bring me back down to earth. "But, you're not bad for a forty-year-old. Let's go to bed. I want that reward you promised me." Ugh, that's the last thing I want right now. I contemplate the 'I've got a headache' line, but figure I may as well get it over with. I promised him, after all.

I follow him up the stairs. We check the kids are asleep before heading to the bedroom. I unzip the dress and hang it on the wardrobe door. Justin pulls off his top and I unbutton his jeans, kissing his hairy chest as I make my way down to his stomach. He's lost his defined abs he had when we first met; I blame the beer. Kneeling in front of him, I pull his jeans down, along with his boxers. Taking his semi into my hand, moving back and forth until he's hard, then I lick at the tip and slide my tongue down his full length. He groans as I tease his erection before taking as much of him into my mouth as I can. Placing his hands on my head, he groans again. After several more strokes, he pulls away and lies on the bed, beckoning me on top of him. I turn the light out before removing my knickers but leave my bra on. I know Justin doesn't find me as attractive as he once did with my changed body. Several rubs, strokes and kisses later, and I direct him inside me.

The dog's whining again. We've left him downstairs this time, but I can still hear him whimpering and scratching at the door. *I hope I can finish this time.* I try to block it out, rocking my hips against Justin. The moonlight peers through the flimsy curtain, casting shadows on his face. I watch him beneath me; his eyes close and his lips press together as he fights his release. *Did I lock my car?* We rock in rhythm and the intense pressure builds in my core. I shut my eyes tight, blocking out all sounds and vision, trying to focus on nothing else but the heat between us, and Callum comes into my head.

The thought of Cal beneath me makes my legs tremble, and my heart rate speeds up. My eyes screw tighter as I picture his face. I'm back in the attic, shamelessly riding him senseless. My sex tightens. *Oh gosh.* I tilt my head back and let the pleasure take me. All the sexual frustration that I've built up over the last few weeks instantly disappears. Justin thrusts one more time before coming inside me. We're both quiet and all I can hear is our breathing and the dog still whining, but I'm so relaxed. I'm not even sorry that I was thinking of Cal just then. I just needed a quick release, and it worked. After climbing off, I lay on the bed on my back for a few minutes. I catch my breath and clean myself up. Justin goes directly to the bathroom and then lets the dog upstairs to stop his whimpers.

THURSDAY COMES ALL TOO QUICKLY and I have a taxi booked for 7.15pm. It's freezing outside, but I don't want to take a big coat. I have a little denim jacket that doesn't actually keep me warm, but sod it—it looks good with my new black dress. I slip on my black peep-toe shoes with a kitten heel and wait for my taxi downstairs by the large bay window. Justin is sitting on the sofa with a can of beer. I don't bother asking him how I look. After his comments the other night, I can't take any more criticism from him. I do enough of that myself.

Headlights flash on the driveway. "My taxi's here. See you later. Bye kids."

"What time will you be back?" he shouts as I walk to the door.

"I have a taxi booked for midnight, so I should be home at 12.45-ish."

"Fine, see you later," he shouts.

"Bye." I close the door and wrap my denim jacket around me as much as I can, pulling it around my neck as the icy wind nips at my cheeks.

I sit in the passenger side of the taxi; the heating is blowing, and the seat feels warm on my bottom. The driver is nice enough but doesn't make conversation, which allows me to catch up on social media. It's not very often I get to have a cheeky look through my socials. I arrive at the club to see Cal outside. *Is he waiting for me?* The creases form around the corners of his eyes when he spots me getting out of the taxi. I walk towards him with my chin down, pulling my small jacket closed to hide my dress.

"Wow." He stuffs his hands into his ripped grey skinny jean pockets, then runs his tongue along his bottom lip as his eyes rake me from head to toe.

"Hi, are we the first here?" I let go of the jacket and lift my chin up.

"Everyone's inside. I thought I'd wait for you."

My eyes widen and I have a smile so big it's making my jaw ache. "That's so sweet of you, thank you."

He's still looking me up and down. I relax my shoulders and stick out my chest, feeling a little more confident about my outfit after seeing his reaction.

"Come on, you soppy sod." He nods towards the entrance of the club.

The bouncer checks our names off a list and pulls the door open for us. We walk through the entrance and tread the wide staircase.

I take in the shiny fixtures and inhale the smell of new carpet and fresh paint. "Everything looks brand new."

"It is brand new. This is the first night the bar has opened." Callum shakes his head and grins.

"I knew that." I bump shoulders with him.

A girl behind a desk at the top of the stairs takes our coats. She must think we're together because she places them on the same hanger. I don't mind her thinking we're a couple; I think about it myself sometimes. Cal opens a large glass door and I step into the main club. The music playing is 'Promises' by Calvin Harris and Sam Smith, giving off a chilled and classy atmosphere. Swirling colours of light flash around the room, highlighting a large dance floor in the middle, surrounded by railings and bar stools. I follow Cal to the large bar that runs along the back wall, walking through a crowd of other guests who I don't know.

"What are you having to drink?" he asks, like I can't

order my own drink or something. Everything is on the house tonight for the VIP launch party.

"Tia-Maria and Diet Coke." He repeats my order to the bartender, and he gets a pint. We scan the club to find the rest of our team sitting on the barstools next to three steps that lead to the dance floor. Kelly looks amazing in her slinky dress that drapes down her back. Everyone scrubs up well to be fair, even our boss Jerry, who's here with his stunning wife. Kelly is sipping a cocktail. "What cocktail have you got?" I ask, having to shout a little over the music.

"Pornstar Martini," she yells, then giggles covering her mouth with her palm. "Here." She thrusts a cocktail menu in my face and I peruse my next drink while trying to listen to everyone's conversations over the music. After studying the menu, I realise that all the cocktails have some sort of sexual reference: Sex on my Birthday, Wet Pussy, Cum in my Panties, Blowjob and the classic Sex on the Beach. There's even one called Sex with Jennifer, whoever she is. While going through the names, I chuckle to myself. "I'm having a Buttery Nipple next," Kelly announces, pointing to it on the menu. "I'm going to work my way through the list."

"I might join you." All the names have me simpering.

It isn't long before Cal is ready for another drink. He leans into me, close to my ear, so he doesn't have to shout over the song. "I'm going to the bar. What do you want?"

I revel in this attentive side of him and take one last look at the cocktail menu. "I'll have a Slow Screw please."

He looks at me as if I'm joking, then notices the dirty cocktail menu in my hand and a smirk surfaces from his lips. "I can give you one of those. And I don't need to go to the bar for it."

My breath hitches and I swat his chest.

He laughs.

"I'll stick with the drink variety, thank you."

"Suit yourself. So, you want me to ask for a Slow Screw?"

I know he will; he's never been shy. "It's that or 'Cum in My Panties'." I bite my lip while I wait for his response.

"I can make that happen, too." He titters, rocking back on his heels with his hands in his pockets.

"Cal." If only he knew my knickers are already damp for him. "Let's start with a slow screw and I may have cum in my panties after." I giggle and look down, trying to hide my flushed cheeks.

His tongue darts out, licking his lips. "I can guarantee it," he whispers, brushing his hot, wet mouth against my ear. He pivots and walks towards the bar, leaving me all hot and flustered.

Kelly turns to me. "You look fantastic in that dress, Steph."

"Thanks, Kelly, I'm glad you picked it out for me." I simper, replaying Cal's reaction to my outfit when I arrived here tonight. Images of Callum unzipping me pop into my head, and a tingle blossoms in the pit of my stomach that travels to my centre. At that moment, Cal appears with my drink.

I take it from him and he shouts over the music, "They didn't have the ingredients for the 'Slow Screw' so I got you a 'Screaming Orgasm' instead." He's looking smug, fighting a laugh. If only he could give me a screaming orgasm.

I suck up the thick creamy liquid and taste a kick of alcohol on my tongue. "This is nice. What's in it?"

"Something mysterious with a dash of sexy mixed with honey, sweat and a shot of cum for good measure."

I take another sip. "Mmm, I love cum. My favourite."

Still looking down at my drink, I flash my eyes upwards to see him grinning with hooded eyes.

He leans into me. "You're filthy." His warm lips brush against my flesh again, making my head light and dizzy as if I'm drunk on him.

"You used to like me being filthy."

"I still do." He tucks his loose wavy lock behind his ear and I want to run my fingers through his mane. I want to unbutton his fitted black shirt and glide my palms over every bit of his chest and stomach.

'Blinding Lights' by The Weeknd plays and I love this song. Kelly must like this song too, because she drags me onto the dance floor. A few of the other girls from the office join us, including Sarah. Several songs and cocktails later, I'm still dancing with the girls, leaving Cal with James and Chris at the top of the steps. My head is dizzy from all the cocktails and I can't stop smiling. Kelly leans into my ear and shouts over the music, "Cal's been watching you dance most of the night, you know."

"Really?" The club is a blur, but when I look over at him and catch his eye, he comes into focus, like he's the only person in the room. He doesn't look away, but studies me while sipping his drink, his other hand stuffed in his pocket. I'd noticed him looking at me occasionally but hadn't realised he's been full-on staring.

"I think he still has feelings for you," she slurs.

A wild laugh escapes my lips. "Well, that's tough shit. I'm married now." I want him to have feelings for me and know what it's like to want someone who doesn't want you back. Even though I want him more than anything, but I would never tell him that.

She laughs along with me and closes her eyes as she sways to the music.

"I'm going to get a drink," Sarah shouts.

"Me too." Kelly follows Sarah to the bar.

I walk up the steps towards Cal and tug on his arm. "Come, dance with me."

He stands stiff like a statue with his bottle of Bud. "I don't dance."

I pout, and he laughs. He never danced when I knew him before, so why I thought he would dance now is beyond me. It must be the drink talking. My head is light and Cal only adds to my dizziness.

I look him straight in the eyes. "So, are you just going to stand here watching me all night?" I gasp at my audaciousness.

He smirks. "I enjoy watching you."

My heart bursts into a frenzy of star jumps. I wet my lips and gulp.

"Especially in that dress," he adds.

My lips part. I swallow the air again. *Is he coming on to me, or just being playful, or is he as drunk as me?* I can't tell. I look around and James and Chris have gone to the bar, leaving Cal and me alone at the top of the three steps that lead to the dance floor. The next song is a more upbeat DJ remix of 'Shape of You' by Ed Sheeran.

I look into Cal's eyes as the music plays. He steps closer. My chest rises and falls heavily with every breath. He licks his lips, and I want to press mine against them. His eyes rake over my body, settling on my heaving breasts. My mouth gapes as his hand rests on my hip and my sight darts to where his fingers roam. My eyes widen as he palms the top of my thigh, digging his fingers into my fleshy behind, forcing me closer to his body.

The electricity surges through me, coating my skin in a layer of moisture. My palms press against his chest, and I look into his dark thirsty eyes that seek out my soul. I'm hot, so hot I may combust as this beast sweeps me off into the depths of his inferno. The seductive tones of the song combined with his body pressed against mine make me doubly aroused. I wonder if he can read my mind, though my body language gives everything away as I lean into him.

Seven

Kelly stumbles against us, snapping me out of Cal's alluring trance. She places the cocktails on the ledge in front of us, and Cal immediately removes his hand from my arse. I take in a deep breath, then grab my cocktail and suck the cool fruity liquid up through the straw, soothing my dry throat. Kelly loses her footing again and falls against the railing. Cal catches her before she goes flying down the steps and she giggles. Hopefully, she's too intoxicated to have noticed where Cal had his hand a moment ago.

The next song is a remix of 'Slow Hands' by Niall Horan, and it's so friggin' sexy. Or do all the songs sound sexy because I'm wasted? I can't decide. Everything is fuzzy, a drunken haze of lustful longing.

I shout to Kelly, "I love this song."

Cal bursts out laughing.

I swat his chest. "What's funny about that?"

"Nothing," he shouts over the music, shaking his head before bringing his lips to my ear. "You would love this song."

"It's sexy."

He smirks, then leans into me again, this time brushing my ear with his lips as he speaks. "I'll remember to play it for you when I fuck you."

"What?" *Oh my, is he serious?* My cheeks flush; my mouth gapes, and my eyes flick upwards.

"You heard me." His lips press together into a thin line.

"Cal, stop it." It shouldn't surprise me he would say that. Part of me likes it when he talks this way, but I can't let him think he can just have me. I'm married. As much as I want him to, it can't happen. "You will never fuck me," I shout over the music, folding my arms across my chest. Then shout the word, "Again." After realising my previous line made little sense. He's already had me about a hundred times or more. My foot taps wildly on the floor while I wait for his response.

He ignores me and walks to the bar. I'm glad though, this flirting and thinking he can just have me is getting too serious and his arrogance just pissed me off. But I'm afraid of what will happen if I continue to talk to him tonight, especially as I'm so drunk. *And horny*, my subconscious reminds me. She's right. I squeeze my thighs together and feel the dampness in my lace panties.

"Was he flirting with you?" Kelly asks.

"I'm not sure." I shrug my shoulders. We finish our cocktails and go back to the dance floor when Tinie Tempah plays. I can't see Cal anymore. James, Chris, Jerry, Sarah, and a few others from the office are near the bar, but Cal seems to have disappeared. He must have gone into the toilets. I'm constantly looking for him. I try to shake him out of my head as I dance with Kelly. A guy tries to dance with her, and it makes me smile as she tries to squirm away from him. She is dating someone now, so she isn't interested in anyone else. We both move away from the creep and get another cocktail. It's been a while and I still don't see Cal. I grab my drink and make my way around the club with Kelly, walking past the seating that lines the wall till we reach a VIP room at one end.

Walking through the doors, the cool breeze from the air conditioning swathes my clammy skin.

Kelly points to an empty table in the corner. "Shall we sit over there?"

The music is quieter in here with a more relaxed atmosphere. Taking a seat, I spot Cal standing near the VIP bar with a girl. Kelly says something to me, but all I hear is a muffled sound. My mouth opens and my eyes cloud as his hand strokes the red fabric of her dress that clings to her dainty hip. Despite the cool air in the room, my body temperature rises. Crescents imprint on my palm as my nails dig into my flesh.

I turn to Kelly. "Who is Cal talking to?"

She shrugs. "Nobody I know, babe."

I have a side view and watch his every movement. He takes a sip of his bottled beer, then tilts his head back, laughing at something she said. His hand leaves her hip, and he runs it through his hair, pulling the waves off his face. I gape as his hand goes to her face. His fingers tangle in her long raven hair, and move her curls from her shoulder, revealing a large rose tattoo on her neck. My eyes widen as his thumb caresses her cheek. I know what follows this signature move of his. My hand hovers over my eyes, but my fingers fail me—parting open—allowing me to peer through the gaps. I don't want to watch, but I can't stop torturing myself. *No, no, please no.* The acid creeps up my throat. "Kelly, I'm going to the loo. I feel sick."

"Shall I come with you?"

"It's fine." I get up and dash to the toilets, my hand covering my mouth in case my body follows through with its threats. Once in an empty cubicle, I lean over, waiting for the retching to stop. I can't bear it; I can't stand seeing him with someone else. Even now, it makes my stomach churn and my hands tremble. I end up sitting on the toilet seat with my head against the cubicle wall and let the tears flow. I pull out some tissue from the holder and wipe my cheeks. How have I got myself into this mess? I need to get a grip.

I call Claire; she's the only person I can talk to about this. It's late, but she should be up still. She never sleeps. I just hope she isn't out partying, although, it's a Thursday, so she should be home.

The phone rings. "Hello, Steph?"

I let out a sigh of relief at her voice. "Claire," I cry.

"Are you all right?"

"Yes, well, no, I'm drunk."

"Where are you?"

"I'm at a work event and I'm sitting on the toilet crying because Cal is all over some tart." Although she didn't look like a tart, she looked nice, which makes me hate her even more.

"Oh, Hun."

"Why do I even care? I don't want to care, Claire… wait, that rhymes." The tissue feels rough against my nose as I blow into it and sniffle down the handset. "I don't want to feel like this. I just can't bear to see him with anyone." *Care, Claire, bear. I can't help rhyming words in my messed up head.*

"Hun, I think you need some sort of closure. Either leave now before you do something you regret or wipe your eyes, pull yourself together, go back out there, and don't engage with him."

"I think I'll just go home. They booked my taxi for midnight, but I can call them and ask for one sooner. I'll just wait outside, try to sober up."

"Hun, I know it's hard, but if you're drunk, it is making

everything seem ten times worse. Things will seem better when you sober up."

"I know you're right."

"Call me when you get home - let me know you're okay."

"Thanks, Claire bear," I wail.

"You take care." She hangs up.

Oh my word, why does everything rhyme suddenly. I can't stop rhyming stuff.

Googling the taxi company, I call and arrange for an earlier one. I unlock the toilet door and sort my makeup out, then get a bottle of water from the bar and make my way back to the VIP room. Kelly is standing with Callum and this random girl. He's leaning against the bar now. His arm is behind her back as she leans into him. The scene makes me want to vomit all over them. Knowing Cal, he'll most likely take her home and shag her brains out. A vision of the two of them pops into my mind; him biting the rose on her neck as he takes her from behind, and I want it to be me. I need to go. He catches my eyes and tilts his head, studying me. Oh no, he can probably tell I'm drunk, or worse, that I've been crying. Gosh, I hope not.

"Kelly, I'm going home."

"I thought your taxi was at midnight, like mine." She looks at her phone to check the time.

"I've booked another taxi."

Cal pulls his bottom lip between his teeth, his eyes still fixed on me.

Kelly squeezes my shoulder. "Do you want me to come and wait with you?"

"No, please, it's fine. I'll just wait outside the club. I'm a big girl." Even if I'm acting like a teenager again, getting jealous and crying over a boy.

"Text me when you get home."

"Okay, bye." I walk away, ignoring Cal. In the cloakroom, I unhook my coat from under his, leaving Cal's on the hanger. I turn around, and he's behind me. "What are you doing?"

"Getting my coat."

"Oh." I glance around for his slut, but she isn't here. I put my jacket on and walk past him to the entrance. Once outside, the fresh cold air hits me, sharpening my mind. Cal stands next to me. I take in a deep breath, clearing my head. "Are you waiting for your whore?"

He furrows his brow. "What did you say?"

"You heard me."

He sniggers, making my blood boil. "Steph, what the fuck are you talking about?"

"Oh, come on, you had your hands all over that slut in there. Don't mind me, fuck whoever you like." I turn away, closing my eyes to fight back the tears. The bridge of my nose stings, and I flare my nostrils using every ounce of strength I can to stop the dam from breaking.

Cal pulls my arm to turn me towards him. "Steph, I'm not fucking anyone."

"Well, I'm sure your girlfriend really appreciates you putting your hands all over some random girl."

"I told you before, I don't have a girlfriend." His grip tightens around my forearm.

"Oh sorry, my mistake, the girl you're *casually* seeing."

"Are we still talking about my *girlfriend* here, or are we talking about you?" He mimics my use of air quotes as he says the word girlfriend. His lips press into a hard line as he looks deep into my eyes.

"What's that supposed to mean?"

"Are you jealous, Steph?" He rocks back and forth on his heels.

"Piss off. And don't friggin' touch me." I yank my arm

from his grasp. A throb hums in my temple, and I rub at my forehead. My fists grip the edge of my jacket, and I wrap it around my body to keep out the cold air.

"Look, I came to wait with you until your taxi comes. You don't look well." He reaches out to put his hand on my back.

I burst out laughing. I'm not sure why I'm laughing. Is it the irony or the relief? Or is it I have to laugh or I'll cry?

His palm runs down my spine, sending a tingle through me, and I quiver.

"You're freezing. Do you want my coat?" He pulls his jacket off his shoulders.

"No, Cal, I don't want your pissin' coat. Save it for rose neck."

He shrugs, pulling his coat back on. Pressing his lips together, he looks down at his feet and kicks the pavement. "What the fuck do you care, anyway? You go home to fuck your husband every night."

"I don't fuck him every night." I've calmed down now after having a minute to regain my thoughts. "More like once a month."

He huffs. "That makes me feel so much fucking better."

"I told you, sleep with who you like." I try to sound like I couldn't give a toss while rolling my eyes.

He furrows his brows. "I would, Stephanie, but the person I want to fuck is married."

My mouth is open, and I have no words. Well, I do actually, and after gaping for a beat too long, I ejaculate them fiercely before my mind can stop my mouth. "Whose fucking fault is that?" I yell, waving my hand in the air. "If you hadn't ended our relationship, I would still be with you, and you could have me anytime you like." I stop myself at that, sucking in a breath and covering my mouth with my hand, realising what I just said and hoping that he meant me when he referred to someone who's married. If he's talking about someone else, I've just made myself look like a complete idiot. He has to be talking about me, surely?

"Are you done?"

I nod and tilt my head down; I don't want to argue with him, and I certainly don't want to make him so angry that he goes and shags some random bird tonight, just to piss me off. He doesn't speak. He must have meant me or he would have contradicted me by now.

My taxi pulls up. I take one last look at him before I go. My body willing me to throw my arms around him to feel his tight embrace, but my mind won't allow it, and I just get into the taxi. He stands watching me go with his hands in his jean pockets.

A long sigh leaves my lungs. I'm safe in the cab, knowing I can't say or do anything else that I'll regret.

I text Claire to apologise for spilling my emotions to her and tell her I'm on my way home, and I text Kelly, too. I can't help but ask her if Callum went home with anyone. She replies about half an hour later and texts, 'No, he's in the taxi with me.'

I quickly text back, 'Don't let him know I asked about him.' I hope it's not too late. I hope he hasn't seen my text. *Why did I ask about him?* Of course, I already know the answer to that. I needed to know he went home alone so I could actually sleep tonight.

She replies, 'Don't worry, my lips are sealed,' with a zipper mouth face emoji.

The cab drops me off and I walk into the house, lock the door, and walk into the bedroom. Justin is already asleep. I take off my dress and collapse into bed in my underwear. I can't even be arsed to take my makeup off. The night's events have left me mentally drained.

The next day I dread going to work. I'm so embarrassed at how I behaved; I don't want Cal to know I'm jealous or even care about what he gets up to. How selfish of me. I can't expect him to not go with anybody else for the rest of his life. Of course, he's going to meet other people. I need to deal with it. I should apologise. No, I should just act as if nothing happened. Oh, I don't know what to do.

I make an extra special effort with my appearance this morning, but nothing can conceal the bags under my eyes. As I step outside, the stiff wind jars my body awake. I can see my breath in the cold air, but the sun is bright, making the throb in my temple worsen. I find my sunglasses in the car and pop them on while I drive to work. The radio pierces my ears and I bang on the stereo, turning it off; my head is too delicate.

Cal pulls up at the side of me; I'm later than usual this morning. It's already 9am. I don't know what to say to him. Will he be pissed off with me? I sit in the car for a moment. My foot tapping against the pedal, my palms sweating and I have a twitch in my lip. Eventually, I brave it and get out of the car just as he does, taking in a deep breath.

"Hey." He looks me up and down as he always does. At least he's talking to me, that's a good sign.

"Hi," I reply, letting out a breath, relieved that he spoke first.

"Rough night?"

"What?" Is he serious? I can't be arsed with him tormenting me this morning.

"You have your sunglasses on in the middle of winter." He points at my Ray-bans. For a moment, I think he's going to touch my face, but he quickly puts his hand back in his coat pocket.

I'd forgotten I was still wearing them. "Oh, yeah." I take them off, chucking them back in my car. "Last night is a blur; I was wasted," I lie. I remember everything, most of all I remember how I felt when he placed his hand on my hip and his fingers trailed down my thigh and the fire crackled under my skin. How his lips brushed against my ear, and the electricity surged through my body… His deep, rough, erotic voice when he told me he would fuck me. I wanted nothing more than him to take me back to his place and have me all night long—I wanted it as much as he did—the arrogant arsehole. He makes me feel every emotion all at the same time. How is that even possible? I feel everything for this man. It's so confusing.

"Yeah, I was wasted too." He didn't seem wasted, although he was back and forth to that bar like a friggin' Yo-Yo. We all were; the drinks were free, and we made the most of it.

In the office, Kelly somehow looks perky. She drank as much as I did last night. How can she look so good? Then I remember, she is about ten years younger, that's how. Everyone is buzzing and talking about last night. Everyone seemed to have had a great time. Cal doesn't mention the club to me again, and he doesn't speak much to me all day really, but I'm also avoiding him out of embarrassment. I'll be glad when the day is over, and it's the weekend.

How dare he want me again after everything? I know I wanted this, but the reality scares me. I don't trust myself. He hurt me—I can't forget that—it's the only thing stopping me from giving in to him. *Yeah, and the fact you're married.* Oh yeah, that as well.

We lasted just over a year; it was around Valentine's Day

when I knew something was off. It wasn't the same beautiful moment as the year before—almost forced—he wasn't himself. He was cruel to me in the hope I would end us, but I'm a hopeful, optimistic soul, so that would never happen. Instead, I put up with his bad moods, convincing myself that somehow things would get better.

One day, one argument. He snapped, and I heard the words I'd been dreading. Those five words shattered my world. He had my heart, and he chewed it up, digested it and shit it out all over the attic bedroom. I didn't want to hear the words. They hit me like a high-speed car crash. Words I never thought would leave his lips. *'I don't love you anymore,'* he said. To add insult to injury, he said he'd felt that way for some time. I sobbed until there was nothing left but a dry desert, begging him not to end it; this beautiful relationship that we had, or the version of it I thought we had in my head. But he'd made his mind up; there was no going back.

We shared our life in that room, our clothes in the same wardrobe, our belongings all mixed. I spent the entire day sorting through our stuff, deciding what was his and mine; books, CDs, and other stuff we'd bought together. I ended up with most things; figured he owed me that much, including his room. I always loved the attic, and he let me keep it out of guilt, I guess. He moved all his belongings into what was my old room a lifetime ago. I got the train home that evening. Staring out the window numb the entire journey.

Once home, I collapsed on my bed. My life was over. I hadn't just lost Cal; I'd lost what came after. My entire future involved him. After living with him all that time, I thought when we left university we'd move in together, and we'd both get jobs in marketing. He always talked about travelling the world: Europe, Asia, America. I never cared for it, but I would have followed him to the ends of the earth, putting his career before my own.

I wanted to marry him, not right then, but years down the line, I thought we'd marry and have children. He said he wanted lots of children eventually and I would have gladly had them with him. It was this loss that tore me apart, memories we had yet to make, the dreams that would never come to fruition. My chest ached. There was a gaping hole left in me, an open wound that wouldn't heal. I spent a week at my parent's house. Friends came to see me and I went out, hoping they could brighten my spirits. On the outside, I would smile and say I'm okay, but on the inside, I was broken. I couldn't even find the pieces to put myself back together. I'm sure they were still in the attic bedroom, trodden on by his big black boots. He'd warned of ruining our friendship at the beginning of our relationship. I should have listened to him. He was right; things were never the same.

After no luck finding anywhere else to live, I went back to university—back to my attic bedroom—only this time, I was alone. I'd never slept up there alone before. The other housemates would be downstairs, laughing without a care in the world, and I'd never felt so lonely. Even when I went down to join them, surrounded by a room full of people and yet I was wandering the abyss, trapped in my mind, my soul lost, searching for his again so we could be one. I couldn't find it; I searched for a long time. We barely spoke; he would avoid me at all costs. Hanging out with his new friends at his bar job, the bar job I talked him into getting. How ironic that he would start work there and then dump me. I know he met *her* there.

The worst thing was that when we eventually spoke, I told him I was fine, and we ended up sleeping together again. I felt used. Or was I using him? I couldn't figure it out. Doing anything I could to feel his touch, hoping if I slept with him enough times he would realise he still loved me and all would be well again, but it was no use. I realised it was finally over when he dated again; to know he hadn't come home and was out with her was the most painful. Normally when two people break up, you don't see them, but I still had to live with him. Those last few months were pure agony, seeing him happy, holding hands with another girl. What made it ten times more distressing was that she was stunning, with a perfect tiny body and a beautiful face. She seemed kind and caring. I bet she was even a friggin' virgin.

I guess I should thank him. The moment he ended our relationship, it shaped the woman I've become. I used to believe in fairy tales—soul mates that belong to each other for eternity—and we were lucky enough to have found each other and all that. I knew once our relationship was over that this sort of thing was all in my head, and that you have to work hard to make a relationship work. There's no such thing as a soul mate; if there was, Cal and I would still be together. My ideals came shattering around me, along with my heart.

Thinking of these awful memories has put me in a grim mood for the rest of the day. I listen to my sad songs on my playlist. Obviously, I love torturing myself. Staring at him from across the desk, I imagine us a couple again and how wonderful that would be. Although I forgave him a long time ago, I'm not sure I could trust him to not hurt me again. My heart couldn't take another wound from him. *And you're married.* Yes, I know. Stop reminding me.

CHAPTER
Eight

"Happy Birthday, Mum." I walk into the local beauty salon.

"Thanks, love." Mum sits in front of the large mirror while Diane colours her hair. My sister Samantha is here too and has her hair in foils under the heat lamp.

She looks up from her phone. "Didn't Cassie want to join our pamper day?"

"She wasn't fussed. I'm glad. I may actually relax for once."

"Take a seat, Steph. I'll be with you in a mo'." Marie, the other stylist says, gesturing towards an empty seat next to my mum.

"What's Justin up to today?" Mum asks.

I sit in the salon swivel chair. "He's taking the kids to that new trampoline park. Probably why Cassie didn't want to come with us. She's had a better offer."

"He's such a wonderful dad, isn't he?" Mum has always thought the sun shines out of Justin's arse. Especially since he shits gold. His family is well off; running their own construction business that Justin now manages, and his nan passed away about ten years ago—bless her soul—leaving him with a nice inheritance. We're not filthy rich or anything, but we are comfortable.

"What are we doing today then, Steph?" Marie asks me as she comes over with a long black cape that she fastens around my neck.

"I want to go darker. A chocolate brown or something more like my natural colour." Although I can't actually remember what my natural colour is anymore, I've been dying my hair since I was fifteen. Callum always liked my hair darker. Not that I'm doing this for him. I just fancy a change. *Sure you do*, my subconscious utters.

Marie brings the colour chart over and I run my fingers over the coloured hair samples in the book, settling on a rich coffee colour.

"Why don't you have this at the roots and fade to a warm auburn on the ends." She shows me the two colours together.

"Love it. Go for it." I say and she pulls my hair from under the cape, teasing it with her comb before sectioning.

"How's your new job, sis?"

I haven't seen my sister in a while, not since I started working at Browns.

"It's really great." I always tell my mum and sister everything, but I can't seem to tell them that Callum works there. I don't know why. They would remember him. They went through all that heartache with me. Mum was the one I would call, crying on the phone when I was feeling low. Even after I graduated and came home, I was still getting over him.

Justin doesn't know he's my ex, and I don't want them to let it slip. I don't even know why I want to hide it from Justin. He has no reason not to trust me. Perhaps it's me. I don't trust myself. But I feel deceitful not mentioning Callum to my mum and sister, but is it deceit to omit telling someone something? I don't know. It's gone on far too long—after working there for several weeks—I can't just mention it casually. *Oh, remember Cal, the love of my life who shattered my dreams. He also works at Brown's Media, and he doesn't just work there. He sits on the friggin' desk opposite me... I didn't mention it, as it's no big deal, really.* I mean, you just couldn't make this shit up. It's such a huge deal. Everyone would think it's odd that I didn't mention it before.

I don't think I would feel comfortable if Justin started working alongside one of his ex-girlfriends, so I think I'm trying to save him from any discomfort. It would be awful for him to have that kind of insecurity about me going to work every day, and I love this new job. I don't want anything to burst my bubble.

I get a French polish while I wait for my hair to cook and a head massage when Marie rinses out the dye. Her fingers are magic and relieve some of the tension I have. I close my eyes and relax into the chair. My head rests in the salon sink, and the warm water pulses around my scalp.

Marie dries and straightens my hair. I turn in the mirror and swish it from side to side. Loving the fading colour and the straight style. I usually curl it so this is quite a fresh look for me.

My sister gets her usual silver highlights in her blonde locks and Mum always goes for a burgundy tint to her short bobbed hair.

We have lunch, more like an afternoon tea at a posh establishment. The hostess brings out an assortment of dainty sandwiches, scones with jam and cream, and beautiful miniature desserts that look like a work of art.

"These are too nice to eat," Samantha says.

"I'll have yours." I give her a smile.

"Stephanie," Mum says. "I thought you were on your slimming programme."

"Ugh, not you as well. You sound like Justin."

"How's your diet going, Steph?" Sam asks.

"How does it look like it's going?" I wave a hand over my body, knowing I haven't lost a damn thing in months. But I've put no weight on either, which is a bonus.

"You look like you've lost a few pounds." She is just being polite now.

"Thanks." She doesn't know my struggle. She's always been the slim one.

We clink our glasses together and toast Mum's 60th and I fill my plate with the crustless sandwiches, shaped into small triangles. My favourite is the salmon and cucumber filling that's tangy and refreshing, and I wash it down with a sip of champagne.

A friend of the family walks over to our table. "Hello Susan. Girls." She nods and smiles at us. I smile back but keep my lips closed, containing a mouthful of bread.

"Julia." Mum says curtly, turning her nose upward, then looks away.

Julia sighs and walks deeper into the restaurant with a man I've not seen before.

"What's going on, I thought Julia was your friend?"

"She was until she thought it was okay to divorce her husband." Mum sips the champagne and swills the glass around in her hand. "Thirty years we've been friends with her and Jack and she's left her husband for that man." She waves her hand in their direction. "Poor Jack is distraught. He has to sell the house." Mum takes another swig. "And don't get me started on the children. I know they're teenagers, but they're still in shock. How can a mother do that?" Mum pulls a face as though the words leave a bitter taste in her mouth. "She's left them too in my book."

I look up from my finger food. "Haven't the boys gone with her?"

"No, she's shacked up with her fancy man and left the

boys with their father. Although it's the best place for them if you ask me."

"Perhaps she loves him." A lump rises in my throat and I swallow it back down with a bite of my sandwich.

"Pft. Family comes first. You make your bed and you lie in it. She should have made it work for those boys, at least. Not go running off with some bit on the side."

"It takes a lot to make a marriage work, Mum."

"Don't you think I know that, Stephanie? It's not all plain sailing. You're lucky you have a good one at home that requires minimal effort and so did Julia."

I roll my eyes at my stuck up mother. "Nobody knows what goes on behind closed doors, Mum."

She juts her chin out and straightens her back. Her overly large mouth takes a small bite of the sandwich and she closes her lips to chew on the tiniest morsel. I shake my head and dive into the desserts. Each bite is like heaven as the sweetness melts on my tongue, tantalising every taste bud. I close my eyes, savouring the moment. Not knowing when I will get to taste such rich, indulgent food again.

The waitress comes over to our table. "Is everything all right with your meal, ladies?"

"Yes, thank you. Delicious. I couldn't eat another morsel," Mum says.

"Me neither," my sister rubs her stomach.

Lightweights.

"I can parcel up the remaining desserts up for you to take away." The young girl says.

"That won't be necessary." I take another sweet; a miniature salted caramel cheesecake.

"Stephanie. How many of those desserts have you had?" Mum asks.

I shrug my shoulders. "About five." Her mouth opens, and she widens her eyes.

"What? They're only bite-size. Five is probably the equivalent of a slice of cake." Honestly, you would think I'm adopted by looking at these two. They have stomachs the size of a pea. I'm still hungry after all the sandwiches and desserts, even if I have had five. "Have you heard from Sebastian?"

"Yes, your brother's coming out with us tomorrow for my birthday."

"He's finally going to visit, is he?" He hardly ever calls or visits, but Mum still thinks he's golden balls.

"He's been working a lot lately. They work him ever so hard in the city." She always sticks up for him.

The lemon meringue tart is staring at me. "Last one anybody?"

"Stephanie. I think you've had enough now."

"Oh, Mum. Leave her alone," Sam says.

"I'm not about to let it go to waste."

I finish the bottle of champers too before we go to a few shops and let Mum choose a new outfit for her birthday present.

Tomorrow we have a meal planned at her favourite restaurant with all the family. But today it's just us girls. It's been nice catching up, even if Mum is a pretentious, busy body.

"MAKE sure you wrap up today, snow's forecast," Justin says while I scoop a spoonful of bran flakes from the bowl.

"We only ever get the tiniest flurry. I can't see it being

bad; it never is, especially at the end of November." I chew on my cereal that resembles cardboard.

"Just telling you what the weather report says." Justin places his empty coffee mug on the side like it will wash itself and pulls on his fluorescent high-vis jacket.

"I'll believe it when I see it."

Stepping out of the door, the dry crisp air bites my cheeks and I wonder if Justin is right. I bounce into my car and feel refreshed after having all weekend to recover from my night out.

When I arrive at work, Cal is already here; he looks up from his Mac. "Morning."

"Morning. Do you want a coffee?"

"Yeah, that'd be good." He reaches over the desk to pass me his mug for a refill.

"You already had one? How long have you been here?" It's not like him to come in early.

"About half an hour. I'm leaving early today. I've got a parents' meeting."

"Oh, okay." I take his cup and go to fill it along with mine at the coffee machine. When I turn around, he's standing behind me.

"Your hair colour looks nice." I hold my breath. He noticed. I've straightened it today as well for a change, so I'm sure everyone will notice how different it looks.

"Thanks." I smile, relishing his compliment.

"I like it curly though," he adds. And just like that, his lovely compliment has turned to a backhanded one.

"Cal," I whine.

"What? I'm allowed to say that, aren't I? Don't worry." He waves his hands in the air to mock me. "I'm not saying I want to fuck you or anything." He grins. "I'm not getting into that again. I'm just saying you look better with curly hair."

Ouch. I nod at him and make a mental note never to straighten my hair again. "Here, get your coffee."

He takes it from me and grabs himself a pain au chocolat. I've had my breakfast already, so I stay clear of the pastries.

Kelly walks in and sits at her desk. "Steph, I love your new look."

"Thanks, Kelly." I sit down at my desk next to her and swivel my chair. "Can I ask, do you think it looks better straight or curly?"

Callum smirks.

Kelly thinks it over while tapping her fingers against her lips. "I think I like curly better. It looks more fun on you, but if you want a more serious look, this is definitely it."

Callum looks at me as though to say, I told you so. Smug bastard.

"How was your weekend?" I ask her.

"It was all right. Ryan was in Amsterdam this weekend for a friend's stag doo and he hasn't texted me once."

"Oh, I forgot that was this weekend. I remember you told me he was going."

Callum pipes up again with a mischievous tone. "I bet that was fun for him."

"Cal. She was already worried about him going to Amsterdam on a stag weekend; she doesn't need you rubbing things in her face."

"Is it as bad as they say?" she asks.

"Yep."

"Take no notice of him, Kelly. It's not bad at all. It's a great place to visit with lots of history. I've been." Not that I saw much history. I spent my time in bars, cafes, and sex shops. I glance over at Cal, to see him smiling, like he's reliving the same memories.

"You were high most of the weekend. I'm surprised you remember it." Cal's right, I was, and he looked after me.

"It's not my fault the joints were strong. I wasn't used to it." After two days of smoking, I decided to just stick with alcohol.

Kelly is looking at us both in disbelief. "I've heard it all now. I can't imagine you doing that."

"I was young once, you know." I chuckle to myself.

"So was I, but I didn't get up to anything like that. I clearly missed out."

"No, you didn't." As a mum now, I don't want to encourage that sort of behaviour. We were wild.

"Yeah, you did," Cal contradicts me.

I turn to my work and make a start on checking my emails; I always have more emails on a Monday. Half are spam though, mainly offering me Viagra pills or a mail-order bride or something to that effect.

At lunch, we all go to the pub as usual. I sit in the middle of the bench on the back wall next to Kelly. James sits next to me on the other side, penning me in. Chris sits down opposite, then Sarah takes a seat. I sigh, wishing I'd taken my usual place at the end so I could sit near Cal. We haven't spoken much since the other night, and I want to get back to our friendly, playful banter.

He walks over to the table with a pint in his hand and Chris instantly scrapes his chair along the wooden floor, making space for Cal. He grabs a spare chair from the table behind and places it directly in front of me. I smile as he sits down, hoping the awkwardness from last week has gone and we can go back to being friends. Even though I still want to run my fingers through his hair and kiss those lips and feel his rough bristles scratch my skin. A girl can dream, right?

"Have you ordered?" Cal asks me.

"Not yet."

"Why didn't you tell me what you wanted? I could have ordered for you."

"It's fine, Kelly hasn't ordered yet."

"I'm going to the bar now. What do you want, Steph?"

I hand her some money from my purse. "Order me a chicken salad please and fizzy water." She nods and goes to the bar with Chris. I'm desperate now to keep on track with my food and rein things in before weigh day. After the amount of alcohol I ploughed down my neck last Thursday, and the afternoon tea on Saturday, not to mention the roast dinner and dessert out on Sunday. I'm optimistic that I may get away with a maintain. Oh, who am I kidding? I bet I've put on half a friggin' stone, but at least my hair looks nice.

"So what did you get up to this weekend, other than getting your hair done?" Cal asks.

"It was my mum's birthday, and we went out for the day Saturday. I got my nails done too." I lift my fingers to show off my perfectly polished nails. He takes hold of my palm and slowly caresses his thumb over the back of my hand. His touch ignites me in ways nobody else can, sending an electric current through my bloodstream that settles at the apex of my thighs. My entire body heats in an instant. His thumb moves slowly down to my fingers and over my French manicured nail. He bites his bottom lip and I imagine it's my lip he's biting and the flicker returns between my legs and my mouth is dry once again.

Kelly and Chris return, and I pull my hand away from Cal's skilful fingers. She hands me my fizzy water and I take a sip of the refreshing drink, trying to quench my thirst and put out this blazing fire inside me.

"Did you get up to much?" I ask.

"I took my girls to the cinema." When he calls them his girls, it sounds so endearing.

"Anything good?"

"It was that fairy godmother film."

"Cinderella?" I look at him, confused.

"A new story about a godmother or some shit. I don't know. The girls wanted to watch it. It was a Christmas movie."

"I know what you mean. My daughter would like to watch that."

"We should go. There's another Christmas film coming out in a few weeks. We could go together and take the kids."

"Maybe." I take another gulp of my drink and feel my temperature coming down slightly now he isn't touching me, but each time I catch his gaze it fans the flames.

The server arrives with Cal's meal, placing it in front of him. My tummy grumbles. I lick my lips as he pours the jug of gravy over the pie, chips, and peas. Lucky sod. I can't remember the last time I had pie.

Kelly claps her hands together, and in true Love Island style, hollers, "I've got a text."

Cal takes his eyes off me and turns his attention to her. "Amsterdam guy?"

"Yes." She reads the message to herself with an elated smile radiating across her face. "He's back in the UK now and wants to take me out tonight."

"I knew he would contact you, eventually. He perhaps had a poor signal in Amsterdam."

"Steph, it's Amsterdam, not the fucking moon. They have phones there, you know." Cal smiles with his annoyingly cheeky grin that I love.

"Trust you. I was only trying to make her feel better. It's what girls do."

My chicken salad arrives, along with Kelly and Chris's meals.

"Give the poor bloke a break, he's been out enjoying himself. It's not like you're married." He takes a piece of pie onto his fork and dips it into the gravy. My mouth waters, watching him eat the pastry; I can almost taste it. I sigh, reluctantly taking a bite of my iceberg lettuce.

"I know you're right. It would just have been nice to get a text, but I'm happy now," Kelly says.

CAIREN SWIRLS his breakfast around in his cereal bowl. "Mum, will it snow today?"

"I doubt it, it's been threatening all week and nothing."

Justin walks into the kitchen, leaving a trail of mud from his work boots.

"Justin, your boots." I sigh, knowing that's one more job I have to do before leaving for work.

"Sorry."

"Why are you wearing them around the house?"

"I've been in the garden. Do you want to clean the dog's shit up?"

"No, but you don't have to trail your muddy boots throughout the friggin' house."

He ignores me and cracks an egg into a bowl, making his usual omelette breakfast that results in half a dozen pots all over the worktop. I mop the tiled kitchen and parquet flooring that leads to the back door, and decide to leave before he makes any more jobs for me.

"I'm going now."

"See ya."

I kiss Cairen on the cheek and give him a squeeze. "Love you, have a good day at school."

"Bye Mum."

Cassie is upstairs getting ready with her music on. "Cassie, bye love," I shout at the bottom of the stairs.

She arrives at the top of the landing. "Mum, can you do me a fishtail plait before you go?"

"Cassie, why didn't you say about half an hour ago? I'm going to be late."

"Can you just do me a normal plait, then?"

"Get me a hairbrush."

She runs down the stairs with a brush and bobble. "We find out what parts we have in the nativity today."

"Oh, that's exciting. I hope you get a good part." I gather her blonde locks into a high ponytail.

"I think I will get the part of Mary."

Once I've secured the bobble, I plait the ponytail. "You may not, sweetheart. Don't get your hopes up." My hand strokes her hair. "There, all done." I kiss her forehead. "See you later. Have a good day and don't get upset if you don't get the part you want."

"Okay, Mum. Bye."

I make it to work barely on time and find Callum at the coffee machine.

"Morning, Steph."

"Morning."

"I've already made you a coffee. It's on your desk."

"Thank you, that's great." Things have been amiable with Callum these last few days—considering how fraught things were this time last week—we've actually been getting on well as friends and I've enjoyed his company. He hasn't been flirty, just friendly. I think he's got the message that there'll never be anything between us. *Have you though?* My subconscious asks. I ignore her.

After a few hours, I look out the window to see it is snowing heavily. Justin was right. He's been saying it's going to snow for about two weeks now and it finally has. I doubt it will settle though—I'm not worried.

When the workday is done, the snow is still falling. I walk to my car covered in snow and Cal helps me clear it from the windshield before clearing his own. I climb in to start the engine. Nothing, it won't start. *Great.* Cal sees my struggle and comes over. He tries the ignition again as though I didn't turn the key right or something. When he hears nothing, he lifts the bonnet.

I watch him as he examines under my hood. "What are you looking at?" He knows absolutely nothing about cars, unless he's digested a Haynes manual on Suzuki's in the last twenty years, I'm doomed.

He bursts out laughing. "Fuck knows. I know shit about cars."

I thought so. He puts the bonnet back down. "You can stay at my place. I'm only a ten-minute walk from here. Looking at the weather, you shouldn't be driving, anyway."

CHAPTER
Nine

I look towards the road covered in the white stuff. The traffic is moving at a snail's pace. The thought of driving home in these treacherous conditions has me clutching at my throat and the sound of my beating heart thrashes through my ears. I hate driving in poor weather. Justin could drive here in his work van, but it would take hours to get here with the current traffic situation. I think about what Cal said. It would be easier to just stay with him, and I wouldn't have to drive back here in the morning. "Are you sure I won't be intruding?"

"Steph, of course not." He puts his hands in his pocket and presses his lips together while he waits for my answer.

I pause, releasing my throat and stroking my neck. How bad can it be? Now we're working together and becoming friends? I feel like we've been able to rekindle the friendship we ruined before. Kelly has already left, so I can't really ask to stay with her.

"Let me call Justin." I sit in my car out of the snow and pull my phone from my bag. Cal climbs into the passenger seat. Justin answers, and I give Cal a wide-eyed look, pleading for some privacy. He rolls his eyes but doesn't move.

"Steph."

"Hi. My car won't start."

He huffs down the line. "I knew that pile of crap would eventually breakdown. You should have got a new car when I offered. Trust it to happen today of all days."

"Now isn't the time for I told you so's."

"Where are you?"

"I'm still at work. It's totally dead."

"How bad is it out there?"

"It's bad. The traffic isn't moving, and some have pulled over and abandoned their cars."

"I don't fancy coming to get you in the van. It's just taken me an hour to get home. I've walked around to get the kids from your mum's. I wasn't attempting to drive down her street."

"Don't come out if it's not safe. I can stay over at a colleague's tonight and walk to work in the morning."

"Good idea. Whose place are you staying at?"

"Callum's here. He's looked at my car but isn't sure what's wrong." I glance at Cal tapping his foot in the footwell, making his leg shake along with the rest of the car. "He said I could stay with him and his girlfriend."

A puff of air escapes through Cal's nose, and he snickers, shaking his head.

"Where does he live?" Justin asks.

"It's a ten-minute walk."

"Fine, makes sense and will save me from coming out. I'll leave work early tomorrow to look at your car."

"Surely you won't be working tomorrow?"

"If it stays like this, we'll shut the site."

"Are the kids all right?"

"They're outside building snowmen. Do you want me to get them?"

"Let them play. I'll call later to say goodnight."

"I'll talk to you later, then."

"Bye."

I let the phone slip from my hand and into my bag. Callum frowns. His finger and thumb pinch his eyebrow where his silver ring used to be.

"I told you I don't have a girlfriend."

I knew that, but I didn't want Justin thinking I was staying with another man alone. He wouldn't understand the relationship we have. I've known Cal my whole life and despite our situation, I would feel more comfortable staying at his place than Kelly or Sarah's.

"Sorry, I meant the girl you're casually seeing, or whatever."

"I'm not seeing her anymore."

"Oh, since when?"

"About a month ago."

"Oh." This is awkward, so he stopped seeing her not long after I started working with him. I try not to read too much into this. It's obviously just a coincidence.

"So you're staying at mine?"

"If that's okay?"

"Yeah, I said it's cool. Come on, it's fucking freezing in here."

"What are you doing with your car?"

"I'll get it when the weather's better. I'm only around the corner. It's not worth driving in this."

We both step out of my Suzuki and I button my coat right up to the neck.

"You didn't have plans tonight, did you?" I pull my gloves from my bag and slip my icy hands into the fabric.

"Nah, the girls are at their mother's."

We trudge through the deep snow. Thick clumps fall,

settling on Cal's coal black hair and dark lashes; a stark contrast against the pure white flakes.

"Was he all right with you?"

"Who?"

"Who do you think, Jack fucking Frost?"

"What?"

"Justin. Was he all right about you staying out? He moaned last time you wanted to go shopping, didn't he?"

"Oh, yes. He seemed fine. I think he's relieved he doesn't have to trek out here to get me, to be honest."

"He was cool about you staying with me?"

"Yes, of course. Why wouldn't he? We're friends, aren't we? Although I think he would have let me stay with the Grim Reaper if it meant he didn't have to come and get me." I laugh and I can see my breath in the cold air. I glance at Cal in his black coat and think he could be the Grim Reaper. He already has my soul.

He meets my gaze. "I don't think I would be so understanding if you were my wife."

"Why not?" I furrow my brow and fold my arms over my body.

"There's no fucking way I'd let you stay with your ex if you were mine. But if we were together, I would've driven all fucking night to get you. He sounds like an arse."

"He's not an arsehole. He trusts me. Besides, he doesn't know you're my ex." The bottom of my trousers stick to my legs as I plod in the thick fluffy snow. I can't feel my toes anymore.

"You haven't told him?"

"No. Why would I? He doesn't need to know that. It's all in the past."

"But if he trusts you. Why not tell him?"

"I don't know. It hasn't really crossed my mind. I don't sit thinking about you at home. I have better things to talk about. What's the point in bringing all that up?"

"Fair enough."

My teeth chatter and I wrap my arms around my body tighter, hoping to keep out the chill.

"You're shivering. Not far now, just round this corner." Cal wraps an arm around my shoulder, rubbing his hand up and down to warm me up. It works to a certain degree. Being close to him always raises my temperature. We turn the corner to fresh, unspoilt snow. The setting sun casts a glowing pink hue as it kisses the ground, illuminating the usually dreary estate. With Cal's arm wrapped firmly around me, the majestic setting reflects my mood, taking me back to our teens.

By the time we reach his home, the bottom of my trousers are soaked.

"Home sweet home." He opens the door to his ground-floor apartment. I step into his small entrance hall that's only big enough for the two of us.

"Let me take your coat. I'll pop it on the radiator." I hand Callum my coat and take off my faux leather boots and drenched socks. He shakes the flakes from his damp hair, wetting me in the process.

"Come through, I'll show you around." He takes hold of my wrist, sending an electric current through my veins, and leads me into the small modern kitchen. The work surfaces are spotless and minimal, with grey appliances and units. I wouldn't have expected anything else from him. He presses a button on the thermostat that's fixed to the kitchen wall. We walk down a corridor and he opens a door. "This is the living room."

I stand next to the doorjamb scanning his nicely decorated lounge—well, nice for him—it could definitely do with a woman's touch. He has modern striped wallpaper along one wall, in a variety of grey shades, a large, black, leather, corner sofa with a grey plush carpet, and accessories.

"What's this, fifty shades of grey or what? Where are you taking me next, to your red room?" I giggle and cover my mouth.

"Red room?" His head flinches back slightly and he squishes his eyebrows together.

I exhale and slump my shoulders. "A spanking room filled with sex toys."

"Got ya." The corner of his mouth curls upwards. "I only have a two-bedroom apartment, but I can spank you over the kitchen counter. I don't need a room for that." He winks at me and it's like my vagina has eyes and ears as my walls clench and my stomach flips. "And you should know I don't need to use sex toys."

I press my lips together, holding back a smile. I don't want to encourage him. But he's right. He was more than enough for me.

"You can sleep in my girls' room tonight." He leads me to the next door, into a bedroom with two single beds, similar to my daughter's room with pink and lilac colours gracing the walls. I step over a doll and place it in the large wooden dollhouse.

"Did you make this?"

"Yeah, Bethy wanted a custom made house. She designed it."

"Cal, this is fantastic."

"Thanks. I'm gonna get changed." He leaves me in the room for a few minutes. My handbag drops on the single bed and I sink down next to it, taking in my new surroundings where I will spend the night. I check my makeup in my compact mirror and re-apply my lipstick.

Cal returns wearing an old plain black t-shirt and some black jogging bottoms, holding a bunch of folded clothes. "Here, I got you some spare clothes, if you want to change out of those wet trousers."

"Thank you." I take the clothes from him and hold up the joggers. "Err, Cal, there's no way I can fit in your clothes." He's taller than me, but my chest, hips and arse are much wider than his.

"They stretch." A cheeky grin plays on his lips.

I swat his arm, laughing. I've always been bigger than him, even in school, but my weight never bothered him and he always complimented my curves.

"I'll just keep my trousers on." I know however much those bottoms stretch; it wouldn't be enough to go over my hips.

He shrugs. "Suit yourself. Let me show you where the bathroom is." I follow him out of the girls' room to the door opposite. "Here." He opens the door to his small bathroom; it's clean with a shower, no bath. We walk to the kitchen, passing another door, which I assume is his bedroom. I can't help but wonder what it's like, probably more shades of grey, but I'm still intrigued. "Help yourself to whatever you want."

"Thank you."

"What do you fancy for tea? I have a few frozen pizzas, or I can do a stir-fry or Bolognese."

"You're going to cook for me?" To be fair, he was always an excellent cook; his mother taught him well.

"Yeah, unless you want to cook." He chortles, most likely remembering that I'm a shit cook.

"I'll have you know, I can cook now," I lie and fold my arms across my chest.

He glances at me with his cheeky grin. I don't think he believes me.

"I'll have whatever you want to cook."

"I'll do a stir-fry; it's easy." He leans back against the counter. "Remember when you cooked that jacket potato?"

"I can't believe you remember that."

"It's hard to forget, seeing as it exploded all over the fucking microwave and I cleaned it up." He titters. "Who puts a baked fucking potato in the microwave for thirty minutes?"

"I didn't know. I'd never cooked a meal in my life before going to university."

He boils the kettle. "Coffee?"

"Yes please, I need something to warm me up."

He looks like he wants to say something or touch me. If we were together, he would have said, *'I'll warm you up'*, and he would have wrapped his arms around me, kissed my lips and within minutes I would be on fire.

"I put the heating on when I walked in."

"I know, I saw. Thank you."

After making two coffees, we both stand facing each other in the kitchen, holding our mugs. The cordiality between us is so familiar. Like we've never been apart. He's holding his drink near his mouth, blowing into his cup before taking a sip. Each time our eyes meet, I get a flutter in the pit of my stomach like I'm eighteen again—one look from him and that was it—I used to sit in class gazing at him, knowing he was mine and thinking how lucky I was.

"Have you warmed up yet?" he asks.

"Yes, a little." I clasp my mug in both hands, feeling the warmth from the hot cup, and take another sip.

"When do you want tea?"

"Whenever."

"I'll start now if you're hungry."

I look at the clock on his kitchen wall and it's almost 6pm.

"Okay, can I help?"

"Yeah, you can show me your improved cooking skills."

Oh no, I shouldn't have offered.

He pulls out a bag of pre-chopped stir-fry vegetables and some pre-chopped chicken breast in a sauce and throws it all into a wok.

"Do you want to stir?"

I smile and take hold of the spatula, poking the food around.

He stands at the side of me and clasps my hand, causing a spark that sends a tingle up my arm.

"Steph. Like this." Scraping the spatula along the bottom of the pan, he flips the chicken and vegetables over and gives them a good stir. "Here, sprinkle some of this seasoning in." He hands me a pot of Chinese spices and I give it a little shake and continue to mix.

"So what happened with your girlfriend, sorry the girl you were seeing?"

"It wasn't anything serious. I go on dates, but I haven't really seen anyone properly since I left the girls' mother."

"Oh, how come?" I stop stirring and turn to look at Cal.

"I just can't be bothered with it all. I'm not the settling down kind of guy." He nods towards the wok for me to continue mixing.

"Oh, yes. No kidding." I laugh.

"I haven't met the right person, or maybe I did and fucked it up." He looks down at the food, almost mesmerised by my circular motions. "I don't want you to think I'm still... you know..."

"What?" I'm not sure what he's trying to say.

"I don't know." He sighs.

"You have commitment issues?" I say it for him; at least I think that's what he's getting at.

"I don't have commitment issues," he groans.

"Yes, you do. I haven't known you to be with anyone for much longer than a year. I was shocked to find you stayed with someone long enough to have two kids. She must have been really special."

"She's okay, but was never the love of my life. She got pregnant within a few months of our relationship and I stayed for my kid. I tried so hard to make it work, but after our second daughter was born, we just didn't get on anymore."

"See? Commitment issues." I smile, knocking my shoulder against his.

He just smiles and drops the subject. If only he could talk about his feelings.

"Is this done, do you think?" I point the spatula towards the food in the wok.

"Looks good to me. Is that your first stir-fry?" He grins and takes the wok from me.

"Hey." I swat him with the utensil. "Could you tell?"

"Yeah. You were just tickling the food instead of stirring it." He chuckles to himself, plating up our meal and places it on the small square table in the kitchen.

"Justin always takes over. I do very little cooking at home."

"Wine?" he asks.

"That would be lovely."

"You like red, don't you?"

"I like any, let's be honest. But yes, red will do nicely, thank you."

He pops the cork and grabs two glasses from the cupboard.

"Here you go." He hands me a large glass of burgundy filled to the brim.

"Thanks. Are you trying to get me tipsy?"

He grins. "No, but if you want to get sloshed, be my guest. You're hilarious when you're well lubricated and even better stoned." He sits down opposite me.

"Cal." I titter. If only he knew I'm already lubricated. Just being near him makes my body react in ways I can't control. I pick my fork up to eat. "Cal, this is tasty, if I say so myself." The onions in the stir-fry have caramelised and the peppers are charred and soft. The combination of the two, along with the diced chicken coated in a sticky soy sauce, tastes sweet and has my taste buds wanting more.

Cal takes a bite and samples my cooking. "Not bad for your first attempt." He glances over at me with a smirk. "Let's keep it real, though. Tesco did all the work, you just tickled it in the wok."

I giggle and kick his foot under the table.

"Are we playing footsie now?" He rubs the sole of his foot up my leg. I lock my knees together and he stops when he can't go any further. My heart is jumping like gymnasts on a trampoline and I almost wish I hadn't closed my legs. He smirks and wiggles his toes between my knees.

"Cal, stop fooling around." My voice is breathless. I fork more stir-fry into my mouth, hoping it will take my mind off the throb between my thighs.

"I'm sorry." He removes his foot and continues to eat.

I take a sip of my wine and it coats my tongue in a thick rich syrupy texture—I savour it—so much better than that low-calorie chateau de shite Justin buys for me, while he drinks the good stuff. "Thank you, Cal. This is a really nice meal."

"It's nice to share a meal with someone." He pushes the remaining bit of food on his plate around with his fork. "I enjoy spending time with you, Steph."

I'm tongue-tied. My fingers ache to touch his skin. I want

to tell him I love spending time with him. But I'm afraid of where it will lead. If he made a move on me now, I'm not sure I could resist. My head is light and not just from the wine.

He picks up my empty plate and takes it over to the sink.

"Let me wash those for you."

"There's no need, Steph. I'll put them in the dishwasher."

"Well, let me rinse them for you first?"

"Nah, it's cool. It'll only take me a minute. You sit and relax." I'm not used to relaxing after a meal. There are always a million pots to tend to.

"I'll call my kids before they go to bed."

"Sure."

I pull my phone from my pocket and call our landline, tapping my middle fingernail on the table, waiting for Justin to pick up.

"Ay-up."

"Hi Justin, is everything okay?"

"Yes, how're you?"

"I'm good. I wanted to say goodnight to the kids. They're not in bed yet, are they?"

Cal sits down and leans back in his chair, watching me intently while swilling his wine.

"No, I've let them stay up to watch the end of this film. Hang on. Mummy's on the phone."

I smile at Cal while I wait for one of the kids to talk.

"Mummy?"

"Hi Cairen, what are you watching?"

"A shark film. It's eating everyone." He sounds enraptured.

"Oh, nice. Is that appropriate?"

"Dad said I could watch it." Of course he did.

"Did he now?" I shake my head. Justin is so soft with these kids.

"It's great Mum. Do you want to watch it with us tomorrow?"

"Err, I'll give it a miss."

"Cassie wants to talk."

"Okay, I love you, I'll see you tomorrow."

"Love you Mum, bye-bye."

"Mum? Can I tell you about Chloe? She's being a bitch again."

"Cassie. Don't use that word." I tut.

"You say it."

"I'm an adult." My cheeks heat again. Cal is chuckling at me getting scolded by my ten year old.

"Listen, Mum, they've given her the lead role in the school Christmas panto, and she doesn't deserve it. I'm sick of her. I should've had that part."

"What part did you get?"

"I'm the star." She huffs. Then in her most whiny tone says, "I wanted to be Mary." She sniffles, and I wish I were home right now to comfort her.

"Sweetheart, Mary doesn't do much except sit next to Joseph, looking pretty. Do you have any lines?"

"I have a song to sing on my own."

"Wow, it sounds to me like you're the *star* of the show."

"That's what Grandma said." She sniffles down the handset. "I hate Chloe. Why does she get everything she wants?"

"Well, you don't do bad yourself. I seem to recall you getting everything you ask for."

"But I want to be Mary." She drawls. Cal must be able to hear her because he's grinning at me.

"We'll talk about it tomorrow, okay. Take no notice of Chloe."

"Will you ring the school?"

"I'm not ringing the school telling them you want to be Mary."

"Nobody cares about me." She huffs again.

"I do, I love you. Now enjoy the rest of the night and don't think about it. I'll be home tomorrow and you can go through your lines with me."

"All right, Mummy."

"I'll let you go then, don't stay up too late watching that film."

"I haven't been watching it, it's boring. I've been on my phone."

"Okay, don't stay up too late on your phone. Love you. I'll see you tomorrow." I rub my chest, wishing I was there right now to tuck them in bed and read them a story.

"Bye."

"Bye, sweetheart. Put your dad on."

"What's up?"

"Is it still snowing there?" I stare out of Cal's kitchen window and I can see the white flakes still falling.

"It's pretty bad, still coming down thick."

"I'll call you tomorrow, see how things are."

"Fine, speak to you tomorrow."

"Night."

"Night."

I end the call and let out a long breath.

"Another bottle?" Cal pulls out another bottle of wine.

"Yes, please. I need one after that. How many bottles do you have in there?"

"I've got a good stash, don't worry."

"Could you hear my daughter?"

He grins as he pours me a glass of red. "Yeah, I heard. She wants to be Mary."

I chuckle to myself. "Veruca Salt would be more fitting, right?"

He laughs. "Bit of a drama queen, is she?"

"You could say that."

"She reminds me of you. You get mardy when you don't get your own way."

"Cal, I do not." I swipe at his hand on the table.

"Do too." He takes another drink and gulps it down.

"This kid called Chloe has the part of Mary. You know who her mother is, don't you?"

He shrugs his shoulders. "Why would I?"

"It's Melanie friggin' Stevens from school." She was my nemesis.

He shakes his head. "Still not a fucking clue."

"You know, that blonde bitch that thought she was God's gift."

"Still nada. I've slept since then, Steph."

"Cal, you must remember her. She fancied the pants off you."

He raises his eyebrows. "Did she? Damn, why can't I remember her?"

"She was a bitch." The bane of my school days, and now her spawn is tormenting my daughter.

Cal scratches the scruff on his jaw. "Did I tap her?"

"No, at least I hope you didn't. She was horrible to me."

"Probably why I don't remember. I wouldn't have shagged anyone who was mean to you." A warm smile spreads on his face, reaching his eyes.

"I've missed you." It's mainly the wine talking. I don't seem in control of my mouth anymore, or my body, for that matter.

"You've seen me every day for the last month." His hand reaches across the table. Our fingertips lightly press against each other and the hairs prick up on the back of my neck.

"But I've missed *you*." I move my fingers ever so slightly, tangling them with his. "The person I knew in school. You're more *you* now than you are at work." I try to make sense; it's hard to find the words. A tingle runs from my fingertip right through my centre. My breathing is ragged and my head is cloudy. "I guess what I'm trying to say is that I miss us chatting, laughing and hanging out."

He rubs his hand over his face. "I've missed you too."

CHAPTER

"**Y**ou were always the one that got away." He lets out a heavy sigh and looks down at where our fingers connect. I settle back in my chair and jut out my chin feeling smug, but there's a heaviness in my chest that aches with sadness for him and me. Us. He pulls at my heart with an invisible cord that always tugs me back to him. His hand moves over mine, while his thumb traces circles on my palm and I somehow feel his touch between my thighs.

"You pushed me away." I remind him.

"I know. I sometimes think about what my life might have been like if I hadn't ended things with you." He stares into his glass of red before knocking back another mouthful.

My mouth is open and I don't really know what to say. It would be so easy to kiss him right now. Would he kiss me back? If I weren't married, I would already be in his bed.

"Do you ever think about me?" he asks.

"No." I pull my hand away to take hold of the stem of my glass. If only he knew I think about him almost every minute of every day. Well, I have since I saw him again. Before that, I would only think of him when I was reminded of him.

"You hurt me when you mailed all our photos and my stuff back to my mum's house." His dull eyes peer into his empty glass, twirling the stem with his fingers.

I take a big swig of wine and swallow. "I'm sorry, but I couldn't keep all your shit. It was too painful. I didn't want to throw it away either. You hurt me, more than you'll ever know. It took me a long time to get over you and I couldn't have photos of you, or your CDs and sweater and stuff lying around." I take another drink, needing to keep my hands busy. I don't want to do anything I'll regret, like wrap my arms around him and kiss those red-stained lips and show him how sorry I really am.

"Did you keep your ring?" He pours another glass and tops up my half-empty one.

"Yes, it's in my jewellery box. I never wear it but I couldn't part with it." I think it's the only thing I kept. "Do you still have the watch I bought you for Christmas?"

"Yes, but it broke, the glass cracked, and I never got it fixed. It's in the box you sent back with the rest of my shit that reminds me of you."

"You kept the box?" I thought he would have chucked everything away.

"Yes, of course I did. That was a year of my life and some wonderful memories. Unlike you, I wanted to hang on to our memories."

"Why? You were the one that ended everything. You said you didn't love me anymore. Do you have any idea how distraught I was?" The pressure builds behind my eyes and I pinch the bridge of my nose to hold back tears. I take another mouthful of the sweet velvet wine to distract my thoughts.

"You know I'm sorry, but just because we weren't together, didn't mean I wanted to erase a year of my life. I know I was wrong. I've had to live with my mistakes."

"Are you saying you wished we were still together?" I peer into his eyes, trying to read them, but I fear I've had too much alcohol to make a good judgement.

"Yes, no. I don't know." He sighs, placing his head in his hands.

"Don't do this, Cal. You can't do this to me. I'm married and I have kids and I'm happy. I was finally happy without you and now you come back into my life and start messing with my head."

"I'm sorry, forget I said anything."

"You've only started wanting me again since I started working with you, and the only reason you want me is because you can't have me. I've been left wanting you since the day you broke me. I've spent a lifetime trying to get over you," I cry.

"Steph." He looks me in the eye and reaches over to put his hand on my face.

"Don't *Steph* me. You can't do this to me. I'm going to bed, it's late, we have to be at work in the morning and I've already had too much alcohol." I get up from the kitchen table, fighting back tears.

"All right, just forget it. I'll see you in the morning." He stays seated, drinking his wine as I make my way down the hall.

Once alone in his daughter's room, I lean my head back against the door and close my eyes. Taking in several long, deep breaths, I walk over to the bed and undress. I pick up the t-shirt he gave me, pull it over my head, and take my bra off. It fits. A little fitted around my chest—okay, more than fitted—let's just say it's snug. It won't go past my hips, so I let it bunch slightly above my silky short style knickers. I look at the joggers again, but I don't attempt them.

THERE'S a thrumming in my temple. I've been tossing and turning for the last two hours. Everything he said plays over in my mind. I rub my hand over my forehead to ease the throb and sigh, knowing if he didn't end things with me at university, he would have eventually. I'm no fool. He would have left me with kids as he did with his girls' mother. That would be me, a single mum.

After staring into space for what feels like an eternity, I get up to get a drink of water. Tiptoeing through to the kitchen so as not to wake Cal. The lights are still off, but the streetlamp gleams through the kitchen window, giving me enough light to see my way around. I rifle through the cupboards, looking for a glass. When I turn around, I gasp. Cal is standing in the kitchen wearing nothing but tight black boxer shorts. My mouth gapes as I scan his delicious ink-covered body.

"Are you all right?" he asks softly.

"Yes, I just wanted a drink of water. I couldn't find a cup." Oh no. I'm standing here with my arse on show in his t-shirt. My heart beats faster with every passing second, and my cheeks flush.

He steps towards me, and I hold my breath as he lifts his arm over my shoulder. My body trembles. *Is he going to kiss me?* I freeze. My chest tightens. He surveys me for a moment, inches away from my lips. I gulp. The cupboard door behind me swings open and he pulls out a cup. I breathe out a sigh of relief when he takes a step back. Though my shoulders drop as disappointment creeps up my spine and I sag against the counter. He turns on the tap and I'm practically drooling over his insanely beddable arse.

I lick my dry lips, wanting to sink my teeth into those toned cheeks. Cal spins back around, handing me the water. I pour it down my parched throat and examine the plastic cup in my hand with a princess design.

"Nice. Beauty and the Beast."

He smirks. "I think it's fitting, don't you?"

"Are you saying I'm a child or that I'm Belle?" I feel like Belle right now being held captive by this devilishly handsome man.

"I'm saying you're beautiful Steph." He leans back against the worktop and surveys my body. His eyes settle on my knickers, and he swallows. Moving on to my breasts, he licks his lips and pulls them between his teeth. I'm sure my nipples are hard and prominent in this tight top.

"That's so cheesy." I let out a giggle and take another sip of water.

He grins. "But you like cheese."

"Is that one of your pick up lines?" I examine his exquisite torso, studying every muscle and tattoo in the dim light. With each heavy breath, the inked phoenix flitters on his chest as if it's about to take flight.

"Only for you."

"Well, if I'm Belle you must be the beast." My gaze wanders downwards until I reach the bulge under his tight boxer shorts and ogle for a beat too long.

Cal clears his throat and I pull my eyes away from his crotch, hoping he didn't notice me staring. "I'll show you the beast if you like."

"Cal." I pant and take another sip.

He bites his lip, watching me drink my water, closing the gap between us. *Is he getting another glass?* I don't move; I want to feel him near me, if only while he reaches up.

"You wore my t-shirt?"

"Yes." I glance down at his snug top that fits tight around my chest. "It was this or nothing."

The warm air from his mouth finds my cheek, but his arm doesn't go above my shoulder; it goes to my waist. His fingers find the hem of his shirt and slip underneath onto my bare skin, igniting my soul.

"I would have preferred nothing." His hand wanders around my back, sending tingles up my spine. His other hand slides over my silky underwear and squeezes my plump cheek. All my senses are heightened and I've never felt so alive.

His fingers electrify my skin as they glide across my back. I don't know what to say, so I say nothing as his lips inch closer. His hand reaches for my breast and I wish I'd kept my bra on; motherhood and age haven't been kind. My boobs are saggy and softer since he last touched me here. I place my hand in front of my stomach to hide my insecurities, but he takes hold of my fingers, moving them gently away. His breath falls into my mouth and he smells like toothpaste. My body melds to the familiar feel of his warm lips brushing against mine. His tongue runs along my bottom lip, parting my mouth like he always would, and my heart races. I'm putty in his arms. He always had this effect on me.

Our lips lock together like magnets, sending an electromagnetic charge into my bloodstream that buzzes through every cell. Our tongues entwine, feverishly lapping each other—I devour him—I've been starved of him for so long. His hand squeezes my breast while his other slips under my silky underwear, holding me tight against him. A moan reverberates into his mouth and his tongue stiffens. I lift my leg to pull him further into me, and his tongue isn't the only thing that's hard. I forget everything, wrapping my arms around him, running my fingers down his back. He holds my leg and lifts my other, placing his erection firmly between my thighs.

Before my mind catches up with my body, he's lifted me. My legs wrap tightly around his waist as he carries me out of the kitchen. Wow, he's still strong. Even with my extra weight, he can still lift me easily. I continue to kiss him, tracing his tongue with mine. He walks into his bedroom. The bedside lamp is on, giving the masculine grey room a soft glow. Cal's slender yet strong physique hovers over me as he lays me on his large bed. The crows on his stomach ripple as he climbs on top of me, resuming our kiss.

My heart is pounding against my ribs like a wildcat trapped in a cage. He pulls the t-shirt over my breasts, but I pull it back down, conscious of my saggy boobs and stretch marks adorning my stomach. I reach for the switch on the lamp. The wire and button hang next to the pillow. He grabs my wrist before I can turn it off, pinning me beneath him, kissing me deeper and grinding his erection between my legs. His fingers unfurl from my arm, only to glide back under the cotton shirt, seeking my nipple. The fabric rides up and I tug it back down, aware of the light still on. I reach for the switch again. Cal grabs my hand, pulling it away from the cord.

"I've been fantasising about getting you in my bed for weeks. There's no way in hell you're turning that light off." The rasp in his voice reverberates throughout my body. My eyes widen and my body stills like a deer caught in the headlights.

"Cal." My voice is barely a whisper, a breathy moan that only he can summon out of me. His tongue darts back into my mouth, circling before he pulls away, sucking and biting my bottom lip.

"I want to see you." He pulls the cotton hem up again. "All of you." His ravenous eyes move from my face to my breasts. I pull him back to my lips to distract his gaze while I squirm and tug the top back down. He laughs into my mouth as I writhe under him and we fight with his t-shirt.

I whimper as his kiss leaves my mouth, and he lifts his head to look me in the eye. "You don't have to hide anything from me, Steph." His words calm me, making my body relax slightly. "I know every inch of this body of yours." His rough hand roams under the fabric and his thumb finds my nipple, circling until he has its full attention.

I gulp. "It's not the same body you remember." I lift my hand to touch his cheek, needing to feel every part of him. My fingers wrap around his unruly locks that have fallen in front of his face.

"No?" His hot breath falls on my lips. He holds his weight above me with one arm, while his other hand teases my nipple under the cotton shirt.

"No, I'm not a young girl anymore." My body trembles.

He smiles and his lips trail along my jaw with small pecks of admiration. Again, he lifts the shirt above my bust and stares at my quivering body, caressing my breast after I lost the battle with the t-shirt.

"No, you're not a girl anymore, Steph." His voice is deep and ragged. "You're a woman. A fucking sexy woman." His words set me ablaze and the fire crackles under my skin. I watch him engulf my areola and lap his tongue around my stiff peak while fondling the other. He comes up for air. "What happened to your piercing?"

"What?" I pant. My head is cloudy and I can't think straight.

"Your nipple piercing, it's gone." The sparkle in his eyes dulls for a few seconds before he continues to lick and nip my soft, bouncy flesh.

"Well, so has your tongue piercing."

He flashes a cheeky smile. "Don't worry about that. I can

still make you come with my tongue, even without my piercing." His eager mouth makes its way to the top of my silk underwear. The tension builds in my stomach and the heat rises between my legs. Knowing what's coming, I shut my eyes tight. He tugs at the elastic, and I lift my bottom to free my knickers. Cal's nimble fingers stroke my skin as he slides my panties off, discarding them on the bedroom floor. His strong hands push against my knees, while his tongue glides up my inner thigh, and I'm so glad I shaved this morning.

"I want to taste you again." He sucks at my flesh. *Oh, please taste me.* I could come from his words alone.

His head burrows between my legs and I feel his warm breath there as his tongue slides from my slick opening up to the bundle of nerves. He groans and the vibration from his mouth brings me close to the edge and I let out a moan of my own. "Fuck, I've missed your taste."

I grab onto the bedsheets as he gets to work, licking, sucking and nipping. His stubbly beard rubs against me and I'm skyrocketed to the clouds. I whimper as he lifts his head away. "You like that?" he asks.

My eyes still shut, my back arched. "Yes," I scream. "Don't stop." I grab hold of his thick hair, forcing him back down to me, lifting my hips to meet his mouth. His fingers slide inside my throbbing and desperate wet heat. Flickering and fluttering, remembering exactly how I like to be touched, and I come undone. "Cal, Cal," I scream, pulsating around his fingers. He holds steady as I ride out my orgasm, licking gently. My breathing slows and I descend back down to earth. His mouth trails up my pillowy stomach, kissing every curve of my body over my round, soft breasts that peek out from under the t-shirt.

"Baby, I'm so fucking hard it hurts." His teeth sink into

my shoulder, and his mouth sucks the sting away. He nuzzles into the crevice of my neck, digging his erection into my fleshy thigh.

I catch my breath. "Do you have a condom?"

He hovers above me, holding his weight with the palms of his hands placed on either side of my head. "Yeah, I do." He reaches to his bedside cabinet to retrieve a small wrapper. He tears the foil with his teeth while pulling his boxers down to his thighs, and I've never seen him put a condom on so fast.

He lies back on top of me, holding his weight with his elbows. His tip presses firmly against my opening. "You sure?"

"Yes," I cry, trying not to sound desperate for the feel of him inside me. I wrap my legs around him and pull him into me. It feels like home. A wave of nostalgia fills me and I let out another moan. "Cal."

"Steph." He pushes further into me. His possessive mouth smothers my moans, kissing me deeper.

After several thrusts, he grabs my waist, rolling over and pulling me on top of him. "Ride me, baby." He lifts his hips while I rock against him. He tugs at the t-shirt and this time I lift it off completely, letting him massage my breasts with both hands. My entire body is trembling. The feel of him inside me is transcendent. He takes me places I'd long forgotten, beyond the borders of this world. He reaches a hand down between us to rub circles around me and I'm transfixed in an emotion of pure joy, ecstasy and fulfilment that exceeds the laws of physics.

"I'm going to come again," I pant. My legs turn to jelly and my body shakes. I press my hands onto his chest to steady myself and throw my head back. He takes over the motions and thrusts into me. Flashes of light fill my mind with each pulse and my walls clench around him.

"Fuck." His arms wrap around me while his greedy lips envelop my nipple, and he bites down as he comes only seconds after me. He rests his forehead against my chest while he catches his breath and sucks at my tender breast before flopping back on the bed. "Fuck, Steph." He exhales, holding onto my shaky thighs. I can still feel him inside me. I don't want to get off. It feels incredibly familiar, like we're made to fit together. I've missed this intimacy between us more than I knew. "Come here." He pulls me down to him and I roll off to his side. "Are you all right?" he asks, placing soft kisses along my jaw.

"I'm more than all right." Gazing into his eyes, I don't want to think about anything else, not tonight. We always had good sex, but this was intense.

He sits up and removes the condom. "Back in a minute." I lean up on my elbow to get a better view of his toned, lily-white arse walking out of the room.

He returns with a wet flannel and pushes against my knees. I open my legs, allowing him to wash between my thighs as he always would. After tossing the cloth in the laundry hamper, he climbs back into bed and pulls the duvet over the two of us. I lay my head half on his chest and shoulder and he plays with my long hair.

"You have more tattoos than before." A flock of crows decorates his stomach, sweeping around his side. "This is definitely new." I trace my fingers over the outline.

"It tickles." He laughs and holds my hand instead. Like me, he was always ticklish. He would tickle me till I begged him to stop, and then make love to me. The memory makes my stomach flutter again.

"So why did you take your tongue and eyebrow piercings out?"

"They didn't bode well for job interviews."

"That's true." I giggle.

"What about you? I was disappointed you didn't have your piercing."

I silently laugh to myself. "I thought you were disappointed. I took it out after we broke up. I only got it to impress you. It wasn't really me." He kisses my forehead and I tilt my head to see an endearing smile like he never knew I did that for him. I never told him. It was just something I thought he would find sexy, so I did it and he loved it. "Plus, I couldn't have breastfed with that in." I giggle and glance up to find a smile playing on his lips.

"You breastfed?"

"Yes,"

"Wow, I never thought I would be jealous of an infant."

I swat at his stomach.

"I always loved your tits." He caresses one, then the other, giving them both his attention.

"They're not as perky as they were the last time you saw them."

He kisses my head. "They're better, fuller. I loved seeing them in my face when you rode me." He grins, and I can see him reliving the moment in his head. "You've no idea how many times I've sat at work staring at your tits."

My cheeks flush again. "Cal."

"It's true. I've dreamt about this moment."

"Me too." I kiss his chest. The dusting of hair covering the phoenix tickles my nose.

His long fingers stroke up and down my arm, while his other hand twirls my hair. I close my eyes, content for the first time in weeks.

CHAPTER
Eleven

A loud high pitch beep pierces my ears repetitively. I roll onto my side, wondering what that ear-splitting sound is. A clang rings out. The beeping stops. I contemplate rolling over again and returning to my previous state of relaxation, but as I slowly open my eyes, the view before me softly comes into focus. I see Callum. Waking up to his face is like waking to a dream. His bicep rests under my neck and pillow. He gazes at me with his bleary eyes and his perfect mouth hints at a smile.

"Morning, Baby Cakes."

A grin spreads across my face. "Morning. You haven't called me that in a while."

"You haven't woken up in my arms in a while either."

The fresh, frosty morning air nips at my feet as they dangle out of the duvet. I pull the blanket tight around my neck and snuggle into Cal's warm body. "Hmm, this is nice."

He tucks a loose curl behind my ear. His hot naked flesh presses against me, and his warm lips delicately touch my nose. "Did you sleep well?"

"Err, yes I did."

"I wish I could wake up like this every morning."

The extremity of the situation dawns on me as clear as the dawning outside. What am I doing? What have I done? I instantly sit up, holding the cover over my breasts. A knot in my stomach replaces the euphoric high from last night and the bile rises in the back of my throat at the thought of my betrayal. Wanting to remove myself from this shameful setting before I succumb to his charms and touch once more, I ask, "Can I take a shower?"

"Sure." He sits up behind me, his rough hands graze along my arms and I flinch as his warm breath falls onto my shoulder, sending me all aquiver. "Can I join you?"

"What?" The knot in my stomach tightens. "No, you can't." My voice is loud, but trembling.

"We've had showers before." He trails his luscious mouth along my shoulder blade, and with every brush of his soft lips against my skin, the tingling blossoms between my thighs, and I relive the sensation of him inside me. He runs his palm down my spine. The knot loosens. I crave him. I contemplate showering with him; the thought is all too tempting. There's an internal battle going on between my mind and my aching vagina. The latter always wins. I have to stop this now.

"I know, but I can't let this go any further." *A bit late for that,* my subconscious reminds me.

"Did you not enjoy last night?" His voice falls to a whisper.

"Yes, of course I did, but that's it, it can't be anything more." He continues to nibble at my neck, trailing his tongue under my ear to the sensitive spot there. Contradictory to my words, I let him continue with his assault.

"Let's make the most of it while you're here." His warm breath against my ear ignites me, and I'm no longer cold. He knows I can't resist him; I never could. But I must. The loosened knot in my stomach entangles more.

"I'm going in the shower." I jump up from the bed, taking the throw with me. The soft fleece texture swaddles my skin, hiding all my imperfections in the dim morning light. My legs scramble out the door and into the bathroom before I do anything else I'll regret. I close the door to the small room and feel it closing in on me, as the guilt weighs heavily on my chest. I take a deep breath. *Breathe, just breathe.*

I fumble with the shower, turning both knobs, but nothing happens. How does this thing work? There must be another button somewhere, and where does he keep his towels? I scan the room to find a single hand towel on the rail that would barely cover my arse, let alone dry me. I give in. "Cal," I shout. He appears in the doorway within seconds. There's a pain in the back of my throat and a lump that won't go down, restricting my airway, making it difficult to get the oxygen I need. The sight of him naked, displaying his morning glory, only adds to my breathlessness.

"Change your mind?" He smirks. The soft morning light peers through the small bathroom window, highlighting his inked body. I take in every line, every rippling muscle. Mesmerised as he walks towards me.

"I... I... I couldn't work the shower." My voice is shaky. He tugs at the blanket clenched around my chest. I resist, gripping it tighter, but the moment his tongue glides between my lips, I surrender, letting it pool around my feet. Once free of the throw, he smooths both hands over my round, full breasts, grazing his thumb over my hard nipple. His fingers accidentally tickle my waist as they make their way to my plump behind and dig into my fleshy cheeks.

With our lips still locked, he steps into the shower, pulling me in with him. He wraps his firm hand around the back of my neck so I can't pull away from him, not that I would now. I have renounced all my previous ideas of escaping his intimacy, for now at least. My hands grip his biceps. He reaches out to touch something behind me and the freezing cold water rains over our heads, trickling down our skin. My mouth sucks in a breath and my body jerks. The chill of the water runs down my spine, but Cal doesn't falter. He quickly wraps his large hands around my back, pulling me further into his embrace.

The heat from his flesh soothes me from the icy blast. His hard tongue dances with mine, kindling the fire inside me. My body temperature rises along with the temperature of the water. I can never resist him like this. He knows he only has to cup my face, bring his lips to mine, and I am at his mercy.

"Let's fuck work today and stay here," he says, in between soft kisses

"We can't, Cal," I pant into his mouth. "It looks too suspicious."

He reaches down and his finger runs along my slit. My body shudders once again. I want to feel him. My hand slithers down the length of his body, over his firm chest and his tight stomach, until I reach his erection. I form a snug grip and move my hand back and forth.

"Steph." He breathes heavily and pushes me back against the tiles, darting his tongue back into my mouth in a lustful frenzy. His skilful hands savagely take my body. He reaches for my knee, handling and lifting my leg up. I instantly wrap it around him as he takes my other leg. I'm pinned between him and the shower wall. He guides himself into me. I'm dripping wet and not from the shower. I draw in a breath as he thrusts deeper, and calls my name, exhaling into my neck, "Steph."

"Cal," I cry, running my fingers through his soaked hair.

"Steph," he pants with each thrust. "I fucking love you."

What? He loves me? It's just a figure of speech, right? Sex talk? I squeeze my eyes tight as I'm about to come undone once more. "Cal," I scream, tugging at his long hair. My head leans back against the tiles. I lose all control of my body as the insanely exhilarating wave of pleasure pulses through me.

"Steph, Fuck, Steph."

My orgasm slowly recedes. I whimper as he pulls out of me, ejaculating over my stomach with one last thrust into my plump belly.

He catches his breath. "Fuck me, Steph."

I smile and joke, "I just did." Although, he was the one doing all the work.

We let out a hint of laughter as our lips collide once more. I savour the long, deep, sensual kiss as though this may be the last time I have him. His stubble scratches my chin and I fist his thick, wet hair that's slicked back from his face. My breasts smash against his chest as he holds my legs around his waist. I hold him tighter, not wanting this closeness to end.

He eventually lets go of my legs so I can stand, unpinning my back from pressing against the tiles. The shower's still pouring down on us into the steamy cubicle. His hands rest on my hips. He pulls away from my lips, looking into my eyes. "Fuck, I've missed you, Steph." His voice is raspy. "I never realised how much I really missed you until now."

My breathing is still erratic. Lord knows I've missed him. I take in a breath. "You only realised just now? What about last night?"

He lets out a small puff of a laugh. "I couldn't fucking think straight last night. Until you were in my bed."

"I was the same." I blush, biting my swollen lip, thinking about how he made me come with his tongue. He was right; he hasn't lost his touch, even without his piercing. The tips of our noses gently brush together before our lips connect.

"I hadn't planned on wetting my hair."

"Ha, it's soaked now. Here." He grabs a bottle of shampoo, flicking the lid open, pouring a small amount into his palm. I inhale the fresh, minty scent. Gazing into my eyes, he rubs the lotion into my long dark saturated hair, just as he used to do when we were boyfriend and girlfriend a lifetime ago. I take some of the shampoo and run my hands through his, relishing the silkiness of his thick hair between my fingers. Delicate kisses trail over my shoulder as we both cleanse each other. He washes the rest of me, running his soapy hands between my thighs and over every curve of my body.

"I have to get ready. Do you have a towel?" He turns the shower off and opens the steamy door. Stepping out of the cubicle, the cool contrast of air swathes my skin. Cal reaches up to a cupboard that I hadn't spotted before and grabs three towels, handing me two. He leaves me to get ready, wrapping the remaining towel around his waist. I step out of the bathroom and look for my clothes, but they're not where I left them. My silky drawers were on Cal's bedroom floor the last time I looked. He's on the phone. I'm not sure who he's talking to, and I can't find my clothes anywhere. I go back into his daughter's room for another look.

Cal appears in the doorway, wearing his jogging bottoms. "That was Jerry. The office is closed today; they can't get in because of the snow. We can work from home." His elbow leans against the doorframe, and he bites his lip. "Don't bother getting dressed." He winks and presses his lips together.

"What... where are my clothes, anyway? Cal?" I whine.

"I put them on a quick wash before I came in the shower. Literally came in the shower." His lip turns upwards in one corner. "I thought you'd want clean clothes for work. They should be washed now; I'll put them in the dryer. Anyway, who says you're getting dressed?" He winks again. With each wink, my centre tightens and tingles. I can't believe this man.

He's insatiable. He still has the same sex drive he had in his teens. I have to get out of here soon. I can't keep doing this. The flutters in my stomach tell me otherwise. The tingles below want more. Cal shouts through from the kitchen, "Do you want a coffee?"

"I could murder a coffee right now." Still wrapped in my towel, I walk into the kitchen and take a seat at his table, waiting for my clothes to dry. I tug at the towel, pulling it over as much as possible; it only just meets. "I have to call Justin."

Cal looks at me with his mouth gaping. "Not yet."

"Justin won't be working in this weather. He can come and get me in his van. The gritters will have been out on the main road by now. I'll walk off the estate and meet him."

"Stay with me for a while longer, Steph."

"I want to."

"Good. I haven't finished with you yet."

My eyes are wide, and I gulp, wondering what else he has in store.

CHAPTER
Twelve

"Come here," Cal says, but I can't seem to move. My body is like a lead weight constraining me to the chair. I hold the towel tight over my naked chest and fold my arms across my stomach to hide the gap where the fluffy fabric doesn't quite meet. With no clothes and worse, no makeup on to hide behind, I duck my chin, hiding my bare face.

He walks over to me with two coffees and sets them down on the table. The chair next to me scrapes along the floor tiles as he moves closer to me and takes a seat. His hand rests on my leg. He leans in to kiss my cheek, and I suck in a breath.

"I can't get enough of you. You're still beautiful, you know. You haven't changed at all." His lips brush against mine before his tongue slips into my mouth. He knows just what to say and do to make me melt for him. The kiss ends with a light peck and my head is dizzy once again.

My voice is a quiet quiver. "You have."

"What?" His head tilts and his thumb strokes my thigh.

"You've changed." Before he can jump to conclusions, I add, "You're sexier and more muscular than I remember."

He smiles from ear to ear. "I wondered what you were getting at for a minute there." His hand goes to my cheek, his fingers wrap around my neck, holding me in place while trailing deliciously delicate kisses along my jaw. He really makes me feel beautiful, even as I sit here with no makeup. With each brush of his lips, my stomach tightens and the tingling blossoms.

"I put your clothes in the dryer. They should only take about 30 minutes."

"Thanks." A smile plays on my lips, and I tap my fingernails against my coffee mug. "So what shall we do for the next 30 minutes?"

Without saying a word, he stands up, takes my hand, and leads me back to the bedroom. My heart is in my mouth, no matter how many times he touches me; each time is like the first. Once in his room, he peels away the towel, letting it drop to the floor. I cease all movement, but when his fingers skim down my arms, all the tension leaves my body.

"Lie down, baby." His deep, rugged voice has me at his will, and I do as he asks. My mouth opens, watching him pull off his joggers. I'm so fixated on his inked skin, I forget to blink. I lie still as he climbs onto the bed. He rests beside me, leaning up on his elbow. His knee bends over my leg, pushing between my thighs. The daylight shines through the window, the light seems brighter, glistening and bouncing off the snow-covered ground, allowing his eyes to rake over my curves.

His large hand caresses my breast, moving to my stomach, then my hips. Roaming every stretch mark and imperfection with his rough palms and his lustrous eyes. "You're the one that's sexier." He kisses me again. My body trembles, my lip quivers against his. This man knows exactly how to make me feel sexy; he makes me feel alive like I'm a teenager again. I forget about everything when he's touching me. The only thing I can focus on is him. His hand slides down to the spot where all my nerves join, cupping my swollen lips there, before he slips two fingers inside me and uses his thumb to circle my swelling bud. "I love how wet you are for me." He was always good at dirty talk. His nimble fingers continue to massage me inside and out while he gently nips at my mouth and jaw.

"Cal," I moan. "Don't stop," I pant.

"I'm not stopping." His fingers flutter inside me, hitting the spot that makes me arch my back and grasp at the sheets. "Don't come yet though," he whispers into my ear as his tongue flickers at the sensitive spot on my neck.

"I'll try not to," I huff out the words. "Cal, Cal. I want you inside me." With a mischievous grin, he reaches over and pulls out a condom from the drawer. Still keeping his fingers inside me, he tears open the foil wrapper with his teeth, and with one hand tries to position the condom. I quickly help him, not wanting him to remove his fingers, not until he can replace them with the full length of him. He holds himself steady while I roll the pink opaque rubber down his large erection. His eyes flicker and his breathing picks up pace as the phoenix on his chest comes alive.

He sits up against the headboard and pulls me onto his lap. I slide onto his erection, and the feel of him is immense. I rock my hips and I'm lost in his blazing brown eyes that mirror the phoenix on his chest, consumed by a raging fire. His arms wrap around my back, pressing our chests together, and we breathe in sync as if he's breathing new life into me. We're connected on another level. Our souls reunite on a spiritual plane. I'm so close; looking into his eyes while we make love is enough to bring me to orgasm without him moving his hand between my legs. Grinding my hips against him, my body shakes.

"Tell me how much you want me, baby. Tell me, like you used to," he begs.

Still gazing into his penetratingly fierce eyes, I fist his

hair and my voice wavers. "I want you. I want you, Cal. I want you so much."

He pants into my mouth and growls. "Baby, I want you. I fucking want you like this every day; your tight pussy wrapped around my cock every fucking day from here on out. I'm never gonna let you go." My hips rock one last time as the orgasm takes me, and my body shakes. Still holding his gaze, I breathe heavily into his mouth and pull on his hair. My nails dig into his shoulder as I come undone. Shimmering sparkles dance all around me, as if the sparks between us have fallen from the heavens itself, igniting us, and like the phoenix, we are both reborn; rising from the ashes of our failed relationship.

He thrusts into me as my rocking subsides and groans back into my mouth with every breath. His eyes are like glowing embers as he finds his own release. "Fuck, baby, I... I..." He tries to catch his breath.

"What is it?" I say, but he doesn't speak, he's still riding out his high and I wish he wasn't wearing a condom so I could feel him surge inside of me. Feel his warm cum spill into me where it belongs. My body stills. I watch his eyes flicker in total wonderment. Amazed I can still have this effect on him, knowing it's me and my body giving him this incredible, mind-blowing, wondrous sensation, fills me with a tingling warmth that spreads throughout my limbs. Was he going to tell me he loves me again? I don't think he does. He stopped loving me a long time ago. He's confusing love with lust. I'm sure he only wants me to relive his youth. Maybe he's going through some sort of midlife crisis and wants to feel young again. *Is that what you're doing?* My subconscious adds. Is it? I don't know. Perhaps I'm an easy shag for him. He obviously knows I can't say no to him. I never could. Am I more appealing because I'm married and he doesn't have to commit? Whatever the reason, I don't care. I haven't felt like this in years. Being with him has reawakened a fire deep in my soul, and I can't seem to put it out.

After he regains control of his body, he kisses me lightly, brushing his lips against mine and flicking his tongue into my mouth.

"I think I need another shower."

"Yeah me too."

"You can't shower with me again. I need to have a proper wash."

"Don't worry, I'm spent. I couldn't go again if I wanted to. I need time to refuel."

"Finally, I've worn you out, have I?"

"Just give me half an hour." He would go again too, knowing him.

I slap his thigh as I climb off. "Stop, I'm serious. I have to go. Would you see if my clothes are dry, please? I hope you haven't shrunk them."

"I can do laundry, you know." He slaps my bottom as I bend over to pick up the towel.

"Cal." I clench my bum cheeks, wrapping the towel around me, and scurry to the shower for the second time today. My body is still shaky after the morning's events. I can't stop thinking about him, how he makes me flutter with one look, his touch, his lips, oh my goodness, his tongue. I stand under the luke-warm, water hoping it will dampen down the flames deep within me. At least enough so I can have the strength to leave and call Justin. The thought of speaking with him makes my chest tighten and my throat close up.

Walking back to the girls' bedroom to grab my bag, I try to shake Justin from my mind. Cal has hung my clean clothes up on the side of the wardrobe and placed my clean underwear on the bed. I'm not sure where he is, but I quickly get dried and dressed. As much as I would love a round three this morning, I have to get back to reality. Luckily, I always carry a bit of makeup in my bag for touching up. I have lipstick, eyeliner, mascara, concealer and powder. I don't use the last two; just sticking with the first three is enough for today. I borrow the girl's hairbrush to detangle my mop of hair.

Once I'm ready, I know I must call Justin. The burn returns in the back of my throat. Beads of moisture gather on my forehead and the palms of my hands are sticky. What have I done? I worry he'll be able to tell from my voice that I've betrayed him. Taking in a deep breath, I tap his name on the screen and listen to the rings, closing my eyes.

"Ay-up," he answers.

"Hi, how are you?" I open my eyes and hold my breath so he won't hear my jagged breathing.

"Good, the kids are off school. I got a text saying it's a snow day."

"I thought they would be. You're not going into work today, are you?" I wipe my sweaty palms on my trousers.

"We've shut the site today. I tried calling your mobile and your office but there was no answer."

"Sorry, I missed your call. I'm still at my friend's. Work's called off. They've asked us to work from home." I clear my throat to dislodge the huge lump there. "Do you think it's safe to drive?"

"Do you want me to come and get you?"

"Only if it's safe." My voice is quiet, and I hope he can't hear the wobble as I speak.

"The roads here look clear, it's just getting off the estate, but I should be all right in the van."

"Don't bring the kids, drop them off at Mum's. It's not worth dragging them out here." My skin itches, and I scratch my neck with my long nails.

"Fine. When do you want me to come?"

"Whenever, there's no rush. I'll text you the street, but I'll walk off the estate as it's quite bad here. You can meet me on the main road."

"Give me an hour, I need to get dressed and I'm in the middle of making pancakes."

"That's fine, shall we say around 11.30?" I glance at the clock to check that it gives him enough time.

"Yes, see you then."

"Love you," I say the words automatically, but after saying them, I retch. It's not how I usually end a phone call. Will he think it's odd? Did he even notice? It's not like he's a bad husband. If he were, it would make this so much easier. He's a good person. I'm so ungrateful.

I take a few deep breaths and walk into the kitchen. Cal is cooking breakfast, his joggers hang deliciously low, showing off his glorious inked back.

"Hey, I wasn't sure what you wanted, so I cooked some bacon, eggs, and toast." He waves the flipper utensil towards the plate with bacon on, then points to the toaster.

"Thank you, that's great. I could get used to this, although I have a perfectly good cook at home who takes care of me." I scrunch my nose up, realising what I said isn't exactly true. Justin may cook for me, but he doesn't make me feel the same.

Cal huffs and turns to slide an egg onto my plate. "If he takes care of you, where the fuck is he now? And why are you fucking me?"

Why am I? I don't know. I never wanted to be with anyone so much in my entire life. Was it closure? The need to feel his approval of me again after he so cruelly rejected me? Was it because I could? He was offering it on a plate after all, but I know deep down the truth; he makes me feel things I've only ever felt with him. *That's his huge penis hitting your erogenous zones.* A nervous laugh escapes me. "I... I don't know, you came onto me and... I didn't have the heart to turn you down." When I'm around him, I can't control myself. I've always been the same. Even after we broke up, I would see him and my entire body would shake, mainly out of rage because he was dating someone else, but he had an overwhelming physical effect on me, even then.

He smirks and tosses the utensil into the sink. "So you gave me a sympathy shag?"

"Yes, something like that." I press my lips together and look down at my feet.

"What about the shower, was that out of pity too?" He strides over to me as he speaks. "And the bedroom this morning? You came on to me that time. I recall you asking what can we do for 30 minutes; you were practically begging for it." His fingers lift my chin, and I gaze into his eyes. Our lips are almost touching, and I can smell the toothpaste on his breath. I lean in to kiss him, but he pulls away, flinching his head back slightly. "Admit it."

"Admit what?"

"Admit you wanted me. That you were desperate." His lips come close again and gently brush against mine. "Admit you were desperate for me to fuck you." Right now, I would admit to murder if it meant I could feel those warm, delectable lips smacked against me one more time.

"Okay, I admit it. Now kiss me." His tongue slides across my bottom lip before slipping inside to meet mine. I throb against him. My body melds to his as he deepens our kiss. His firm grip around my waist tightens, and my breasts smash against his chest. I'm still whirling from before. Every time I think of him, a tingle spreads through my centre. As our kiss lingers, I feel him smile, and my fingers trail up his spine.

He eventually pulls away and taps my bottom. "Get your breakfast before it goes cold." He grabs a top from the dining room chair and pulls it over his head, then sits down to eat with me.

I glance at the large clock on the kitchen wall, which reminds me that my time here is limited, and I sigh. "We can't do this again, Cal. You know that, don't you? I won't leave my family." I want to be clear about that. Whatever this is between us, he needs to know where he stands. I could never leave Justin and the kids.

He runs a hand down his face. His eyes have lost their fire and all that's left are the cinders of our passion. "I expected as much." He has a monotone voice. "I don't want you to leave him for me." He looks down at his plate and shovels a fork full of beans into his mouth. "I... I just miss you, that's all."

I've missed him too. I never realised how much till he walked into work on my first day. We eat the rest of the breakfast in silence; I don't know what to say. The longer I sit here, the hotter I get, making my skin itch again. Not really knowing where to look, I glance around the room. I'm flustered and confused after what's happened between us, not to mention ashamed of my actions as the sickening guilt intensifies deep in my stomach. The time is almost 11am. I know I have to leave soon and my palms are clammy. I'm absolutely shitting myself at the thought of seeing Justin. What if he can tell something is off? He can't find out about this, he just can't.

How do people do this? I wouldn't recommend this to anyone. The stress alone is a total turnoff. But then I think back to last night and this morning and wonder, was it actually worth the stress? Without hesitation, I want to relive it all again. I hum as I let out a long breath and look over at Cal loading the dishwasher. Even doing that is turning me on. The long sleeves of his top are rolled up to his elbows. His hair falls in front of his face as he bends over, and his top rides up. I see the muscles of his swift arse under the fabric of his joggers. I lick my lips, wanting to place my hands under the elastic waistband, and squeeze his succulently sinful cheeks.

I glance at the clock as I stand, needing to go before I do anything else to add to my ever-growing list of fornication. "I'm going to wait at the top of the estate."

"Don't go yet, it's freezing out there." He's right; I can't wait out there for 30 minutes. "Stay, I'll put the kettle on."

"Okay, I'll have a quick coffee."

"What was that? You're staying for a quickie?"

I can't help but laugh and swat at his arm. He smirks before pulling me in for another kiss. I let him, knowing this will definitely be the last time.

"I could go for a quickie, now I've had breakfast." He wiggles his eyebrows and the cheeky grin on his face is adorable.

"Stop it, Cal, I have to go soon."

"I'll settle for another kiss then." He swipes his tongue between my lips and I part my mouth for him, letting him have full control as I always do. He consumes me and I go limp in his arms. The kiss ends with light pecks of his lips. "I'm sorry. I know I shouldn't keep doing that."

"Don't apologise. I just don't want you to get the wrong idea. I'll never leave my family. As much as I want you, I just—"

He cuts me off by pressing his lips to mine again.

"I get it, it's cool."

"Thank you."

He hands me a coffee, and I sit back down at the table. "I had a great time last night, but it can't happen again, Cal."

"Sure." He smirks.

"I'm serious," I shout.

"Yeah, yeah, keep your knickers on." He chuckles. "Or don't." He shrugs and laughs. I can't help but smile, he always makes me laugh, but as each minute draws closer to 11.30am my laughter turns to nausea as realisation and panic set in.

"Okay, I'm really going now. I'll walk off the estate and meet him on the main road. I'll see you on Monday if we get no more snow."

He looks at me with dull eyes. "Yeah, see you then." He doesn't hug me or come closer, but leans against the doorjamb in the kitchen, watching me go down the hall. I'm glad there was no big parting farewell, but I almost wanted a goodbye kiss. Dammit, what's wrong with me?

I step out into the cold, close the door and don't look back. The snow covers my faux leather boots on my way to the main road. Trails of grey slush and black ice line the middle and the edges of the tarmac. I try to put the events of last night and this morning to the back of my mind. The chilled icy crystals soak into the bottom of my trousers, and my feet and hands have grown numb. But I don't care. The harsh weather and biting wind whips at my face, but I feel nothing. My heart is as hard as the stained snow that crunches underfoot; mimicking the harsh reality I face this morning.

After a five-minute wait, Justin pulls up. I try to act as though nothing happened, but can't stop the throbbing memory between my legs. Climbing into the passenger side of his work van, I shiver. The leather seat is as cold as the chill outside and my teeth chatter.

"I suppose I need to fix your shitty car?"

"I don't think you'll be able to access it with the snow. Plus, it will be totally covered; let's just go home." I hold my hands in front of the hot air blowers. "We can sort it when it's better weather."

"Fine." He turns right at the lights to head home. "So how did you sleep last night?"

"Fine, I slept in the girls' room. They were at their mum's house."

"I would have come for you, but I didn't think it was safe." *Yeah right. He couldn't be arsed more like.* For once, I'm grateful for his selfishness.

"I know, and honestly, the traffic was at a standstill. Everyone had ground to a halt. I don't think you'd have got far had you attempted to come last night," I say, trying to justify my sleepover. Justin nods and agrees.

It's Friday afternoon now and I've done no work at all today. I need to check my emails, at least make it look like I've done something. After doing some baking with the kids and helping with a bit of homework, I open my laptop to check my emails on the company server. Callum emailed an hour ago and my heart races. My back straightens. I click on the envelope next to his name, but when it opens, it's just a document with some brand guidelines for a logo we've been working on. He hasn't even said hi. I sigh and slump back on the sofa, but I can't help thinking it's for the best.

After our evening meal, I aim to get the kids in bed early so Justin and I can have some alone time. Wanting to recompense for my sins, I open a bottle of red for both of us. My plan doesn't work; the little shits won't go to sleep and Justin opens a can of beer instead, leaving me to drink the full bottle of wine on my own, which I do gladly and retire to bed half pissed.

He's downstairs watching darts or some other sport I

couldn't give a shit about. I collapse into bed, the kids still awake and running wild on the landing. One's firing Nerf bullets all over the house and the other is singing into a karaoke machine.

"Bedtime," I shout, only to be ignored for the third time. Just because there's no school, they figure they can stay up all hours. I pull a pillow over my head to drown out the din and drift off to sleep thinking of you know who...

"You're up early." Justin walks into the kitchen wearing his 'Mr Potato Head' lounge pants and top that says, 'Couch Potato'; a Father's Day gift from the kids.

"I thought I would cook you a Sunday roast for a change." I peel another carrot.

He huffs. "I'm surprised you knew where to find the peeler." I glance at the potato on his t-shirt, then at the potatoes on the worktop, and I want to throw one at his face. Normally I would never attempt to cook, but I wanted to do something nice for him in the hope it will make me feel less terrible.

"Of course I know where the peeler is." *I will peel his friggin' face off in a minute.* I smile through gritted teeth and carry on preparing the vegetables.

He shrugs and makes himself a coffee. "What's brought this on?"

Oh no, It's too much. I should have stuck to our normal routine. I'm like one of those husbands that come home with flowers out of the blue after they've been banging their secretary. My blood pumps so loud I can hear it pounding in my ears. "I just fancied cooking you a meal; what's wrong with that?"

"Fair enough. Are you sure you're not up to something?"

I freeze and I can feel the colour drain from my face as a cold, sticky sweat covers my forehead.

"After a new car, perhaps?" He raises an eyebrow, then takes hold of his coffee and walks to the table.

A sigh of relief escapes my lips. Yes, that's it. Even though I haven't thought about my broken-down car at all this weekend.

Justin sits down in our large kitchen, pulling his feet up onto the opposite chair, and picks up the Sunday newspaper that was posted this morning.

Each time I look at him, my stomach turns, and I have to stop myself from retching. "Ouch."

Justin peers over his paper. "What's up?"

"I'm okay." I run my finger under the cold tap water. "The peeler sliced my finger and took half my nail off."

"I told you, those long nails aren't practical." He continues to read the paper and my body slumps against the counter, watching the blood run from my finger. Staring at the running water, I relive my nails digging into Callum's back. The thought gives me a flutter in my core. I'm sure he appreciates my long nails, even if Justin doesn't. Justin clears his throat, snapping me from my trance and the bile rises again in my throat. I scurry to the bathroom, thinking my body will follow through with the sickness it keeps threatening.

After drying my hand and wrapping a plaster around my finger, I walk back into the kitchen and continue with dinner. I need to redeem myself; I want to be a better wife, the wife that Justin deserves.

"What are your plans today, Justin?"

"I think I'll watch the telly. Seeing as you're cooking dinner." He chortles and shakes his head.

"What's that for?"

"Nothing. I'm going in the shower."

I let out a long breath. How friggin' hard can it be to cook a pissin' meal?

Cairen walks into the kitchen all bleary-eyed in his football pyjamas. "Morning sweetheart." I scoop him up in my arms and give him a big hug. "Do you want some breakfast?" He nods and I toast some chocolate pop tarts and fill a glass of milk for him.

Cassie strolls in. "What can I have to eat?"

"What do you want?"

"I want some pop tarts."

"I don't have any left. They were the last ones."

She stamps her foot. "That's not fair. Why does he get everything he wants?"

"Sweetheart, I can't help it. I'll buy some more."

"Now?"

"I'm not going out now. Have something else."

She whines. "Nobody cares about me. You only care about him." She storms off to her room. "Daddy…" she whines to Justin upstairs, and I smile. She's such a daddy's girl. At least she isn't crying to me. I already have a headache.

An hour later, Justin pops his head in the kitchen. "Right, I'll take Cairen to football and leave you to it, shall I?"

"Yes, everything is under control. The veg is cut, and the chicken is seasoned, ready to go in."

"See you later, then. Cassie is coming with me too."

"Oh?"

"I promised her a breakfast cob from Maccy's. She said there were no pop tarts left."

I smile. He's such a softy with her. My skin itches again and my chest tightens, thinking of how I've betrayed my family. If they found out what I'd done, the kids would never forgive me, especially Cassie; she always takes her dad's side.

"See ya."

"Bye." I almost choke on the word with the growing pain in the back of my throat.

Once alone in the house, I sit on the sofa with a coffee and pick at a frayed cushion. I don't know how long I've been sitting here, but when I take a sip of my drink, it's cold. I place it on the coffee table and rest my head back on the settee.

"Steph." Callum's calling my name. His gruff voice has me quivering beneath him.

"Hmm"

"Steph." I open my eyes to see Justin standing above me with a scowl on his face.

"What's wrong?"

"What's wrong? You haven't even put dinner on. I knew I should have dealt with it myself."

"Why, what time is it?"

"Chuffin' dinner time, that's what time it is."

"Justin, I'm so sorry. I must have drifted off to sleep."

"Obviously."

"I'll turn everything on now." I jump up and run into the kitchen to turn the oven on. "Do you want a sandwich to tie you over till dinner's ready?" I shout.

"I'll wait," he groans. I hear the TV and keep myself busy while dinner cooks. One thing I'm good at is the laundry. I can't possibly mess this up. Sorting through the clean clothes, I come across my silky knickers from the other night and I remember how Cal pulled them down my leg and grazed my inner thigh with his tongue. Ironing Justin's shirt, I picture Callum licking my body, worshipping me like he always would in our attic bedroom. The tingles start in my centre and work their way through my bloodstream, reaching the tips of my fingers and the ends of my toes.

"Steph, what are you doing?" Justin yells.

"What?" I look around, then glance at the ironing board. Moving the iron, I see a brown, smouldering mark on his shirt. I suck in a breath. "Justin, I'm sorry."

"What in the world's got into you today?"

"I'm just tired."

"Have you kept your eye on dinner?"

"Yes, of course."

He turns to check the oven. "Argh, Steph. The chicken is cooked and you haven't even turned the veg or potatoes on." He turns the knobs on the hob and pulls the crispy chicken from the oven. "For frig's sake, Steph."

"I'm sorry. I'll do better."

"I'll do it."

"No, I said I'll cook today; you watch your sport."

"Fine." He walks back into the lounge with a can of beer.

My timings are off and dinner is a disaster. The roast potatoes are like crisps. The chicken has gone cold, and the Yorkshire puddings resemble burnt cardboard. I'm totally inadequate.

We sit at the dining table, and I wish I hadn't got involved with the cooking. Not that I'll eat much, anyway. I can't seem to stomach food at the moment.

"Where are the Yorkshire's?" Cassie asks.

"Your mother burnt them."

I pick at the food on my plate, moving it around, watching everyone else eat.

"Are you feeling all right?" Justin asks.

"Yes, why?"

"I know the meal isn't great, but it's not like you to leave food."

Cheeky twat. I cut a piece of chicken and fork it into my mouth. Any other time he's telling me not to eat, you'd think he'd be happy. "I have a bit of a dodgy stomach."

"Ugh, stay away from me then. I don't want your bug."

I exhale and wish I was somewhere else. I wonder if Cal's thinking about me? What am I going to say to him tomorrow? Will things be awkward?

"Why don't you go to bed if you're not well. You've gone all pale."

I nod at Justin, put my fork down on my plate, and take myself to bed, but I can't sleep. I'm dreading Monday.

———————

JUSTIN'S TAKEN some time off today to drive me to work. I look out of the passenger window at the wet roads. At least the snow has gone. Only grey slush remains along the edges and patches of white hard clumps along the grass verge. We pull up at Browns Media early. The snow has slid halfway down my window, but the bonnet is clear. Callum's car has gone. He must have got it over the weekend.

Justin wipes the remaining snow from my windshield and sits behind the wheel. He puts the key in the ignition, ready to turn the engine.

"I told you, it wouldn't turn over when I tried. I got nothing." Why do men always think they have some sort of magic touch? Of course, he still has to try himself. He turns the key and the engine miraculously starts. Perhaps Justin has the touch after all. *Not bloody likely*. I stand with my mouth agape. "I can't believe it. It didn't do that Thursday." A million things go through my head. Did Cal do something to my car on purpose? Was it all part of his plan to get me to sleep over?

Justin lifts the bonnet. He actually knows how to fix a car, unlike Callum. "It looks like you have a new battery."

"That's weird, Cal must have sorted it for me." It's the only explanation. Nobody else even knew about my car not starting. I stand baffled, looking under the bonnet.

"Cal who's house you stayed at?" Justin asks, like there's another person called Cal that I work with.

"Yes, it's the only thing I can think of."

"Why would he do that?" He inspects under the hood for evidence of anything else that has been tampered with.

"I don't know, to help me out I guess."

"Don't you think it's weird?" Justin frowns, and slams the bonnet back down.

"It's not weird. I do work with him. He was probably just being kind."

"I don't like some bloke messing with your car."

"He isn't some random bloke. I work with him. We're friends. If he was a woman, we wouldn't be having this conversation." I play the feminism card as a last resort.

He clenches his jaw. "You'll have to find out how much we owe him."

"I will."

"At least it's sorted." He dusts off his hands. "See you later, then."

"Bye." I walk into the office in a bit of a daze. Nobody is here yet, not even Sarah, who works in reception. Luckily, the cleaners let me in. I catch up on the work I should have done Friday and get so engrossed that I don't notice as the office fills up around me… until Cal appears, that is. He walks in with Kelly and Chris. I peer across the desk as he sits down, looking sexier than ever.

"Did you have a good weekend, Steph?" Kelly asks.

Callum smirks and tilts his head, leaning on his elbows.

"Yeah, Steph, how was your weekend? Did you enjoy your day off on Friday?"

"Friday was okay." I try not to make him any more big-headed than he already is.

"Just okay?" His eyebrows lift, and he's grinning like a cartoon villain.

I glare at him, trying to tell him to shut up with my eyes. Which only makes him laugh more. Nobody else seems to notice or is even remotely interested.

When the crowd around the coffee machine has dispersed, Callum makes his way over there. I follow and grab a mug.

"Did you fix my car?"

"Yeah, I got a friend of mine to look at it for you. Remember Dean from school? He's a mechanic. I don't know shit about cars."

"I thought so. That you fixed it, I mean. Plus, I know you know shit about cars." I smile and bite my lip. "Thank you. What do I owe you?"

"It's cool. I got you a new battery; no big deal." He shrugs.

"Please, it is a big deal. I'll reimburse you. How much?"

"I told you, it's fine. You don't need to reimburse me." He pours the coffee into a cup.

"Justin says he'll pay you—"

He cuts me off. "I don't want his fucking money."

"Cal, please, it's too much."

"You buy me lunch. Then we're even." Is this his way of manipulating me into spending more time with him?

"Maccy's it is then." I giggle and look down at my empty mug.

"Sounds about right. I can't today though. I have to leave at 11am."

My eyes flick back to his arresting face. "How come?"

"I'm taking my lunch early so I can watch Olivia at her school dance show."

"Oh, another day then." I dip my chin, disappointed that I won't get to spend lunch with him, but I admire how he is with his girls.

"Give us your cup."

I pass my mug to him, and he places it on the table, then takes my hand in his.

"What's this?" He inspects the two plasters around my poorly finger.

"I sliced it with a potato peeler. It's fine, really."

"Nice choice of plasters." He titters, examining the design which has a collection of zoo animals printed on a bright green background.

"I know. I didn't have any others."

He brings my finger to his lips and kisses the tip. My breath hitches, and his kiss travels from my nail straight to my centre. I want to feel those lips against my mouth. I want to press my naked body against his and make love to him in every position possible.

"Steph, baby." His low whispering voice makes my core muscles clench.

"Callum."

"Can I just grab a drink?" James says from behind me. How long has he been standing there? I lose all sense of time and place when I'm with Cal. He has me mesmerised with those dangerously divine eyes of his.

"Sorry, James."

Callum pours me a drink and goes back to his desk. I scan the pastries. I've somehow got my appetite back, and I'm ravenous. *Ravenous for him, you mean.* Yes, of course, but I will have to settle for a marmalade tart.

Each time I glance up, Cal is smiling at me, making my

heart flutter. The things he said to me last week made me fall in love with him all over again. At least I think this is love, or is it lust?

I'm glad when 11am comes, and he disappears so I can finally concentrate. We haven't spoken much today. What is there to say? *Oh, by the way, I had the most incredible night and day of my entire life, but we can't do it again, ever, no matter how much I want to.*

I stay in the office at lunch and try to catch up on some more work that I missed Friday. Everyone goes to the pub for a meal, but without Callum, I'm just not bothered. I get a sandwich from the corner shop and pop my earpods in to listen to my playlist. I add a few more songs to it too, including 'Physical' by Dua Lipa, and 'You're making me high' by Toni Braxton. Listening to the words is turning me on again, and I relive my memory of last week.

I'm humming away, lost in my own world, when firm hands rest on my shoulders. Long fingers dig into my flesh, massaging at my neck and collarbone. I know these powerful hands. His touch electrifies me; I stop all previous thoughts. His warm breath on my neck sends goose bumps across my skin. His stubble brushing against my cheek reminds me of his jaw rubbing between my thighs and my head swims, drowning in lust. "What are you listening to?" His words are soft with a hint of a smile.

I glance around the office. We're the only ones here. I turn slightly towards him and my lips almost touch his. My heart is racing. I gulp, wanting his tongue to run along my bottom lip once again. Before my brain can form a sentence, my mouth runs away with me. "It's your playlist."

"What?" He tilts his head.

"I mean, it's my playlist."

He smiles, swiftly wheeling Kelly's office chair close to

mine. He sits facing me, pulling closer. His knee moves between my legs. "You made me a playlist?" He raises an eyebrow.

I bite my lip while I think about what to say. "It's just some songs that remind me of you, that's all."

Without asking if he can listen, he takes the pod from my left ear and places it in his. The words to 'Secret Love Song' by Little Mix flash up on my phone as it lies on my desk.

A puff of laughter leaves his mouth. "I should have known you'd listen to something like this."

I swat his chest, and he stifles a laugh. My hand slides over his pecs, and I can feel his chest rising and falling.

"Listen to the words. It reminds me of us."

He licks his lips, gazing into my eyes. His hand on my outer thigh slowly moves over my hip, then to my waist. My breathing speeds up, making my mouth dry and my head cloudy.

His lips are close to mine, and I can feel his warm, heavy breath on my face. As the song builds, our lips collide. I move my hands to his face, splaying my fingers on his neck and my thumb on his cheek. Lustfully caressing his tongue, sparks of magic ignite the atmosphere. I don't want to break the kiss, not knowing if I'll ever get the chance to feel his sinfully skilled tongue again. The song ends, and he slows the kiss down with delicate touches of his lips against mine. I'm glad I haven't reapplied any lipstick since this morning, as it would no doubt have smeared after that. He pulls in his bottom lip and tucks a lock of hair behind my ear as the next song starts. He pulls out his earpiece.

"Fuck, Steph."

"What?" I gulp. "Have I done something wrong?"

"Nah, I just… Fuck, you're driving me crazy… In a good way," he adds, before sweeping his lips against mine once more and flicking his tongue in my mouth. The tingles bloom again between my thighs as I relive the sensations from last week.

"Send me your playlist."

"What?" I'm still not able to think straight or form a cognitive sentence.

"Share your playlist with me. I want to listen to it."

"I don't know how." It's true I don't.

He picks my phone up, presses a few buttons, and scans the rest of the songs on my list with a smirk. "'Hotter than Hell', that's me, right?"

I swat his arm for being so big-headed, but he is hot. There's no point denying it.

Chris walks in from lunch, followed by the rest of the gang. Cal winks at me and goes back to his desk.

I make my way to the ladies' toilets. I need to check on my makeup and calm myself down. Looking in the bathroom mirror, my cheeks are flush, my lips are pink and slightly swollen, and my hands are trembling. I pat my face with a cold wet paper towel, touch up my makeup, apply my crimson lipstick and try to compose myself before going back to the office.

Sitting back at my desk, still flustered, Cal has his earphones in and is no doubt listening to my playlist. I start mine from the beginning, hoping it will be in sync. He occasionally glances over, undressing me with his come to bed eyes and a hint of a smile forming in the corner of his mouth. Several songs later, 'A Thousand Years' plays by Christina Perri. Gazing into his eyes, the words are beautifully profound. I've loved this man for a millennium and a part of me has perished every day that we were apart. Being with him again has awoken my soul from an eternal winter. Every cell and synapse is bursting with a new lease of life. I could spend an eternity with him like this, sharing our favourite songs, reading together, and making love with him. The thought that all these things can never be breaks me all over again. I close my eyes to hide the sadness and try to focus back on my work.

We walk to our cars to go home. "Thanks for sorting my car, Cal," I say before I get into my silver Suzuki.

"Don't mention it. See you tomorrow." I want to kiss him again, but everyone is in the car park, so I buckle up and go.

I WALK INTO THE HOUSE, slip off my shoes, and walk into the kitchen to see Justin adding seasoning to a casserole. The smell is divine and always reminds me of my mum's cooking and cosy winter nights.

"Did you find out who tampered with your car?" Justin asks.

I'd completely forgotten about the battery. "I would hardly call a new battery being tampered with."

"If they did it without permission, it's technically tampering."

"It was Callum. I paid him for the battery." I have to lie. Justin wouldn't like another man paying for my car maintenance.

"How come he did that? I still think it's weird."

"I thought it was kind. You don't need to be jealous. He's just a friend and a colleague." I shift in my seat and avert my eyes from his stare.

"I wasn't jealous, but I am now you've said that."

"Are you serious?" Justin isn't normally the jealous type. Having another man mess with my car has clearly got him riled. He must have been thinking about this all day. Shit.

"Justin?" I scratch the back of my neck that's suddenly hot and itchy.

He shrugs. "I just think it's odd that you spend the night and then he mends your car."

The divine smell from the casserole now makes me want to heave, and I swallow the acid creeping up my throat. "I spent the night with him and his girlfriend, who was equally nice." I can't stop lying. "Can we stop talking about this, please?" The kids have made an appearance, wondering what time dinner is. He says no more on the subject.

———

A FEW DAYS PASS, and I still haven't repaid Cal with lunch because of meetings and a client that wouldn't go. I ended up having a late lunch; a sandwich that Cal picked up for me, which I found really thoughtful. I haven't been alone with him since Monday, and I'm relieved in a way. After lying through my teeth to Justin the other night, it's not something I want to make a habit of.

I don't go straight home tonight. It's time to face the scales. If I've lost nothing this week, I'm quitting. I haven't been able to stomach food, if only I could lose weight as easily as I lose my self-control. I step on the electronic weighing platform one foot at a time, standing perfectly still, awaiting my result.

"Four pounds off, Steph," Laura says in her most high-pitched squeal.

I exhale and form the biggest smile that I can't seem to remove as I float to take my seat. I've obviously done something right this week, even though I feel like a complete fuck-up.

Lindsey sits next to me.

"Have you had a good week?" I ask.

"Shocking. You?"

I can't even look sympathetic; I'm elated by my whopper. "Four pounds off," I say.

"Well done, that's great."

"What did you do? Do you want to talk about it?"

"I bought some chocolates to put away for Christmas gifts, and I opened them."

"Oh dear." Knowing how fatal this is, I wipe away my smile and chew on the inside of my mouth. "How many did you have?"

"I only had a few on Friday."

"Right, well that's not too bad."

"No, but it was Saturday and Sunday that did all the damage."

"Oh no, perhaps you should get rid of them if they're too much of a temptation for you."

"I got rid of them, two entire boxes full."

"Well done. Did you give them away?"

"No, I ate them." She sighs and looks down at her lap, twiddling her thumbs together.

"Oh, I see. At least they've gone now." I smile, trying to be positive for her.

"Yep, no more temptation."

"That's true." I think about all the things tempting me and it's not just food I have to contend with. Laura begins her weekly round-up, kicking off with a motivational quote.

"It will hurt.

It will take time.

It will require willpower.

It will require dedication.

It will require sacrifice.

There will be temptation."

Is she still talking about food?

She continues, "I promise you, it will be worth it."

Oh, it was so worth it...

"To start off the celebrations this week, I'll come to Steph first. She is our biggest loser this week with an impressive four pound weight loss." Everyone cheers and claps their hands together. "Tell the group what you've done this week, Steph." I look around the room to see everyone's gaze resting on me, and I freeze. What can I say? *Oh, you know, just cheated on my husband having the best sex I've had in years; talk about a work-out. But I've been sick as a dog all week with guilt. I would recommend it to anyone needing a kick up the arse. So much more effective than cutting out carbs.*

"I just cut down on my portion sizes," I say, when really, I've had my cake and eaten it.

I have that Friday feeling, singing along to the radio on my morning commute. I pull into the usual parking space that I've claimed as mine. Cal always parks next to me. We step out of our cars at the same time.

"Hey." He bites his lip, looking me up and down.

"Hi, I thought I would take you for lunch today to say thank you for my car."

"I look forward to it." He grins and winks at me.

We have our usual morning briefing. Jerry tells us about a new client—a well-known sports company—who wants to hire us for their rebranding, and we're going to London for a presentation. It sounds exciting. I don't go to London very often.

Sitting back at my desk, I think about where to go for lunch. I wonder if I'm doing the right thing. I don't trust myself to be alone with him, and yet there's nothing I want more. Since our passionate night together, I can't stop thinking of him and our kiss right here in the office. Were we on camera? I hadn't noticed the security cameras before. I can't help but gaze at him. He catches my eye and smiles, making his eyes crease in the corners. His cheeky smile makes me think he planned this, fixing my car so he can suggest I repay him with lunch. I have to just get through today, be strong, and resist him. It's just lunch, surrounded by other people. How bad can it be?

Cal grabs his coat. "Where do you want to go for food?"

James says, "Aren't you coming for sushi with us?"

"Nah, I hate that shit." Cal huffs, shrugging on his coat.

I smile. I'm glad he doesn't like it; it was never a thing when we were young.

Once everyone has left, I turn to Cal. "Seeing as it's my treat, let's go to that refurbished pub down that country lane, 'The White Lion Inn'. I don't know what the street name is."

"I know where you mean. Let's go." He pulls his keys from his coat pocket and leads the way.

"Are we not going in my car, as it's fixed now?"

"Nah. I'll drive." He opens the door to his black Audi A3 saloon, and I climb into the passenger side. I only know that's what it's called as he told me. I know nothing about cars and frankly, I'm not interested, but his car suits him, and he looks good behind the wheel. How can he turn me on so much just by driving? He smiles, pulling out of the car park.

"I haven't been able to stop thinking about you all week." His warm hand squeezes my thigh and a tingle blossoms there. The heat from his palm radiates through my body, and I cross my legs, pressing them tightly together. "Crossing your legs won't make the ache disappear, you know."

"What?" I gulp. He knows me so well.

"It's all right. I'm the same." He grabs my hand. I think he's trying to hold it, but he places it on his crotch, showing me exactly how aroused he is. He keeps my hand there and presses it down firmly against him.

"Cal," I cry, but he just laughs before releasing my hand. All the awkwardness I've felt since we were last intimate has disappeared now we're alone again, and all I can focus on is him. We pull into the car park. I get out of the car and walk towards the entrance. Cal takes my hand. I like his forcefulness; how he laces his fingers with mine. I doubt I'll see anyone I know here. We're miles away from where I live, and I don't know anyone from this town other than my work colleagues. He smiles, maybe a little shocked that I let him hold my hand, but he should know I can never say no to him. He's always been the dominant one in our relationship.

Walking into the restaurant, I scan the modern décor and industrial copper lighting. We're shown to a small rustic wooden table and the server hands us two menus and lights a dinner candle in a stubby gin bottle, giving off a flicker of light in a dim quiet corner. Cal reclines into the soft grey furnishings in the booth while perusing the menu. "So, what are we having?"

"I'm going to have the duck." I hand my menu back to the server without even looking at it.

"How do you know that's on here?" Cal scans the list of meals. "Oh yeah, it's there."

"I worked on these menus." I giggle.

"Right, I forgot. I'll have the lamb, and a pint of Stella." He tells the server.

"Just a small wine for me please and a glass of sparkling water."

The waiter nods and walks away.

I settle back into my seat. "So what've you been up to this week?"

"Besides thinking about you?" He laughs. "I've had my kids this week. We built snowmen, and I took them sledging while the snow was still about."

"Kids love a bit of snow, don't they?"

"Yeah, I bet our kids would get on. How old are yours again?"

"Ten and my son is seven. What are yours?"

"My girls are nine and seven."

"Is that what that tattoo is on your wrist?"

He glances at his wrist and nods. I take hold of his hand and turn it over to find three names and dates. Olivia, Beth and Jax. I run my thumb over the scroll. "Who's Jax?"

He pulls his hand away like I've burned his skin. "My son. He died before he was born." His voice wavers, and I can hear him choke up. I know that pain only too well. I want to hold him and tell him I understand. His hands go under the table, and he shifts in his seat. I don't push the subject, seeing how his eyes have glossed over, and he's slipping into the darkness.

"I'm so sorry, Cal." I hold out my palm.

"It's fine. I'm fine." He places his hand back on the table, and I hold it in mine. "It was a long time ago." His thumb caresses my fingers, and we gaze into each other's eyes for a while. "So, tell me, how much you've been thinking about me this week?" The corner of his mouth curls upwards.

I can't help but laugh; he's so friggin' cocky and sure of himself. But he's right. I haven't stopped thinking of him inside me. I smile, dreamily reliving our three escapades.

"What are you thinking about? Tell me." His tone is demanding, but he has a cheeky grin as he squeezes and tugs on my hand.

I lean over the table slightly. "You."

"Yeah, what am I doing?"

"Last week, when we were… you know," I whisper.

"Which time?"

"That's what I can't decide." I bite my lip while I think about it again. "I can't decide which is my favourite. The bedroom, the shower, or the bedroom again. What was yours?"

He grins and thinks for a moment, scratching his stubbly

jaw that elicits something so primal deep within me. "The car."

"What? We haven't done it in the car?"

"Not yet." His voice is rough. I suddenly get the pull in my stomach and have the urge to cross my legs again, but nothing can stop the throb I'm feeling.

Finally, my drink arrives, and I'm desperate to take a sip. My mouth is so dry, and I gasp for breath, thinking of getting back into his car.

My index finger rims the edge of my glass. "So tell me what you're going to do in the car." The small amount of wine has made me a little brave—or is it him? He makes me say things I wouldn't normally say.

"It's not what I'm gonna do, it's what you're gonna do."

"And what's that?" I'm practically breathless, panting out each word. I take a big gulp of wine, hoping it will calm my nerves and stop my fringe from sticking to my forehead.

He grins, leans over, and whispers into my ear. "You're gonna sit on my lap and slide down my big cock and ride me while screaming my name."

I almost spit out my wine, then try to swallow, but it goes up my nose. We both burst out laughing at my reaction.

"Would you like that, Steph?" he asks in a sultry tone, looking rather pleased with himself.

"Yes. You haven't changed one bit. You're still as filthy as ever."

"Only with you. You fucking love my dirty mouth." He smirks. He's not wrong.

My cheeks are sizzling right now. I run my hand over my forehead to remove the moisture gathered there, but I can't stop the dampness seeping into my knickers.

"You're wet now, aren't you?" His tongue darts out, licking his scrumptious lips.

"Cal." I look around the room to check no one is privy to our conversation.

"Tell me, Steph." He commands with his low, gravelly tone that I can't deny.

"Yes." My voice trembles.

"How wet?"

"Cal, stop."

"Come here, sit next to me." He nods to the space beside him in the booth.

I do as he asks and slide around to the corner of the padded seat. Our knees knock, and he places his hand on my leg. I get a hint of his scent, like a fresh ocean spray with a hint of mint. My lips part. I'm intoxicated by him. The flickering light from the candle highlights a smirk on his lips and the dancing flame reflects in his eyes.

His agile fingers slip under the fabric of my skirt, trickling upward to the apex of my thigh. He tugs at my tights, and the fabric tears. My eyes widen. I lean into him more and open my legs slightly. He slides his hand under my panties and slips his finger inside me, keeping eye contact with me the entire time. If I could, I would mount him right now. His thumb presses against my sensitive spot. He repeatedly pushes his fingers in and out of me, making my eyes flicker. I let out a small moan of his name. I try to hide the pleasure on my face by resting my forehead on his shoulder. He kisses my hair, and I notice the server walking over with two meals.

"Cal, stop, look." He spots the waiter and removes his hand from between my thighs. He sets Cal's plate down and places my meal in front of me, and Cal thanks him before he goes.

Cal pulls his hand from under the table and puts his finger

in his sinful mouth and sucks it seductively. "You taste so good, Steph."

I'm left so aroused I can't think straight.

"I'm sorry about your tights." He titters. He's not sorry at all.

"You better be. You just ripped a massive friggin' hole in them, you know."

"I hate those fucking things, but I'll buy you a new pair."

"I can live with one less pair of tights, but you better make it worth my while," I half-joke. I can't wait to feel him inside of me again.

He grins. "Don't I always?"

I smile back. He's right, he does. "The food looks amazing. Is your lamb good?"

"Yeah, but I'm so ready for dessert." The way he looks at me makes my cheeks flush. I could easily come from his words and the way he looks at me alone.

"You already had dessert." I bring a piece of succulent duck to my mouth.

"Not enough. I'm hoping it snows again. I might have to sabotage your car so you'll have to stay over another night."

"Is that what you did last week?" The duck is coated in a plum sauce and has a kick like a rich luxurious wine on my palette.

"What, you think I sabotaged your car?" He scoops up a forkful of his creamy mashed potato and shovels it into his mouth.

"It had crossed my mind." If he did, I hope he does it again.

"I didn't. I didn't plan any of it." He takes hold of my wrist just as I'm about to take another bite of duck. "You believe me, don't you?"

I nod. "I believe you." My mouth opens to take the meat

from my fork, and he leans in and takes it from the metal prongs with his teeth.

"That duck tastes almost as good as you, Steph."

"It's good, isn't it?" I take another piece and let it roll around my tongue. "If you tampered with my car, I'm not mad."

"Steph, I never fucked with your car. But I will if you want me to."

I laugh and bite into a roasted chantenay carrot with a honey glaze. "Mmm Cal, this is lovely, here try one of these." I place a piece of carrot on my fork and position it in front of his mouth. He wraps his lips around the metal prongs, and I wish I was that fork right now.

"That's delicious. You picked a good place here. I totally forgot about it being tucked away."

"Do you know anywhere to go in your car after?" It's all I can think about.

"Yeah, don't you worry your pretty head about that." He grins.

"I can't wait much longer. Hurry with your food or we won't have time." Gosh, I sound desperate. *You are desperate.*

He laughs. "I don't need long."

"How long?"

"I can make you come in five minutes."

"Can you now?"

"Yeah, next time I'll make it longer when we have more time." He is so sure of himself. I want to say there won't be a next time, but who am I kidding?

"Next time?"

"Yeah, next time." He smirks and takes another bite of mash. "I read a book I think you might like."

"Oh, what's it about?"

"Dying."

"Great, my favourite genre."

"It's much more than that. You used to love me reading my books to you."

"I loved you reading my books more." I flash my eyes upward to meet his gaze.

"Yeah, I bet you did, you filthy minx."

I giggle and cover my mouth with my hand while I chew on a roasted potato.

"You have an e-reader, don't you?"

"Yes, of course."

"I've read a few books that I know you'd like."

"Send me the list and I'll download them and take a look."

"I'll send it to you later. I don't want you getting distracted now." He grins.

"Honestly, nothing could distract me right now." The pressure between my legs is intense. I eat the rest of my food so quickly I think I might give myself indigestion. "I need to go to the restroom."

I look in the mirror at my flushed face and check my teeth. Luckily, my skirt hides the hole in my tights. The combination of him and the wine has me in a salacious mood. I place my hands on my cheeks and the heat emanates to my palms. My chest is pounding so hard I fear I may need a defibrillator by the time I'm done.

Cal is waiting for me near the entrance, leaned up against the wall with his hands in his pockets. "Ready?" He pulls his car keys out, tossing them in the air and catching them again.

I nod and take his hand as we walk out to the car, interlacing my fingers with his and adoring the affection in public, like the familiar feeling of coming home. Once in the car, Cal pulls out of the parking bay. I'm dizzy. Everything is a haze, and all I can think about is getting him back into my pants.

"Where are we going?"

He glances at me and smiles as we turn down a woodland lane. His hand rests on my knee, and I watch it slowly disappear up my black skirt. His fingers dig into the inside of my thigh. I can't wait much longer.

"Cal, pull over." I pant.

"Soon." He reaches further up to my apex, and I open my legs for him. Shuffling my hips to meet his fingers as they creep through the hole he made in my tights. He lifts the elastic of my knickers, crooking a finger into my heat. My eyes screw shut. The pleasure he's giving me intensifies, and I tug on the seat belt, moaning his name.

"Fuck me, Steph. You're sexy as fuck like this." The car suddenly swerves and comes to a stop. I open my eyes, and we're down a dirt road surrounded by trees. Cal pushes his seat back, and I waste no time in undoing his jeans. He helps me as I fumble with his belt, and he pulls his boxers down along with his Levi's. I climb on top of him.

"Eager." His erection springs free, and presses against the fabric of my underwear. He grabs my waist, stopping me from rubbing myself against him. "What happened to not doing this again?"

"What?" I'm still panting and desperate.

He holds me above him. "You said we couldn't do this again."

"Cal, please, you're wasting time."

"Tell me how much you want me."

"Cal, stop teasing me." I can feel the tip of him pressed against my inner thigh. "I want you," I huff in my hazy, panting state. "All of you. Inside me. Right now."

"Fuck, I want you, Steph." His lips collide with mine and

our tongues entwine. He pulls my waist to his and tugs at my knickers, pulling them to one side at the apex of my thighs.

I moan into his mouth as I slide onto him, rocking my hips back and forth. "Cal."

"Fuck, Stephanie."

"Cal, I love it when you call me that."

"Stephanie, Stephanie."

"Callum." Our mouths lock again. He stops my hips from rocking and pulls back from my lips.

"Fuck," he shouts.

"What's wrong?"

"I haven't got a rubber."

"You've got to be kidding me." My mouth is gaping.

"Hang on." He opens his glove box and rummages through. "Fuck."

"It didn't bother you in the shower last week."

"I could pull out in the shower."

"Well, pull out this time."

"I can't exactly pull out when you're on top, Steph."

"Leave it then. I'm on the pill, anyway." There's no way I'm getting off him now.

"Are you sure?" He looks into my eyes with desperation.

"Yes, it's fine. You don't sleep around, do you?"

"Do you really want me to answer that?"

"Ugh, Cal. I mean, you're not diseased, are you?"

He frowns. "No, Steph. Fuck. I don't shag anyone without a johnny, not since my kids anyway."

"Good." I pant. "Then fuck me harder, Cal. I want to feel you, every inch of you." He lets go of my hips so I can move against him, and he moves his talented arse in rhythm with me.

I pull the band from his hair and run my fingers through his waves, fisting his black mane as I reach my pinnacle.

Rough kisses line my jaw and he sucks my neck. "Fucking-hell, Steph. I can't last much longer," he huffs into my shoulder.

I fist the fabric on his shirt to steady myself and hold his hair tight in my other hand, rocking my hips faster. "Don't you dare come yet, not until I'm done." He reaches a hand down to rub his thumb in circles to rush me along. It works. A few more rubs and thrusts, and I come apart, screaming his name. The car is spinning in donuts around me, and everything is blurry. Everything except him. I wrap my arms around his neck and rest my head on the headrest behind him as I get my breath.

He kisses my cheek. "I told you I could have you screaming my name in five minutes." He must have come when I did; I was so lost in my gratification that I didn't notice. He kisses me again and moves my hair from my face. "I love it when you're a bossy bitch."

I laugh. "Glad someone does." I lean my forehead against his. "I don't want to get off."

"You just got off." He titters.

I giggle and peck his lips.

"It's all right. There's no rush. We'll just make up some bullshit if we're late back."

I kiss him again, knowing it will be the last time, for today at least.

"You have me breaking all the rules here, Cal."

He cups my face. "What rules?"

"You know what rules. You don't need me to spell it out."

"Rules are made to be broken, baby. You have me breaking my own rules too."

"What?"

"Fucking without a rubber is one. But I would never normally go with a married woman."

I look down and take in a deep, pained breath.

Cal lifts my chin. "Hey. In your heart, I know you're married to me. You always have been. Don't you feel guilty about what we have." His tongue laps mine again, and I lose all previous thoughts. My desire for him outweighs my contrition.

"I need to clean myself up, Cal."

He reaches behind him and pulls a sweater from the back seat. "Here, wipe yourself on this." He holds it for me. I lift myself up from him, and he wipes between my legs with the jumper. He even makes that sexy. I sit back in the passenger seat after sorting myself out. Cal zips up his jeans and tucks his shirt in before starting the car. "Same time Monday?" He has a hopeful, cheeky grin.

"Piss off." I laugh. I can't believe I let this happen again, but then, of course, I should have known. "Is this why you fixed my car? You planned this, didn't you?"

He chuckles. "Hey, you came on to me, remember? I just came for the free lunch."

I stare at him, not knowing whether to laugh or scowl at my weakness. Though the grin on his face is adorable and has me smiling along with him. I touch up my makeup in the passenger mirror and he backs up into his usual parking bay next to mine. "What did you do with the tie for my hair?"

"Here, it's wrapped on my wrist." I watch him pull his hair back into the black elastic band, and I draw in a breath. As fond as I am of his hair down, I also take pleasure in seeing the stubble along his chiselled jawline.

"What's up?" He smiles as I gaze in awe.

"Nothing, I... I love looking at you." I avert my eyes.

He glances around the car park, then lifts my chin towards him. "You just shagged me in the car like a fucking animal and now you go all shy telling me you love looking at me." He kisses me softly on my forehead.

Back at the office, I try to ignore him. I have to get some work done. On the way out, he squeezes my arse as we approach the door. "See you Monday."

I glance around to check nobody saw him do that. "Cal, you can't touch me like that, not here." We both walk to our cars.

He smiles. "I couldn't resist. You know I love your arse."

"You love shagging my arse."

"Yeah, that as well." He presses his lips against the flesh under my ear, and I feel it in my stomach. Luckily nobody saw, I hope.

The entire drive home, I can feel him still inside of me. A tingling sensation fills my entire body as I think of him. What am I doing? I park on the drive at home and walk into the house. My legs are unsure. The guilt rises in my throat when I look at Justin.

"Hi."

"Hi, good day?"

"Yes, the usual, you know," I say, trying to play it down.

"Drink?"

"Yes please. I'll have a cappuccino." I sit at the dining room table as I do every day when I come home. Only today I'm squirming in my seat, knowing I have an enormous hole in my tights. My knickers are damp, and there's a phantom throb from my earlier exploits. Justin makes a hot drink, and we both chat about our day.

"Justin, I'm going to have a bath while you do tea, if that's all right?"

"Yes, I'll shout you when it's done." Everyone always comments how lucky I am to have a man that cooks, and I know it. He is a good husband and father. I can't do this with

Cal anymore; I have to have some self-control. What is wrong with me? The guilt roiling in my stomach every time I look at Justin is intolerable. It's okay for Cal; he's free and single, and doesn't give a shit. Arsehole.

"I've got you those skinny sausages you like for tea."

"Thanks. Although I wouldn't go as far to say I like them."

"You need them." He sniggers and I let out a breath and scramble upstairs before I ram the skinny sausage down his throat. Peering into the kids' rooms, I find them getting along for once. They're playing on their games console together. "Hi." I get two grunts back, and they're not even teens yet. Such darlings.

I run my bath and take my clothes off, chucking my tights in the bin. The hot, bubbly water is so relaxing. I could go to sleep in here, but every time I close my eyes it's his face I see. How can I get him out of my head? I need help. I can't talk to Claire. Not about this. She'd never approve.

CHAPTER

It's that time of year again when the shops are full of Christmas spirit. The smell of mint candy canes, oranges and cinnamon fill the aisles. Houses twinkle with multicoloured flashing lights and dazzling window displays.

The local town hall lights were switched on last week and the kids keep pestering me to put our tree up. Every year around this time, I get the urge to re-decorate, just because—let's face it—I haven't got enough on my plate.

"Remind me why are we doing this again?" Justin huffs, opening a tin of paint.

"I like the house to look perfect and cosy, ready for Christmas. You know that."

"Can we re-decorate in September next time? Why is everything last minute with you?"

He's right. I shouldn't be re-decorating three weeks before Christmas, on top of all the Christmas shopping and everything else. But at least it keeps me busy and helps take my mind off Cal.

I ignore him and listen to the joyful music playing on the radio. Our antique furniture matches perfectly with the new gorgeous damask wallpaper I've selected. The kids stripped the old paper last night, so everything is prepped. It was fun until they started fighting over who held the wallpaper steamer. Cassie blasted Cairen in the face with the steam and Justin stepped in.

Justin has already set up the pasting table and is giving the walls a fresh coat of paint while I paper the feature wall around the fireplace. I've been looking forward to finally getting it done, though when the alarm went off this morning, I didn't want to get up. I was having the most amazing dream, lying on a private beach with Callum rubbing sun cream into my back, the gentle sea breeze blowing in my hair, and a 'Sex on the Beach' cocktail in my hand. His palms made their way to my bottom. He pulled down my swimsuit and massaged my plump cheeks. Kneading them as if making a rich dough. His fingers slipped between my thighs and I let out a moan before his teeth sank into my flesh there and I awoke. I've honestly never woken up more disappointed in my entire life.

My dad calls round and offers to take the kids and dog out for a walk so we can decorate in peace. After I have hung two lengths of paper, I stand back and admire my handy work.

"What do you think?" I ask Justin. He hands me my third coffee of the morning.

"Fine." He shrugs and takes a sip of his drink. Happy to go along with whatever I choose. He never gets involved in what wallpaper, curtains, or furniture we have. As long as he has a comfortable chair to sit in and a big TV to watch his sport, he's as happy as a pig in shit.

"We need to do a shopping list." Justin hands me a pen and paper, and I plan my meals for the week.

"Don't forget I'm not here Thursday, so you and the kids can buy pizzas or order a take-away or something, whatever you want to do." I tap the pen against my chin.

"I forgot it was your London trip this week. Are you prepared for your presentation?"

"Yes, everyone else will do the actual speaking. My role

is to put the visuals together." Justin nods. He knows I hate public speaking. "Hopefully, I won't need to do a speech or anything." I continue to jot down food items for the rest of the days that I'm here. Watching my weight, I always like to plan my meals. It's been hard managing my weight while having a pub lunch most days, but I'm finally getting a handle on it. I haven't been snacking in the evening; Justin has seen to that, which is fine, as I've not been interested in food while at home lately.

The wallpapering is almost finished when my dad calls back with the kids. He looks at my handy work and I beam, standing proud with my hands on my hips, awaiting his praise. "You have put this on upside down."

"What? I haven't."

"The fleur-de-lis should be the other way." Dad points to the pattern on the wall, and an unsettling feeling swells in my stomach. Still hopeful, he could be wrong. I Google the wallpaper pattern—holding my breath—and sure enough, the photo on the website is the other way up.

I exhale, passing the phone to my dad. "You're right."

"I know I'm right." He has a hint of a smile.

I dare him to laugh with my frown. "I've spent all morning doing this." Burying my head in my hands, I flop on the sofa.

"Nothing a bit of time and money can't sort out," Dad says.

Dad is more of an optimist than I am. "I'm pissed off. I'd planned on glossing this afternoon but that won't get done now."

"Leave it, it looks fine to me," Justin says.

I'm almost tempted to leave it, but I can't. Not now it's been pointed out. "It has to come off." I scowl at Justin for suggesting we can just leave it. "I have an extra roll. Do you think I'll have enough?"

"You should do," Dad says, looking at the spare rolls.

Dad helps me pull the paper off the wall. I huff, starting again from scratch. It doesn't help that I started my period this morning and already have a serious case of ratty bitch syndrome. I blame Callum. If it wasn't for his pleasurable fingers distracting me, I may have been able to concentrate on the task at hand.

Before I can take my foul mood out on Justin, he leaves to do the food shop while my dad helps me rectify the wallpaper situation. My dad is always to the rescue, every time I call him; even just for a chat, his opening line is, *'What've you broken now?'* The kids think he's some sort of genius or God. He really can fix anything, my dad. *Anything but a broken heart.* Cal has wormed his way back into my thoughts again. I wonder what he's doing now; surely he has to be having a better day than me. I look over at my phone on the windowsill. I'm tempted to call him, but then look back to Dad; thank goodness he's here. Callum already thinks I'm desperate. I vow to not throw myself at him anymore. *Have some dignity woman.*

With Dad's help, we have the wallpaper hung in no time; Justin has been shopping and put the food away.

"Shall I start on tea?" he asks.

"I'm starving." I haven't eaten since this morning when I had scrambled egg on toast. "Shall we have chip shop instead?"

"Do you think that's wise with your diet?"

"I just can't be arsed to cook anything." I sigh.

"Since when have you ever cooked anything?"

"What I mean is, I'm so hungry, I can't be bothered to wait for you to cook something. Let's just go to the chippy."

"Fine." Justin shrugs his shoulders. I think he's happy for a night off cooking, especially after the busy day we've had. "What do you want, Steph?"

"Hmm, get me haddock, chips and mushy peas, please."

The kids are happy too; they both order a battered sausage, chips and ketchup. I love a battered sausage—no pun intended—I really love batter.

Justin arrives back with our take-away and dishes it out. My mouth waters at the sight of the large battered fish as Justin peels away the newspaper wrapping. In one swift motion, he tears off the battered coating and throws it into the bin.

My mouth opens and my lip twitches. "What are you doing?"

"What? You don't want to eat the batter, do you?"

"Well, I did, yes." His sacrilegious actions have my blood bubbling.

"You can't have the batter, Steph. It's bad enough that you're having chips."

I slant my eyes at him and flare my nostrils. He hands me the plate, and I snatch it from his grip. I make my way to the living room, breathing heavily through my nose. If I speak, I'll scream. I'm sure I'll thank him one day, but right now I want to murder him. *Maybe he'll choke on a fishbone.* If only.

I eat my naked fish. The grease from the chips combined with the salt and vinegar satisfies me. I relish in my simple pleasure and forget about the batter.

"That's enough for today," Justin says.

I sit on the covered sofa in my scruffs and silently applaud my decorating achievements. "Yes, I need a wash."

"I can smell you from here."

My eyes squint in his direction. Callum always liked me sweaty. I sure worked up a sweat with him, that's for sure.

After my tea, I fill the bath, adding bath salts for aching muscles. I'm getting too old for this decorating stuff. Relaxing into the hot, soapy water, I close my eyes, thinking of my dream with Cal and all the times we've shared a bath together. I rub the soapy flannel over my breast and catch my pert nipple. The stiff peak grazes my palm and I imagine it's his hand caressing me. I glide over the suds down to the apex of my thighs and slip two fingers beneath my folds, arching my back, saying his name over and over in my head. His sultry voice tells me how wet I am while circling my nub. My hips lift as my fingers push inside my slickness. A small moan escapes my lips and I flex my fingers.

"Mum." The door opens and Cassie bursts in. I instantly sit up and wrap my arms over my breasts. We really need to get a lock on this door. I can never go to the toilet in peace, let alone bring myself to orgasm.

"What's wrong, sweetheart?"

"Cairen's being mean to me and keeps coming in my room while I'm playing with my dolls."

"Cairen," I shout. "Stay out of her room."

He ignores me.

"He's not listening, Mum."

All my frustration comes out in my voice and I shout, "Cairen. If you annoy your sister again, I will take your TV out of your room."

"Okay," he shouts.

"Right, if he does it again, tell your dad. Let me bathe in peace."

She walks back into the landing, leaving my bathroom door open.

"The door," I shout. She returns and closes it and I sink back into the bubbles to resume my previous position, but the moment's gone. I exhale and wash my hair.

MONDAY AT WORK, everyone is frantically trying to get everything completed for our London trip. I'm like a swan; calm on the surface, but underneath, I'm paddling like mad just to stay afloat. I know I shouldn't panic though; everything is under control. While I haven't been to London for a big client presentation like this before, I have given many presentations at a local level and chaired many meetings with designers and clients.

I need another caffeine hit. Walking to the coffee machine, Callum follows me with his mug. I hold my hand out to take his cup from him and he grabs hold of my wrist, examining my forearm.

"What's this?"

I look underneath my arm and find a long white streak of gloss. "Oh, I didn't know that was there. I showered this morning, honest."

"Have you been painting?"

"Yes."

"You're supposed to paint the walls, Steph, not your arm." He grins.

"Ha-ha, you're so funny." I give him an eye roll.

His firm hand still grips my wrist, and I don't want him to let go. Goosebumps prickle up my arm, and the hairs on my skin stand to attention from the electricity between us.

"I put the wallpaper on upside down."

He chuckles, letting go of my arm. "That's so typical of you."

"It's not funny." I swat at him for laughing. "I was so proud of it too until my dad pointed it out."

"Have you left it?"

"What do you think?"

He hums for a moment, tapping his finger against his lips. "I think you re-did it."

"Yep, it took me all friggin' day to paper one wall." I laugh. "Twice."

"Were you away with the fairies again, Steph?"

"No." I daren't tell him I was thinking of him and the amazing dream I had, especially since I'm not doing this with him again. I will be strong.

"You are ditsy sometimes."

"It's true. I have no common sense, but then neither did Einstein."

"You haven't seriously just compared yourself to Einstein?" He raises his brow.

"You're only jealous because I'm more intelligent than you." I pour him a refill.

"Yeah, okay then," he says with a warm smile. His all-consuming eyes have me in a trance. Deep rich shades of brown swirl, stimulating me just as the circulating coffee in the pot motivates my senses. He gazes upon me for a beat too long before his eyes rest on my lips.

"Did you have a good weekend?" I hand him his coffee.

"Yeah, it was just the usual, you know." He looks down, then back up at me, pulling in his bottom lip. "I want to see you at dinner."

"Cal, please, no. I'm not doing this with you anymore. Please." I don't know what I'm actually saying please for. Is it for him to stop coming on to me, stop looking at me that way and turning me on with his sex eyes.

"I just want to talk."

"You know full well we can't just talk when we're alone." I walk back to my desk and avoid him for the rest of the day, partly because I need to have some self-control, but mainly nothing can happen as I'm on my period.

———

"Morning," Cal shouts as we step out of our cars. He's waiting for me again.

"Morning." I yawn, taking in the cold, fresh air.

"Tired?"

"I didn't sleep well last night." Same as most nights, but being hormonal just adds to my troubles.

We enter the office. "You sit down. I'll get you a drink. Do you want any food?"

"No thanks. I've already eaten this morning."

He hands me a strong coffee. "I thought I'd drive today. It doesn't make sense for us to go in two separate cars." We have a meeting with a client this morning, a local coffee shop that wants a new logo, signage and menus.

"Thank you, that's great." I nod, blowing my hot drink and check my emails before heading out.

"You ready to go?"

"Yes." I yawn again.

He passes me my coat and pulls his keys from his jacket pocket. I open the passenger door to his Audi and slide in as he starts the engine. His car feels familiar already and I relax into his grey leather seats, watching him drive out of the car park. Once on the straight road, he moves his hand from the gear stick to my thigh. As much as I crave his hand on my skin, I'm being strong.

"Cal, we agreed we weren't doing this anymore."

"I didn't agree to shit." He narrows his eyes at me while waiting at the traffic lights.

I pick his hand up and place it back on the gear stick.

"How far is this café?" I don't know how long I can resist him.

He taps his fingers on the steering wheel. "It's just around this corner."

"We could have walked here."

"We could, but then I wouldn't be able to do this." His hand strokes my leg and tucks under the fabric of my skirt. His long fingers dig into my inner thigh and my walls clench, reminding me of my period.

"Cal. Stop." My eyes widen at his impudence.

He chuckles and pulls up on the kerb.

"We're here now, anyway." His hand squeezes my leg before he gets out of the car.

He walks around to my side and takes my hand. Tingles sprint up my arm, racing to my centre. I unhook my fingers from his and hold my bag with both hands. He frowns and holds the door open to the café.

A familiar face stares at me. He runs a hand over his shaved head. "Steph, is that really you?" He strides over and gives me a hug that lifts me off my feet.

He's bigger than I remember. His overalls smell of engine oil.

"Dean, my clothes." I giggle.

"Sorry." He lowers me to the floor until my kitten heels click on the tiles and I steady myself.

"It's good to see you, Steph. Have you been keeping this one on his toes?" He playfully punches Cal in the stomach. "Ay up mate."

Cal pats Dean on the back. "How's it going?" Cal looks at his hand. "What the fuck is that? Mate, you're covered in shit." He wipes his hand on Dean's greasy sleeve.

"Soz, mate. Some of us actually work for a living." Dean chortles, scratching his unshaven jaw. There's more hair there than on his head.

"Yeah, yeah. Cheeky fucker."

"Thanks for sorting my car battery, Dean." I flash a glance at Cal and see him smiling.

"No problem. I checked your brakes over too and everything else. Cal wanted me to give you a good service." Dean laughs. "Not that sort of service. He'd already seen to that. But you know what I mean."

My stomach drops like it's been hit with a sledgehammer. The heat shoots straight to my face, ringing the bell in my ears like a high striker at the fairground. I look at Cal, shuffling on his feet, with a big cheesy grin on his face.

The girl behind the counter hands Dean a bacon buttie and he pays. Another lady comes through. "Morning, Callum."

"Morning, Sally, this is Steph. She'll be working on your project with me."

I shift from one foot to the other and shake her hand. "Nice to meet you."

"Come through into the back." She waves a hand towards a quiet corner of the café, through a small archway.

Cal nods his head towards the back. "Go on. I'll be there in a minute."

I turn towards Dean. "Nice to see you again." I follow Sally through the archway and take a seat at a table, while Cal stays behind to chat with Dean.

"Can I get you a tea or coffee?"

"I'm fine thank you."

Cal walks through. "I'll have a coffee please, Sally."

She smiles at Cal. "Are you sure I can't get you anything, Steph? We have some homemade cakes behind the counter." Now she's talking.

"Steph will have one of your caramel shortbread tart slices," Cal says.

"No problem." Sally disappears behind the counter.

My eyes turn to thin slits. "I might not have wanted anything."

"You can thank me later. The caramel tarts here melt in your mouth. It may even cheer you up."

"What's that supposed to mean?"

He shrugs. "You haven't exactly been Little Miss Sunshine these last few days. What's up with you?"

"Nothing. I can't believe you told Dean about us."

"Calm down. He guessed when I told him you'd stayed over."

Him telling me to calm down makes my nostrils flare and I grind my teeth together. If we weren't sitting in this café right now, I would scream.

I pull out my notebook and pen. "Do you need a pen or anything?"

"Nah, I've got one." He opens his jacket and pulls a pen from the inside pocket.

"Wow, you *really* have changed." I glare at him while I chew on the inside of my mouth.

"Yeah, borrowing your pink fluffy pens isn't really a good look for me." His shoulder nudges mine, and he hints at a smile.

Sally walks back into the room with a caramel slice for me.

"Thank you, this looks delicious."

She pivots on her heels. "I'll just get your coffee, Callum. Back in a minute."

"Eat your cake and cheer the fuck up." His lip curls in the corner and I don't know whether I want to smack it, kiss it, or both.

"If you're not going to eat it, then I will." He grips the plate and pulls it towards him.

I pull it from him. "You should have got your own."

Sally walks back in and takes a seat opposite us.

I pick up the fork, break off a piece of the crumbly shortbread base, and taste the buttery biscuit. The caramel topping coats my tongue and sticks to the roof of my mouth. I treasure the sweetness while listening to Sally's ideas for revamping her quaint little coffee shop. Cal is listening to Sally and taking notes, occasionally adding his own ideas to the mix. The sugar from the treat seems to have sweetened my heart. I can never stay mad at him for long. He was right about this dessert; it's divine. Almost as scrumptious as him —almost.

CHAPTER
Sixteen

After the meeting, I get back in his car. He turns right at the lights, heading in the wrong direction for work. I don't recognise where we are.

"Where are we going?"

He smirks. "Not far."

"Cal, please, take me back to work right now." What's he playing at?

"Calm down, I just want to talk."

"Like that's going to happen." My heart rate speeds up and I feel it pulsing between my thighs, just thinking about being alone with him, knowing I don't trust myself, let alone him.

"You've been avoiding me all yesterday and this morning. Have I upset you?"

"No."

He pulls up at an old abandoned building in a desolate car park. "Then what's wrong?" He turns the engine off and turns sideways to look at me.

"Cal, I'm married."

"Yeah, So?"

"So, I have kids. I can't keep doing this." I wave my hand between us.

"You weren't complaining last week, or the week before."

"Please Cal, I'm trying not to do this anymore, but you're making it so hard."

"You're the one that's making things hard." He grabs my hand and thrusts it onto his crotch so I'm aware of just how hard he is, and he leans in to kiss my neck.

I pull my hand away. "Cal, stop it, please."

His tongue licks at the spot under my ear, and then he sucks at the flesh there. How can he touch me there, and I feel the flicker of his tongue in my panties? His breath on my neck sends tingles through me and his warm mouth is heaven on my skin. He knows my resistance will crumble with his lips against my flesh. I'm drawn to him like a moth to a flame. He's luring me back into this sinful cycle. His hand goes back to my thigh and his fingers trail up my skirt as his kisses run along my jaw, making their way to my lips. I want to kiss him; more than anything, but I need to stop this now.

"No, Cal." My eyes plead with him, but he ignores me and continues his tender assault on my lips. I don't have the strength to stop him. I'm tortured by the temptation that is Callum Richards. Even though I know nothing good can come of this, yet I contemplate letting things go further. He slips his tongue into my mouth, giving me that familiar sensation that I adore. His fingers tug at the elastic between my legs and I remember I'm on my period.

I squirm and push him off me. "Please Cal, stop. I'm on my period."

He smiles, probably thinking that's why I don't want him right now—nothing to do with the fact that I'm married. Perhaps if I wasn't on my period, I would have already given in.

"So." He shrugs his shoulders. "We've done it loads of times before when it was your time of the month." He goes back to nibbling my ear and his hand back on my thigh like he doesn't give a shit. I can feel the heat between my thighs rush to my face and I know if I was in my home right now I would shag his brains out, period or not, but I'm not doing it in his car and wiping myself on his sweater again, that's gross.

"Not in the last twenty years we haven't." I squirm in my seat. My mind willing him to stop, but my body betrays me, letting him continue with his seduction.

"So, I'm not bothered about a *bit* of blood." How can he make talking about periods sound sexy?

My entire body writhes under his touch. "It's a lot heavier since I had kids," I whisper the words, locking my knees together. The heat in my cheeks intensifies, and I push his hand away from the top of my leg.

"All right, I'm not bothered about a *lot* of blood." He continues licking and nipping at my neck.

"Cal, I'm serious, not happening." I push him back to his side of the car and finally, he gets the message.

"Suck me off then." He unbuckles his belt like I'm a sure thing.

"What?" *You heard him.* My mouth opens, watching his dick burst from his pants.

"You got me all hard and worked up."

"Are you serious? I haven't touched you, you got yourself all worked up." My eyes are fixed on his bobbing erection that's waiting for my special attention. I'd love to give it the red carpet treatment. *No, no, no. Be strong.* I shake my head.

"You had to wear that top, and I swear, I can see your fucking nipple through it," he yells, gesturing to my breasts.

"Where?" I gasp, looking down, curling my shoulders inwards.

He runs his thumb over my nipple. "There, see." My erect

nipple protrudes through my lace bra and is prominent under my silky shirt.

"Cal." I sigh. "I'm not sucking you off. Can we go back to work now, please? I'm not doing this with you anymore. Please, I'm begging you, help me out here."

He throws his hands into the air. "Help you out? Do you have any fucking idea what you're doing to me?" His voice is harsh and raspy. He tucks himself back in his boxers and buttons up his jeans. "I go to bed dreaming about you. I wake up thinking about you. I sit at fucking work staring at you. Now I've tasted you again, I need more. You're like a fucking drug to me."

My mouth gapes. He takes his frustration out on the steering wheel, clenching his fists around the leather. I want to tell him I feel exactly the same, but that won't help our situation. "I hope it hurts you to look at me and think of me, because you've no idea how much it hurt me to watch you leave. To live with you and watch you date another girl killed me inside. If you're suffering even a tenth of what you put me through—I'm glad."

"You'll be fucking thrilled then, because it hurts like hell. You're in every cell of my body, in my veins, my bones, my mind. There's no escaping you now. I have to have you, Steph."

"You can't do this to me, Cal. If you cared for me at all, you'd stop now. I'm married."

"I don't care. Call me a selfish bastard. If anything, he stole you from me. You were mine first, Steph."

"You discarded me. You lost your claim on me the moment you tossed me aside."

"You'll always belong to me, Steph. I know I have your heart even if you won't admit it to yourself."

"Yeah, well, I want it back. You can't keep it. It isn't yours to toy with anymore."

"I can't give it back. It belongs to me. You gave it to me, forever mine, remember."

"And what of your heart? You never gave me yours."

"I fucking did."

"Then where is it? Because I no longer have it. You took it back with force, ripping me open in the process and left me bleeding out." The sadness drains through me. A tear forms in the corner of my eye, but I won't allow myself to cry in front of him. My mouth is dry. I take in a deep breath and pinch the top of my nose to stop the tears from flowing.

"I'm sorry." He grips the steering wheel.

I stay silent. If I speak, he'll hear the tremble in my voice. The memories of him leaving me still haunt me to this day. He left me a shadow of myself, and Justin brought me back into the light. He was the sun and water I needed after Callum tore me from my root and left me wilting.

Cal starts the car. He huffs, sounding more pissed off than before. Is it because I haven't spoken, or is it because I wouldn't blow him? I look out of the window as Cal drives and I recognise the road. A line of trees runs along the grass verge that leads back to work. I'm proud of myself for resisting him, though I'm not sure how long I can keep this up. If he keeps pushing me, I'm bound to cave and succumb to him again.

We arrive back at the office, and before I get out of the car, I turn to him. "I'm sorry."

He doesn't speak, giving me a taste of my own medicine, no doubt. He gets out of the car and doesn't even look at me.

AFTER WORK, I go to my slimming group at the local village hall. Standing in line ready to be weighed in, I sweat. This won't be pretty. My skirt is tight from my bloated stomach, one of my many menstruation symptoms. And the greasy chips over the weekend didn't help matters. I hate this. You'd think the thought of standing on these scales every week would be enough to make me stop putting shit in my mouth. *A moment on the lips is a lifetime on the hips.* One of the many phrases our group leader likes to quote. I smile as her irritating voice plays out in my head.

The queue goes down, and only Lindsey is in front of me now. Like me, Lindsey is a serious yo-yoer. Standing back enough to give her privacy, I watch as she mounts the scales. It can't be good news. She's taking off her watch, now her earrings—why the earrings I'll never know—they're studs. We're not exactly talking Pat Butcher here. Oh, wait... the necklace is coming off now; a thin chain with a small heart pendant. Like that's going to matter.

"Well done, Lindsey. You've lost half a pound," our group leader says, singing with excitement. Who knew?

Unseen, I unclip my bracelet, letting it fall into my bag. Every little helps I guess. I pat Lindsey on the back as she walks away, elevated by her minuscule loss. My turn. I drape my cardigan over an empty chair, slip off my shoes, and step onto the scales, looking straight ahead. I'm sure you weigh less if you lift your chin up.

"Half a pound on Steph," our group leader whispers.

What else can I take off? No, I'm turning into Lindsey. Suck it in and let it go. I nod. "Thank you," I say, although why I'm thanking her I don't know. It's like when you go to the dentist for a filling and you thank them for putting you through the worst pain since childbirth. I scurry away with my shoes and cardigan. Not staying for a confession, not tonight. I would sooner confess to murder, murdering a chocolate fudge cake, that is.

I have too much on my mind. I can't stop thinking about my fight with Cal. He hasn't spoken to me since this morning. I hope things will be all right tomorrow. We fought many times when we were together, but never stayed mad at each other for long. We'd have blazing rows about something or nothing as couples do and in mid-sentence, he would kiss my mouth to shut me up—and it worked. Half an hour later, he would make me a cuppa or cook my tea and would act as though nothing had happened. I don't want him back. I won't leave my kids, but I would give anything to go back to that time, to spend one more day with him the way it used to be; just the two of us in the attic bedroom, no worries or cares, with a lifetime of wonder and opportunity ahead of us.

AFTER OUR MORNING BRIEFING, Cal goes to the coffee machine. He would usually offer to get me a refill, but he still hasn't spoken to me since yesterday morning. He hasn't even looked at me. As the day progresses, I'm getting worried that I may have to drive myself to London tomorrow. Lunch comes and goes and I accept I'll have to drive. There's no room in Jerry's car and I won't grovel to Cal after he was the one being a dick. Come 5pm I'm still on the phone with a client and the office empties around me. *Great.* Any chance of catching Callum about London tomorrow has definitely gone now. I finish my phone conversation and gather my things together. As I walk out to a half-empty car park, Cal leans against his car, looking at his phone. I walk over to my car. "I thought you'd gone."

"I wanted to see you before I went." He puts his phone in his pocket, along with his hands.

"Oh?"

"Do you still want a lift tomorrow?" He looks down at his feet, pulling in his bottom lip.

Relief fills me, and I exhale a deep breath. "Yes please, although I can drive if you don't want to take me."

"Course I want to fucking take you." He lifts his head and his eyes are a dull sepia shade. "You should know that."

"Well, it's just, you haven't spoken to me in two days."

"One and a half, actually." His lips turn upwards in one corner. "And only because you told me not to."

"I didn't tell you not to speak to me, just not to come on to me."

He bends his knees slightly to gaze at my face. "I can't speak to you without coming on to you, you should know that too." He reminds me of a lost puppy dog and I can't resist showing him affection.

"I'm learning." I step closer and grab hold of the front of his jacket. He rests his forehead against mine and our noses touch. I move in to kiss his pouty lips, but he pecks the tip of my nose instead.

"I'll pick you up early as planned."

"Are you sure you don't want me to drive to yours? It seems daft you backtracking to get me."

"It's cool. I don't mind adding another hour on my journey," he says with a hint of sarcasm and a smile.

"Okay, see you then." He winks and gets in his car. His eyes crease in the corners as he smiles at me through our car windows. It's the first time I've seen him smile since our fight. What a fucking adorable bastard he is. Why did I ever bother fighting with him?

Today is the day of our presentation in London. We have an evening dinner booked with the clients and an all expenses paid hotel for the night. I don't want Cal to meet Justin, so I hurry to get dressed. As soon as he arrives, I want to be ready to go. I pack my clothes, makeup and hair products into a suitcase.

The doorbell chimes. Oh no, he's early. I bet he's come early on purpose.

Justin shouts up to me, "I'll get the door."

Adrenaline shoots through me. I get a sudden case of vertigo and hold on to the dressing table to keep my balance. *Calm down.* Justin never knew Cal, and he saw no pictures of him from when we dated. I mailed them to his mother's house. Hopefully, Justin will be none the wiser. "Come in, mate," he says.

I frantically rush around the bedroom, packing the rest of my belongings.

Cal's voice carries up the stairway. "You must be Cassie." Both my kids are shy creatures. I have visions of them gawping, not saying a word. "And you must be Cairen." I don't hear the kids speak back, but I hope they at least nodded. I smile at the thought of them making him feel awkward.

"Do you want a cuppa?" Justin asks.

I pop my jewellery on and squirt my perfume before tossing it into my bag.

"No thanks, I'm good. I've got a Starbucks in the car," Cal replies. I hope he's picked one up for me.

"You didn't need to fix Steph's car. I would have sorted it." Not this again. I run down the stairs carrying my belongings.

"It was no big deal. Technically, it was our mate Dean from school that fixed it. He's a mechanic."

"Our mate?" Justin folds his arms over his puffed up chest.

I stand in the hall with all my stuff. "Hi, I'm ready."

Justin waits for Cal to reply, and I widen my eyes to Cal to keep his mouth shut. He's already said too much.

"My mate from school."

Justin nods, but I can sense something ticking over in his brain as he stares at Cal.

"Shall we go, then?" I can't wait to get out of here—fast.

Both men grab my suitcase at the same time. Justin grips the handle firmly, forcing Callum to let go. I hand Cal my portfolio and a small holdall to take, then kiss the kids goodbye. They wipe away my kisses, still bleary-eyed and not fully awake at this time of the morning.

Cal waits at the passenger car door for me as Justin walks back up the drive. He stops me by placing his hands on my shoulders and kisses my lips. "Hope it goes well."

"Thanks." I swallow a breath of air. Justin never kisses me in public. I glance at Cal, who is watching our interaction. "I'll call you when I check-in."

"See you soon."

Cal opens the passenger door for me as I approach; he's not usually this chivalrous. My heart is still racing, and I'm coated in a sticky, cold sweat. I get in the car and settle into the seat, waving to Justin as we drive off.

"This seat is lovely and warm."

"I had the heating on for you on the way here."

He is so thoughtful, heating the passenger seat up for me.

"Here I got you a Starbucks." He pulls it from the drinks holder and hands it to me.

"Thanks." I knew he would get me one. "What did you get me?"

"Caramel Latte." He knows me so well. Even though I always have Americano for the low calories, caramel latte is my favourite. "I got you a brownie too, in the bag." He points to a Starbucks paper bag sat in the centre console. *Gosh, I love this man.*

"Thank you. And thanks for coming to pick me up. I really appreciate it." I pull the brownie from the bag and smile.

"No problem." His firm hand squeezes my leg, and I tense as a shiver of pleasure emanates from my centre. He turns off my street and heads towards the bypass.

I bite into my brownie. I can't remember the last time I had one of these. It's still warm too and gooey. "Oh my goodness."

Cal chuckles at me devouring the chocolate cake. I'm sure I have chocolate around my lips and between my teeth; I try not to smile in fear I'll look like an extra from a horrible histories episode.

"Watch your fingers," he says, which makes me burst out laughing and I check my teeth in the pull-down visor mirror.

"That was so good."

"I could tell. You were pulling your sex face."

"I don't have a sex face." I slap his thigh and he catches my hand, holding it on his leg before I get the chance to pull it back. His touch feels warm and tender, and the familiar tingle blossoms in my stomach.

"So that was Justin?" he smirks.

"Yeah, so?"

"Nice guy." His smirk widens.

"Yeah, he is nice. Nicer than you."

"Ouch." He puts his hand on his heart to mock me. "I was being sarcastic, by the way. I think he's a tool."

"Callum. Stop. He wasn't happy that you messed with my car, that's all."

"That's not all I've messed with." He titters.

"Oh my goodness. Callum. Stop.

"Does he fuck you like I do?"

"Cal," I cry, and swat at his chest with the back of my hand. He's smirking still. "He's... he knows his way around a bedroom."

"But does he fuck you like I do?" He glances over, taking his eyes from the road for a second.

What's he talking about? Nobody has ever taken me the way he does, like I'm the sexiest woman he's ever had, or the only woman in the world, like he might die if he doesn't have me. Justin's ok, but he doesn't have the same passion and intensity as Callum. Everything is heightened with Cal. Maybe that's the rush of having an affair; he's dangerous and sinful. "Yes, he does," I lie.

He grins as though he knows otherwise. I don't get wet at the touch of Justin's hand on my thigh like I am now. My heart's never skipped a beat when he holds my hand.

I had planned on not letting anything happen between us on this trip, but who am I kidding? One squeeze of my leg and my heart is racing and my knickers are wet. I'll be lucky if I make it to the hotel room without having him at this rate. Should I ask him to pull over somewhere? I sip on my latte and imagine what we can get up to at the hotel. He'll be pleasantly surprised if I make the first move. I'm always fighting the urge to be with him. I'll surprise him by taking the lead and sucking him off as soon as we check-in.

"What are you thinking about?"

I gulp down the sweet caramel. If only he knew what I was thinking about. "Nothing." I smile.

"You're such a fucking tease." He touches my leg again. "I'm glad you haven't worn any tights."

"I'm a tease? Cal, stop stroking my leg or it'll be a long drive."

"Are you wet already?" He glances over at me with an eyebrow raised.

I swallow my drink. "Piss off, and concentrate on the road."

He grabs my hand and places it on his crotch. The trousers he's wearing makes his stiff erection easier to feel under the light fabric.

"Oh," I squeak, then cough to hide my embarrassing high-pitched sound.

"You turned me on as soon as I got in the car, when I saw your skirt ride up your thigh." He's biting his lip now.

"Pervert."

"You know me." His hand goes back on my leg, poking under my skirt where the small front slit has opened up, stretching across my flesh. He's wrestling with my tight skirt to reach my panties. I grab his hand and interlace our fingers, hoping this will satisfy him for now.

"You need to concentrate on the road, not on my vagina."

"I can't help it. I can't keep my hands to myself when we're alone, you know that."

I smile and lean over the centre console to whisper in his ear. "I am wet."

"Why are you whispering?" He glances at me. "You know there's only us two in the car, right?" He's laughing now.

I sink further into my seat and feel the heat again in my cheeks.

"So, tell me, are you still surfing the crimson tide?"

"What?" What's he talking about? What's the crimson tide?

"Have you still got the painters in?"

I look at him, confused.

"Code red?"

"What are you talking about?"

"Are you still on the rag?"

"Cal," I whine at his vulgarity. "You can say the word period you know."

"So are you still on your *period*?" he mocks the word period in my voice.

"No."

A grin spreads across his face. Probably because he knows he has a better chance of seducing me today.

"Good. You're one mardy bitch when it's your time of the month."

I swat his chest. "And you're one miserable bastard when you don't get a blow job."

He chuckles to himself and glances at me before pulling his bottom lip between his teeth. "I'm gonna fuck you so hard, Steph. You'll be screaming my name and everyone in that hotel will know it's me making you come."

"Cal," I gasp, but his words travel straight to my core, and I shift in my seat to stop the throb between my thighs.

"I love it when you go all shy on me."

"I love it when you talk dirty, even though I'm blushing."

"I know you do." His hand goes back to my thigh, tucking under the split. His fingers press into my flesh and it sends an electric current up my leg. "You look nice today."

"Thanks, you don't look too bad yourself." I scan his body, wetting my lips.

"You look nice every day, Steph. What I meant was you look foxy as fuck in this black skirt and that red top."

"This is good stuff, keep it coming."

"Red has always looked good on you." His thumb rubs circles on my skin where the split rides up my thigh.

"You should wear a suit more often, too. It looks good on you."

His eyes flick to me, then back to the road. "What are you wearing tonight?"

"What for? The business dinner, or do you mean after?"

"The dinner, of course. We both know you won't be wearing anything after."

A smile plays on my lips and he looks pleased that I'm not contradicting him for once. "You'll see." I have a black dress. It's classy, falling just above the knee with a sweetheart neckline.

"No tights, I hate those things."

"I need tights, Cal. My legs are so white." I look down at my legs that haven't seen the light of day in months. Next summer I should really work on my tan.

"I like your milky skin, plus nobody is going to be looking at your legs during dinner." His hand moves further up my thigh, revealing more of my chunky flesh, and he glances between me and the road.

"What does it matter to you if I wear tights, anyway?"

He shrugs. "They make access difficult."

"I can just take them off, back at the hotel room."

"I might not be able to wait that long." He has a cheeky grin on his face; no doubt imagining something perverse.

"Are you going to finger me under the dinner table again?"

"Maybe." He bites his lip.

"As much as I would love that, it's not happening during a business dinner. I'm definitely wearing tights."

"Fair enough." He smiles and winks at me, and I can't help but smile back. My stomach flutters at the thought. His hand still rests under my skirt, and he has no idea what he's doing to me. I'm aching for him, willing his fingers to move up just a few more inches. My breathing is jagged and the outside world seems to have blurred, as if we're travelling at the speed of light. I turn to him and watch him drive.

"Your kids are cute."

"Thanks. Did they speak to you?" A loose strand of his hair has come out of the bobble. I tuck it back behind his ear and stroke the stubble on his jaw. It's neater today, like he's had a groom for the occasion.

"They nodded."

"They're shy."

"Yeah, I got that. They reminded me of you. You were always shy in school. I know you put on this outgoing, fun and loud exterior, but it's all an act." His head turns slightly and his lips brush against my fingers, sending goosebumps up my arm.

"You're right. I've been acting confident all my life." I place my hand back in my lap and rest it on top of his hand that holds my thigh.

"They don't look like you, do they? Your son is the spit of Justin."

"I know, everyone says that."

"Yeah, it's the blonde hair and blue eyes." He slows down as we come to some traffic and removes his hand to shift the gear stick. "Neither of them have your dark auburn hair and green eyes."

"Nope, they both take after him. Thank goodness they haven't inherited my fat gene."

"You're not fat, Steph."

"I'm not skinny either." I laugh, trying to make a joke at my misfortune in the gene pool.

"You have a fucking delicious body. I've always loved your curves, you know that."

I cringe. But I love the way the sweet words roll off his tongue like syrup. Justin doesn't compliment me like this. I'm always on a constant diet. Cal slaps his hand on my thigh where the split in my skirt has parted and rode up, showing even more leg than I would like.

"I love it when you do that."

"What, slap your leg?"

"No." I giggle. "I love it when you give me compliments."

He squeezes my flesh and digs his fingers into my skin. "I could give you compliments all day long."

I gaze at him as he drives, resting my cheek against the headrest. "What happened, Cal?"

"What do you mean?"

"You're here, saying all these incredibly nice things and constantly wanting to get into my pants, but you broke up with me. You had me, all of me. I would have done anything for you. What happened?"

"I don't know. I was a dick." His hand rubs over his face, and he scratches at the stubble around his jaw. "I regret breaking up with you every fucking day."

"Since when?"

He takes his eyes off the road for a split second to look at me. "Since I saw you again."

"What about before?"

"I thought about you then, too. I checked out your profile on social media a long time ago."

"You did?" My eyes blink rapidly as I process what he's saying.

"Yeah." He exhales a long breath.

"I looked you up too, but you're not on any socials."

"I don't do that shit. Dean from school said he'd added you as a friend, and I couldn't help but see what you were up to."

"What was I up to?"

"It was about ten years ago. You'd just had your daughter. You looked really happy."

"I was happy, I mean, I am happy still."

He glances at me again. "You've no idea how many times I wished we never broke up. I wished it back then when I checked out your profile, and I wished it was me that was making you happy. I wished it was me you had a kid with."

"I wished for that too, before you broke my heart." I turn to look out of the window at the rolling English countryside.

My neck feels stiff, and I rub my brow to ward off the onset of a brewing headache. I'm sure I was happy and content before he came back into my life.

I envy his freedom to do as he pleases. My actions would hurt so many people. The nausea returns, thinking about my kids. It would destroy them. They would never forgive me, nor would my parents, our friends, or the church. Everyone sees Justin as this amazing husband and father who's loyal, hardworking, and wonderful. There's no denying he's hardworking and a wonderful dad, but how can you justify a feeling? How can anyone understand how I feel about Callum when I don't understand it myself? The acid rises in my chest and bile burns in the back of my throat.

"We have to stop sleeping together, Cal. I can't keep doing this and hurting my family." My forehead rests on the glass. I continue staring out the window at the passing fields.

"You're not hurting your family, nobody knows."

"If anyone found out—"

He cuts me off. "No one is going to find out."

"Cal, please."

"All right, we'll stop after this trip." The smile in his voice tells me he has no intention of stopping.

"Cal, I'm serious. I would lose everything, and my kids would grow up split between two parents. You know first-hand what that's like. I wouldn't have thought you'd want that for me."

"I don't want that for you. I know how that shit can fuck you up as a kid." His fists clench the steering wheel, and he stares straight ahead.

"If you care for me at all, you'll respect what I say and try to leave me be. We can just be friends."

"You know as well as I do, we can't be friends. It's all or nothing with us. I'm not willing to give you up this easily."

I hold back my tears. I shouldn't have stayed over at his place. Justin should have picked me up, even if it took all night. I've been fighting him ever since, and I can never find the strength to say no to him. Cal signals to turn off the motorway.

"What are you doing?"

"Services." He pulls into a parking bay in the far corner of the car park. A row of trees shields us from the road in front. He turns off the engine and faces me. "Steph." His voice is soft.

I swallow a gulp of air.

"Steph, look at me."

I can't look at him; if I do, he'll see my glossy eyes and a tear rolling down my cheek. He unbuckles his seat belt so he can reach over to me and his large hands cup my face, pulling me towards him. He swipes his thumb under my eye, then strokes it gently over my lips.

"Cal—"

He silences me with his thumb on my mouth. His forehead rests against mine and the tips of our noses touch.

"If you tell me you don't feel the same, I promise you, I won't touch you again." His lips are inches from my mouth, and I want nothing more than to feel them on my skin. "Tell me, Steph. Tell me you never want to feel my touch again."

"I can't, I can't say that." It couldn't be any farther from the truth. What was I thinking? The thought now of him never touching me again makes my chest ache and my throat close up. I want to feel his touch every day. I need him more than I realised. My hand rests over his on my face and I part my mouth, inching towards him. I brush my tongue between his lips. His grip on my face tightens and his tongue stiffens and our kiss becomes a deep, passionate song.

After a long sensual kiss—that lasted far too long for someone saying we need to stop seeing each other—Cal asks, "Are you all right?"

I nod, but I'm not all right. I'm in a constant daily battle with my head and my heart, but the heart wants what the heart wants. To deny Cal would be to deny myself. He kisses me again and all previous thoughts are removed. I lose myself in him and all I can focus on is his lips and hands.

He pulls away to look at me. "I won't stay away from you, Steph. Not while you want me as much as I want you. I've stayed away for too long already and I won't waste any more time without you."

CHAPTER
Eighteen

I kiss him again. "Did you want something from the services?"

"Nah, I just want you, Steph. Only you."

"I want you, Cal." I take in our surroundings. The next car is a few spaces down; the owners must be in the services. He must know what I'm thinking because he pulls the lever under his seat to slide it back. I climb over the centre console and straddle him. He must think I'm a lunatic after what I just spouted contrasted with my actions. My body trembles as I hold him, wrapping my arms around his neck. His hands glide up the silky lining of my skirt till they reach my lace knickers. He tugs at the elastic between my legs and crooks a finger inside of me. I pull the bobble from his hair and run my fingers through his unruly waves.

"Don't push me away, Steph. Promise me." I will promise him anything while he has me like this. I breathe heavily while his gifted fingers work their magic. His other hand fists my hair, pulling my head back. "Tell me," he growls into my shoulder and nips my neck.

"I promise." Our lips collide, furiously lapping our tongues together. His fingers pull out of me to unbuckle the metal clasp on his belt. I look down between us and watch his erection spring out of his trousers. "Cal," I gasp, sliding onto his full length. I needed this; I needed him to remind me how much I actually need him.

This is more than sexual gratification. Each time my body's wrapped around his and the flush of rose paints our skin, everything falls into place, as if the universe exists just for us and this moment. Gazing upon him, my heart finds a rhythm that only he can match. I rock my hips against him. He feels something too; I can see it in his eyes that shimmer like glitter in a snow globe. His heavy breath falls into my mouth as our lips brush against each other. Time slows down, transcending into psychedelic realms of orgasmic possibility. The sun's rays filter through the car sunroof, lighting up the space around us on this dreary day, just as Callum lights up my soul where there was darkness.

I know what we have is rare. After having my share of boyfriends and sexual partners over the years, I know this feeling is unique. Only Cal can evoke this level of ecstasy in me. My back arches, forcing my head back. I Fist his hair with both hands, and bring my lips to his. My body stops rocking against him as the pleasure takes over, turning me into a quivering jelly.

He lifts his hips to thrust into me and exhales into my mouth. "Fuck, Steph, baby." With another thrust, I feel him surge inside of me. I come back to earth as my orgasm slows down, and I kiss him again, not wanting to move just yet. He smiles into my mouth, then buries his head in my chest, catching his breath. Now I'm back from my euphoric communion, I scan the car park. We're good, apart from a young couple sitting in a car five spaces down, eating what looks like a burger. Did they see us? At this point, I couldn't care less as long as they're not the fun police.

Cal's gentle lips kiss my chest where his head rests. "You

have some sort of disorder, you know. I can't keep up with you."

"What do you mean?"

He looks up at me. "What do I mean? One minute you're talking about fucking me in the hotel, then you're saying we can't see each other again. Then you ride me in the fucking car... again. I'm sure you'll go back to telling me to stay away from you before the night's out, but we both know that's not gonna happen." I take in a deep breath and exhale before burying my face into his neck.

"I know. I'm a wreck."

"Don't worry, baby. I'm here to tow you away, and take care of you." He takes my face in both hands and gently presses his lips against mine. The tip of his tongue runs along my lip and I'm lost in him once more.

"I rather like your car. It's a good job you have a saloon. I don't think this would work in my little Suzuki."

"If this is gonna be a regular thing, I may upgrade to a Volkswagen camper." A puff of laughter leaves his lips, falling into my mouth. "We could have the bed made up ready. You'd just need to draw the curtains. Or leave them open if that's your kink."

"Cal." I kiss his succulent lips one more time.

"We'd better get going or we're gonna be late." He reaches behind him and grabs a sweater to wipe between my thighs.

"Is that the same jumper that you used last time?"

"Yeah, so?"

"Please tell me you washed it."

He laughs.

"That's gross."

"I forgot. It's just been behind my seat. It's not like I've worn it or anything." He gestures for me to lift my bottom and he swipes the jumper between my thighs. His eyes don't leave mine and the act feels as intimate as the sex we just had.

I sit back in the passenger seat and sort myself out, checking my makeup and hair in the pull-down sun visor mirror. "I need the loo before we get going."

"Yeah, me too." We both get out of the car and walk towards the services. He takes hold of my hand, and I melt, cherishing these small, intimate gestures. I've lost all my inhibitions since reaching this state of equilibrium with Cal. His fingers interlace with mine and I'm walking on air. We get to the toilets and he kisses my cheek before going our separate ways into the designated gender-specific areas. When I return, he's waiting for me. "Do you want anything?"

"I could do with a bottle of water." We go to the newsagents and I grab a magazine, water, and a packet of crisps. Cal picks up a couple of bars of chocolate, crisps and a bottle of coke for the journey. He flashes his credit card before I get my purse out. He's always been generous with his wallet as well as himself. I'm still on a delirious high walking back to the car and I reach for his hand this time, making him smile and kiss my cheek. The rest of the journey is uneventful but much more relaxed since I've given in to the inevitable. I have to stop torturing myself with this conflict between my organs because my mind will never win the battle. Not against my beating heart and the pulsating organ between my thighs. It's two against one. It isn't a fair fight.

WE FINALLY ARRIVE at the hotel on the outskirts of London. It's good to get out of the car and stretch my legs. My bum has gone numb during the last stretch of the journey. Although thanks to Cal's heated seats, I'm nice and toasty, which only makes the damp air seem cooler against my warm body. Cal grabs our bags and we check-in. The lobby is spacious and modern. Cal asks for two key cards for each room, and I agree. He takes a card for mine and gives me one of his. Our rooms are on the second floor. We step into the lift and once the doors close I can't help but press my lips to his, running my hands under his coat, breathing in the rich aroma of peppermint and that fresh coastal scent that he wears. We walk down the corridor, finding our rooms, which are at opposite ends of the hall. Cal drops his bag in the first room, then carries mine further down the corridor.

I point to a door with my number on. "Here's my room. What a shame they're not next to each other."

"It makes no difference. I'll be sleeping in your room tonight, regardless." The thought of being able to spend another night with him makes my stomach tighten and a warm, fuzzy tingle fizzes through me. I smile and kiss him one last time before he retreats to his room to unpack. Although when he's gone, I think he may as well have unpacked in here. I take out my clothes, hanging them in the wardrobe. The room is comfortable, clean and classy, with added luxuries that include an array of high-end toiletries, bathrobe and slippers, complimentary bottled water and a hospitality tray.

Long arms wrap around me from behind. I close my eyes, enjoying the closeness as Cal nuzzles into my neck. "Are you ready for the meeting?"

"I'm just going to finish unpacking and freshen up."

His mouth sucks below my ear. "I can't wait to get you back here later."

I turn around and press my lips against his. "I can't wait either."

"If we didn't have to go to this meeting, I'd bend you over this bed and take you right now."

"If we didn't have to meet in the lobby soon. I'd let you."

He lies on my bed and watches me unpack the rest of my things. Once I'm ready, I grab the large portfolio case and we head to the reception area. The rest of the team is waiting there, and Jerry asks if we have everything for the presentation. I tap my hand on the black leather portfolio. James holds up his laptop, and we're all set.

Two taxis arrive and Cal, Kelly and I share and the others take the second one. The weather isn't great in London. It's milder than it was at home, but it's now drizzling. I hope it doesn't ruin my hair—I don't want to have to re-do it again before tonight—I spent ages curling it this morning. The driver makes conversation with Callum about where to go, then the weather, and Callum asks the usual taxi questions like, 'have you been busy?' 'What time are you on til?' So cliché.

Kelly stops the embarrassing line of questioning. "Was your drive down here okay, Callum?"

"Yeah, good." He glances at me and I can see a hint of a smile in the corner of his mouth.

"How was yours?" I ask.

"Cosy," she says. "I was in the back between James and Chris."

"Like a rose between two thorns. You should have come with us."

Kelly looks at Cal. He presses his lips together in a hard line, furrowing his eyebrows.

"What?" I say.

She slumps her shoulders and leans back in her seat. "Cal didn't want me going with the two of you. It's fine, I get it."

My eyes grow wide. What does she get? Does she know?

I look at Cal with my mouth open and wind the window down to get a breath of fresh air. Has he told her what's going on? My heartbeat picks up a pace along with the throb in my temple. The thought of someone else knowing about my deceit makes it more real. I could almost live a lie, knowing it was just between the two of us. The acid rises in my throat, and I try to swallow it back down. I don't have time to focus on this now. I'm already anxious about the meeting.

We pull up at a grand old building in the centre of Soho. Modern signage and lighting enhance the exterior. The area looks vibrant, surrounded by other shops, offices and an array of bars and restaurants. A lady greets us at reception and an elderly man comes through to welcome us. He and Jerry seem to know each other. They exchange pleasantries and show us into a large conference room.

I set the large A2 mount boards with our ideas on an easel at the front of the table and James sets up the slideshow he has prepared. Cal pulls the seat out for me, and I sit down. I'm still upset with him, but I want to get the full facts from Kelly before I kick-off.

The room fills up with three more people from the company and the director introduces us. Jerry takes the lead in the presentation and goes through our proposal. I take notes of everyone's comments. Cal stands to go through the visuals and brand identities for the new products. He's confident, self-assured, and one sexy bastard, standing at the front of the conference table pitching our idea.

It's probably the smartest I've ever seen him, dressed in a dark grey trouser suit, white shirt, and a matching grey tie. His hair is neatly pulled back off his face. I haven't got a clue what he's saying anymore. I just see his lips moving in slow motion and can't wait to be pressed against them again. His charms would dazzle anyone. Wait, I'm still flamin' mad at him. I look over at Kelly taking notes—good thing too, as I just zoned out.

I glance around the room to see some of the other women gazing at him. I can't say I blame them. He always had girls throwing themselves at him. My centre tightens, knowing this scandalously seductive man was mine this morning, and I can still feel the phantom throb between my thighs. I slip off my little black jacket as the thought makes me hot all over again.

I'm thrilled at the end of the meeting when the company expresses how much they love our ideas; we've worked so hard on this project. We have free time before the dinner this evening. I leave the boards in the office, and Jerry takes the portfolio case back with him. I walk out onto the streets of Soho with Cal.

"Shall we go back to the hotel now and try out that bed?" He wiggles his eyebrows and bites his bottom lip.

I can't let things simmer any longer. I stop walking. "Why did you tell Kelly she couldn't travel with us?"

He takes in a breath and exhales. "Because I didn't want her coming with us, there was room with the others." He stuffs his hands into his trouser pockets.

"You shouldn't have told her she couldn't come." I fold my arms over my chest.

"For fuck's sake, Steph. Forgive me for wanting to be alone with you."

"She knows, doesn't she?" My foot taps on the pavement.

"Knows what?"

I glare at him; he knows exactly what I'm talking about. "That we're sleeping together."

"Yeah, she knew anyway."

My mouth drops.

His hand waves in the air. "For fuck's sake, she isn't blind."

"What do you mean she knew, anyway? You told her?" My ribs tighten around my lungs, and I struggle to take a deep breath.

"I didn't tell her shit. She guessed something was going on before." He points towards me. "When you texted her that night at the club, asking if I went home with that girl."

"She told you I texted her? She promised me she wouldn't say anything to you." My brow furrows. Wrapping my arms tighter around my body, I clutch my elbows.

Cal skims a hand over his face. "She didn't tell me. I saw your name flash on her phone while we were in the taxi, and I snatched it from her to read your text."

"Why didn't Kelly tell me?" My voice cracks.

"Probably to save you any embarrassment. She's a good friend to you, Steph."

"So she suspected something was going on? But nothing was going on then." I try to put the pieces together in my head.

"She knew I had feelings for you and with your text, she knew you had feelings for me." His hands glide down my arms. "Can we go back to the room now?"

I step back. "No, let me get this straight. Are you saying, when you said she couldn't join us in the car today, she guessed we were shagging?"

"Yeah, basically." He shrugs like it's no big deal.

I stare at him and shake my head. "Who else knows about us?"

He sighs. "Nobody."

"Tell me the truth, Cal."

"All right, Chris knows." He kicks the pavement and looks down at his feet.

With each new revelation, my heart shrinks. "Oh my

goodness, Cal, this is so embarrassing." My voice is a weak echo as I gasp for breath.

He puts his hand on my cheek, and I flinch away. "Come on, Steph. Let's go back to the room. You can yell at me all you like there."

"I'm not going anywhere with you. Why would you tell Chris?" My hands curl around my clenched stomach. "I'm surprised you didn't tell Justin today. You've told everyone else."

"Chris was in the front seat of the taxi after the club and overheard."

"I thought he knew something, how he moved the other week for you to sit opposite me. Why would you tell anyone?" I yell, but my voice is faint.

"I didn't tell them fuckers; they guessed."

"So basically everyone in the office knows we've been sleeping together." My hands cover my face.

"Not everyone. I haven't told Jerry. I don't know if they've told anyone."

"I can't understand why Kelly didn't tell me?"

"I told her not to."

Tears threaten my eyes and my lip quivers.

"Steph, come on, don't spoil today. We only have one night together." He reaches his hand out to hold me, but I step away.

"You're the one that's spoiled it." I storm off down the street. Cal follows.

"Where are you going?"

"Away from you," I shout.

He grabs at my arm. "Steph, come on."

"No, Cal." I yank my arm from his grip. "I can't trust you. Everyone knows about us, and you didn't tell me."

"I didn't want you to feel uncomfortable, and I didn't want you to stop seeing me."

I continue to walk away.

"Steph, please. I love you."

"You've got a funny way of showing it."

"Steph, come on, let's go back."

"Leave me alone." I walk faster, but I can't out-walk him. A group of people jump out of a taxi. I get in and ask the driver to go, not knowing where to, but I need some space. Cal chases the taxi as it pulls away. He stops and throws his hands into the air, no doubt cursing me.

"Where to my bewty?" the driver says in a Cornish accent —which sounds strange being in London—it isn't what I was expecting.

"Covent Garden, please." I may as well do some Christmas shopping while I'm here.

"Dreckly," he says. I'm not entirely sure what that means, but he continues to drive and turns left. My phone rings. I glance at the screen to see Callum's name flashing in green. I cancel it. He rings again. I press cancel and huff.

"He's a persistent laddy," the driver says with his Cornish twang.

"Yes, he is." I flare my nostrils.

"What's he done, my lovey? He ain't been cheatin' on you, has he?"

"No, nothing like that." Ironically, it's me doing the cheating, I think to myself.

"Ah, it'll all work out in the end you'll see."

"I hope so." I sigh. My phone rings again and I turn it off.

Arriving at Covent Garden, I pay the driver. An enormous Christmas tree stands proud in front of the Plaza, illuminating the surrounding shops. A brass band plays out joyful sounds and the smell of hot chocolate wafts through the air from a nearby vendor. I scan the luxurious boutiques that you can only find in the city. Walking into a fragrance boutique, the store oozes opulence with its signature black and white branding. Candles and perfumes line the walls. I can't help but smell every product, eventually settling on a refreshing citrus fragrance for my sister. Moving on to other high-end stores. I buy a scarf and bag for my mum, body products for Justin's mum, a few books for my dad and a mindful book for Claire.

Walking by a decadent, artisan craft store, the smell of chocolate grabs my attention. I sample a few tasters they have on display. It reminds me of my first day at Browns Media when Cal fed me my favourite caramel centres. Thinking about him again makes my shoulders drop, and I take a few more samples for comfort while purchasing a couple of boxes as gifts. The next store to grab my attention is a lingerie boutique. I decide to buy myself a red and black two-piece set with stockings and dainty suspender clips. They're for Cal more than me. After my retail therapy, I know I'll forgive him when I get back.

I get a taxi to the hotel. It feels good to sit down. My feet are killing me. I put on these new shoes this morning, not thinking I would do any walking today. Because I stupidly omitted the tights, my feet have been rubbing against the hard fake leather material. I knew I should have worn tights. At least it stopped raining while I was shopping—one saving grace—my curls are still intact.

I walk down the corridor of my hotel floor, laden with bags. My feet are sore, pinching with every step. My legs are throbbing and my arms ache with the amount of bags I'm carrying. I walk past Cal's room and wonder what he's doing. My phone's been turned off since the taxi ride. I struggle to get my key card out of my bag, but eventually, I swipe it and walk into my room. Cal is sitting on my bed with his phone in his hand. He jumps up, shouting, "Where the fuck have you been?"

My mouth drops. "Excuse me?" I drop the bags on the floor.

"I've been calling you non-fucking stop." He's waving his mobile in front of me to show me the calls.

"I... I went shopping."

"Yeah, no shit, Sherlock. I can see that." He looks around my feet at all the bags.

"What's your problem?"

"I didn't know where the fuck you were. I even had Kelly ring you, but she said she couldn't get through either."

"I'm sorry, okay." I wince as I sit down on the end of the bed to take off my shoes.

"Sorry, you're fucking sorry, is that all you can say?" He throws his arms in the air.

"What do you want me to say?"

"The least you could have fucking done is text me back to let me know where you were."

"Calm down, you're not my friggin' husband."

"You didn't just seriously say that?" He hovers over me, pressing his lips into a thin hard line, and I can see the storm brewing in his eyes.

"I'm sorry." I pull off a shoe and blood paints my toes where the fake leather has rubbed at my skin.

"Fuck, what's happened to your foot?"

"My shoes." I pull the other shoe off to reveal the same raw skin and blood.

He kneels in front of me and takes my feet in his warm hands, as if the sun itself is massaging my cold limbs.

"If I were your husband, I would give you a good fucking seeing to right now."

My breath hitches. "You can still give me a good seeing to."

His eyes are whirling with bolts of lightning. "I should spank you for not answering my calls." He flashes a sinister grin, rubbing his thumb against the sole of my foot.

I bite my lip. "Perhaps I should get you riled up more often."

"You get me riled up one way or another every fucking day." He brings my bloodied foot up to his lips to kiss my poorly toe better.

"Cal, don't kiss my feet. They're sweaty. I need a shower."

"Your feet are a mess." He runs his hands up my calf, over my knees, reaching under my skirt. His lips press against my shin and he trails kisses along my leg, working up to my knee. I pull off my coat and let it drop onto the bed behind me, not wanting to move as his hands work their magic on my tired limbs.

"Cal," I moan, tipping my head back as he continues to kiss my leg. "I need to get ready for dinner."

"What? It's not for another two hours." His fingers trail up my skirt and roam the top of my thighs, followed by his lips.

"I need to get ready." I close my eyes as the familiar tingle blossoms in my bud.

"It's gonna take you two hours to get ready?"

"Yes, plus I really need a shower."

"You can have a shower after." His fingers reach my panties and hook under the elastic as he sucks at the plump flesh on my inner thigh.

"Do you want to come in the shower with me?"

He looks up, then presses his lips against my panties, where I'm already tingling. His palms press against the bed on either side of me, and he pulls himself up. "Nah, I'll run us a bath."

"Come on." Cal pulls me from the bed and leads me into the bathroom. My fingers twist in my curls. I worry we won't both fit in the bath, but when I walk into the room, the large corner tub is almost as wide as it is long. My eyes flit towards the heavens, and I'm thankful for this luxurious hotel room.

Cal turns on the hot water tap and undresses. I love his confidence and how he feels comfortable walking around stark-bollock naked with me. He leans over the bath to pour some complimentary bathing products into the running water. He has the perfect arse, and I delight in watching his inked skin move as his muscles flex. I undo the buttons on my top and he helps me undress by unzipping my skirt, his gentle fingers graze my waist, and his lips delicately brush against my cheek. My clothes fall to the floor, leaving me in my baby pink underwear.

He looks me up and down. "You're so fucking sweet, Steph." His tongue licks my lips and I part my mouth. He unclips my lace bra and glides his fingers along my arm, pulling the straps down. "Like cotton candy."

I run my fingers through his black hair. "You're like liquorice; a sweet, delicious poison."

He nips my breast. "You're a fluffy pink marshmallow."

I giggle. "Stop talking about food; you're making me hungry."

He smiles, pecks my lips and climbs in the bath, sitting down as the water pools around him. I hide my pudgy stomach with my hand and the other holds my saggy breasts.

He flicks hot water at me. "Are you coming in, then?"

I pull down my knickers and climb in. He pulls me towards him and I end up sitting between his legs with my back resting on his chest. He takes his hair tie from his hair and gathers my long curls into his hands, styling a messy bun on top of my head. "There, you don't have to worry about your hair now, you've got more time."

"Thanks."

"Lie back. I've got you." His forceful hands grip my shoulders, pulling me back to lie on his chest. He slides his hand between my legs and feels the slickness inside my folds. His face nuzzles into my neck, sucking and licking at my skin.

"Mmm, Cal." I moan, making myself comfortable against his body.

"Does this mean I'm forgiven?"

"For now." A smile plays on my lips.

His lips widen against my neck. He presses his erection into the bottom of my back and I moan again as his massaging fingers flicker and tease while his thumb runs rings around me.

"I love how you're always wet for me, Steph. I want to make you come every day."

"Cal," I murmur in my dizzy haze. "I want that too, but my kids."

He rubs his erection against the top of my ass, making my thoughts scatter. His teeth nip my lobe and he groans into my ear, "I love your soft, plump, wet cunt."

"Cal." I cringe at his choice of words.

"Sorry, pussy." I can hear the smile playing on his face.

"Cal."

He continues licking and sucking my neck.

"I'm not sure I like the word pussy either."

"Your slit, then."

I'm desperate now and so close. "Call it whatever you like." I pant. "Just don't stop." The hot water still running and lapping around me adds to the pleasure. The back of my head rests against his shoulder. He kisses the side of my face while using one hand to squeeze my breast and the other between my legs.

"Your pussy is mine. I know it's my hand you imagine there when you touch yourself."

"I don't touch myself."

"Yeah, you fucking do. I've watched you."

I sit up. My mouth opens. "You've been spying on me?"

A grin spreads on his face. "I've still got the video."

"What?" My eyes widen and I realise he's talking about when I let him film me touching myself. The thumping in my chest drowns the sound of the running water.

Cal laughs. "I'm joking. You got rid of it, remember."

I splash water on his face. "Stop talking shit. I'm still mad at you."

"Relax, baby. Let me make it up to you." He gets back to work, pulling me back down, nibbling at my ear and tweaking my nipple.

"That's nice." I relax back into him, rocking my hips against his hand between my legs.

"That's it, baby." His throbbing erection pushes and rubs against my cheek as I move back and forth. "So fucking sexy," he groans, pulling on my ear with his teeth.

I close my eyes and images of Callum spin through my

mind like a movie reel getting faster with each flick of his finger. My toes curl and my back arches. My body heat rises and it's like corn popping through every cell in my body, leaving me gasping for breath. Moments later, the odd popcorn still pops in my centre, and the movie reel slows down, bringing Callum back into focus. I turn my head towards him and open my eyes. My lips press against his while my hand finds his erection.

"Lay back down." He pulls me back to his chest. "You can play with my cock later." He places some soap into his hands and palms my breast, lathering me up in foam.

I can't remember the last time I felt this relaxed. "I could go to sleep."

He lifts my arms one at a time and rubs the soap along my skin while kissing my hair before wrapping both arms around me. Not wanting to remove myself from his arms, I turn the tap off with my foot. My fingers trace over the ink on his wrist where his three children and dates of birth are written.

"I lost a baby too." My voice is quiet.

He sits up, pushing me up with him, causing the hot waves to splash against my breasts. "Steph. I'm so sorry. I had no idea."

"I'm fine now, but I wanted you to know that I understand loss." I glance at him, then look down at his arms wrapped around me.

"Do you want to talk about it?" His lips brush my skin where his head rests over my shoulder.

I take in a deep breath, and my voice trembles. "I miscarried at around 14 weeks. It was like on Marley and Me. Have you seen that film?"

"Yeah." His lips kiss my neck.

"Where they go to the hospital and the heartbeat isn't on the ultrasound."

He squeezes me tighter and brushes his lips against my cheek. "I'm sorry you had to go through that."

"I'm sorry you did too."

He lays back down, pulling me back with him. "My son was stillborn at full term. We found out afterwards that he had a heart condition and his heart stopped beating. My girlfriend had to give birth to him. It was the worst time of my life." His arms wrap around my chest, and I continue to caress his skin.

I run my finger over the scroll on his wrist. "Was it the same mum as your girls?"

"No, it was someone I dated before." His chest rises and falls beneath me. "She said she was on the pill, so I stopped using a johnny. Somehow she got pregnant." He sighs. "The worst thing was that I didn't want it, though I never told her that. I played the doting dad, but I wasn't ready to be a father." His voice breaks. "Sound familiar?"

"Cal. We don't have to talk about it if it's too painful."

He lets out a long, jagged breath. "We got our own apartment, and I got a new job. I'd just got used to the idea of being a dad, then we lost him. I always felt it was a punishment for me not wanting him."

"These things just happen, Cal. It's nobody's fault." I continue to stroke his arm, watching the beads of water run over the ink there.

"I know you're right. It's just easy to blame myself. I liked the pain. It was all I had left of him."

Tears form in the corner of my eyes and my chest aches. If I could take this pain for him, I would. I wouldn't wish this on my worst enemy, let alone the man I love most in this world.

"I'll never forget holding him at the hospital." His voice wavers. "Rachel, my girlfriend, dressed him in some preemie baby clothes that her mum bought and we held his lifeless body."

I lift his hand to me and I press my lips to his wrist where his son's name is. The tears escape me, but Cal doesn't see me cry.

"What happened after?" My voice is quiet and shaking.

Cal presses his lips against my head. I turn slightly to meet him and kiss his cheek before he continues to speak. "We broke up. It's ironic that I never wanted a kid while she was pregnant, but the minute he was gone, I would have done anything to have him back. I couldn't stand the guilt. I drank and smoked weed. She got sick of my moods and left."

I turn my head again. This time I meet his lips. I kiss him softly and gently and hope the touch of my lips will help him forget the pain just for this moment. I lay my head back on his shoulder and he kisses along my hairline.

"About three years later I got an email from Priya saying she's travelling to Europe and visiting England."

"Who's Priya?"

"The girls' mum."

"Oh."

"You know I went to Australia not long after leaving uni. I met her over there. She was a teacher. We were just friends, and we kept in touch after I moved back to England when my mum was sick."

I nod along and continue to glide my fingers along his soapy arm.

"She'd always wanted to come to England. I offered to meet her and take her sightseeing as she did me when I was in Sydney. We met in London and she came back to Nottingham with me. One thing led to another, and she ended up getting a job here. Three months later, she was pregnant. It was a complete shock. I'd always used a rubber, the story of my life." He lets out a huff, and his warm breath tickles my shoulder. "Looking back, one had come off. Another time I hadn't used one, but thought I'd pulled out in time. Anyway, Olivia was the result. There was no way I was fucking this up. I was glad to have another chance, and I thanked my blessings every day."

"So why did you and Priya separate?"

"I liked Priya. I thought we could actually make it work. We even got engaged." He lets out a small laugh.

"Really, you got engaged?" I sit up and turn my head to him. He smiles and his hand soothes my back.

"Yeah, I realised after a while we weren't compatible. We argued more than we got on, especially after Bethy was born. I think it was because of our different cultures. Her family hated me, which put a strain on the relationship. She was always trying to please them. They were in fucking Australia. We didn't even see them that often, but somehow they were always coming between us."

"I'm sorry things didn't work out."

"Yeah, at least I can say I tried. I swear I tried my fucking hardest."

I slide my body around in the tub to face him. "I'm glad you told me."

"I wanted to tell you about Jax so many times. I just didn't know how." He cups my face and lightly pecks my lips.

I wrap my arms around him. My breasts press against his chest and I deepen our kiss. "I'd best get ready."

"Come on, then."

I stand up, covering my stomach and breasts once again. Cal shakes his head as I climb out of the tub. He smiles, watching me hide my body with my arms. "Why are you always hiding from me?"

"Because." I look down and wrap a towel tight around me.

Cal steps out of the bath. The water drips down his body over his stomach like rain drizzling over the flock of crows there. He tugs my towel and pulls me closer.

"You never have to hide from me. I love you."

I freeze, trapped in a moment of stillness. The rush of blood pulses through my veins as it surges straight to my heart. His lips press against mine again before he pulls the hotel robe around himself. He gathers his belongings in his hands. His eyes are sad as he goes back to his room, leaving me with a ringing in my head. His words, I love you, echo through my eardrum. I wanted to say I love you too and I mean it. I never stopped loving him, but I just can't seem to say the words.

———

I PULL the bobble from the messy bun that Cal fashioned. Most of the curls are still intact, but I run over it with the curlers and add smoothing balm. Thoughts of Cal holding his son's tiny body flash through my mind. If I could take away his pain, I would. I can't imagine what that must have been like. It was bad enough when I miscarried. The scan showed my baby hadn't developed past ten weeks and I had to take tablets for my body to expel the tissue. I pray his poor girlfriend found peace after losing her boy. My eyes water as I apply fresh eyeliner. I leave my makeup for a moment and try to think of something happy.

The new underwear I bought, along with the stockings and suspender clips, lay on the bed. I pop them on and look in the mirror. Cal will explode when he sees me in these. I'm tempted to show him before we go to dinner, but I think that would be cruel. We need to be focused on the clients tonight, not on each other. I re-do my makeup for an evening look, adding shimmering eyeshadow, fake lashes and my bright red go-to lipstick. Zipping up my black dress, I think of Cal taking it off later, and the lingering feel of his fingers inside me makes my core tighten once again.

I wince, sliding on my black kitten heel peep-toe shoes. They don't normally hurt, but tonight my sore skin rubs against the material. Walking around the room applying the finishing touches to my outfit, the flesh on my feet stings. The door opens and I draw in my breath. Cal looks so friggin' handsome. The burn on my toe is replaced with a scorching desire for him.

CHAPTER
Twenty

Callum walks into the room wearing black trousers that fit snug around his gifted arse. The tattoos on his torso are visible through the white fabric of his fitted shirt. His top button is open, showing a hint of chest hair, and I'm practically drooling like a spaniel with a new toy.

He pulls out a small box from his black jacket that's draped over his arm. "I got you some plasters." He waves them in front of him. "How are your feet now?"

"Err, fine." I'm still taking in his appearance and forget all about the pain in my feet. I walk towards him and flinch as my shoe rubs. "They're not fine actually, they hurt. I really do need some plasters. I can't believe you did that for me."

He wraps his arms around my waist. "You look beautiful."

"Thank you, you look good too."

"Here, sit down." He gestures for me to sit on the bed, and he kneels down in front of me, running his hand up my leg over my stockings. "I thought we agreed on no tights."

"No, you agreed on no tights. I said I'm wearing them." I daren't tell him they're not actually tights. He would bend me over the bed right now and we'd be late for dinner. Although I need to take them off to get the plasters on, I'll go into the bathroom. As the thought enters my mind, it's too late. His hands are already up my dress, and he's tugging on the dainty suspender clips.

"What the fuck is this?" A grin spreads across his face, and his eyes are wide like a kid at Christmas, ready to delve into Santa's sack. He frantically tugs at my dress, trying to lift it up.

"Cal." I wrestle with him, pulling my dress down.

"You sexy fucking tease, let me see." His hands ride up my thighs.

"We have to go." I giggle and squirm as his fingers tickle my thighs.

"I'm not going anywhere till you show me what you're wearing under there."

"Cal, we have like fifteen minutes till the taxi comes."

"And five minutes till I come." He pulls at my dress again.

I swat his chest and stand up. He stands up too and grabs at my waist, leaning in for a kiss.

"Cal, my lipstick."

He stops and instead of kissing my lips, he delicately kisses my nose. "I want that lipstick smeared all over my dick."

I gulp. My mouth is dry once more, and I decide to let him see my new underwear. "If I take my dress off, do you promise to look and not touch?" I slowly unzip my dress.

"Err, fucking-hell-no."

I stop pulling the zipper down and pull it back up.

"All right, all right, just lose the fucking dress already." His chest rises and falls. He licks his lips as the zipper travels down my side. I pull the strap down my arms slowly, revealing my new satin and lace bra that holds and lifts in all the right places, making my boobs look damn near perfect if I say so myself.

"Fuck, Steph. Go on..." His breathing is heavy and his eyes are still wide. He opens and closes his fists as I shimmy the dress down over my hips and slide it to the floor, revealing my black full knickers with red lace. His mouth gapes. His eyes follow the dainty straps attached to the trim around my panties and down to the thigh-high, sheer fabric of the stockings.

I gulp again, letting his eyes rake my body. I suck in my belly to appear thinner, and place my arm over my stomach to hide my stretch-marks, but I don't think he cares. Judging by his reaction, I don't think he's looking at my stomach. His eyes dart from my breasts, then to my thighs and back to my chest again. I press my lips together, waiting for him to say something. He doesn't speak; he just stares, breathing heavily.

"Well, don't you like it? I pout.

"Like it? I fucking love it." He steps closer, placing his hand on the lace that covers my nipple.

"Ah-ah, no touching."

"Baby, I have to touch you."

"No, you promised." I smirk, placing his hands back at his sides. "Sit on the bed." He does as I say, and I kneel in front of him. I undo his belt and his zipper, freeing his throbbing erection from his black boxers. I run my tongue along the bulging vein there, up to the glistening tip.

"Steph, ahh, baby." His voice is raspy. Cupping and massaging him, I take his full length in my mouth and hear him suck in a breath. I look up to see him watching my mouth intently. He leans back slightly, his hands rest on the bed, then a hand moves to my hair, forcing me to take him deeper. The tip of him presses against the back of my throat, and I try not to gag. "Steph, baby, fuck, Steph." He pants. I pull back to swallow and grip his shaft, licking at the salty tip before engulfing him again, feeling him along my palette, my tongue and the back of my throat as I suck and lick and squeeze.

"Baby, harder. I always loved fucking your mouth." His words spur me on, wanting to take in as much of him as I can. I let out a moan of my own as I get aroused, knowing I'm having this effect on him. My lipstick's marked around his length. His eyes flicker, watching my every move.

"Baby, I won't last much longer." He fists my hair, forcing me to go deep again, and he lifts his hips, pressing at the back of my throat, making my eyes water. His shaft throbs against my tongue. The salty liquid pumps through him as he fills my mouth, pulsating through my lips. I swallow before he thrusts again, squeezing and squirting every last drop onto my tongue. His grip on my hair loosens, and his breathing slows. "I'm gonna make you come over and over again, baby. You won't ever want to leave this room."

I climb up and straddle him, wrapping my arms around his neck. "Promise?"

"I promise." He pulls at my shoulders, gesturing for me to meet his lips. "Come here." His tongue slips into my mouth. "Mmm salty."

I laugh against his lips as he kisses me again.

"I can call Jerry and tell him we're sick. We ate something dodgy at lunch, and we can stay here all night."

"Cal, no, besides I would have got dressed up for nothing."

"Baby, you got dressed up for me, and I can appreciate it right here in this hotel room." His large hands squeeze my bottom. He groans into my mouth as he kisses me again.

I pull back and tuck his hair behind his ears. "As much as I would love that... we can't."

"You would?" His hooded eyes are still dreamy from his

eruption a moment ago. I gaze into the sparkling amber hues surrounding his pupils like a red sky on a summer's night.

"Of course I would. I love being alone with you." His facial hair scratches the palms of my hands and my thumb swipes between his tasty lips. "Come on, we need to go." I reluctantly climb off of him.

Callum goes to the bathroom while I take off my stockings. He returns and kneels in front of me and places the plasters on my raw skin. His lips press against the lace on my knickers, just below my stomach. My muscles tense as he tugs at the fabric, and I draw in a breath.

"Let me tongue-fuck you before we go."

My walls clench and I bite down hard on my bottom lip, wishing I had more time. "Cal, we really have to go."

His rough palms slide up my thigh. "Later, then."

"You can do anything you like to me later." He has a naughty grin; perhaps I shouldn't have said *anything*. I pull my stockings back on; Cal helps me attach them to the suspender clips, teasing me the entire time with kisses along my thigh as he fumbles with the straps.

I pull on my dress, rinse my mouth and touch up my makeup. Cal takes my hand and interlaces his fingers with mine as we walk to the lobby. I've missed this. Justin never holds my hand or shows me any type of affection in public, not even in front of our kids.

Everyone is waiting for us near the reception area. I immediately untangle my fingers from his, but he tightens his grip. I widen my eyes at him, and he frowns. I pull my hand away and he lowers his head, but says nothing. Even though they probably all know about us, I'm not about to make it blatantly obvious.

INSIDE THE RESTAURANT, I'm drawn to the funky neon lighting. A spectrum of dazzling colours illuminates the walls, transforming the old rustic building into a vibrant den. A waiter shows us to our reserved seating. The further we walk into the restaurant, the buzz of clinking glasses, chatters and laughter drowns out the ambient atmosphere. Jerry stands back talking to Cal near the pink cherry blossom tree in the middle of the room. I sit at a long table next to Kelly, hoping to save a seat for Callum on my other side.

Kelly turns to me. "Is everything all right with you and Cal?" Her voice is a whisper, but loud enough to hear over the soft Spanish music playing in the background; reminding me of my summer holidays.

"Fine." I fiddle with the napkin ring, twirling it around.

"Steph, I'm sorry. I wanted to tell you I know about you and Cal."

"It's fine, Kelly. I wasn't mad at you. I hope we can still be friends."

"Of course, why wouldn't we be friends?"

I sigh. "I don't want you thinking any less of me, that's all." My chin dips. I stare at the napkin ring between my fingers. "I know I'm a terrible person for doing what I'm doing."

She has a sympathetic look as she smiles at me. "I understand. And I don't think any less of you. I just hope you know what you're doing. You've so much to lose. But I can see how much Callum cares about you."

I suck in a breath. "You can?" My eyes widen as I wait for her to elaborate.

"I've known him for the last ten years and I've never seen him this happy with anyone, not even Priya."

Our conversation stops when a guy from the earlier

meeting takes a seat in the spot I was saving for Cal. "Hello again," he says.

"Hi." I smile politely.

"Stephanie, isn't it?" His grey suit matches his steely eyes and his short highlighted hair is styled to perfection around his model-like features.

"Yes, I'm sorry, forgive me, I'm terrible with names."

"Michael." He holds out his hand, and I accept. He has a firm grip as he shakes my hand.

"Do you come here often, Michael?"

"Not too often, but it is one of the best tapas restaurants in the city."

The large rectangular table fills up as the rest of the company arrives. A woman sits opposite me. Callum is still talking with Jerry. He notices the table filling up and comes to claim his seat opposite Michael.

Michael continues to make small talk, and the woman across from me talks to Cal. The server brings several bottles of wine over to the table and Michael asks, "White, red or rosé?"

I eye the bottles, all excellent wines, no doubt. "Rosé please."

"And *wine* not?" He chuckles at his little joke, pouring me a glass of the pink stuff. "You have beautiful hair?" He fingers a ringlet as he says the words. "I bet you get that all the time."

"Err, thank you." Is he hitting on me? Cal stares at Michael like a praying mantis waiting to strike. Michael brushes his hand over my long curls that fall down my back. Cal's eyes turn to thin slits and his lips press together. The woman next to him continues to talk, and his eyes turn to her. I let out a breath.

"Tell me about yourself, Steph."

"Not much to tell, I'm afraid. I'm quite boring." Even though my life is anything but boring at the moment. It's dangerous, scandalous, complicated. I would take boring any day over this.

He waves a hand in the air. "I'm sure that's not true."

I turn to face Michael. "Tell me about you. Do you live in the city?" My elbow leans on the table, and I rest my chin on my palm.

"Just a tube ride away from work. I live in Brixton with my husband."

His husband? I smile; he wasn't flirting with me after all. "How long have you been married?"

"Only a year, but we've been together for longer. My husband is an artist. He would love to paint you with your full-figure and gorgeous features." Michael caresses my hair once more, and Callum's fist clenches into a tight ball around his napkin. I smile and continue chatting with Michael while I peruse the menu. He tells me all his favourite dishes, and we order a selection to share.

"Do you want a top-up?" I ask.

"Don't *wine* if I do." The silly pun makes me burst into a fit of laughter. The silliness from the first glass is already taking over.

I turn to Kelly. "Rosé?"

"No thanks, Steph. I'll stick with white." She's talking to another lady from the meeting, whose name has also evaded me.

Cal is deep in conversation with the woman sitting next to him. I watch him pour her a glass of red. She swills the wine around the glass, licking her lips before bringing it to her pert mouth. The woman is pretty. No, pretty isn't the right word. Pretty is what you call an innocent young girl, and this woman is far from innocent the way she is flirting with my man, flicking her slick dark hair like something from a shampoo commercial. He's always been a sucker for a brunette. And how she sticks her breasts out like a bird puffing out its chest to attract a mate. She bats her long, full lashes at him and he smiles. It's like watching a David Attenborough episode, talking us through the mating rituals in the wild. Her hand strokes his. I can hear part of their conversation. "Are you involved with anyone?" she asks. Straight in for the kill. No messing around. I hold my breath to zone in on his response.

"No, I'm free and single," he says. What a dick. My temperature rises several notches as my blood heats. If this is the game he wants to play, I can play it too. I turn back to Michael and continue our conversation; he's very touchy-feely, which helps my plight.

The food arrives, an array of tiny dishes line the long table and the smell of Spanish cooking makes my taste buds prick up in anticipation. Michael reaches over, placing some sort of mini fritters onto his plate. "Try these." Before I can reply, he thrusts his fork into my mouth. I bite into the crunchy battered coating to taste heaven itself on my tongue. A mixture of aubergine and halloumi tantalise my senses.

"Mmm..." I moan as the melted cheese glides down my throat. "I loved that."

He fills my plate with wonderful nibbles, some I've never tried before. The wine seems to have replenished itself. I was too engrossed in my potato bravas to notice the server. One thing I notice, though, Cal is being spoon-fed paella by this hussy. She's moved closer to him. His eyes are on her pumped chest. I'm sure her top is lower than before. She leans into him with her petite body and curves in all the right places. She is the perfect woman for him, his type, and no wedding ring, which is always a bonus. I gulp down my wine.

"Top-up?" Michael asks, holding the bottle ready to pour.

"Yes, please." I hold out my glass.

"Doesn't *wine* fly when you're having fun?"

Another fit of laughter and I join in with the silly jokes. "You had me at rosé."

We both giggle like children. "Scarlett seems to have taken a shine to your colleague." He nods towards Cal and this woman.

Scarlett eh? *More like harlot.*

"She had her eye on him at the meeting today. Her and the other women were fawning over him."

"I bet they were." My blood boils—mixed with the wine in my veins—I'm bubbling over.

"Can't say I blame them, he's quite the catch." Michael takes another swig of his drink.

"She's digging her claws into him all right." I stare at the two of them. My jaw tightens.

Michael laughs. "She has a rep in the office as a bit of a man-eater."

"I can see that." What makes it worse is that I know she is the type of woman he likes. She oozes confidence. He's lapping it up. If he thinks he's sleeping in my room tonight after flirting with her, he has another thing coming.

Mini desserts arrive, my favourite part of any meal. I take a small dish of crema Catalana—Michael told me the name. It looks like crème brûlée to me. Must be the Spanish version. I spoon out the custard texture. The taste of the warm burnt lemon flavoured cream takes my mind off Callum as I experience my first tapas orgasm, savouring every mouthful... until this woman feeds him a churro. I'm brought back down from my lofty realm. I slump in my seat, watching as she wipes the chocolate sauce from the corner of his mouth, and he licks the cream from her finger. My nostrils flare and I fist the fabric of my dress under the table. Does he know I'm sitting right here? Has he forgotten about me already?

I scoff down several bite-sized balls that taste like almond and coconut—I don't even enjoy them—I'm just eating now to suppress my anger. I inhale another glass of wine and demolish a slice of lemon cake.

Michael licks the tips of his fingers. "We're all going to a club after. Will you be joining us?"

"Yes, I will, why not." I force a smile. Callum can piss right off.

Michael smiles, lifting his glass up to clink against mine. "*Wine* not." And he makes me laugh again.

"If you can't be with the one you love, love the *wine* you're with." I chuckle. The sweet taste of the rosé turns to a bitter residue in my mouth when I glance at Callum and this floozy. Her hand goes under the table and my eyes pop. Where is his hand? The thump in my chest subsides when he pulls her hand back on top of the table. He glances at me, then back at her. The acidity from the wine regurgitates in my mouth, almost choking me. I've had way too much alcohol.

After excusing myself, I head to the ladies' room. The cubicle spins. No more wine. I make a mental note to drink water from now on or I'll end up embarrassing myself like I did the last time I was out. More electric-red lipstick reapplied and out of the toilets I slump, only to see Callum leant up against the wall.

CHAPTER
Twenty one

Callum stands up straight with his hands in his pockets when he spots me walk out of the ladies.

I squint my eyes at him as I walk by.

He clamps down on my arm and pulls me tight against him. "Hey, what's got into you?"

I glance at his tight grip on my arm, then at his face. "Are you friggin' serious?"

"What? You're the one that's been fucking flirting all night."

I roll my eyes. "Ugh. What do you want, Cal?"

"I saw that sleaze follow you. I'm making sure he keeps his hands to himself."

My brow crinkles. "Michael?"

"I don't know his fucking name, the guy sat next to you."

I smile, knowing that Callum has a better chance of seducing Michael than I do.

"He isn't a sleaze, he's a nice guy."

"Nice? Steph, you're so fucking naïve. He's all over you and I don't like it."

"And what about you?"

"What about me?"

I wave my hand towards the tables. "That fluffed up flamingo out there is all over you."

He laughs. "Are you jealous again, Steph?"

"No." I peel his fingers from my skin and cross my arms over my chest. "Don't mind me, if you fancy her—go for it."

He growls into my ear. "Why are you being like this?"

I push against his chest to put some distance between us. "Because you're lapping up all her attention."

He stuffs his hands in his pockets again. "I'm only being polite."

"Polite my arse, you were getting rather cosy with her." I lift my chin and shake a loose curl out of my face.

"Yeah, Steph. Polite." He speaks through gritted teeth. "She's our client after all."

"Oh, please." I wave a hand in front of me. "I heard what you said."

"What did I say?" His tongue pushes against the inside of his mouth.

I mock his husky voice. "I'm free and single."

His head tilts back slightly, chuckling again. "I am free and single."

"Well, if you're so free and single, you can sleep in your own hotel room tonight." I turn to walk away and he pulls me back, gripping my arm.

His sultry voice whispers in my ear. "The only way I'll be sleeping in my hotel room is if you're in there with me, and you know it."

Michael walks out of the men's toilets and nods at the two of us. I smile, trying to look nonchalant. Callum loosens his grip on me and waits until Michael is out of range before speaking again. "You think I give a shit about anyone else here."

"I don't know, I thought—"

He cuts me off, gripping me tighter. "There's nobody in this restaurant that could compare to you." He shakes my arm. "Look at me, Steph." He lifts my chin with his other hand; I look him in the eyes. "You don't need to be jealous of some client. Hell, there's no one in this city or fucking country that could tempt me away from you."

"Cal, I—" Before I can speak anymore, he presses his lips to mine.

"Cal, my lipstick."

He rolls his eyes. "You and your fucking lipstick." He pecks my lips again, then pulls back to inspect my mouth. "Your lipstick is fine."

I gulp and gaze into his eyes; I can't seem to stay mad at him. "Michael is gay."

"What?"

"He's gay, so, you don't need to be jealous either."

He grins. "Is he now? He could have fooled me."

I giggle and cover my mouth with my hand. "He fancies you more than me."

Callum titters and wraps his arms around me, leaning his forehead against mine. "Do you want to go into the disabled toilet?"

I flinch my head back. "No, I've been to the toilet."

He wiggles his eyebrows and nods towards the disabled door.

"Ew, I'm not doing it with you in some toilet, I'm not that desperate."

"I can get you desperate." His tongue licks my neck and his hand squeezes my bottom. I squirm from his embrace, knowing a few more minutes of this and I'll be begging him to take me right here.

"Come on, everyone will wonder where we are."

He smiles, pecking my lips again. "Come on, then." His hand rests on my lower back as we walk to the table. I take my seat next to Michael and pour myself a glass of water.

Callum takes a seat at the end near Jerry. Everyone is mingling now the meal is over.

"Everything all right?" Michael asks.

"Yes." I smile.

"Are you and him... together?" He nods towards Cal down at the bottom of the table.

"It's complicated, but let's just say he will be in my bed tonight, not Scarlett's." Oh no, I should have kept my mouth shut. Damn that wine.

"I see. You lucky girl." He grins and pours another drink.

A little while later, the restaurant is closing around us and the others are moving on to a club. I whisper to Cal, "Are we going to the nightclub?"

"I don't want to go to a fucking club."

"No?"

"No, all I've been thinking about for the last few hours is ripping that fucking dress off your back and licking your sweet cunt." He stares at me with a sinister smile manifesting in the corner of his mouth, like he's picturing exactly what he's going to do to me.

"Oh." My head had finally stopped spinning from the alcohol and now my entire body is spiralling from his words as if I'm on an infinite helter-skelter.

"Are you ready to go?"

"I just need the loo." Walking into the ladies', I find an empty cubicle. Voices rise over the partitions.

"Scarlett, do you think you'll go home with erm, what's his name?"

Oh my goodness, they're talking about Callum. I stand still with my head against the door, listening to every word.

"No, that ship's sailed. He hasn't spoken to me since the meal. Michael says I have no chance. He's involved with the girl that was sitting opposite me."

"Which one, the fat one or the slim one?"

I hold my breath. The fat one? I bury my head in my hands. I'm back at school again in my senior year; a bunch of girls are talking about me in the toilets. *'She doesn't know she's fat', 'Yeah, she acts like she's slim', 'As if she can compete with us'*, they said. All because I was friends with a boy they liked. I spent the rest of the day hiding. I thought these girls were my friends. Being overweight gives you thick skin, but words can still penetrate deep and infect old wounds. I should be used to it; I've always been the fat one, next to my sister's perfect body and my brother the Adonis. Growing up, I was always the intelligent one or the funny one, never the pretty one or the sexy one.

"The one sat next to Michael. She is chubby, that must be his thing." She laughs. That one derogatory comment is like a block being pulled from a game of Jenga, and any confidence I have built up over the years comes tumbling down. It's strange how one word or sentence can make you feel so shit, no matter how many compliments you receive.

"His loss," the other woman says, then the dryer comes on and their voices muffle. I rest my head against the cubicle door and wipe a tear as it rolls down my cheek. I take in a deep breath. The top of my nose stings. I close my eyes tight, holding back the remaining tears. This won't ruin my night, and I don't want Cal to know I'm upset.

I know what they're saying is true. I am the fat one, but I would hate for Callum to hear that. He doesn't seem to notice just how chubby I am, or does he? Is that his thing? I wait until they've gone before stepping out of the cubicle. The last thing I want to do is ruin the client's relationship with the company I work for. After a few more deep breaths, the coast is clear. Callum is waiting for me and I look around to find everyone else has gone, thank goodness.

Cal takes hold of my hand. "Are you all right?"

"I'm fine." I hide my face, looking down. If I look at him, I know I'll cry.

"You sure?" He entwines his fingers with mine and brings them to his lips, kissing the back of my hand. Somehow, his kiss makes everything better.

I nod. "Yes, let's go." I can't get in the taxi fast enough. On a brighter note, I'm much more sober now. The fresh air has helped. The taxi is one of those big black cabs with a sliding window behind the driver for privacy. I think about what *harlot* said. I mean Scarlett. *'That must be his thing'*. The words play over and over.

I look at Callum and wonder if he has a fetish for big girls? His girlfriend before me was chubby. The girl he left me for wasn't, though, but I don't know what his other girlfriends look like. I can't help but think that's why he likes me so much. I thought it was because he liked *me*, everything on the inside regardless of what I look like. That's why I love him after all. I love his personality, his intelligence, his humour, his kindness. But most of all, I love how he makes me feel. That I find him attractive is a bonus, but what if he only likes to sleep with me to satisfy some sexual fetish he has? A fantasy of shagging fat girls: he's always grabbing my arse and saying how much he loves my big boobs. It all makes sense now. I gasp for breath. He called me a fluffy marshmallow earlier tonight. I thought it was cute, but all I see now is the Stay Puft Marshmallow Man.

He places his hand on my leg, and I flinch. "What's wrong?"

"Nothing." I look down and fiddle with the hem of my dress.

He takes my hand. "Is this about earlier?"

"What do you mean?"

"Something's wrong with you. I thought we'd sorted all that bullshit out earlier. I told you I wasn't interested in anyone other than you." His grip on my hand tightens, as though he's never going to let me go. "I've done my fucking best to avoid her for the rest of the night."

"I know." My voice is quiet.

"Then what's wrong? Tell me."

"Nothing's wrong." He cups my face. "I know you, Steph, and I know when something's wrong. Just tell me what I've done now."

"You haven't done anything, have you? Unless there's something you think I should know."

"I've done nothing, but that doesn't stop you from blaming me for shit."

"I'm fine, really." He holds my face and brings his lips to mine. I part my mouth and melt into him. I put all my previous thoughts on hold for now. If this is a fetish for him, I'm happy to oblige, for tonight at least. He can have me tonight to do whatever he likes, and I'll deal with everything tomorrow. He wraps his arms around me in the back of the taxi and I nuzzle into his chest, soaking up the smell of him. I place my hand on his.

"You're freezing." He tucks my hand under his shirt so I can feel the heat from his body. "I'll warm you up." He pulls me closer, tightening his arm around me. He would always warm my chilly hands and feet. His body seems to burn at a much higher temperature than mine.

My palm on his tight stomach lights a fire inside of me, and I hum into his chest and close my eyes.

"I love you, Steph," he whispers.

I draw in a breath. That's the third time he's said those words today. "You don't have to say it back, I know how you feel."

I glance up at him. "You do?"

"Yeah, I know you don't love me the same as you did before, but that's okay."

I don't love him the same as I did before; I love him more, so much more.

"I want you to know, I've fallen in love with you all over again, even if you don't feel the same."

"You're wrong." I sit up and look at him.

"What about?"

"You don't have a clue how I feel about you if that's what you think."

His fingers skim my cheek. "So tell me, how do you feel?"

"I feel the same as you." I still can't bring myself to say the words. He kisses my forehead and we pull up at the hotel. He pays the driver and we make our way to the room.

"My room or yours?" He gets the key cards from his wallet.

"Mine."

Once inside, he closes the door and I go clammy, knowing what's coming. I swallow the air as my legs teeter beneath me. He steps closer. His mouth turns up in the corner. His eyes are as fierce and wild as a tiger ready to strike.

"The things I want to do to you." His untamed fingers graze down my arms.

My breath quickens. Our lips touch, his savage tongue dips into my mouth and in his kiss is the promise of love, hunger and all his desires.

Everything fades away as I kiss Callum. Nothing else exists other than the two of us. I'm no longer Stephanie Bailey; I'm simply his, and he's mine. His fingers tickle my side as he unzips my dress, and my skin tingles. I unbutton his shirt while his gentle hands caress the curves of my back. He grabs at the soft material, pushing it over my wide hips, letting it fall in a puddle at my feet. With trembling fingers, I unbuckle his belt. He swats my hands away and takes the rest of his clothes off, quickening the process.

I crawl to the middle of the bed in my underwear and stockings and lie on my back. My gaze rests on his glorious body covered in that majestic ink.

He climbs on the bed and growls, biting into my spongy thigh. I giggle as he nibbles my flesh and pulls at the suspender clip with his teeth.

"My cock's been aching most of the night, thinking about you in these stockings." He glides up my body, teasing me with his tongue and planting soft kisses against my squishy stomach. I tug on his hair, bringing him to my lips. I can't get enough of his tasty mouth, sickeningly sweet and warm like apple pie. His tongue swirls around mine, adding a kick of spice, while his hand caresses my body and squeezes my breast. He pulls down the cup of my bra and sucks my pebbled nipple.

After circling the hardened nub with his tongue, he pushes away, flips me over, and straddles me. My body floods with warmth as I'm reminded of our days in the attic and how he would massage me like this. I sink into the pillow as his hands roam my back, kneading the tense muscles before unhooking my bra. He moves my hair to one side to kiss my neck and under my ear, sucking, licking, and nipping at the flesh there. A delightful shiver sails along my spine. His palm navigates the curve of my hips and I moan into the fluffy cushion. Warm tingling waves wash over me in a pulsing rhythm as he worships me, trailing his hot wet lips down my back little by little, licking and sucking along the way.

I suck in a breath as his hand runs between my thighs and lifts the elastic to my knickers. I grip the sheets as he dips a finger into my slickness, and I clench around him. Any other time, he would tell me how wet I am with that dirty mouth of his, but he stays silent as his dexterous finger glides in and out of me.

"On your knees." His gruff voice is more of a command than a request. He wraps his arm under me and pulls my bottom up so I'm on my knees with my head still buried into the pillow. I try to turn on my side, not wanting my big arse in his face, but he pulls me back into position.

There's a ringing in my ears and all I can think about is how big my bum looks bent over like this. How can anyone find this attractive? My chest tightens as I'm reminded of his potential fetish. "Callum, not like this."

"Hush, baby. Let me take care of you." He slips inside me again, this time with two fingers. Using his free hand, he tugs at the elastic at the top of my knickers, pulling them halfway down my cheek, and sucks at my newly exposed flesh.

My body trembles and my knees weaken. "I'm not comfortable like this, Cal." My voice is quiet, but breathless as my mind battles with my need for him.

"It never bothered you before. You always liked it this way." He continues moving his fingers, pleasuring me at a leisurely pace.

"It bothers me now, especially with the light on." My voice quivers.

He stops, and I whimper as his fingers slip out of me. "Is that what you're worried about?"

I turn my head back to see his smouldering eyes cloud over, smothering the fire deep within, like I've wounded him or something.

"Steph, it's me. You don't need to be worried with me." His hands smooth over my back.

"I'm not. I just don't want my big arse in your face… or anyone's face for that matter."

He leans over me and kisses my neck. "What's he done to you?"

"What do you mean?"

"You're much more self-conscious than you were before." His thick erection presses into my round cheeks, making it hard to think.

"I'm chubbier than I was before, Cal." My voice is barely a whisper, and I bury my head in the pillow.

"I don't give a shit about the size of your body. How many times do I have to tell you? Just relax. Let me show you how much I love you." His soft lips run along my spine. He pulls my panties completely off and I try to turn again so I'm not exposed.

His fingers dig into my hips, holding me in place. "I love this juicy arse of yours."

I turn my head to face him. "I get it, you've got a fetish for big boobs and big arse, I know."

His eyes widen and he lets me go, allowing me to roll onto my side. "I don't have a fucking fetish."

I sit up on the bed and curl into a ball, hiding my middle area.

"I've told you before, you never have to hide your body from me. I love everything about you, Steph, including your full-figure, your beautiful arse, your stretch marks, and everything else that you think I don't like." He lifts my chin to look me in the eye. "I only love *your* big tits and big arse. I couldn't give a fuck about anybody else's. I love them because they're part of you." His words wash away all my anxieties and my shoulders relax. The tears that clung to my lashes fall and I blink them away.

"Cal."

He smothers my mouth, sliding in his tongue. Any thoughts I had on the subject have vanished completely.

"I wish you could see yourself as I do." His thumb wipes the wetness from my eyes and I beam at his exquisite face that reads nothing but love for me.

"Now, are you gonna get back on your knees so I can give you a good fucking?" He smirks and pecks my nose. His hand fists my hair, holding my head in place as his tongue greedily tastes me. "I don't want to hear you spout any more of that fetish shit."

My palms press against his jaw. "I'm sorry. I should've known you'd never think that."

"Yeah, you know me better than anyone. Now let me remind you just how fucking sexy you are." He pulls me into my previous position, tickling my waist, and I let out a giggle. I relax with his touch and he sucks my fleshy behind.

He hushes me, smoothing his palm along my back and

strokes his full length between my legs—I'm greedy for him —forcing my bottom against him. He digs his fingers into my hips and drives forward, plunging himself into my heat. "Baby."

I bury my head in the pillow, using it to muffle my moans and cries as he fills every inch of me.

"Steph, I love listening to your sweet fucking cries and breathy moans." Rocking in and out of me at a steady pace, he groans. "You feel so fucking good, Steph. I'm gonna fuck you over and over. You're gonna be so fucking sore by the time I've done with you."

I hope so. His words stimulate me like an aphrodisiac. I could do this all night. I want to do this all night.

His fingers move in circles around my throbbing nub while thrusting deeper; the combination has me panting his name.

"That's it, baby, come for me."

A few more strokes and my walls tighten, my legs tremble, and my voice runs away with me. I cry out a deep sense of completion as a million party poppers go off simultaneously, leaving me breathless and shaky.

"I fucking love feeling you come around my cock." He increases his pace, pounding into me fast and hard. His hands tighten on my hips. He releases deep into me with a low, guttural growl that makes my walls clench once again.

I lay blissfully dazed, flat on my front. Cal leans over and presses a kiss to the centre of my back before collapsing next to me, brushing the wayward hair from my cheek. Rolling to my side, our lips collide, and our tongues entwine. I live for these beautiful intimate moments after sex where he holds me and makes me feel like I'm the only woman in the world.

He pulls my bra away, tossing it to the floor. I pull myself closer to him, my breasts smash against his chest. My knickers are still attached to the stocking clips, fitted snugly around my thighs. I try to slide them off, but Cal grabs my wrist.

"Leave them on." He pulls the underwear back up, and our legs tangle together. His arms wrap tightly around me and he peers into my eyes. "I'm yours, Stephanie. I'll always be yours." His voice wavers.

I graze my lips against the stubble on his jaw. "A part of me has always been yours too, and that's never going to change." Even after all these years, he still has pieces of my heart. I drag my fingers through his thick, wavy hair as I always would.

"I fucking love it when you do that."

"I love your hair." I muse.

The corner of his mouth curls upwards. "Yeah, what else?"

I run my finger to his temple that creases as his smile widens. "I love your eyes." Then swipe my thumb along his lips. "And these lips." Planting a kiss against his perfect mouth, I move my palm onto his chest. "I love this body." I grip his bicep. "And these arms." My fingers trail down his spine, and I squeeze his delectable arse. "And this bum." I kiss him again, and he smiles against my lips. My hand strokes his inked stomach, moving down. "I love your big dick." I cup my hand around him, and he pushes his tongue into my mouth. My hand moves back to his face, and I run my thumb over his forehead. "I love this the most."

"What?" His eyes sparkle.

"Your mind." It's what made me fall in love with him before.

"There's nothing I don't love about you, Stephanie."

Our lips touch in a chaste kiss. I could lay here all day with him like this. He leans over to the bedside cabinet, reaching for a bottle of water. "You brought your book?" He gulps down the drink.

"Yes, of course."

He titters. "I doubt you'll get much time for reading while I'm here."

"Well, I'm at an exciting part and I'm desperate to find out what happens."

"You could have read it in the car." He hands me the water and I take a sip.

I shake my head. "It makes me nauseous."

He picks up the book, props up the pillows and slumps against the headboard, holding an arm out for me to cuddle up to him. I nestle my face against his chest; the bit of hair there tickles my cheek. The sound of his heart comforts me like the soft beating drum of rain on a window or the pulse of the ocean. My head rises and falls with each breath of his, like waves crashing and swelling. Reading the male character's point of view in my romance novel, his deep, resonating voice kindles the fire still burning inside of me. We would often cuddle up in the attic and read to each other. His fingers draw circles on my skin, trickles of excitement fill my veins, and I'm practically purring beneath his touch.

After reading for a while, the chapter gets steamy. He stops speaking, and grins, his eyes still fixed on the page.

"What's wrong? Why have you stopped?"

He smirks, laughing under his breath.

"You've not gone shy on me, have you?"

"I've not gone shy." He has a naughty grin and continues scanning the words.

"What are you doing?" I reach for the book and he holds it up over his head.

He chuckles and closes the book.

"Read it to me then, we were getting to a good bit."

He pulls his bottom lip between his teeth. "I'm going to do more than read it to you. I'm going to do *it* to you."

"What?" I gulp, knowing how the rest of the sex scenes go in this book. I'm clammy and gasping for air.

"Bend over," he growls.

"What?" My eyes bulge, taking in his dominant voice.

"You heard me. I want you bent over my lap." He sits up straight and gently throws the book to the bedside table. "Now."

When he puts it like that, I scramble to obey and kneel over his legs.

He runs his hand under my lace panties, squeezing my flesh. "I want to leave these on, they're such a turn on."

"Leave them on then." I'll feel more comfortable if my bare arse isn't on show again.

"They have to come down though." He tugs at the lace, pulling them underneath my cheeks.

"Okay." I pant as he grazes a finger between my folds, sliding into my wetness. His thumb presses firmly against the tight rosette there and I moan.

"I'm going to spank you now." I whip my head to the side to see him biting his lip. He withdraws his fingers and my eyes clench tight as I anticipate what's coming. Although I always loved it when he was rough with me during sex, it's been so long.

I gasp as his hand slaps my cheek. It's not so painful, but sends a shockwave of pleasure through my centre. He spanks me again, and I cry out, not in pain, but pleasure. Or maybe a mix of both, I can't decide. Swiftly slapping my flesh again, harder this time, he lets out a grunt of his own. I glance at his wild eyes and notice his mischievous grin like a lion toying with its prey. He hardens beneath me and I can see he's just as turned on by this as I am. After the fourth slap he doesn't remove his hand, but palms my cheek, stroking and kneading the sting away. He slides his fingers into me again, massaging me from the inside. "You liked that, didn't you?"

"Yes," I pant.

"I'm gonna do it again."

I brace myself, tensing my bottom. He slaps the other side with a hard, swift swipe. The sting burns, but with each hard spank, a jolt of ecstasy ride up to my core. I moan as he re-enters me, rewarding me with his massaging fingers, while his thumb presses firmly against my tight rosette.

"I'm going to go off-script now."

"What do you mean?"

His sinister grin makes the hairs on the back of my neck prick up. "In the book, he fucks her, but I'm not ready for that yet. I'm gonna fuck you with my tongue first."

My jaw drops and I'm panting like a dog on a hot summer's day.

"Lie down." His voice is demanding, possessive, and consuming. Everything I want in a man. I lay opposite him on my back. He unclips my panties and slides them off my legs, leaving the stockings on. His strong hands push against my knees, spreading my legs wide. He licks his lips, taking in my aching sex. "I love licking your sweet cunt."

I lean up on my elbows and watch his tongue glide up my inner thigh. His warm breath blows across my bundle of nerves, and he presses his lips there, gently kissing along my folds. The heat from his mouth combined with his firm wet tongue circling my opening makes me a quivering mess. I tip my head back, close my eyes, and enter a state of bliss. My body trembles as his tongue laps inside me, sucking, licking and kissing as though it were my mouth.

"Ca... Cal... Callum... that feels so good." I arch my back, grasping the sheets. He places his hand on my pubic bone, using his thumb to massage circles around my bud. "Come for me, baby. I want to feel your quivering cunt around my tongue."

"Cal," I scream, convulsing as the orgasm takes over. His tongue stiffens, reaching in as far as he can. Enraptured by his touch, my back arches once more and I lose all sense of time, space and consciousness. All I can sense is the heat of his mouth, the softness of his lips, and the pressure of his tongue. Cells of pure ecstatic delight explode all around my body.

As my orgasm subsides, I unclench the sheets and lie in a state of relaxation. He softly kisses my tummy before making his way to my face. The tip of his erection presses against my inner thigh. "Cal." I exhale into him as he presses his lips to mine and I taste my own flavour.

"You like that, don't you?"

"Yes." I move the hair from his face and kiss him again. "Would you like me to do anything to you?"

"I just want to bury myself deep inside you until I can't see straight."

"How do you want me?"

"Like this." He lifts my leg over his shoulder and I'm almost doing the splits. I've never been bendy and I'm less flexible now than I was before, but when he thrusts into me, the pleasure of having him deep inside outweighs any discomfort in my leg. He slides in and withdraws slowly, grinding and pushing deeper. "Steph." He nips at my calf. "Steph, you do things to me that nobody else can. You're gonna be the end of me." His voice is raspy and trembling.

"Cal, you do things to me too."

"What things?" He moves in and out of me at a steady pace.

"I don't know exactly, you do things to my soul that I can't understand."

His hot mouth soothes the bite mark on my leg. "You're the only person I ever want to be with."

"Cal." My fists clench the sheets

"Tell me, baby." He pushes deeper into me.

"Tell you what?" I lift my head to gaze into his eyes.

"Tell me I'm the one you want to be with."

"You are, Cal. I want to be with you. You're all I want."

He thrusts hard, and his eyes shut as he finds his release. I watch in awe as this man falls apart on top of me; watching him come gives me a rush, knowing it's my body giving him this pleasure. I wipe away beads of sweat lining his forehead and push his hair back from his face. He collapses next to me and pulls me in for a kiss. His fingers wrap around my neck as he continues the bold caress of his tongue.

He pulls away, tucking my hair behind my ear. "It's always been you, baby. You showed me what actual love is. I've travelled the world searching for a love like ours, and it doesn't exist. No one's ever loved me like you did, Steph."

"I still love you, Cal. I never stopped loving you." My voice breaks and the tears form in the corners of my eyes.

A smile spreads across his face and his eyes sparkle, filling my soul with warmth as if his happiness is radiating through my entire body.

"Steph, baby, I love you. I love you so fucking much."

I kiss him again before snuggling into his chest. "It's always been you, Cal."

CHAPTER
Twenty three

"Steph, wake up, baby." Something presses on my shoulder, jigging me from my dream. "Stephanie." A deep voice, a sexy voice in my ear, warm, soft, wet...

"Ugh, Cal."

"I thought that would wake you." He laughs.

I open my eyes but quickly close them again, pulling the duvet over my head to shield me from the daylight. Cal peels it away from my face and I blink, trying to acclimate my eyes to the light pouring through the window. "Morning, sleepyhead."

"What did you do? Was that your tongue in my ear?"

He chuckles again. "Yeah, you wouldn't wake up."

"What time is it?" I roll over to my side, hugging the duvet around my body.

"We have to vacate the hotel room in thirty minutes."

"Why didn't you wake me sooner?"

"I haven't been up long myself. I thought I'd let you sleep in, while I had a shower." He leans over and brushes the hair from my face.

"You had a shower without me?" I sigh.

"Yeah, I didn't think you would... fuck, I can go in again."

"I wanted morning sex with you before we go." I frown at him, pouting my lips.

"Didn't you have enough yesterday?" He kisses my nose.

"I can never have enough of you." I peck his lips, getting a hint of his fresh breath.

He stands. "I'm just gonna get my stuff from my room and bring it in here."

"Are you all packed and ready to go?"

"Yeah, don't worry. I'll pack your stuff while you get ready." He walks out of the room.

I pry myself out of the warm, soft bed and into the bathroom to clean my teeth. I'm wearing the stockings I'd forgotten to take off last night and nothing else.

Cal returns. "Foxy."

"Are you being sarcastic?" I quirk a grin and place my toothbrush on the sink.

"No, you look hot as fuck in nothing but those stockings."

He walks over, takes my face in his hands and kisses me with breathless urgency. The feathery strokes of his tongue have me dazed. His greedy mouth takes possession of me, and for the first time in a long time, I don't have the urge to hide my body.

"Hello, housekeeping," a lady shouts, knocking on the door.

"I need a shower." I wring my hands together, hoping I can get more time.

Cal pecks my nose. "I'll get rid of her. You jump in the shower." He slaps my arse as he goes.

After I've showered and dressed, I walk into the room. Cal is tidying away all my things. I love this man and everything he does for me.

"I'm packing these stockings in my bag." He holds up my garments.

"Why?" My eyebrows squish together. "Something

you're not telling me?" I titter. "If I'd have known, I would have bought you a pair too." I laugh harder.

His eyes draw thin and he isn't laughing, which makes me stop, press my lips together into a thin line and blink rapidly.

"I can't stand the thought of you wearing them for him."

"Who?"

"Father fucking Christmas. Who do you think?"

I flinch my head back. "Justin?"

"Yeah, Justin the jerk. You've no idea how much it bothers me, knowing he touches you. I can't fucking stand it."

"I won't wear them for him. I promise. You don't have to take them. Do you know how much they cost?" I giggle, trying to not make a big deal out of this, but when his jaw tightens, I add, "But if you want them, have them."

"Do you promise you won't wear them for him?"

"I promise." I get up and place my hands on his jaw and kiss his lips to reassure him he has nothing to be jealous of when it comes to Justin and me.

"Have you worn sexy underwear for him before?"

"Not stockings. I've never owned a pair until yesterday."

"I'm glad I'm the only one who gets to see you in these, and I was the only one to see you with your nipple pierced too."

"Only you, Cal."

"I can't bear that he gets to touch you whenever he likes."

"You shouldn't be jealous. I haven't been intimate with Justin since before the snowstorm. Plus, he doesn't do the things you do to me."

"Doesn't he know you like to be fucked with tongue and have your arse whipped?"

"Cal." I swat his chest, biting my lip as I look at him, reliving the memory of last night. "He's never spanked me, I've only ever let you do that to me."

"I fucking love you." He kisses me again and with his brutal strength in this moment of passion, he lifts me onto the bed. His kiss is aflame with everything he desires while his nimble fingers unbutton my clothes. "As much as I like you in these tight fitted jeans. I want to peel them off you."

He hasn't seen me in casual clothes since our teens, although they're a little too tight this morning. I must have overdone it with the tapas and wine last night. "I'd wear them more often for you, but it's not exactly work attire."

"I prefer your skirts, sans tights." He quirks a grin and kisses me again.

"Well, I would wear my stockings at work, but I can't if you take them."

His mouth opens, and he sucks in a breath.

"Housekeeping," the woman shouts, knocking on the door.

"For fuck's sake," Callum shouts.

"Cal, we best finish packing." He pins me to the bed, holding my wrists above my head.

"Not until I've finished." His tongue dips and swirls into my mouth and I'm drowned in his lust.

A knock at the door again, "Housekeeping."

"Ignore it," Cal says.

"We can't, she'll walk in any minute, thinking we've gone."

I walk over to the door. "Can I just have a few more minutes? I'm sorry."

She mumbles something under her breath, no doubt cursing me, and moves down the corridor.

Callum reluctantly packs the stockings in my case. "I'll take these bags to the car." He picks up my suitcase along with his holdall and we walk out the door.

"Do you think Jerry and the others have left already?"

"Yeah probably, we were late getting up."

The young waitress shows us to an empty table for two, and it is a buffet breakfast. "Do you want a coffee or juice?" Cal asks.

"I'll have one of each, please." I walk over to the buffet and help myself to scrambled egg on toast with sausages and tomato. It smells amazing. My tummy rumbles. I sit down at the table, ready to dive in. Cal returns with his full English piled to the rafters.

"You hungry?" I'm so jealous of his hollow legs.

"Yeah, I need to replenish my energy after last night." He grins, wiggling his eyebrows. "You wore me out."

The heat goes straight to my cheeks. "Cal." I widen my eyes, signalling for him to keep his voice down.

"What, it's true." He chuckles.

I bite into my thick pork sausage. He licks his lips, watching me. I'm sure he's picturing his dick in my mouth right now instead of this meat. I smile, thinking of Justin's skinny sausage and how this is so much more succulent.

I take a sip of my fresh orange juice. "Do you want to get going after this?"

"Err, No."

I wipe my mouth with my napkin. "What did you want to do?"

Cal shrugs and swallows his mouthful. "Did you want to go sightseeing while we're here?"

A smile lifts my cheeks. "Do you?"

"Yeah, I don't want to go yet."

"I would like that." I don't want my time alone with him to be over just yet.

He sips his coffee. "Where do you want to go?"

I move the scrambled egg around on my plate while I think. "Let's go to the National Gallery,"

"All right, if that's what you want to do." He continues to eat his food, dipping a hash brown into his beans.

"Cal, I would really love that." I almost choke on the words as a warm fuzziness fills my chest.

"Did you ever go to Florence? I know you always wanted to live there."

I sigh and look down at my half-empty plate. "No, I haven't even been to visit."

He studies me for a moment. "Why not?"

I shrug my shoulders. "Because Justin hates looking at art. It's not his thing at all, and the kids wouldn't be interested."

He reaches across the table and takes hold of my hand. "Let me take you. Tell him you're going with some of your girlfriends or ask Kelly to cover for you."

If only it was that simple. I smile at the wonderful idea, knowing it will never come to pass. "Have you been?"

"Yeah, I went travelling around Europe. It was busy with tourists in Florence, although not as busy as Venice. Tuscany is nice though."

"I went to Rome for the day." I bite into a slice of toasted granary bread.

"I stayed in Rome for a few weeks. Did you see much of it?"

"We did the Colosseum, Trevi fountain and Spanish steps and had lunch and ice cream. That's all we had time for. It was a day trip while we were staying at a nearby holiday resort."

"I suppose there's only so much you can do in a day." His thumb strokes my hand.

"I went to Salvador Dali's house in Spain." Maybe I've been to one place he hasn't ventured to.

"Oh, really. Was it good?"

"Amazing, you'd enjoy it. You've seen pictures right, with the weird egg shapes lining the top of the building?"

"Yeah."

"The entire castle is filled to the brim with his work and most of it was dedicated to his one true love. It's beautiful. I went with my friend Claire, years ago before I had kids."

"I'd like to go travelling with you, Steph. Where else have you been?"

I chew on my toast and try to think about where I've been. Most of the places I've visited abroad are family holiday resorts, where the only culture I've sampled is the local food and drink. "I've been to Barcelona and Paris too. I adored Paris."

"Yeah, Paris is nice. But you'd like Vienna."

"Oh, Cal. I've always wanted to go there."

"I want to take you." Sadness fills me, thinking about all the things we'll never get to do. I'd love to go away to Florence with him, Vienna, Tuscany. It's nothing more than a dream, a wistful fantasy. Listening to his travel stories makes me regretful, like I wasted my youth.

I pull my hand away from his. "Cal, we know it can never be."

"It can, Steph. We still have the rest of our lives. We can certainly make up for lost time, and we can start today."

"Cal, please. My kids. Where do they fit in while I'm gallivanting halfway around the world with you?"

He drops his fork onto the plate, and it makes a clatter. "I just don't understand why you're so intent on staying with him." He spits out the words and leans over the table slightly. "If you love me like you say you do, then leave him."

"I won't leave my kids, please stop asking me to." I wipe my mouth with the napkin and fist it into a tight ball.

Cal runs his fingers through his hair and exhales. "Fuck, I've ruined the morning now, haven't I?"

"Can we just forget about everything and enjoy the rest of the day?" He nods and finishes his man-sized breakfast.

CAL TAKES hold of my icy hand as we walk out of the tube station. The rough feel of his skin on mine makes me wish we'd slept together one last time. He wraps his woolly scarf around my neck, shielding me from the cool crisp air.

"Thank you. I didn't bring a scarf or gloves."

"You brought that great fucking suitcase, and you're telling me you didn't think to pack a scarf?" I see his breath as he huffs the words.

"I didn't think." I wrap his scarf tighter around my neck and tuck it into my coat. The smell of his peppermint aftershave on the fabric sends me into a blissful haze. Squeezing his hand, I kiss his cheek. I commit every sense of him to my memory.

He stops in his stride in the middle of the street, pulling me into him. His warm lips against my cold skin heats my entire body. His tongue enters my mouth, and the feeling reminds me of his tongue entering me elsewhere. The tingling from the memory blossoms again, and I'm spiralling into a vortex of heady sensations. He slowly ends the kiss, but not before several light pecks against my lips.

"Come on. We're just around the corner from the gallery." I see the enormous fountains in front, and I'm surprised it isn't busy, most likely because everyone is doing their Christmas shopping. We climb the steps leading up to the extensive building and walk through the lobby. Cal picks up a map. "Is there any particular work you'd like to see?"

"I'd like to see Botticelli."

He holds the map out in front of him. "Right, he's in room 58. That Arnolfini portrait that you liked is in room 63 and Monet is gallery B."

The smile on my face makes my cheeks bulge. "You remembered Jan van Eyck?"

He quirks a smile. "You mean Dick Van Dyke?" His shoulder bumps mine. He would always get the two confused. I burst into a giggle, remembering how he would always take the piss in our art history lesson. I'm sure he only signed up for the class to annoy me.

"I've seen that Arnolfini wedding painting tons of times. I did my art history essay on it. Where's room 58?"

Cal studies the map again and looks around the lobby, getting his bearings. "Up these stairs on level two and to the left. Route A according to this map."

"Do you want to see anything?" I ask.

"Baby, I'm happy to go along with you." I take his hand as we climb the ornate staircase. Walking past artwork by Bellini, Michelangelo, Leonardo, Piero, Raphael and finally, I see Botticelli's Venus and Mars adorning the wall above a gold chest in the large room. The painting is bigger than I thought. I point to the image, showing Cal which one it is. We sit on the bench in front and wait for a tourist to disappear and take his camera with him.

"Why anybody would take a photo of this is beyond me," Cal huffs.

"Don't you like it?"

"Yeah, I do, but why take a photo? I'm sure there are much better photos online. Why do people feel the need to take their own photo?" I nod and hope the happy snapper hasn't heard his rude comments, but I agree with him.

"I love this painting."

"What is it you like about it?"

The guy with the camera moves along, giving us a full view of the masterpiece.

I point to the woman on the canvas. "Venus. I love how Botticelli used the same model, Simonetta Vespucci, for a lot of his paintings. He was said to have been in love with her. He asked to be buried at her feet, but she was married."

"She's shagging Mars in this painting. Look at him. He looks well and truly fucked. A bit like me last night." He chuckles to himself, and his shoulders rock next to mine.

"They're having an affair."

Cal glances between the painting and me. "Who, Botticelli and the model?"

I shrug my shoulder. "I don't know about that, but Venus, the goddess of love and Mars are having an affair here, in the painting."

"No wonder he's fucked then." A cheeky grin spreads across his face.

"It's supposed to be symbolic that love conquers all. They're in love."

"She looks annoyed to me." He lets out a puff of laughter.

"What, like he came before she finished?" I join in with his tittering.

"Maybe, perhaps she wanted round two, and he fell asleep."

"Perhaps he showered without her that morning and didn't wake her until late."

"Look, I didn't wake until late myself. I tried to wake you, and you just rolled over. So I jumped in the shower quickly, then went to my room to get some clean clothes and you were still fast asleep. You know you're mardy when you're tired."

My eyes roll. "I don't think she's mad at him. I think she's watching him sleep because she loves him."

Cal kisses my cheek, then moves his lips to my ear whispering, "See, she loves him so she's letting him sleep."

A smile plays on my lips.

Cal kisses the spot below my ear. "Did you like how I woke you up this morning?"

"No, that was weird, don't do that again." I giggle.

"What this?" His tongue goes in my ear again.

"Ew, that's just wrong." I wipe my hand over my ear.

He's laughing. "All right, all right, I know you like it here." He kisses below my ear again. "Don't you?" I nod and turn my head to him and take his lips to mine. Our tongues tangle together. Slipping and sliding, licking and lashing, he pulls away to look at me. "I love kissing you. How do you expect me to see you every day and not kiss you?" I sigh; I know he's right, as I don't think I can do it either.

We peruse the gallery hand in hand, looking at Monet, Leonardo de Vinci, and many other famous paintings, though none so intently as Botticelli. The afternoon seems to go by in a flash and we head back to the car—parked at the hotel—to get a head start before the Friday rush hour. I buckle up and turn on the sat nav to navigate us onto the motorway. I text Justin to let him know I'm setting off and catch up on my socials.

I turn sideways to look at Cal. Watching him drive stirs something inside me; his strong stubbly jaw excites me as I relive the memory of it scratching at my inner thighs. His bicep is more prominent as he grips the wheel and I can't help picturing him pinning me under him. He glances at me and smiles, then places his hand on my thigh, squeezing it before shifting gears. I yawn.

"Tired?"

"Yes, are you?" I yawn again.

"Err, yeah, you could say that. I told you, I feel like that dude in that painting. I'm totally fucked." He chortles.

"Is that why you didn't want to go again this morning?" I flit my eyes to him and then back to his hand on my leg.

"I could've gone again, but I reckon I broke the record yesterday for the number of times I've come in one day." He's grinning as though all his Christmases came at once.

"We must have had it more times than that in a day when we were younger, we were always at it."

"Maybe." He sneaks a glance at me and moves his eyes back to the road. "Which was your favourite?"

"From yesterday, or overall?"

"Yesterday."

My cheeks flush. "I liked it when you spanked me, then rewarded me with your tongue." I smile as the memory lingers between my thighs.

"I liked that too." He's still grinning. "I always loved slapping your arse."

My head is light and the houses outside blur into one as we drive through the suburbs.

"I didn't hurt you, did I?"

"No" I interlace his fingers with mine as they rest on my thigh.

His thumb strokes the back of my hand. "You're not sore or anything?"

"No. You didn't hit me that hard. It was fun."

"Good." He pulls my hand to his lips and kisses my fingers. "That was better than some fucking nightclub, right?"

"Yes." I yawn again.

"Go to sleep if you're tired."

"Are you sure? I feel bad going to sleep while you drive all the way home."

"It's fine, baby." He squeezes my hand. "I'll listen to the radio."

"If you feel tired and want me to drive or anything, wake me, and not by sticking your tongue in my ear."

He laughs. "All right."

CHAPTER
Twenty four

"Steph, baby."

"Hmm?" I open my eyes, blinking as I come around. "Are we home already?"

"We're about an hour away. Did you want something to eat?"

"What time is it?" I look around for a clock on his dashboard.

"Teatime, I was gonna stop at the next services."

"I'm hungry." I stretch my arms, yawning. Taking a deep breath, I try to wake my body.

Cal grabs food while I go to the restroom. We walk back to the car together and he interlaces his fingers with mine. The touch of his skin awakens my body, and I'm no longer tired.

"Mmm." The mayonnaise on the chicken burger is warm on my tongue and the tantalising taste of the fast food isn't something I have often, so I appreciate it that much more when I do. I hope with all my nocturnal activities this weekend, I may have burned off a few calories, but I doubt it.

"You're pulling your sex face again." Cal wipes a bit of mayo from the corner of my mouth.

"I don't care, this food is amazing."

"Only you and my kids can get excited about fast food."
He titters.

"You used to get pretty excited when I would come home
from work with a box full of nuggets. You used to stay up and
wait for me." I lean over and peck his lips.

"I wasn't waiting just for the nuggets. I was waiting up
for you, and other treats." The naughty grin on his face makes
me smile.

"I thought so." There was nothing better than coming
home to him after a day at uni and an evening of flipping
burgers. I guzzle down the diet coke.

He finishes the rest of his food and licks his fingers. "Did
you enjoy today?"

"I had a fantastic time. Justin never takes me to art
galleries." I dip the salty fries into the pot of barbecue
sauce.

"So, if you and Justin have nothing in common, why are
you together?" He sucks on his strawberry milkshake.

"We have lots of other stuff in common." I sigh, knowing
that's not really true.

"Like what? I can't think of one thing."

"He makes me laugh." Well, he used to anyway. That's
one thing I liked about him.

"I make you laugh." He leans back against the door. "It
surprised me when I saw him. He isn't your usual type."

"He isn't like you, you mean." Justin was safe. Complete
opposite. My heart couldn't take another Callum. I couldn't
date anyone who reminded me of him. "He was friends with
my brother and our parents have been friends for years, so it
just made sense."

"You settled."

I shrug my shoulders. "Whoever I ended up with, Cal, I
would have settled. Nobody can compare to you."

"Stay with me, Steph. You don't have to go home. You can come back to my place."

"I have to go home. Justin will wonder where I am." My stomach curdles at the thought of going back to him.

"I mean, stay with me. Leave jumped-up Justin."

"Cal, I can't." Even though there's nothing I want more.

"You can, it's simple. Tell him you don't love him and move in with me. Hell, I'll even come with you and do it for you if you want me to."

"It might be simple for you. You're practically an expert at loving and leaving, but I'm not made that way, Cal. I can't leave my kids."

"Bring them too."

"Don't be ridiculous. Where would they sleep?"

"How can you say you love me if you won't even consider it? Or do you love him more? Are you just using me?"

"How can you say that? You think I'm using you?" My shoulders curl inwards.

"No, I didn't, but what's the point in this if you're never gonna leave him? What are we gonna do, have the odd fuck in the car or whenever there's a chance to come on a business trip?"

I know he's right. I gaze down at the empty wrapper on my lap.

"It doesn't make sense. If you love me, be with me like this every day." He runs his palm over his face and sighs.

"You think I don't want that?" I wave my hand between us. "I've wanted this life with you for the last twenty years, Cal, and where were you? Fucking around in Australia and Timbuktu or wherever else you went trotting off to."

He leans over the centre console and places his hand on my thigh. "I'm here now."

"For how long? You'll get bored with me as you did before."

"I didn't get bored with you." He straightens his back.

"You stopped loving me, Cal. You once told me you'd always love me, then you stopped."

"And you told me we'd always be friends. You lied." His fist squeezes the cardboard cup in his hand.

"You told me you didn't love me anymore." My voice wobbles. I choke back the tears, remembering those dark days.

"I was scared, okay. I got fucking scared. Things were moving too fast, and I couldn't handle it. But I never stopped loving you."

"You were scared? All this time. You had me believe it was me, and the truth is you got scared? I thought I was some sort of clingy, lazy, materialistic bitch, so unlikable that you couldn't stand to be around me anymore." I cover my face with my hands.

He peels my fingers away. "Why would you think that?"

"Because you said I was all those things."

"I don't even remember saying that. But if I did, I never meant it. You kept wanting to know why I didn't want you any more, and I must have spouted that shit to shut you up."

I wave my hand in the air. "You expected me to be friends with you after you said all those hurtful things to me?"

"I thought you'd be friends with me and the breakup would be amicable, but you wouldn't let me go."

"Cos I was in love with you," I shout with my trembling voice. "Why would I let you go when you were everything to me? I wanted to fight for us."

He slams the empty cup on the dash. "I want to fight for us now." He tries to wrap his arms around me, but I stay put with my back to the seat, doing my best to not let the tears take over.

"I hate you."

"I love you." He kisses my cheek.

"You told me you loved me before. Justin will never leave me. He's safe. You'll get bored with me again in a few years."

He retreats to his side of the car. "You'll never trust me again, will you?" He buries his face in his hands.

"I'll always be waiting for the day you tell me you don't love me. I can't live like that, Cal. My heart just couldn't take you leaving me again." I can't hold back the tears any longer.

"Marry me then. If that's the reassurance you need from me. I'll marry you."

I huff. "Like a piece of paper will stop you from leaving. And in case you've forgotten. I'm already pissin' married."

"Yeah, to the wrong fucking person. Leave him and marry me. I know it will be hard, but I know I can make you happy. I'll spend the rest of my life making you happy." He gathers the empty wrappers in his hands, crushing them into a ball.

"Cal, please. I can't do that. I told you, we can't be anything more. This has to be it now." My heart aches. Is this really it?

"I can't stop this, whatever this is. I don't think you can stop either."

"We have to. It's going to destroy us."

"You've already destroyed me." He storms out of the car and slams the door shut. The sun stripped from my flesh, leaving me cold and alone. I watch him take the rubbish to the bin before he disappears into the services.

I always wanted to hear those words from his lips. Marry me. Trust him to say them when I'm already married. That's so typical of him. He's only about fifteen years too late. His words play over and over in my head like a broken record, haunting me, knowing I can't marry him, even though there's nothing I want more in this world than to be Mrs Richards. I wanted it back then and I want it still; to be his wife and have him worship me like this every day. Was it even a proposal or just his manipulative way to get what he wants?

He returns to the car, and slides behind the wheel. I try to read his expression. His jaw clenches, and he breathes heavily through his nostrils as his fists grip the steering wheel.

I swallow the lump that's filled my throat. "Everything okay?"

He shoots me a glare and starts the engine. "No Steph. Nothing about this fucked-up situation is okay."

Turning to look out of the window, I wrap my mouth around the straw and suck the last of my fizzy drink. Gazing at the fields alongside the motorway, I wonder what my life would be like to move in with him; to wake up in his arms, go to work together, spend our evenings doing normal family stuff. Could I really live with seeing my kids for half the week or alternate days? I know my parents would disown me, although I've always been the letdown in the family. No matter how much I try, I can never compete with my perfect sister and golden brother.

Cal doesn't speak to me, he doesn't even glance in my direction. I hate arguing with him. Fifteen friggin' years since I married, I haven't looked at another man and here I am, a few months with Cal and I'm wanting to leave Justin and marry him. Although, I know things wouldn't stay like this. Eventually, even if it's years down the line, he would most likely get bored with me as he did before. Nothing stays lustful, exciting, and passionate forever. Does it?

We don't speak for the rest of the journey. I stare out of the window, trying to focus on anything other than him. The closer I get to home, the tighter the knot becomes in my stomach and the lump in my throat grows, bringing with it the acidity. The car comes to a stop at the end of my driveway and Cal pulls on the handbrake. I have to force my legs to step out of the car. Every bone in my body wants to stay wrapped in this bubble with him. Before I get out, I turn to him. "Cal."

"What?" He snaps his head to the side.

I know he's hurt, but so am I. I've been hurting for a long time. My fingers fiddle with the fabric of my shirt. "I do love you."

He huffs. "Sure you do." The car door opens, and he steps out.

I get out of the car. He opens the boot and gets my suitcase and all my shopping bags. I try to take some from him, but he bats my hands away. "I'll carry your stuff to the door."

I turn to him at my front door, wanting to kiss him goodbye, but I can't. "I could be happy with you as a friend, as long as you're in my life."

His nostrils flare and he huffs. "I don't think we can be friends, Steph."

I open the door and he drops the bags down in the hall. Cairen comes running down the stairs shooting a Nerf gun. "Mummy's home."

"I'll see you Monday."

He walks back to the car without saying goodbye, and I close the door. Normally, I'd do anything to see Cal happy, but I have to protect my heart. I begged him to take me back before and he wouldn't. He's brought this on himself. I take a deep breath and shake it from my mind.

I give Cairen a big hug. Lord knows I need one right now.

"Mum, that's too tight." He squirms his way out of my arms, giggling.

I ruffle his hair. "Where's Daddy?"

"In the garage mending my bike." He fires another bullet in the air.

"Why, what's wrong with it?"

"Cassie ran into me on our bike ride today."

"Are you all right?" My hands cup his face and I check for bruises.

He moves his head away and points to his elbow, and I see a graze. "She broke my wheel." I kiss his poorly better and walk through the house. Cassie is watching TV.

"Hi sweety."

"Hmm." She doesn't even look up, continuing to stare at the screen. I go into the garage through the back door.

"Hey, I'm back."

Justin glances up from the workbench. "Did you have a good time?"

"Yes, I went Christmas shopping. I got your mum a nice gift."

"Good." Justin always leaves it to me to buy everyone's gifts.

I lean against the wall and watch him lift the wheel to Cassie's bike. "What have you been up to?"

"Not a lot. I finished early today so picked the kids up from school, then we went for a bike ride. The kids went on the bikes, I walked with the dog."

"Oh, nice."

He glances back at me. "How come you're so late back?"

My throat closes up, and there's a pounding in my ears. "We went to the National Gallery."

"Who, you and that Callum bloke?"

"And Kelly." I scratch the itch on my neck and avert my eyes from his.

"I thought Kelly was driving down with you."

"She was. She did." My shoulders tense.

"Is she a ghost? Because she wasn't in the soddin' car."

"We picked her up on the way. Have you done?" I don't see why I have to keep explaining myself. I pick at the red nail varnish on my finger as my heart rate speeds up and a cold shiver shoots down my spine.

"I thought you'd have called me last night. What were you doing, Steph?" He wipes his oily hands on a cloth and throws it on the workbench. "The kids were waiting for you to call and say goodnight." His words tug at my heartstrings.

The pressure builds behind my eyes and a sharp stabbing pain pounds in my temple. "I had too much to drink at the business dinner. I'm sorry."

"I should think so." He tosses the spanner back in the toolbox.

"Have you eaten?"

"Not yet. I'll throw some pizzas in the oven. Have you eaten?"

"I grabbed a burger on the way home."

He shakes his head at me.

My shoulders straighten. He makes me want to scream. "I'll put your pizzas in the oven?"

"I've nearly finished up here. There's some salad in the fridge if you're still hungry."

Piss off. I walk away before I say something I'll regret. I was trying to be a good wife, but do shitty husbands really deserve a good wife? To think I've just turned down a life with Callum for this.

After everyone has eaten, I cuddle up on the sofa with Cassie and Cairen and watch a family film. I kiss their heads and wrap my arms around them.

"I missed you Mummy." Cassie squeezes me tighter. The guilt of not calling them weighs heavily on my chest.

"I'm sorry I didn't call you last night."

Justin comes into the living room with a can of beer, slumps in his chair, and pulls out his phone.

"I'm sorry you were waiting for me to call."

"We weren't waiting. Dad made us go to bed early."

The lying twat. I glare at Justin for making me feel bad. Using the kids to manipulate me. He doesn't even notice and continues to stare at his phone.

After the film, I tuck them both in bed and call it a night. It's been a long day and I'm physically and mentally exhausted. I sink into the mattress. As much as I enjoyed last night, there's nothing like my own bed. I'm about to drift off to sleep when the mattress dips. Justin climbs in. He scoots closer to me and drapes his arm over my stomach. His semi grinds into my plump cheek and he reaches for my breast. My chest tightens and my stomach turns. I grip his wrist before he can touch me, moving his hand away. "Not tonight, Justin."

He huffs. "When? You never want to do anything anymore. What's wrong with you?"

"Nothing, I'm just tired."

"You're always tired. You need to see a doctor or something." He rolls over and straightens his pillows and I relax a little. I can't bear him touching me, not when it's Callum's hands I want, and his face I see making love to me.

***

MY TEETH CHATTER. I sit on my couch draped in a blanket, sipping a hot honey drink. I haven't been able to drag myself out of bed for the last three days; Justin rang in sick for me. It started Sunday with a banging headache and a sore throat. There's only so much mindless TV I can watch. I'm not even sure what's on right now; my head is pounding, my body aches, and my throat is ablaze with each swallow of my drink. All I need now is to start my period and I really will be living the dream.

On top of this virus or cold or flu or whatever this is I'm suffering with, I'm also feeling sorry for myself. Reminiscing about Callum and how our paths have crossed again. I almost wish I'd never met him so I could continue with my mundane life, blissfully unaware of how unhappy I actually was.

How I would love to go back to the woman I was six months ago before I stepped foot in Browns Media Co. That woman was innocent. She lived each day for her family, and now I live each day to see Callum's face; to have his hands graze my skin and hear his words whispering in my ear. When Justin talks, I don't even hear him anymore. I'm listening but nothing registers, my mind is elsewhere.

I hear a melody; it takes me a moment to realise it's my phone buzzing. I search my body for the phone. I'm sure it was on my lap a minute ago. Lifting the blanket, it's slid between the folds. As I look at the screen, Cal's name lights up before my eyes. A flash of excitement fills me. I swipe right. "Hello."

"Steph?" My name rolling off his tongue is as sweet as this honey drink in my hand.

"Cal. Hi" There's a flutter in my stomach saying his name out loud.

"I wanted to check you were all right. Jerry said you've been sick all week." His voice is soft and not the biting tone he had the last time we spoke.

"I'm fine, well, I'm not fine. I feel like shit." But hearing his voice has perked me up no end.

"I thought you were just saying you were ill to avoid me."

"Why would you think that?" The mug in my hand warms my palm, and I slurp my drink, waiting for him to speak.

There's a sigh. "After last week."

"Well, I'm not trying to avoid you."

"What's wrong with you, then? I mean, what are your symptoms?"

My hand strokes my swollen neck. "My throat feels like I'm swallowing razor blades."

"You sound bad. Your voice is hoarse. Kinda sexy though." I can hear a smile in his voice.

I can't help but smile into the handset. "I have a high temperature and I can't get warm."

"I hope you get better soon."

"Thank you, I think I was run down from the trip to London." I fiddle with a loose thread on the blanket draped over my legs.

"Yeah, I feel I'm to blame. I shouldn't have kept you up all night."

"Yes, you should. I wouldn't change our night together for anything. I don't think me walking around London with no tights, hat, scarf or gloves helped matters."

"Probably not. Again, my fault. If we hadn't argued, you would've been with me instead of shopping that afternoon." I should've spent the afternoon with him. I'm such a stubborn cow sometimes.

"I've missed you this week."

"Cal, we shouldn't do this anymore." I exhale into the handset. I can't keep stringing him along like this, even though I want him.

"What? Can't I miss my friend at work?" I can hear him laughing under his breath and I smile, wishing he were here now to look after me like he used to whenever I was poorly.

"You said we couldn't be friends."

"I'll be friends with you until you come to your senses."

My eyes flick to the ceiling. "I want us to be friends, Cal."

"Whatever you say."

My chest aches and I press the hot water bottle against the chill in my heart. "Have I missed anything at work?"

"Nothing you need to worry about. I saw your client for you today."

I rest my forehead against my palm. "Oh, I forgot I had a meeting lined up. Was it the florist?"

"Yeah, I've taken notes so will get you up to speed when you're back."

"Where are you, anyway?"

"I'm sat at my desk. Everyone's at lunch. I came back early to call you."

A warm fuzziness fills my heart. "It's nice to hear your voice."

"Yeah, it's nice to hear your voice too, your husky, sexy voice." He chuckles.

"Who knew my flemmy throat would turn you on." I giggle.

"Everything about you turns me on. You should know that by now."

"You know I feel the same way about you, don't you?" Oh no, I shouldn't have said that—so much for trying to be friends.

"I know, baby." And there it is, those words. He only has to call me baby in that sultry tone of his and it's like his words vibrate around my body, tantalising and teasing with every syllable from his lips. I close my eyes. If we can't even keep things platonic in a telephone conversation, how can we do it when I return to work?

"Cal, promise me we will be friends."

He breathes out a long sigh. "I promise."

"I'll let you get back to work."

"Get better. See you soon."

"Okay, bye."

Moving my fat arse from the sofa, I slump to the kitchen to flick on the kettle. Opening the cupboard while I wait for it to boil, I raid the kid's snacks, spotting a half-full packet of chocolate biscuits. I take one out and bite into the crunchy, crumbly texture. Getting the chocolate hit as it melts on my tongue, taking all my troubles away, if only for a second. I pour the hot water into my mug and sit back on the settee with a hot chocolate and the remaining biscuits.

I've written off any chance of losing weight or sticking to my slimming goals this week. Right now, I really couldn't give a crap; I mean, who am I slimming for, anyway? I thought it was for myself, but I've realised it's for Justin, always wanting to receive a compliment from him and feel good about my body and myself. Callum never fails to make me feel sexy. I sigh and fragments of the biscuit fall from my mouth all over my fluffy pyjamas that I'm still wearing late in the afternoon. Teddy, our dog, nuzzles his head in my lap, licking up the crumbs. At least I don't need to get the hoover out.

After Claire's advice, I'm still writing things down on my laptop. I open the case and type in everything that happened with Cal on our London trip. Getting everything out helps, therapeutic almost. There's no way I want to forget these memories ever.

The front door opens, followed by a clatter in the hall. My mother has collected the children from school all week while I've been ill. Mum walks into the lounge, "How are you feeling, love?"

"I'm feeling a little better."

Cairen hands me his school bag, then runs off to play, and Cassie retreats to her bedroom.

"Why don't you have a bath? I'll stay with the children," Mum says.

"It's all right, I'll have a shower later."

"No, I really think you should have a bath now." She insists, moving her eyes over my messy hair to my stained pyjamas. I roll my eyes when I realise she's trying to say in the most polite way possible that I look a complete mess. My exterior reflects how I feel on the inside. The empty biscuit packet falls to the floor as I get off the sofa. I put it in the bin before I saunter to the bathroom, taking my mum up on her offer. I'm glad the packet was only half full, or I fear I would have eaten the lot.

Floral aromas fill the bathroom as my bath oils mix with the hot water. Sinking into the bubbles is like being wrapped in a thick blanket of cotton wool, as if I'm sitting on a cloud and the weight of the world seems to have lifted for this moment. Nothing like a warm bath to soak one's troubles away. I should never have let things get this deep with Callum. Revenge is bittersweet; I longed for him to understand the pain of wanting someone and not being able to have them. But I've only made myself want him more. Sleeping with him again has reconnected our souls after searching for one another for two decades. How can I separate them again? To be parted from him once more will be like splitting me in two.

Teddy barks as the letterbox clanks, and I look out the large bay window to see a woman walk down my drive. Her long black hair blows in the wind, revealing a rose tattoo on her neck. She looks familiar, but I can't think where I know her from. A man waits for her on a motorcycle. The scar on his face sends a chill through me. I watch as she mounts his motorbike with a smirk plastered on her face and they both pull on their helmets.

Walking into the hall, a large white envelope hangs in the door, addressed to me. Has Cal sent me something? I don't see people like that on my quiet estate. As I open the envelope, I shake the thought. Surely he wouldn't risk sending anything to my home. I hear Justin turn the shower on and I walk into the kitchen, pulling out the contents.

Sucking in a breath, I stop in my tracks when I see pictures of Cal and I. Flicking through—each one more incriminating than the last—I gasp for air. A handful of images showing me in Cal's car, talking at first, then kissing. The thought that someone was watching our most intimate moments makes the acid rise in my throat and I lean over the kitchen sink and retch, bringing with it my morning coffee. My shaking hands grip the evidence. I need oxygen.

The pounding in my chest spreads to my temple. It's bad

enough that someone has taken photographs of us, but to have pictures of us making love in the car is violating and desecrating the moment that we shared. How many other times has someone been watching us and for what purpose? I wipe my mouth and retch again, but nothing comes up. My entire body erupts in a cold sweat. My hands won't stop shaking.

The kids are in their rooms having a lazy Saturday morning and I can still hear the shower. I reach for my phone and scroll for Cal, pressing all the wrong buttons before I eventually tap on his name.

"Hey."

"Cal" My voice quivers.

"What's wrong?" His voice changes to a more abrupt tone.

I can barely get the words out. "Cal, I'm scared." I wipe my forehead.

"Baby, what's happened?"

There's a bang. I jump. My heart races. I run to the front window again, but see nothing. Another bang comes from Cassie's bedroom, making me flinch. I let my shoulders drop when I realise she's dancing. I stutter down the handset. "Someone has just posted some photos through my door."

"What kind of photos?"

I swallow the acid back down. It burns my throat. "Photos of us together… intimately."

"I'm coming over." He growls out the words in that gruff voice that usually has me panting, but now I'm hyperventilating for different reasons.

"No, Cal, Justin." As much as I want to see Cal right now, having him show up here will make things worse.

"Meet me then, the lay-by off the A1. I'll be there in 15 minutes."

"I'm not dressed. Give me half an hour."

"Does it say anything?" I can hear the anger in his gruff voice.

I scan the sheets again. "Nothing. Cal, they were watching us make love. They know where I live. Who would do this?"

"Some sick, twisted fucker," he shouts.

"I can't stop shaking. Cal, they didn't look like the sort of people you'd mess with."

"You saw them? What did they look like?"

"A man with a scar on his face, and a woman with long black hair and a rose tattoo on her neck."

"I'm gonna deal with this, don't worry. I'll see you in half an hour."

"Do you know them?"

"I have an idea who they are, yeah. And it's nothing you need to worry about."

"But I am worried. They were just at my house, my kids Cal, Justin."

"Please trust me, you don't need to worry."

"I feel ill, Cal."

"Baby, get ready and meet me."

"Okay. Bye." I stuff the photographs back into the envelope and shove them in the glove box of my car before running upstairs to get dressed. Justin walks into the bedroom with a towel wrapped around his waist.

"Are you all right? You look pale."

"I'm fine, Claire's called. She needs someone to talk to so I'm going over."

"Is she all right?"

"I don't know." I walk into the bathroom to clean my teeth and wash my face. The cold splash of water sharpens my senses for a moment. I apply my eyeliner with my trembling hand and don't bother with the lipstick. I have more important matters to think about than my appearance right now. "Bye," I shout, walking out the door.

I'm on autopilot, watching from a distance this fallen woman who has made a mess of her seemingly perfect life. To the outside world, I have the perfect family, home, bank account. Perhaps that's why I'm an easy target. What if they want money? I don't just have spare cash lying around, it's tucked away in our savings. Justin would know if I drew money out. I could take some out of my wages, but where does it end? If I hand money over, would they want more?

Justin would go ballistic if he knew I was being blackmailed. He's not one for fighting, but being a builder, he's strong. I've seen him in the middle of a few brawls in his time, usually splitting up a fight or sticking up for one of the lads on an all-day drinking binge. But if he knew the reason for the blackmail, our marriage would be over. I don't see a way out of this. I hope Cal can find out who's behind it. But I worry, that bloke looked rough. Although he's right, he can handle himself too. He did kickboxing growing up and was always getting into fights at school.

As I approach the lay-by, I pull up in front of Cal's car and watch him walk over. For the first time since receiving the images, I relax a little and let out a long breath. He clambers into the car. His hand goes straight to my cheek and I flinch, wondering if we're being watched right now.

"It's good to see you. Are you feeling better?"

"I was until I saw those photos." I Pull away from his hand and point to the glove box, not wanting to touch those dirty photos again. "They're in there."

He opens the clasp, pulls out the envelope, and scans the images front and back. "We're just kissing. Thank fuck." He lets out a sigh of relief.

"Cal, someone was watching us. No matter what we were

doing, that's an intimate moment between the two of us and I don't want to share it with anyone, least of all Justin, not to mention that scum."

"I know, I know, baby." He tears the picture in two and again as his anger gets the better of him. "I'll sort it, you don't need to worry." He stuffs the small pieces back into the envelope.

"You won't pay them off, will you?"

"Fuck no. They're not getting a penny out of me, or you. Fuck, I haven't even got any money, have you?"

"Only in savings. Cal, how do they know about us? They know where I live. I'm frightened."

He places his hand on my neck, stroking his thumb over my cheek. "Baby, you have to trust me with this."

"I do."

"Then trust me when I say they won't be bothering you again, not when I've finished with them."

"What are you going to do?"

"Nothing you need to worry about. It's me they're trying to get at, not you."

"But it's my mess. If I wasn't having an affair, they wouldn't be doing this."

"I seem to recall myself in those pictures. It's my fucking mess and I'm gonna clean it up."

"I'm sorry Cal."

"You've nothing to be sorry about, don't apologise. Come here." He pulls on my neck, beckoning me closer.

"Cal, someone could be watching us right now." He presses his lips to my forehead.

"I'm gonna go, don't worry, yeah. I'm glad you're better." He takes the envelope with him and gets back into his black Audi, leaving my chest a little lighter than before, allowing me to breathe at least. But nothing can dissipate this rhythmic throb in my temple.

———

I ARRIVE at work and go through my long list of emails and my heart races when I hear his voice.

"Hey."

I swivel my chair and look up to see Cal's smile beaming down on me. Seeing him again brings back all my troubles— not that they went away—I haven't slept much this weekend, but now everything has come to the surface. "It's good to have you back… at work I mean."

"Thanks." I'm not sure how I feel about being back, but I can't hide away forever, especially as I'm no longer ill.

"Have you caught up with your emails? I have some work for you."

"Just give me half an hour."

"Steph, good to see you back," Kelly says as she sits next to me at her desk.

"Thanks, Kelly." I swivel my chair to face her.

"How are you feeling?"

"Good, I'm much better now thanks."

She taps a pile of paperwork on her desk. "I have some stuff to go through with you later."

"Oh, you as well." I'm going to be snowed under with all the work I've missed.

After the usual morning meeting, Kelly hands back some work she was doing for me in my absence. I make my way to the coffee machine. The sweet fresh smell of donuts fills the air and they're all too tempting. Cal stands behind me. My hand trembles as I lift the jug.

"Here, let me." He takes the pot of coffee from my grasp and fills my mug. His hand is swollen and bruised. I look back at his face and notice a cut at the side of his eyebrow. Brushing back a lock of hair, the side of his eye is red and slightly swollen around the cut.

"Cal, what happened?"

"I told you I would sort it."

"Did that guy hurt you?"

A small laugh puffs from his mouth. "He looks much worse than me." I want to kiss his wound better, take his swollen hand in mine and soothe it, and throw my arms around him to thank him properly.

"Here." He hands me my coffee. "They won't be bothering you again."

"Who are they?"

He sighs. "They're friends of Dean's."

"Your mate Dean from school?"

"Yeah. Don't freak out, I was seeing her before. She found out I was seeing you and she's jealous, just trying to cause trouble. The bloke is her druggie brother, who probably thought he could make a few quid." I knew it. Somehow, I just knew she'd been with him. My stomach churns at the thought of them together, and I no longer want a donut or a coffee, for that matter.

"I thought she was your type." My nostrils flare. I place my drink down on the table before I'm tempted to throw it on him, and I chew on the inside of my mouth.

"I don't have a type."

I wave my hand in the air. "Of course you do. You love a girl with dark hair and she had the perfect figure and everything." All I can picture is him kissing the rose on her neck. I gasp, covering my mouth with my hands. "She's that girl from the club?" the memory of him caressing her face comes flooding back and acid creeps into my mouth.

"She was there, yeah." He clamps both hands on my

shoulders. "Steph, I ended it with her because I wanted you in my bed."

Tears form in the corner of my eye and cling to my lashes. "You said you didn't have a girlfriend."

"I don't. I didn't. She was just someone I fucked."

My stomach curdles. "I can't believe she took those photos of us." I stamp my foot and clench my fists at my side.

He pinches his eyebrow where his piercing used to be. "You don't need to worry. They have no more photos of us. I deleted them all."

I dab the corners of my eyes with my finger, removing the drops of moisture from there. "I haven't been able to stop thinking about it."

"I can tell. You look like shit."

"Thanks." My palms graze over my face and grip my neck.

Cal moves my hair from my ear and whispers, "Even when you look like shit, you're still beautiful." The words course through my blood, igniting each cell one by one, and I draw in a breath. He smiles and walks back to his seat without a care in the world. I hope I've got nothing more to worry about. The thought of someone violating our private moments is excruciating.

I stay in at lunch to catch up on work, and Cal brings me a sandwich from the corner shop. He also sits at his desk, working through his break.

"Why didn't you go to the pub with the others?" I bite into my egg mayo on brown granary bread.

He types away on his keyboard, and his eyes don't leave the screen. "I have a lot of work to catch up on."

"How come?" I say with a mouthful of bread.

"Just busy." He's not giving much away. I continue to do my work. We're alone in the office, and I miss him trying it on with me. After all the moaning I did, wanting us to be friends. Now all I want is for him to take my face in his hands and kiss me. I'm such an idiot.

Concentrating on work seems impossible. I think of all the things I want to do. I may as well have gone to the pub, as I won't get much work done. He tucks a loose black wave behind his ear, making me want to run my fingers through his hair while he's on top of me, or beneath me. I'm not fussy. But I'm grateful to him for respecting my wishes, which only makes me love him more.

I stand to get another coffee. "Do you want a refill?"

"Yeah, please."

I corner the desk to get his cup and glance at the florist project on his computer screen. "Weren't you going to hand this over to me?"

He waves his hand, batting me away from his screen. "It's cool. I'm doing it now. You have too much on."

"Is this why you're here working through lunch?"

"It's all right. Kelly gave you enough. You've plenty to catch up on."

"Cal, you didn't have to do my work for me, I can deal with it."

"I've started now, so I'll finish. I wasn't gonna let you sit here and catch up with all that work on your own."

"Thank you."

I get him a fresh coffee and continue with my work. He was always the same at university, helping me. He put more effort into my work than his own; always selfless like that. One of the many things I love about him.

CHAPTER
Twenty six

It's been ten days since he's kissed me; ten long boring days, and with each day I find it only gets harder. I know it's for the best, but my body tells me otherwise. It's the last week before Christmas, and I'm still catching up at work. But I need a break. I go to the pub for lunch today. My shoulders and neck are killing me from sitting at my desk for so long. Kelly fills me in on her love life; things are still going strong with her latest conquest. Callum seems to give me space and sits a few seats down next to James. Everyone is talking about the office Christmas party, which is on Friday—the last day before breaking up for the holidays.

I turn to Kelly. "I'm not sure what to wear."

Cal buts in. "It's nothing special. Everyone gets drunk in the office, and we have a buffet, then we go to a club after."

Kelly rolls her eyes at him. "That doesn't mean we don't want to look our best." She pulls out her phone and scrolls through her photos. "I'm wearing a silver, sparkly dress. It's Christmas after all." She shows me the dress she bought online.

"That's stunning." I chew on my lip and think about what I can wear.

Chris takes a swig of his pint, leaving a frothy moustache above his mouth. "I can't believe Jerry's using this Christmas bash as your leaving party, mate. Talk about a tight bastard. I thought he would at least give you a proper send-off after working here for all these years."

Cal immediately looks at me. I watch his Adam's apple bob as he gulps. He turns to Chris. "Yeah, tight fucker."

I look at Kelly, squishing my eyebrows together, then glance at Chris. "What do you mean?"

Chris wipes his frothy lip. "What about?"

"Whose leaving party?" There's a ringing in my ears, and my throat's gone dry.

Chris widens his eyes at Cal, and his mouth gapes. He looks back at me. "Don't you know?"

My heart rate picks up a pace. "Know what?" I glance between Cal, Kelly, James and Chris, waiting for an explanation. My breathing speeds up with every passing second as my mind fills with many scenarios.

Cal clears his throat. "I handed my notice in."

I blink rapidly, seeing spots in my vision. "When?"

He sighs. "Last week." A hand runs down his face. "When you were poorly."

My mouth gapes. Moisture builds on my hands and face. "So when are you leaving?" I pick up my drink and the ice cubes rattle against the glass. I gulp the liquid down my dry throat, wondering how many more weeks, days, hours I will have left with my man.

He scratches his unshaven jaw. "Friday. After the Christmas party."

The pressure builds behind my eyes. The rest of the room seems to have blurred, and the only person I can see is him. Nobody else matters.

"Were you ever going to tell me?" My voice wobbles.

He lets out a breath and bows his head. "Of course, I was gonna tell you."

"When? You could have told me last week."

"I didn't find the right time to tell you last week." He lifts his pint to his mouth, knocking back the remaining liquid, and wipes his lips on his sleeve.

"Why? I mean, why are you leaving?"

James pipes up. "Yeah, why are you leaving, mate? You're like part of the furniture."

He shrugs. "I was just ready for another challenge. I've been here too long."

"I thought you liked it here," James says. I watch the two of them as they talk.

"I did. I mean I do, just time for a change." Cal's eyes don't leave mine.

"Jerry's a cheapskate. Make sure you get your fair share of booze. I would take a couple of bottles home with you, his best whiskey." James laughs.

"So, do you have another job?"

"Yeah, I got a job in the city."

My heart sinks. Just when I was getting used to us being friends. Well, I wasn't getting used to it, but still. I try to keep my composure and eat my lunch.

Back at the office, I haven't been able to think straight all afternoon. I can't believe he's leaving and worst of all, it's been an entire week, and he hasn't mentioned it.

"How long has he been looking for another job?" I ask Kelly when Cal leaves his desk.

"He said he'd been looking for about six weeks." My heart breaks even more, knowing he's been looking to leave for so long.

We don't speak for the rest of the day, and when I walk into the car park, he's parked next to me again. My palm slams on the roof of my Suzuki. The flesh stings against the cold metal. I'm not even sure why I'm upset. Is it because he's actually leaving, or because he didn't tell me?

The car park is emptying, and he's the last one out. I can't go home without saying something. I have to know. "It's me, isn't it?"

He stops next to his car door, not too far from me. "What do you mean?"

"The reason you're leaving. It's because of me, isn't it?"

He sighs. "Yeah."

"When did you start looking for another job?"

He shrugs his shoulders. "It was ages ago."

"After I started working here?" My throat closes up.

"I had an interview after the club event." He leans back against his car.

"Before we slept together?" The thought of him wanting to leave because of me stabs me in the chest.

He folds his arms. "Yeah, but what's that got to do with anything?"

"I'm just trying to work out why you wanted to leave. It seems odd that you started looking for another job as soon as I started working here."

"I started looking for another job because I couldn't stand to be around you."

My entire body tenses. "If you couldn't stand to be around me, then why did you even sleep with me again?" I choke back a sob.

He stands straight, and his hand strokes my arm. "I meant because I can't bear to see you every day."

"That makes little sense." I gaze into his tired eyes. The cut and bruise has almost healed from his temple.

"I can't stand to see you every day and not be able to touch you. Before we slept together, I wanted you. I'd already fallen back in love with you."

A tear escapes me, and he places his hand on my cheek and wipes it away with his thumb. I lean my face into his hand and kiss his palm.

"You make it so easy to love you, Steph. And so damn difficult at the same time." His hand trembles against my cheek.

"Cal," I whisper, inching closer to him. Our lips almost touch. I want to kiss him and tell him he can touch me whenever he likes and that I'm his. I've always been his. His breath reaches my lips. My heart races, and my breathing is heavy. I brush his lips ever so slightly, hoping he will kiss me.

He pulls his head back slightly. "You made me promise we would be friends."

"Kiss me," I beg.

His hands cup my face, and his thumbs wipe the tears from my cheek. "Friends don't kiss each other, Steph."

"You know I always say stupid stuff."

"Yeah, idiotic stuff. You don't know how hard it is to keep my hands to myself." Oh, but I do. I know all too well.

As much as I want him, I respect him for being stronger than I am. I bury my head in his shoulder. My fist clenches, and I hit his solid chest. I love this man, but I hate him for how he makes me feel. I hate wanting him. He left me and we could have been together this whole time if he wasn't so friggin' selfish. I wouldn't have to worry about my family seeing photos of us, or carry this guilt that seems to have become a part of me. "I wondered how long it would be before you left me again."

He holds me tight, his lips brush against my ear, and his breath falls on my neck. "I'm doing this for you, Steph. I want you to be happy. All I do is make you miserable. I won't fuck up your life again." His arms wrap around my back.

"I love you."

When he doesn't say it back, the emptiness grows in my chest. I kiss his shoulder, where my head rests, then move up to his neck. The hint of his aftershave lingers on his skin, and I press my lips against his flesh there, before grazing my lips along his stubble. He stays still like a statue, like every bone in his body is fighting me. How the tables have turned. It's usually me fighting off his affection. I sigh and hug him. He holds me tighter.

I eventually and reluctantly pull away. "I have to go."

His eyes are glossy. "I'll see you tomorrow." He gently kisses my forehead.

"Yeah, see you." I turn and get in my car. As I drive, the tears drip like a leaky tap. The worst thing is that I can't talk to anyone about this. Not even Claire. She thinks I'm still battling with just working alongside him every day. Kelly's loyalties are with Cal. I'm sure she blames me for his leaving. She already said she hopes I know what I'm doing. Of course, I don't have a clue what I'm doing. I'm being ruled by my heart, not my head. I know this is for the best; it will make things so much easier to not have to see him every day and worry about people finding out, and the shame I feel may actually become tolerable. But knowing I've caused him to leave a job that he loves only amplifies my guilt; it should be me going, not him.

ARRIVING at my slimming class from work, I touch up my makeup before entering the hall so I don't look like a panda. Several deep breaths later, and I take my place in the queue. I'm not anxious today; I really do have bigger fish to fry. My stomach grumbles, thinking of fish; I may call at the chippy after weigh-in. I neatly place my coat, cardigan and bag on an empty chair, slip off my shoes and step on the scales, looking down to see the damage—I'm pleasantly surprised.

"Three-pound off, Steph," Laura, the group leader, sings my praises. "Well done, that's fantastic."

A smile spreads across my face for the first time today. "Thank you." On my mini-high, I decide to take a seat in the group. I watch as everyone else mounts the dreaded weighing scales, one by one. Some cheerful faces, some sad, some angry. The struggle is real. June, an older woman, sits next to me. "Have you had a good week, love?" she asks.

"Not really." I sigh. "I was poorly last week, and now I have a ton of work to catch up on, and I just found out my colleague is leaving..." Then I realise she meant weight-wise. Poor woman. I was offloading all my problems onto her. "I lost three-pound. How about you?"

"Ooh, fabulous." She smiles. "I managed one pound off this week."

"That's good."

Laura talks to the group, her usual spiel. This week is all about planning for the Christmas period, seeing as this is the last weigh-in before the festivities begin.

She continues with her guilt-free holiday survival guide.

"Number one, when you go to your work Christmas party or you're going to family members or friends for that Christmas buffet, take a salad with you, or another veggie type of dish, some cucumber and celery sticks."

Yeah, like that's going to happen.

"Or eat before you go."

Right, because that's going to stop us attacking the buffet. That would just result in eating twice. I don't think so, Laura.

"Number two, when you're at that party, drive. This will stop you drinking alcohol, cutting down on your calories and when you're sober, you're much more likely to stay in control."

I nod. This one makes sense. I might do this. Usually, when I'm out, my mouth says wine, but my dress is crying out, 'for the love of God, WOMAN, drink water.'

"Number three, make time for physical activity. This will make you feel better and help with your weight loss."

True, I know I always feel better after a good workout, not that I work out. *The only activity you do takes place in the bedroom or Cal's car.* My mind wanders, thinking about how good it felt to be with him, how his touch ignites my very soul like a jolt of electricity bringing me back to life. His hard tongue lapping around mine makes my body melt into his and we are one. When he makes love to me, we meet on another plane, a spiritual realm not of this world. A surge of light strikes through my centre, and it is so beautiful, magical, and utterly rapturous.

Laura's voice snaps me out of my moment. She's wrapping up her speech. Damn, I missed it.

"Remember." She waves her finger. "Nothing tastes as good as being thin feels."

She's clearly never had one of my mum's chocolate orange cheesecakes.

She goes around the group, celebrating or commiserating everyone's results. "And a round of applause for Steph; she's lost three-pound this week." The group all clap and oooh and ah, and I smile at Laura. It's nice to get praise, although I don't feel I've earned it. "Tell us, Steph, what've you done to lose three-pound?"

My hands crumple the hem of my skirt around my knees. "Well, I've been poorly. I couldn't eat much at all last week. I couldn't even swallow."

"Oh, I'm sorry to hear that, but it seems to have benefited you."

I always said I needed to sew my mouth up. Perhaps she's right, a sore throat works just as well. "Yes."

"Think about the holiday survival guide and hopefully we will all see *less* of you when you return." I doubt that.

"Thank you." I nod politely. There's no way I'm missing out on all the lovely treats that Christmas offers; it only comes but once a year. Everyone is so focused on what they're eating between Christmas Day and New Year's Day. It's all the stuff they eat between New Year's Day and Christmas Day that they should worry about.

A FEW DAYS PASS, and I still haven't got used to the idea of Callum leaving. I hope the Christmas break will help take my mind off him and make it easier. I need to wrap everything up before the holidays. The office empties. I'm still catching up with work from when I was ill.

"Aren't you going home?" Cal asks.

"I have to finish this off. I promised the client they would have it today."

"Do you need help?"

"It's okay, you go."

"I'll help you. What are you working on?" He stands behind me and looks at my screen.

"These brand guidelines. I need to complete the last three pages."

Chris is the last one to go. "See you tomorrow, folks."

"Bye," we both say in unison.

A shooting pain goes from my neck to my arm. I rub the

back of my shoulder and sigh, massaging the pain in my aching muscle.

He moves my hair to one side. "What's wrong?"

"My neck and shoulder hurt. I've been sitting at this desk for too long." Although I've had this pain since I received the photos of us. The stress of it all seems to have manifested itself in the crook of my neck and nothing I do relieves the tension.

His fingers graze my skin, sending sparks of electricity down my spine.

I turn my head towards him. "What are you doing?"

"Shh." His large hands massage my shoulders.

"Cal," I moan as his fingers dig into my neck and every muscle in my body relaxes under his touch. "You said we weren't doing this anymore."

"I just want to give my woman a massage." My woman. I want to be his woman in every way.

My thoughts have already positioned our lips together. His thumb rubs at the back of my neck and my head leans back into his warm chest. Bending forwards, brushing his lips against my flesh, his hair tickles my shoulder, making my thoughts scatter.

He moves my bra strap and nips my skin there. "Does that feel better?"

"Yes." I moan and turn my head, wrapping my fingers around his neck, drawing his lips to mine. He pulls away and stands straight. I stand along with him, my hands clasp his neck to bring him back to me.

He resists. A smirk plays in the corner of his mouth. "It sucks to want something you can't have, doesn't it?"

Ugh. This is like uni all over again, only fewer tears.

"Cal." I try to kiss him again. "Stop teasing me."

"You can't have your cake and eat it, Steph."

"Isn't that what you do with cake?" I stand on my tiptoes and trail my lips along his jaw. "I've never understood that phrase."

He chuckles. "You can't have two good things, Steph."

I flinch back to take in his expression. Is he serious or just teasing? "I like a traditional jam sponge, but I love fudge cake."

"And I'm the fudge?"

"Death by chocolate." I giggle, then try to kiss him again, but his lips stay shut.

"I told you before. Friends don't kiss each other, Steph."

"Cal, you teased me. That's not fair." My shoulders curl forwards.

"You're the one that keeps trying to kiss me."

I swat his chest. "Only after you kissed my shoulder."

"I didn't kiss your shoulder, I bit it." He laughs.

"Same thing." Suddenly my face feels incredibly hot. Is he seriously turning me down?

He runs his hands up and down my arms. "I couldn't help myself; your body was crying out to be touched."

I fist his shirt and pull him towards me. "You know I can't resist you when you touch me like that."

"I want to touch you like that every fucking day; that's the problem. You're like a strawberry tart."

"Hey." I swat at his arm.

He grips my waist. "You're red velvet cake with butter frosting." His lips press against my nose. "Or a passion fruit cheesecake."

I wrap my arms around him and hug him tighter than I've ever hugged him. How can I live without him again? His arms wrap around my waist, and he kisses my hair.

"Baby, you drive me crazy. You know that, don't you?" He sighs. "The sooner I leave this job, the better."

I squeeze him tighter. I can't think about him leaving work, not yet.

He lightly pats my bottom. "Email me the work, and I'll finish it for you tonight. You get off home to your kids."

"Cal, I can sort it."

"Go home. I've got nothing planned tonight. It will only take me half an hour."

His chocolate brown eyes draw me in like a bee drawn to nectar, and I agree with him. If only he was offering something else. "Thank's Cal."

Once home, I look through my wardrobe for an outfit to wear tomorrow for the Christmas party. I have a red dress from last Christmas that's perfect; I hope it still fits. Pulling it from the hanger, I unhook it and try it on. Phew, it fits better than it did before. My tummy looks flatter, and it isn't as tight around my arse. It just needs an iron.

Justin is watching TV and notices me ironing. "Can you iron my clothes for Saturday night while you're at it, love?"

"What are you wearing?"

He waves a hand. "Anything, just pick a shirt, I'm not fussed."

I run back upstairs, looking for something for Justin to wear to his annual Christmas jolly with the lads from the building site. A white shirt with a faint blue pattern will do, and his smart dark denim jeans. After ironing and hanging up our clothes, I find the stockings that I'd tucked away in the back of my underwear drawer. I know Cal won't be able to resist me in these.

CHAPTER
Twenty seven

Justin's in the bathroom, investigating a small leak in the shower. He's finished work for the Christmas break and school has already broken up.

I stand in the bathroom door. "I'm off then."

"Are you still driving?"

"My slimming group advised it best to drive, so I'm not tempted to overindulge. I can enjoy myself without having a drink. Besides, you don't want to be dragging the kids out tonight if it's late."

"Good idea." He doesn't look up and continues to glide his hand over the pipes.

I slip on my red suede wedge shoes that pair with my red wrap knee length dress. The sleeves come past my elbows and it crosses over where my cleavage is, showing a little of my breast. Justin barely noticed the effort I've made, and I wonder if I made the right choice in my outfit. "Bye, kids," I shout. They're both watching a Santa film and grunt.

I arrive at work to find most people already here. I meander towards the coat stand behind Cal's desk, inhaling his fresh minty scent. His eyes look me up and down as he tucks his unruly hair behind his ears.

"Wow. You look..." He pauses and smiles. I wish he'd finished the sentence. After all, I only wore this dress for him.

I never put this much effort in at my last job. Justin thinks it's because this job is high powered and trendy, but it's not much different, really. Except Cal—he's the difference—the real reason I jump out of bed and into the shower each morning, and rush to get here, even if it is just to see his smile. I doubt I'll have the same enthusiasm when he leaves.

After hanging up my coat, his hand catches my leg. His fingers glide up my thigh over the soft fabric of my dress. I bite my lip and hold my breath, gazing at him over my shoulder. His thumb catches the outline of my suspender clip. He sucks in a breath, and his eyes widen.

Cal follows me to the coffee machine. I collect a cup and pour a drink. The hairs prick up on the back of my neck when he stands behind me.

"What the fuck do you think you're doing, wearing these on my last day?" He twangs the stocking clip at the back of my thigh, and it thrums in my centre.

Turning around, my chest heaves. I'm so close to his lips. "Call it a little leaving gift." I bite my lip. "You look good too, by the way." He looks more than good in his signature black skinny jeans, a crisp white shirt, which is open at the neck and rolled up to his elbow, revealing his tattooed sleeve. I tap his chest with the palm of my hand, feeling the taught muscle there, before I swagger back to my desk. My work needs to be completed by 5pm today as I won't be back until after New Year. As I go through my emails, I get a new one from Cal. He sends emails regularly with work-related stuff, but when I catch his eye, he quirks a grin. I click on the little envelope. 'So when do I get my leaving gift?'

A smile spreads across my face and I type back, 'You said I can't have my cake and eat it.'

He replies within seconds. 'You know what those stockings do to me, and every time I look at you, my cock twitches.' The heat rises in my cheeks and goes down to my… erm. How can I respond to that?

Like an idiot, I type, 'You know our emails are copied onto the server, right?' Dammit, I wish I could have sent something back equally hot, but I can't think of what to say, and I'm shitting anyone seeing these emails. He's still smirking. No doubt he's logging on to the server right now to delete said emails. I hope so anyway.

The afternoon is busy. We're all on a high and everyone is laughing and chatting away as we finalise everything. By the time the drinks are out, I'm done with enough time to send personal emails to all my clients wishing them a merry Christmas and a happy New Year.

An array of wine, champagne, spirits, soft drinks and bottled water adorns the breakfast table. Kelly places a glass of prosecco into my hand. I don't deny it; one glass won't hurt. The taste is exquisite, and I can tell it's expensive. Other departments have joined us and gathered around the drinks table, helping themselves. The lights go dull and music plays.

Cal comes over to me; I haven't seen him for the last hour. Everyone wants a piece of him on his last day. "Hey, you're fucking killing me in this dress." His palm rests on the small of my back.

"Hi, nice to see you too." I smirk and silently reward myself for choosing this outfit today.

"Let me get you another drink."

"I'm driving."

He looks at me like I've grown another head. "I thought you'd get a lift tonight."

"Did you now? You thought you could get me drunk and take advantage, didn't you?" I giggle.

His warm breath carries the scent of whiskey. "You know

me too well." He leans in closer, his lips brush my ear. "I can still take advantage without getting you drunk."

I gasp, but I love this naughty side of him. "How do you plan to take advantage of me when we're just friends now?" I glance up through my long lashes to see the corner of his mouth curve.

"I'm gonna take you into one of these conference rooms, bend you over the table and fuck you in this dress." The throb in my knickers returns, and I hope he will follow through with this.

"But friends don't fuck each other, Cal." I bite my lip to stop my smile from widening. What an idiot I am. One glass of champagne, and I lose all self-control. Or is it his dirty mouth that makes me so unrestrained?

"This friend does, just for tonight. I'm gonna fuck your brains out one last time."

I suck in a breath. The bubbles in the champagne have gone straight to my head, making me dizzy. He's still waiting for a response, most likely thinking I'll reply with something to contradict him as I did before our London trip, but I can't. This may be my last night with him. My mouth speaks for me before my brain can gather the words. "Do you promise?"

His eyes go wide, like I've just given him a backstage pass to a rock gig. "Fuck Steph, yes I can assure you."

My lips brush against his ear as I whisper, "I'm so wet right now."

He grins. "Stop it. You're making me hard."

The smile etched on my face is now making my jaw ache. "I want you to feel the throb between your legs like I am."

"I told you to stop it. Don't make me spank you later." His gravelly voice makes my muscles clench.

"Oh, please, please spank me." I pant the words as a flicker surges through my core just thinking about it.

His eyes widen and gleam like a bronze bauble on a Christmas tree. "You want me to spank you?"

My body temperature increases like the heat rising up a chimney from a crackling log fire. "Well, it is Christmas."

"And you're on the naughty list." His sinister grin has me crumbling at his mercy.

"I can't wait much longer, Cal." I bite my lip and glance into his mischievous eyes.

The caterers arrive, wheeling in two long tables of buffet-style food. "You'll have to wait, baby. I need food." He winks and grabs a plate.

The smell fills the air, and it looks delicious. My tummy rumbles. I follow Cal, piling my plate with mini salmon skewers, mini sliders, quiche, not forgetting a handful of salad just to look healthy and not like a total pig. The sweet treats look even better, and I grab a selection of desserts. With both hands full, I make my way to a spare table in an empty conference room. Cal follows me in along with a bloke from finance and a lady from HR.

The salmon is cooked to perfection, coated in a chilli glaze. The mini quiche is still warm with goat's cheese and bacon filling.

"I didn't see them salmon skewers, let's try one." He goes to take one from my plate, and I tap his hand away.

"No way, you know I don't share food." I bite into the remaining quiche.

"You won't want to share one of my cheese, bacon and sausage rolls, then?" He bites into a small pastry, and I watch the melted cheese strings fall from the middle of the casing and my mouth waters.

"How did I miss them? I thought they were sausage rolls. Can I have one?"

He laughs. "No, I don't share food."

"Swap?"

He picks one of the cheese rolls from his plate and brings it to my mouth. I take a bite. The pastry flakes off, crumbling and melting on my tongue, and the cheese is strong with chopped salty bacon mixed in.

"I thought you'd like that."

I pick up my salmon skewer and watch him bite it from the stick bit by bit. With every bite, I imagine him nipping my flesh.

"Are you not eating your salad?" he asks.

Does he know me at all? "No, do you want it?"

He slides it from my plate onto his ham roll. "Do you remember the last Christmas we were together?" He tucks into his ham salad filled cob.

"Yes," I lie. I remember bits, but not much. I can't even remember what he bought me for Christmas. It must have been another memory that I erased from my mind. It seems I erased all the good times and focused more on the bad. In my head, I had to hate him. It made it easier to get over him, but I wish I could remember.

"I can remember New Year's, and your twentieth birthday."

"It was a good night, wasn't it?" He chews down his food.

"It's one of the last wonderful memories I have before everything went sour." I pick up a miniature chocolate log and stare at Rudolph's face on the end.

"Don't talk about it." Cal wipes his hands on a napkin. "I don't want to think about any of that shit that I put you through, not tonight, baby."

I swallow down the cake and nod in agreement, not wanting to bring up those memories, either.

"I'm gonna get another drink."

Our other colleagues leave the conference room, and I

bite into Rudolph's face. Cal comes back with a small glass of whiskey and a bottle of water for me.

"Thank you."

"Why don't you just stay at mine tonight?"

"I can't, Cal. I told Justin I would come home."

"Does he not like you staying out?"

"It's not that. He's expecting me home, that's all."

"Call him, tell him you've had a drink, and you're staying over."

"Cal."

"What? I'm gonna fuck you, anyway. What's the big deal?"

"I don't want to put us in another predicament like before. What if someone is watching us?"

"I told you, that's all over with. You don't need to worry about that. Nobody is watching us, Steph, I promise. You can trust me on this."

Cal kisses me below my ear. "Tonight you're mine. I want this dress on my bedroom floor." The classic line. Although cheesy, it still makes my spine tingle. Why didn't I arrange to sleep over? Justin would never know. I should've told him I was sleeping at a colleague's.

"Call him." He plants soft kisses along my jaw. "Tell him you're staying at Kelly's." His desire to seduce me is enough to make me want him.

"Cal." I scan the room one more time to check we're alone before pressing my lips to his. He slips his tongue into my mouth, and it's what I've yearned for. The tingling in my stomach multiplies. My head clouds. I can't get enough of his lips, like a hot Christmas pudding set aflame. My tongue swirls around his, and I taste the alcohol, reminding me of a warm brandy sauce.

He stands, pulling me with him, and leads me to a small

office that's been turned into an informal meeting room. A soft glow from the street lamp illuminates the room, shining through the trees outside the window. Cal locks the door behind him and draws the opaque blind. As I step back, my thighs collide into a desk. I lean against it as he comes towards me. Our lips lock once more, sending sparks of elation through my bloodstream, exciting my very soul.

He reaches down with both hands and lifts my dress, feeling my stockings as his hand glides up my thigh. "Fucking hell, Steph." Breathing heavily into my mouth, he digs his fingers into the top of the elastic of my lace knickers and tugs them down. I shuffle my bottom on the desk. He unclips the straps from my stockings and my panties drop onto the floor.

I tug his shirt, pulling him closer. "I'm ready for my spanking now, Santa." A giggle escapes me and I bite my lip.

His sneaky smile makes my breath hitch as two fingers slide into my slick opening. "You're so naughty… and wet. So fucking wet."

I let out a moan into his mouth as his fingers go deeper. After unbuckling his belt, I try to pull his jeans down, but they're tight. He removes his fingers and I whimper at the loss of his touch. He grabs hold of the denim fabric, yanking them down along with his boxers. With his powerful arms, he lifts me off the desk, flipping me around so I can feel his hardness pressing into my bottom. His lips brush along my neck while a hand goes back to my folds. His other hand digs down my dress into my bra to squeeze at my breast. "I've missed these puppies."

He sucks the skin on the back of my neck. My dress bunches around my waist. "Bend over," he growls. Removing his palm from my breast, he pushes me down, pressing his hand between my shoulder blades. My palms rest against the cool wooden desk. He spreads my legs with his knees and rubs his erection against the tight tulip between my cheeks. A spasm rocks through me, feeling him there. He moves his length down into my wet heat. "You've got me right where you want me." He rams into me. "Haven't you?"

"Yes." I suck in a breath before moaning his name, then cover my mouth, hoping nobody is outside the room.

A loud snap jolts my core as his hand collides with my arse. The sting sparks a mini-explosion like the banging of a Christmas cracker deep in my centre.

Elvis rings out through the office floor, 'Santa Claus is Back in Town'. *He certainly is*. Cal holds onto my hips and pushes in deeper.

"You knew what you'd do to me in this dress and these fucking stockings." He pulls out slowly, then pounds hard. "Didn't you?" he growls.

"Yes." My breathy voice is something between a moan and a whisper, trying to keep my cries contained to this room.

Slap. His palm smacks my arse cheek, forcing me further up the desk. The strike vibrates around my body, reaching my toes.

His finger circles and pinches my clitoris, causing me to bite down on my hand. "You're so fucking bad, Steph, tempting me like this." His thrusts get faster and deeper. "Aren't you?"

"Yes." The pressure builds, and I rest my head on my arm, screwing my eyes shut.

Crack. His palm burns my flesh and the heat travels through my body, creating a chemical reaction that has me salivating for more. He was right. I always liked it this way, bent over like this. He grunts each time he pushes deeper, driving into me with hard, swift strokes. His fingers twist in my hair, and he tugs my curls, making my walls clench.

"Stephanie." He spills into me, and I contract around him, panting his name. He leans over while my orgasm abates. "Stay with me tonight, Steph." His voice trembles.

My body rests limp on the desk. I turn my head to look into his deep, rich eyes with a hint of heat, swirling around his pupils like a spicy mulled wine warming on the stove. "I want to."

"Then stay with me, just one more night." He pulls out of me and picks up my panties, using them to wipe between my thighs.

I kiss his lips tenderly now the rush of passion has ceased. "I'll stay."

A smile spreads on his face, reaching his twinkling eyes. Still holding my lace knickers in his hand, he pulls up his jeans and stuffs them in his pocket. I reattach my stockings to the clips on the garter belt and tidy myself up, while I think about calling Justin. I'm not ready to make that call yet.

Another drink, a glass of champagne; I have some catching up to do now that I've decided I'm not driving. But I don't want to drink too much, if this is my last night with Cal. I want to remember it; every detail of him touching me, every kiss, every stroke, every word to leave his lips. I want to remember it all.

"I thought you'd gone, Steph," Kelly says while I get a champagne.

"Not yet." I bring the sparkling liquid to my lips.

She gives me that look, the one where the corner of her mouth turns upwards. "Where did you and Cal disappear to?"

I smile, reeling from the memory of him inside of me, and I'm now conscious of the fact that my dirty knickers are in his jean pocket. Hopefully not the same side to where he keeps his phone. That could be awkward if he got a call and pulls out my red lace panties along with his vibrating mobile. "I'm staying at his tonight."

"Is that why you drove?" She pours herself a wine.

"No, not at all. I didn't plan it, but I figure this will be the last time." I sigh, looking down at my drink, not wanting this to be the last time, knowing I've been miserable these last few weeks. Maybe I can leave Justin. My heart races at the thought. I have to get past Christmas first. I can't spoil the holidays for everyone.

She points her wine glass towards me. "You said that after London."

I look down and shuffle on my feet. Cal must have confided in her the week I was poorly. "I'm sorry Kelly, I know you must hate me for all this."

"I don't hate you, Steph. I just don't understand you."

"What don't you understand?" I pull my eyebrows together.

"I don't get how you can say you love your husband, but yet you sleep with Callum and say you love Callum but won't leave your husband. You want the best of both worlds."

I know she has a point. "I love Callum more than I've ever loved any man, but I love my kids more. It's them that tie me to Justin, and Callum knew from the beginning I wouldn't break my family up."

"I'm trying to understand. Cal is my friend, and I don't enjoy seeing him hurt, that's all." She picks at the buffet table and pops a mini scotch egg in her mouth.

How ironic that it is now me doing the hurting. "I know, and I'm sorry. I never meant for him to get another job. It should be me leaving."

"We'll miss him. I just hope he'll be all right. I've never seen him so down like he was when you were off sick, not even after he broke up with his ex."

"He will be fine, he's a big boy." I giggle. If only Kelly knew how big he actually is. Maybe she does. "Have you and Callum, ever... you know?"

"Ew, gosh no, gross. He's well and truly friend-zoned, believe me." She laughs and I laugh along, letting out a sigh of relief.

Cal walks over after topping up his whiskey. "What are you two giggling about?" His eyes are vibrant. I could get lost looking into his hypnotising, fierce, brown eyes that mesmerise my soul as specs of red and amber dance around his dark pupils.

"Nothing, I was just asking Steph where you got to. I thought you'd gone."

He grins again, biting his lip, looking between the two of us. I glance at his jean pocket. Red fabric pokes out against the black denim. My eyes go wide. I try to signal to him. It takes several nods and bulging eyes before he realises and tucks them further into his pocket while laughing. He pulls me to one side and whispers, "You've no idea how much my cock aches knowing you're not wearing any knickers right now."

I sip on my champagne and glance down at his crotch and smile at a larger bulge than usual. "The fact that you have my knickers in your pocket is turning me on too."

"You're not getting them back, you know."

"What?"

"I'm keeping them as a souvenir."

I spit my drink back in the glass and the bubbles fizz up my nose. "You know, this is becoming a regular thing. First you wanted to keep my stockings, now my knickers. If there's something you want to share, you can tell me."

He smirks. "You can make fun all you like but I'm still keeping them."

"You can have them, but promise me you'll wash them."

He laughs with a mouthful of alcohol, but manages to swallow. "I will."

"Are you sure? I hope you washed that sweater from your car."

He laughs again.

My hand rests firmly on my hip. "You haven't, have you? I bet it's still in your car, isn't it?"

"Yeah, it's still tucked behind the seat." He looks down, chuckling away to himself.

I swat his arm. "You filthy bastard."

"I'll wash it, I promise. I keep forgetting about it."

I wait a few more hours, a few drinks of Dutch courage later, before giving Justin a call. The dial tone matches the ringing in my head, and my ears are burning.

"Steph. What's up?"

"I ended up having a few drinks." My voice is quiet and I hope he can't hear the tremble.

"It's a bit late calling now. I can't drive, I've had a drink." His tone is deeper than usual.

I put on a cheery voice, but it comes out a little high-pitched. "It's okay. Kelly said I could stay at hers."

"Oh." There's a long pause. "I could order you a taxi."

"It's all right. I don't mind staying at Kelly's. She has a spare room, and I'll just drive home tomorrow." The back of my neck itches, and I take in a deep breath.

"So you're staying out again? You're never home lately."

I wipe my sweaty palm on the side of my dress. "Well, I don't moan at you when you go on one of your lads' weekends." He was always out before we started a family. "I'm sorry for wanting to have a life."

"I haven't been on one for ages. I'm too busy babysitting our kids." He huffs out the words.

My body leans against the toilet door. I rub my chest, knowing I should be home. "Justin, I'm sorry. I don't want to argue. Are the kids up?"

"They're asleep."

"I'll come home early in the morning."

"Fine, see you tomorrow then."

"Bye."

I relax my shoulders after spilling my lies. My throat burns with shame, but there's nothing I want more right now than to be in Callum's arms. After pulling myself together, I finally emerge from the toilets and find Cal scanning the room. I walk towards him. His smile reaches his eyes when he sees me.

"Hey, I was getting worried." His arm wraps around my waist.

I flinch my head back to gaze into his eyes. "What for?"

"I thought you might have changed your mind."

"No, are you ready to go?" I want to be alone with him again and make the most of this evening.

"If you want to go now."

"There's nowhere else I would rather be, and I don't want to waste any more time." I grab my coat and sneak out, waiting for Cal to say goodbye to everyone. The night air is crisp, fog materialising with every breath. I button up my knee-length black coat and tie it with the belt around my waist.

He emerges from around the corner with his coat on his arm. "Can you believe Jerry came good with a nice cheque for my leaving gift?"

"I thought he would. You don't have to steal his best whiskey now."

He pulls out two bottles of single malt from under his coat and grins.

I suck in a breath. "You thieving git."

He chuckles. "I didn't nick 'em. He gave them to me." Cal hands me the bottles so he can put his coat on as we walk down the road. "James said it was your idea for everyone to pay towards the boxing club membership?"

"Well, if it was left to James he would have got you a lap dancer for your leaving gift." I raise my brow and glance at him.

"I would have preferred a lap dance, but only if it was you doing the dancing." He bumps my shoulder and titters.

"There was no way you were having a stripper. Besides, I figured with me not around you may not get to workout as much." I hope not anyway.

He takes one of the bottles from me and holds my hand. "I'll definitely use it. I can picture Justin's face while hitting the punch bag." A smile forms in the corner of his mouth.

"You know, they do self-defence classes for kids, too. You could take your girls with you."

"I think they would like that." He interlaces his fingers with mine.

We don't speak for the rest of the way. We don't need to talk. The way his hand clasps mine is enough communication for me to know what he's feeling. I remember what happened the last time we took this walk when the ground was thick with snow. The gymnasts in my stomach are back, only now they're on steroids. I squeeze his hand tighter, and he leans over and kisses my cheek. His lips are hot compared to the cold air biting my face, and the warmth from his kiss radiates throughout my entire body.

Cal pulls out his keys and unlocks the door. He takes the bottles through to the kitchen and places them on the worktop, then takes my coat and hangs it with his.

"Can I get you a drink? I've plenty of whiskey." He nods to the bottles and titters.

"I'm fine, thanks."

His hands rub down my arms and tremble slightly against my skin. "Do you want a hot drink to warm you up?"

"You can warm me up." I pull him close, tugging the hem of his shirt and press my icy hands against the hot flesh on his stomach.

His muscles tense.

"Sorry, too cold?"

He smothers my hands with his. "It's okay, leave them."

He pecks my lips. "I've put the heating on, but I can get you a jumper. Do you want any food?" My fingers circle his chest, hoping to calm his nerves.

"Cal, I'm fine. The only thing I want right now is you." His lips brush against mine. My mouth opens, allowing his tongue to slip inside. The kiss is slow and lingers before he ends it with a peck.

He clears his throat. "Do you want to go to bed?"

I smile and bow my head, but glance up at him through my lashes. "Unless you're going to take me on the kitchen counter."

"That can be arranged." He smirks and the cocky tone of his voice travels straight to my centre, making my cheeks flush. He takes my hand and steers me to the bedroom. I'm almost disappointed, but he's already had me over a table tonight. I want him slow. He turns on the lamp and closes the bedroom door behind us. His hard body presses me against the wall, and his heavy breath falls on my mouth, carrying the scent of whiskey. "I don't want to fuck you tonight."

My chest heaves, matching his ragged breathing.

His hand caresses my cheek, and his thumb runs along my lips. "I need to make love to you."

CHAPTER

"Cal." My eyes gloss over and I gulp as he turns me around. My back rests firmly against his chest. He moves my hair to the side and nuzzles into the crevice between my neck and shoulder, sending a cascade of tingles down my spine like a waterfall rushing straight to my core.

He pulls at the zip that runs along my back. "This dress. When I saw you in this dress, I had to have you tonight." He slides the fabric off my arms, letting it bunch around my hips. His fingers stroke my back as he unhooks my bra, making me squirm and giggle.

"Cal that tickles."

My bra falls to the floor, and he kisses my neck. Cupping both breasts, he tweaks my nipples. I shimmy the dress over my hips and let it pool at my feet.

His hand flows over the lace garter belt around my stomach and slips between my folds. "Does that tickle, too?" He circles the area where all my nerves meet and I moan, resting my head back on his shoulder. He sucks and nips at my earlobe and the spot on my neck that sends a stream of goosebumps gushing over my skin. I need to feel his naked flesh against mine. I turn around and unbutton his shirt with my fumbling fingers. He lifts my chin, forcing me to gaze into his sparkling eyes as if I'm gazing at a sea of stars.

Once I undo the last button, he lets his shirt fall off and presses his chest against me, pinning me against the wall. My breasts smash against him as he takes possession of my mouth. He steps back, taking in several deep breaths, and peels his jeans off along with his boxers, revealing the ink on his toned thigh. Every inch of his body is a work of art. His fingers interlace with mine and he pulls me with him as he walks backwards until he reaches the bed. He slides on top of the sheets and leans against the headboard, pulling me on top. I struggle to take off the suspender belt around my waist.

"Let me." He unhooks the lace belt, tossing it to the floor. Our lips lock. His tongue strokes in slow circular motions. Not the passionate rage that we've become so used to. I roll my hips on top of him, feeling him between my thighs, circling my clitoris on his erection, pressing and rubbing and grinding. Holding his face in my hand, I move my thumb along the scruff of his jaw. Planting soft kisses under his ear.

"Kiss me, Steph. Kiss me like you used to."

I raise my head to look into his pleading eyes. Taking his face in my palms, my lips hug his and my tongue dips and swirls. The sweetness of the alcohol lingers in his mouth and I lap it up, whirling around as if licking the cream from a Yule log. Kissing him like this has me spiralling into the night sky. My head is light and my thoughts scatter. My hand reaches down between us to direct him into me.

"Not yet, baby." The tip of his erection teases my entrance. His hands grip my hips, stopping me from lowering onto him.

His tongue presses flat against my nipple before taking it between his teeth. "Fuck, I wish you still had this pierced."

I giggle, wishing I'd found the silver bar and hoop and worn it again for him. Although I'm not sure I could get it in again after all this time. My bottom wriggles, greedily trying to feel more of him. "Please, Cal. I want you now."

"Soon. Let me take care of you first. I won't last long once I'm inside of you." He lifts me up and turns me over so he's on top. His hair tickles my skin as his gentle lips sail down my body. He takes the hem of the stocking with his teeth and teases them off with the help of his fingers. When he pulls them from my feet, he takes my toes in his mouth and sucks hard. I squirm and giggle, pulling my foot away.

"What's wrong? Does that tickle too?"

"Yes, you know my feet are really ticklish." His smile reaches his eyes, making them twinkle. He trails his lips along my leg and kisses my knee before his gifted tongue makes its way to my swollen bud and he teases me, sucking, nipping, licking at the slickness between my thighs. I watch him get to work. My eyes flutter when he catches my gaze, and he groans into me, making the vibration resonate throughout my entire being.

"Callum." I tug at his unruly hair that's now splayed across my stomach. He stops as I near my climax. I take a breath as he slides up my body.

He comes back to my lips. "I'm going to make love to you now." I wrap my legs around him and pull him into me, the missionary position, but it feels so familiar, like our first time.

My mouth opens and my eyes go wide at the feel of his full length inside me. No matter how many times I have him, I'm always awestruck. He's slow and sensual, moving back and forth, trailing his lips across my jaw.

His breath is hot on my neck. All my senses heighten. Tonight will be trapped in my memory like a jewel locked away in a hidden cave until the last sunset falls. The way his lips feel against my collarbone and the way his fingers dig into my breasts and how he moves his hips, pressing into me slow and gentle. The kind of lovemaking that's truly powerful, filled with devotion, evoking my highest self.

"Steph... Stephanie." The way he pants my name is captivating, mouthing it as he marks my flesh, sucking and nipping at my chest and neck. I move my hand to his forehead and pull his hair back from his face before fisting his thick wavy locks, forcing him to look at me.

"I need you, Cal. You're like oxygen to me."

"Stephanie," he groans, sucking and nipping at my bottom lip. "Fuck, Stephanie. I can't go much longer."

Our bodies move in sync. His eyes don't leave mine. Is this really our last time? I can't bear to think about it. I don't think I can give him up. Not now I've had a taste of what my life could be with him. I can't live without him. He's my North Star, the one that brings me home.

"I'm yours, Cal."

"Stephanie, I'm yours. Always."

His words leave me overflowing with pure divine pleasure. I tighten around him as the joy radiates throughout my body. Fisting his hair tighter, I cry out. My legs weaken and my orgasm takes over. Closing my eyes, colours swirl and dance all around me like a starry night painting brought to life, bringing hope to a dim future.

His movements slow and his dark lashes flutter into focus. He spills into me, nipping at my bottom lip. "Are you all right?"

"I'm more than all right." I bite back at his lips. He stays on top of me, holding his weight with his elbows for a little while longer.

"There are no words to describe my feelings for you, Steph." His lips brush against my cheek.

"I love you." A tear rolls down my temple. Cal wipes it with his thumb before climbing off and laying at my side.

He slides his arm under my head and pulls me into him, stroking my arm just as he used to. "Baby, I love you doesn't come close to how I feel."

We stay like this for a while. I soak up each breath, the rise and fall of his chest, and inhale the scent of his skin.

My fingers trace the feathered bird on his chest. "What are you thinking about?"

"Just stuff." He breathes a long sigh.

I kiss his neck. "What stuff?"

"Us. I always wondered what our kids would be like and who they'd take after."

"I'm not having any more kids." I titter. "Two is more than enough for me. I've just got some of my life back, now they're older."

His stomach muscles shake as he silently chuckles. "I don't mean now, I just think if you'd actually been pregnant that time when you were late, or if we hadn't got the morning-after pill that first time. If we'd got pregnant maybe we'd still be together."

"Right, you would've still left and probably hated me even more than you did."

"You still think I hated you? I never hated you." He sits up and takes a deep breath, running his hand over his face. "I was fucked up." He lets out a breath as he lies down on his back, running his fingers through his hair. "I was going through some fucking mid-life crisis."

"At twenty?" I giggle, making my body rock against him.

"Yeah." I can hear a smile in his voice. "You had us married off. It wasn't enough that we already lived together. Shit, you even planned out how many kids we'd have.

You practically booked the fucking church, and I hadn't even proposed."

"No, I had not." I lift my head and slap his chest. Then snuggle back into him. "Okay, I did have my life planned with you, but you're exaggerating about booking the church. You never complained when I would talk about us moving in together after uni and what sort of future we'd have. You used to talk about it too."

"Not as much as you, and I wasn't ready for all that shit. When you thought you were pregnant, shit got real. I was bricking it."

I sit up, pulling the throw over my chest. "You think I wasn't scared too?" My voice is loud. "I didn't want to be a parent." I take a deep breath and exhale. "Cal, let's not argue about the past."

He grazes my bare back as I sit on the bed. "I got scared, that's all. When you weren't pregnant, I felt like I had a second chance. It was such a close call, and I needed to go. I didn't want to be tied down. I felt suffocated, like my life was over before it began."

Pulling my knees to my chest, I wrap my arms around them. "I thought that's why you left. Amy and Scott thought it too. But you waited two months before ending things and you were mean to me, so mean." My voice trembles and a tear escapes me.

"Come here." He beckons me back into his arms. "I'm sorry." He kisses my forehead as I lie on him. "I'm so fucking sorry, Steph." And at those words, I'm once again putty in his arms. Our legs intertwine. My arm wraps around his chest, and I close my eyes. Before my brain can catch up, my mouth runs away with me yet again.

"I have thought about leaving Justin. I think about nothing else, but it would devastate my kids."

"I can't stand to leave you with him, but I don't want you to choose between me and your kids. Maybe when they're older."

"Cal, what are you saying?"

"I'm saying when you're ready, come find me. Maybe one day I'll get the chance to ask you to marry me like I should have done years ago."

"Cal."

A droplet lands on my forehead. I look up. His eyes are red and glassy. He kisses me again softly, where his tear fell. Closing my eyes, I see a flicker of hope and snuggle into his chest.

SOMETHING TUGS at my hair and tickles my nose as I stir. The soft thrumming, hypnotic sound I listened to as I drifted off to sleep is now bringing me back to consciousness. Opening my eyes, I look up to see his face. I could get used to waking up like this. My head resting on his chest, hair twirling around his fingers, his leg pushed against the apex of my thighs and his morning glory firm against my hip.

"Morning, baby. Did you sleep well?"

"Yes, did you?"

"Best sleep I've had in a while."

"Me too." All life's woes seem to disappear when I'm with him. Even though he causes my emotional turmoil, I'm safe in his arms. "What time is it?" I have to get back to reality at some point.

Cal untangles the lock of hair from his finger and reaches for his phone on the bedside cabinet. "It's just gone eight."

"I have to shower and get going." I sigh and my stomach tightens, thinking of going home.

"Not yet." He pulls me closer, kissing my forehead. "It's still early." His leg pushes further between my thighs while grinding his erection into the fleshy curves of my hip. Bringing his lips to me, he slides his tongue in to caress mine.

"I need to use the bathroom."

"In a minute." He rolls on top, pinning me beneath him while rubbing himself against me, planting kisses of want and need along my jaw. Moving downwards, he engulfs my breast, and laps my nipple with his tongue before taking it between his teeth.

"Cal, I really need to pee."

He smiles, holding my wrists on either side of my head and presses his erection harder against me, which pushes on my stomach, making my need for the bathroom more intense.

"I'm serious, unless you want a golden shower."

He laughs and rolls off. I sit up, gripping the throw from the bottom of the bed and wrap it around my body. Cal tugs at the blanket.

"Hey." I pull the blanket back around me, out of habit more than anything.

"You don't need to take the throw."

"Everyone will see my bare arse, I'm naked." He's right, I don't need the blanket. I'm not crossing any windows on the way to the loo.

He sits up behind me and peels away the sheet. His rough hands massage my breasts as he kisses my neck. "There's only me here, and I love your arse." He pulls me down and leans over and bites the cheek of my bottom.

I giggle. "Cal."

His fingers tickle my waist and he growls, biting down again on my padded cheeks, then sucks the red mark.

"Cal, I really do need to go to the loo."

He lets go of me. I saunter towards the door, leaving the

blanket on the bed. Standing in the doorway, I look over my shoulder at his gorgeous face smiling at me. His eyes wander over my naked body, and I give him a wink before heading to the bathroom.

Using my finger and some toothpaste to clean my teeth, my mouth is fresher, but I need a shower; I wonder if he will join me like he did before. "Cal," I shout.

"Yeah?"

"Do you want to take a shower with me?"

"No, come back to bed."

I contemplate a shower or bed. I'm not comfortable getting back in bed with him without a wash, at least. Remembering which button I need to press from last time, I turn the shower on and quickly wash. When I return to the bedroom wrapped in a towel, Cal's dressed in joggers and sat on the edge of the bed next to a large box.

He taps the cardboard. "I got you something."

CHAPTER Thirty

I stand gawking. "You got me a Christmas present?" I haven't even thought about getting him anything.

"It's not a gift. I haven't bought anything." He opens the brown box. "I thought you might like your stuff back."

I look at the old tatty cardboard. "What stuff?"

"The stuff you sent back to me."

I peer inside. It's full of keepsakes and memories from our teens. He's kept them all these years. I hold a black sweater that I wore of his, and bring it to my nose, breathing in the old familiar scent. I lift out the watch that I bought him and inspect the cracked glass. "How did this happen?"

"I was in the park with the kids and the metal bar on the swing caught my wrist."

My chest swells. "You still wore this when you had your kids?"

"Yeah, I fucking loved that watch. I was gonna get it fixed, but my ex bought me another before I got a chance and I never got round to it."

I pick up a pile of photos of us I'd returned; I'd forgotten most of these memories. "Look how long your hair was here."

He leans towards me and chuckles. "You said I looked

like Chewy. There's one in there with your ridiculous fringe too."

I giggle and swat at his arm.

"I'm keeping that one." He snatches a photo out of my hand with my short fringe.

The next photo is of us at the seaside. "We looked so happy, Cal."

"We were happy, Steph." His lip twitches and his eyes gloss over.

I peck his cheek and look at the next photo of us in bed. "We look like we've just slept together."

"You were always taking photos with that camera of yours."

"I like this one of us." My hair is wild, and he's smoking a joint while I kiss his cheek.

"I want that one." He snatches it out of my hand and smiles, gazing at the image. "You look totally fuckable here."

"Cal." I snatch it back. "You look fuckable too, that's why I like it."

His hand rubs my back. "If we were together, we wouldn't need to argue over who gets them."

My smile turns into a frown. I want that for us. Wiping the tears falling down my cheeks, I select a few of my favourites. I spot his journal that he carried everywhere, but he takes it before I can look inside.

"What's in that thing, anyway?"

"Just notes from class." He stuffs it at the top of his wardrobe.

I spot his old book, *The Green Mile*. "What's your book doing in here?"

"I can't read it without it reminding me of you." He takes the book from the box and scans the tatty cover. "You sobbed your heart out while I read this to you."

I smile at the memory, looking back into the box. "My favourite CD, I wondered what happened to this." Alanis Morissette, *Jagged Little Pill.* "You hated this album, I'm surprised you kept it."

"I wanted to burn all your stuff when you posted them back to me, but I couldn't bring myself to."

"I'm glad, thank you." There's one of my lip balms, probably mouldy now. I smile as I continue to look through. Tickets from the cinema and concerts, a teddy he won for me at the seaside. I pull out a large business studies book. "I can't believe you kept this, all this time, Cal." I open the cover, knowing what was inside the last time I looked. Six pressed roses from the first bouquet he bought me on Valentine's Day. I had wished I could keep them forever, and he placed a few roses between the pages of this thick book.

More tears flow. I look into his own glistening brown eyes and he holds me. I sob into his chest, crying over all the wonderful memories that I'd suppressed for years. I sigh and look down at my feet. "It feels like we're breaking up all over again, and we're not even together."

"I know, baby, I know. I'm here." He holds my head tight against his chest, stroking my cheek with his thumb. I cry for the life we'll never have, until there are no more tears left in me. Cal wipes my stained cheeks and kisses my swollen lips.

"I have to go."

He wraps his arms around me. "Stay. Just a bit longer."

"I told Justin I would be home early."

"I'll cook you a bacon and egg sandwich."

My tummy rumbles at the sound of food. "All right." I wipe my stained cheeks with the towel. "Can I have a coffee too, please?"

"Yeah, I'll do it now." He kisses my puffy lips.

"I'll just sort my hair and makeup out and then come

through." He kisses me again before leaving the room. I pack a shoebox with some photos, my CD and I take the book too with my flowers in. I also sneak his watch, hoping I can get it fixed for him.

After applying a bit of make-up, I brush my hair with my fingers and a little smoothing balm that I carry in my purse. I zip up my dress and pull on his old sweater that fits snug, swaddling me in the familiar feeling of comfort and safety. Cal has made me a coffee and sandwich and he's sitting at the table eating his. I sit down with him. "What do you have planned today?"

"I'm picking my girls up soon." He wipes his mouth and swigs his coffee.

"Listen, Justin is out tonight with his work friends. I was going to see if you wanted to do something later, but... I didn't realise you'd be busy with your girls."

He takes both my hands in his. "You're my girl too."

"Cal." His words send a tingle down my spine. I lick my lips and taste my salty tears.

"Do you want to go to the cinema with my girls and your two kids? We can see that Christmas film we talked about."

"That would be nice. Let me check the times." I take a deep breath. I can't believe I'm going to meet his kids tonight. The gymnasts that have taken up residence in my stomach are practising their forward rolls. "Will you give me a ride to my car soon?"

"Yeah, give me a minute to put some different clothes on."

I bite into my sandwich and the runny yolk runs down my chin and I thank my blessings that Callum didn't see me make a mess of myself. Luckily, it didn't drip on his jumper. I don't think I'm ever going to wash it.

Cal walks back into the kitchen, wearing old jeans and a grey jumper. I grab my purse and pop my shoes on.

I peck his lips before getting in my car. "I'll meet you at the cinema later."

"Yeah see you soon."

<hr>

PULLING INTO THE DRIVEWAY, my stomach roils. The cool air blows up my dress as I walk to the door, reminding me I'm knickerless. I hold the small shoebox under my coat along with Cal's jumper and open the door quietly, hoping I can sneak upstairs.

"You remembered where you live, then?" Justin huffs as I walk into the hall.

My shoulders slump and I stop on the first tread. "Sorry about that. There was so much alcohol. Everyone was drinking, and after a few glasses of champagne the room was spinning." My hands sweat, and I'm suddenly hot.

He shakes his head. "So much for not drinking and staying on track with your diet." His teeth grind together, but he won't argue while the kids are in the living room.

"Please don't, Justin. Not now. I already feel bad and rough." Even though I wasn't drunk at all last night, unless being drunk on Callum counts. "I'm going to get changed."

Once in my bedroom, I take out the watch, then hide the box at the back of my wardrobe. I change out of my dress and put some jeans and a t-shirt on. My curls from yesterday—while a little looser—are still intact. I pop the watch into my pocket and go down to see Justin and the kids.

"What are you up to today, Justin?"

He shrugs and glares at me. "Nothing much. I'm out later. I might stay out all night."

"Please yourself. I need to go into town."

"I'll come with you."

"No, you can't." I snap.

He looks perplexed.

"I need to get your Christmas present."

"You've left it a bit late, haven't you?"

"I've had a lot going on at work." Of course, I have his Christmas gift. I've had it for about three weeks wrapped and everything on a shelf at the top of my wardrobe. I have an excellent gift for him too; it's a new power drill that he's been going on about.

"Okay, I'll just hang out here with the kids. Again."

"I'm sorry. I won't be in town long. If you want, I can take the kids with me." I wrap my arms around his big chest and kiss his cheek, hoping I can soften him a little. Even though doing so makes my insides shudder.

"It's fine. Are you hungry?"

"No, I had a sandwich at Ca-elly's." Just as I say the words, Cairen runs down the hallway, screaming. Cassie is hot on his tail, giggling. Probably the only time I'm grateful for their silly games. "I'm going then, see you later."

"Yeah, see you later."

After parking in town, I make my way to the jeweller's first. An old-fashioned family business that specialise in watch repairs and antique jewellery. They can repair the watch within a few hours. With a bit of time to spare, I have a look around. I buy a shirt for Justin, and I look at shirts for Callum, but decide against it; it's too personal to buy him clothes. I get a few stocking fillers for the kids and treat myself to some new underwear. There's another hour left before I can collect the watch, so I go to a cafe and order a cappuccino. A carrot cake calls my name from the clear glass counter. Diet starts January the first.

I text Cal. 'Are you eating before, or getting food at the cinema?'

He replies minutes later. 'Do you want to get a Maccy's? Meet there around six.'

'Yes. Do you know where Maccy's is here, as it's nowhere near the cinema?'

'Not a fucking clue.' His message makes me laugh, and I text him the address.

'Shall we meet at five? Give us a bit of extra time.' I text.

'Yeah, see you then.'

I put my phone away with my trembling hand; I'm more nervous now about meeting his kids than I was when I saw him at work on my first day. What's wrong with me? They're just kids. I suppose I want them to like me, but it doesn't matter if they don't. It's not like I'll be their future stepmother. I shake it off and go back to the jewellers. The watch is fixed. The lady has also cleaned it up, added a new battery and placed it in a gift box for me.

"Thank you, so much." I make sure I pay with cash; I don't want Justin seeing a bill for this on the credit card statement.

Back at the house, I put the gifts away and make myself another drink. Justin is watching football.

"Hi, I'm going out tonight with the kids. I'm taking them to watch that new Christmas film."

"Fine." His eyes are fixed on the screen and I'm not sure if he's listening while the footballs on, or if he's just not bothered. Either way, I couldn't give a toss and I go to tell the kids we're going to the cinema tonight.

"Kids, we're leaving soon. Make sure you look nice." I shout as I frantically start changing myself. There was nothing wrong with what I was wearing and it's not like he will see my underwear with the kids around. But I put my new underwear on anyway, a cute matching lacy set in bright pink. I pull on some tight grey jeans, which pull me in, in all the right places, and a black jumper that falls slightly off the shoulder, revealing my hot pink bra strap. After touching up my hair and makeup, I zip up my black ankle boots, spray my favourite perfume and I'm done.

"Justin, I'm off," I shout, standing in the living room doorway.

He looks over at the kids and me. "Where are you going again?" I knew he wasn't listening.

"Cinema," Cairen shouts.

"I've hung your clothes for tonight on the door."

"Thanks. Have a good night."

"You too, and don't get wasted." I smile, knowing he will get wasted. The only difference now is that I couldn't really care less if he does or not, but I always say that.

"Yeah, yeah." He waves us off.

As I drive to the restaurant, my hands stick to the steering wheel and those bloody gymnasts are at it again. Somehow, tonight feels like a date. Even if we have got the kids in tow, it's nice to do normal stuff together.

Cassie leans against the back of my seat. "Who are we going with?"

"It's my friend from work and he has two girls, Olivia and Beth, the same age as you two."

"Have I met them before?"

"No, but I'm sure you'll like them." Please, please like them.

"I can't wait for a milkshake, can you, Cassie?" Cairen says.

"No, can I have a chocolate milkshake, Mum?" Cassie asks.

"Yes, you can have whatever you like." I'm sweating as I pull into the car park. I don't see his car yet, so I just go into the restaurant and find a table big enough for the six of us.

CHAPTER
Thirty one

"Are you ordering our food?" Cassie asks, champing at the bit to get her milkshake.

"Not yet, let's wait for Cal."

"Who's Cal?" asks Cairen.

I run my fingers through my fringe to stop it from sticking to my forehead. "Callum, my friend." I'm not exactly sure why I'm so anxious. Is it meeting his kids or him meeting mine properly? *Or that Justin will find out who you've gone to the cinema with.* That annoying girl in my head is there again. I'm not actually doing anything wrong, though. We're meeting tonight as friends, after all. Obviously, nothing's going to happen with the kids around.

Within five minutes, he walks in holding hands with two beautiful dark-haired girls. The corners of his eyes crease when he sees me. "Hey." He gestures for his girls to scoot into the booth. "Girls, this is my friend Steph, and her kids, Cassie and Cairen."

"Hi." I smile at the girls. My kids smile too but in true Cassie and Cairen style, don't speak. They take a while to warm up.

Cal sits opposite me. "Have you ordered?"

"Not yet. I was waiting for you. Shall we order?" He nods

and we walk over to the large digital menu. I stand behind the touch screen and if I pop my head around the side, I can see the kids in front of me, chatting away, and I relax my shoulders.

Cal stands behind me. I scroll through the menu, letting his hands roam over my waist and down to my arse. He palms my cheeks. I suck in a breath when his hands squeeze hard over the denim fabric. "Your arse is so fuckable in these jeans." As he speaks, his lips brush my ear, creating a flicker between my thighs, and my heart races.

My jumper has fallen off my shoulder slightly, revealing my bra strap. He presses his lips against the hot pink fabric. My breath quickens. I want him to wrap his arms around me and nuzzle into my neck. Licking my lips, I turn my head to look at him; my throat is dry as I swallow the air.

"Cal." I pant. He knows what he does to me. He sends me wild with one touch. I bite my lip, imagining our naked bodies in a divine dance.

He rolls his eyes. "I know, I know." Leaning into my ear again, he whispers, "I just want you so bad."

I gulp. "Me too." Then I step aside so he can tap in his order. I glance over at our table where the kids are still talking, and it's a lovely sight to see them getting along. Cal pulls out his wallet from his black skinny jeans and swipes his card on the screen.

We both sit back at our table opposite each other while we wait for our food. He takes off his leather corporal style coat, revealing an AC/DC t-shirt. "Did you do much today?"

"No, well, I went shopping, you?" My hand rests on the table, and he brushes his thumb against my little finger. It's barely noticeable, but powerful enough to set my skin alight.

The corner of his mouth turns upwards. "Just picked the

girls up, then here. I've just got them tonight. I'm dropping them off at their friends in the morning."

"I'm going to a party tomorrow." Olivia looks up at me with her big brown eyes, surrounded by long dark lashes.

I smile, pleased that she feels comfortable talking to me. "Are you, who's party?"

"My friend from school."

"It's a birthday party. Poor kid, it's her birthday on Christmas Day." Cal laughs at the kid's misfortune.

"Oh no, that's bad, isn't it?"

"Yeah, it's bad enough being born in January."

I'll have to think of something for his birthday. I slump against the back of the booth when I realise he won't even be working with me on his birthday. "What are you all doing on Christmas Day?" I glance at the girls, then back to Cal.

"Steve's coming round with his dog, Buddy," Bethanie says, smiling at her dad.

"I'm dropping the girls back at their mum's Christmas Eve, then I'm picking them up again after lunch on Christmas Day." He smiles back at Beth, but I can see the sadness glaze over his eyes. My chest aches to know he will wake up on Christmas morning alone. Before I realise, I'm wrinkling my brow and my hand is holding my throat.

"I'm going to my sisters in the morning; she's doing Christmas dinner for me and Mum."

I relax a little knowing he won't be alone for lunch but can't imagine what it must be like to not wake up with my kids on Christmas morning and see them open their presents.

"Who's Steve?" Cassie asks.

"My mum's boyfriend."

I look at Cal to see how he feels about that. He's smirking.

"Are you my dad's girlfriend?" Beth asks, gazing at me

with her beautiful innocent brown eyes full of hope and wonder. I haven't been anybody's girlfriend in about fifteen years. I look to Cal for help. My mouth won't form the word no. I imagine myself saying yes and what it would be like to be his woman.

"Stephanie is just my friend, Bethy." He gazes into my eyes. "My best friend."

I choke back a sob. He's always been my best friend.

Cal leans over the table and whispers in my ear, "With benefits." I swat him away and my eyes go wide at him for talking like this in front of the kids. But they couldn't have heard him and don't appear to be remotely interested in anything we say.

He chuckles, leans back in his seat, and I silently mouth, 'fuck you.'

He titters. "Yes, please."

I roll my eyes. Trust him to make a joke out of a beautiful moment, although it stopped me from crying at least.

The food arrives. "Hmm," I moan, "This food is amazing."

He looks at me like I have a screw loose, making sex noises over a mozzarella stick. The kids are giggling at me too, which makes me smile. "If you love it so much, why don't you have it more often?"

I roll my eyes. "You know why, I only have to look at a chip and I put a pound on."

He laughs. "You never change."

Bethy is colouring one of the puzzle sheets. "Wow, Beth, that's great colouring."

Cairen hands me his picture. "Look at my drawing, Mummy." The tears threaten again when I see what he's drawn. "That's you, Daddy, Cassie, me and Teddy."

"Darling, that's beautiful." I swallow and blink, trying my

best not to get emotional and avoid looking at Cal. If I look at him, I know I will cry.

Cassie asks, "Can we have ice cream?"

"Sure." I get up to order everyone ice cream, glad of the distraction.

At the cinema, Callum buys two boxes of popcorn for everyone to share. The kids are already on a sugar high, but it is Christmas. My kids sit next to me and Cal's next to him, so the two of us are in the middle. Cal lays his coat over the armrest. It falls onto our laps, like a blanket. I squish my eyebrows together and glance at him, wondering what he's doing. Does he think I'm cold? His arm slides under the leather and he takes hold of my hand under the coat, lacing his fingers with mine. He strokes his thumb along the back of my hand with such tenderness. I struggle to focus on the movie after that. Our hands rest at the top of my thigh and all I can think about is his hand elsewhere.

The film finishes and I have his watch to give him in my handbag, but it just doesn't feel like the right time. I want to get him alone; I could ask him back to the house, knowing that Justin will be out till midnight. Not that we can do anything, obviously the children won't be going to sleep anytime soon after their sugar consumption. But I can't ask him to the home that Justin and I share. That would be the ultimate betrayal. I decide to leave it for now.

We walk out to the car under the crisp night sky and he's parked next to me; the children get in and buckle up. I stand near the boot and discreetly hold his hand. "I had a really lovely time tonight."

"So did I."

"You've no idea how much I want to kiss you right now," I whisper.

He leans into my ear. "Yeah, I do. I know the feeling, believe me." He pulls my hand to his groin.

"Cal."

He smirks, letting go of my hand and opens his car door. "Have a good Christmas, Steph."

"Merry Christmas. Bye, girls." I wave as they drive off.

***

ONCE HOME, I change into my fluffy pyjamas, and the kids get changed into their nightclothes. "Did you like Olivia and Beth?"

"I don't like girls," Cairen says, laying down in his bed. I smile, padding into Cassie's room.

"What did you think of the girls tonight?"

"I liked them. Can we go out with them again?" A warmth floods my body and I think maybe we can make this work after all.

"Maybe." I pull her duvet around her shoulders, then pad downstairs and flop on the sofa. As I scroll through my phone, I can't seem to stop myself from pressing the call button next to Cal's name.

"Hey, everything all right?"

"Yes, can you talk?"

"Yeah, the girls are just getting into bed. Are you all right?"

"I'm fine, I just wanted to hear your voice again."

"Baby, I love hearing you say that."

"I want to see you again. Can you meet me somewhere?"

"Yeah, of course. When are you thinking?"

"When do you drop the girls off at their party?"

"Tomorrow morning. Do you want to meet after that?"

"I'm not sure I can get away for long, but I could meet

you off the A1 somewhere. Shall I pick a place and send you the location? There's a nice cafe down a country lane there."

"Yeah, anywhere, just let me know."

"What time can you get there?"

"I drop the girls off around ten, so I could be with you around half past."

"Okay, I'll see you then."

"I love you, baby."

"I love you."

I flick on the TV and put a film on, 'The Best of Me'. Justin walks in near the end to find me bawling my eyes out, covered in tissues. He's used to me like this. I broke down watching Pocahontas. I just couldn't take it when John Smith was shot. But this film resonates with me.

"What's up with you?" Justin asks with his slurry words and red eyes.

"A sad film." I wipe my eyes with one of the many crumpled tissues that surround me.

He shrugs and goes to get a drink of water. Cairen comes running downstairs. Of course, he isn't asleep yet.

"Dad, I broke one of my figures. Can you mend it?" He fists an army dude in his face.

"Not now, mate." Justin scoops him up.

"In the morning, can you please, Dad?"

"Sure, come on, you should be in bed now. It's late, you know."

"I'll take him up, I'm going to bed myself." He puts him down, and I take Cairen's hand and lead him upstairs.

"Have you been crying, Mummy?" Cairen asks.

"Yes, Mummy watched a sad film." I wipe my eyes again.

"Why do you watch films that make you sad?"

"I don't know, I'm a masochist." I chuckle.

"What's a machosict?"

"Never mind. Get in bed." I pull the blanket over his slight frame and kiss his forehead. "Love you."

"Night Mum, love you."

I check on Cassie. She's already asleep with her TV still on. I go into the bathroom and see a panda staring back at me; my makeup is smeared everywhere. I really should start wearing waterproof eyeliner and mascara with the amount of crying I've been doing lately.

PULLING ON MY BLACK TIGHTS, I smile at how much Cal complains when I wear tights, but I don't plan on doing anything with him today. I just want to give him his watch. I have a gift to drop off for Claire too, which is my excuse to go out. After slipping on a blue wrap dress with long sleeves, I curl my hair the way he likes it and add some perfume. It's almost ten and my stomach is in knots. I pull on my brown knee-length boots, throw on my black coat and shout, "See you all later." Clutching my handbag and Claire's gift, I walk out the door.

Justin is still hungover and in bed. "See ya," he shouts.

Beads of moisture gather on my forehead. Driving to the location to meet Cal, I turn the heating off and put the blowers on to cool myself down. When I see him, I know I'll be fine, but the thought of him always makes me flustered. I'm a little early and wait in the car park of a small country cafe nestled next to woodland. The place isn't too busy today. Most people are doing their last-minute Christmas shopping, no doubt.

Cal's car pulls into the car park, and I can't stop the smile spread across my face. Pulling up at the side of my car, his face beams. We get out at the same time. Our hands rest at our sides and our fingers brush, sparking an eruption of goosebumps that trail up my arm. "You look good, Steph." He whispers into my ear, "You smell good too." His gravelly voice incites a flicker in my panties. "What do you want to do?"

"Do you want to grab a coffee and go for a walk?"

"That's not what I had in mind."

"Oh, what did you have in mind?"

A sinister smile plays on his face, and I already know what he's thinking. "We could get in my Audi and find a quiet place down one of these country lanes."

A shiver shoots down my spine when I remember the photos of us in his car.

"Or we can get a coffee," he says, when I don't jump for joy at his first suggestion.

After ordering two coffees to go, we walk along the woodland trail. Twigs and crisp leaves crunch and rustle underfoot. The sun's rays warm my cheeks while my hot drink heats my hands. The cool wind blows my hair and I inhale the fresh pine scents of the forest.

"So, what did you get me out here for? I know you didn't just want to go for a walk."

I bump shoulders with him. "I wanted to see you again, that's all."

"You miss me?" He raises an eyebrow and the corner of his mouth turns upwards. "You can't live without me, admit it."

I roll my eyes again and put on my most sarcastic voice. "I don't know how I'm going to get through the Christmas holidays without you." Although, there is some truth to it. I've got so used to seeing him every day, I'll miss him and not just over the holidays. I'll miss him for the rest of my life. I sip my coffee, which has cooled a little, and I fuss over a cocker spaniel with big floppy ears that's taken a shine to me.

"I have a dog just like this." The dog runs back to its family.

"I know you do." Cal looks down, then back at me.

My brow furrows. I thought Teddy was in the garden when he came to pick me up that day. "How do you know?"

He smirks. "I saw pictures."

"Where?"

He clears his throat. "Your social media account."

"Creep." He's stalked me.

He chuckles. "I looked through all your photos."

"That's really stalkerish." I swat his chest. "Have you seen that Netflix series 'You'?"

He shakes his head. "Nah, what is it?"

"You, that's what it is, you friggin' stalker."

He's laughing louder now. "You know full well if I had an account, you would've done the same. You would've been adding me as a friend and poking me and shit."

I take another sip of my coffee. "I don't think you can poke people anymore."

"Pity."

"I thought I had my account set to private." I make a mental note to check my settings later in case a real stalker tries to look through my photos.

"It was. When you were sick, I went on your computer to get a file and your social media account was open."

"Oh."

"Are you mad?" He has an adorable grin. I could never be mad when he looks at me this way.

"No." I smile, although the thought of him looking through my photos feels a little weird, and I hope there wasn't anything embarrassing on there.

He takes a gulp of his drink. "I liked the photo of you dressed up in your naughty nurse outfit the best."

Oh no, there are embarrassing photos on there. I gasp, but can't help laughing along with him. "It was my friend's 30th."

"I'm surprised Justin let you go out like that."

I cover my face with my hand. "Oh my goodness, was it that bad?"

He wraps an arm around my shoulder. "Oh, it was bad, but not in the way you think."

I turn to look at him. "What do you mean?"

"If you were mine, you would've never gone out like that. You looked so fucking sexy. I wouldn't want anyone else seeing you that way, only me."

A rush of warmth tingles through my centre.

"Do you still have the outfit?" He raises an eyebrow.

"No, I don't, you dirty sod. And even if I did, it wouldn't fit me anymore."

"That's a shame. I'll have to get you a bigger size." He chuckles to himself.

"Perv." The deeper into the woods we get, the fewer visitors there are. I drink the last of my coffee and spot a bin.

Cal puts his empty cup in there too. "I made you a playlist."

"You did?" I turn to look at him with wide eyes. He tucks his hands into his jean pockets and sucks on his bottom lip.

"Are you sharing?"

"Yeah, I'll send it to you." He pulls his phone out, holding it in the air, positioning it in different directions. "There's no signal here."

"Well, let me look at the list." I reach to grab his phone, but he puts it behind his back. "Cal, let me see."

"You have to listen, you can't just scan through the list." He laughs. I reach my arms around his back and he steals a kiss; pressing his lips against mine. I succumb to him, holding onto his jacket as my tongue slips into his warm mouth.

He puts his phone back into his tight jean pocket and, grabbing my hand, he leads me off the path and into the trees. Walking faster than me, and taking bigger strides with his long legs, I have to break into a run to keep up with him. He ducks under a huge tree branch and weaves in and out of some overgrown foliage.

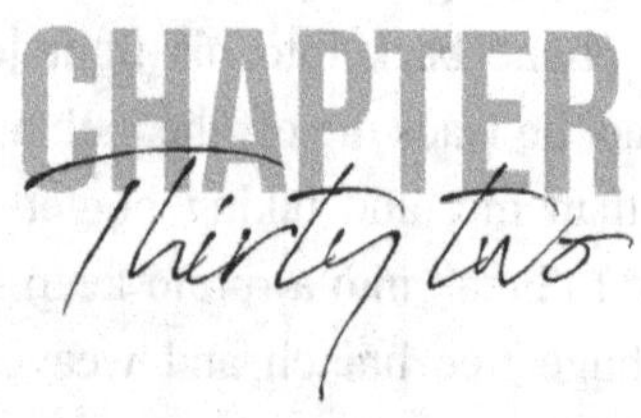

"Cal, where are we going?" His grip on my hand tightens. The overgrown ground snaps and claws at my feet as my heartbeat picks up a pace and my breathing speeds up. The light pours through the veil of branches and plays with shadows and colours between the trees. He stops in front of a huge fallen trunk in the middle of the forest, away from the beaten path. Taking hold of the top of my arms, he draws me closer to him. His lips press tight against mine. He slides his tongue between the seam of my mouth. I place my hands on his face and then run my fingers through his hair, lapping my tongue against his. Closing my eyes, I lose myself in the moment and a low moan escapes into his mouth. "Hmm, Cal."

He breaks the kiss. Finishing with several light pecks of devotion.

I sit on the fallen tree trunk and use it as a bench. Cal sits next to me, scooting as close as he can without actually sitting on me.

He takes my hand in his. "You're wearing your ring again."

I look down at the amethyst flower set in a silver ring on my middle finger. "Yes." I can't remember the last time I wore it, probably when we broke up.

I tuck my hands under his clothes against the hot skin on his stomach.

"Your hands are cold."

"Sorry." I pull away.

"No, no, it's fine." He takes both my hands, tucking them back under his jumper. "I love feeling your hands on me, even if they are colder than a polar bear's arse."

"Have you ever felt a polar bear's arse?"

His stomach muscles shake against my palms as he laughs. "No." He kisses my nose. "Cold hands, warm heart, Steph, that's you." He rests his forehead on mine.

I run my hand up to his chest, feeling every muscle on his perfectly toned torso. He wraps his arms around me and kisses me with his tongue again. The heat returns to my hands and other parts of my body and I pull away, ending our kiss with light brushes of my lips. "I got you something."

He leans back and looks at me. "What?"

I smile and open the zip on my small bag draped across my body and pull out the box with his watch in.

"You got me a gift? Why didn't you say? I haven't got you anything."

"You haven't got me a gift? Are you shittin' me?" I giggle so he knows I'm teasing. "It's not a gift, here open it."

He takes it from me with a curious look on his face and pulls off the lid. Taking the watch between his fingers, he examines the back, and he reads the old inscription. '*Forever Yours x*'

His eyes widen and sparkle like a smoky quartz jewel. "You fixed my watch?"

I nod my head. "I took it the other day when I took the rest of my stuff from yours."

He gazes at me, then back at the watch. "Baby, I can't believe you did that."

I shrug as though it was no big deal. "I wanted you to wear it again."

He puts it on his wrist. "Come here." He cups my cheeks and his lips are on mine once again. "I wish you'd said you were doing this. I would have got you something."

"I don't want anything." Even though I do. I want him, forever.

He nods and bumps shoulders with me. "You can have the playlist."

I smile. "Please tell me it's not full of Black Sabbath and Rob Zombie."

"I toned it down for you." He pecks my forehead.

"I have to get going soon." My chest tightens. I fear this is the last time I will see him.

"Come on, then." He stands, pulling me off the log, linking his fingers with mine as we walk back to the path. "I saw your face yesterday, when you realised I won't be spending Christmas morning with my girls."

"It crushes me that you will wake up alone." The thought sends a shiver to my heart.

"It's not every year. We alternate. But I get it, Steph. I don't want that life for you. It's fucking horrible to miss out on so much while they're young."

I bury my head into the knitted fabric of his jumper, running my hands around the back of him under his coat. My fingers find the hem of his shirt and I press my palms against the warm skin on his back. "What are you saying?"

"I'm saying I understand why you won't leave and I don't want you to. I don't want you to choose between me and your kids, so I'm making this easy for you and saying this is it now."

"Cal, I can't shake my feelings for you, no matter how

many times I tell myself this is for the best. A part of me just won't let go."

"You said not that long ago, if I cared about you at all I would leave you be."

"I take it back."

"Steph, look at me." I lift my head to look into his eyes. "I love you." He lets out a long breath. "I want you to be happy. I'll do whatever it takes to make you happy."

"I don't think I'll ever be truly happy without you." The pressure builds behind my eyes, and I wish I had invested in waterproof mascara.

"You will, you'll go back to your happy married life and your happy family, back to the woman you were before I came back into your life."

I kiss him one last time before we get into full view, keeping hold of his hand a little longer. As we walk, I can't help wonder why fate has woven our destinies together, only to be ripped apart again. We get closer to the cafe where more people are visible, and I can't seem to pull my hand away.

We arrive back at our cars. A tear rolls down my cheek and he catches it with his finger. I inch closer to his lips; I hover, waiting for him to kiss me. If I only have a few more stolen moments with him, I don't care who sees me. I need to feel his lips one more time. I wrap my fingers around his neck, holding his head in place and plant light kisses around his jaw.

"I can't kiss you Steph, if I kiss you back, I won't be able to stop myself from dragging you in my car, taking you home and chaining you to my bed."

I let out a weak laugh as a puff of air escapes my swollen lips, drenched in my own tears. He wipes my face with the sleeve of his jumper and pulls me closer into a tight embrace.

"So this is it, then?"

"Yeah, I guess so."

He kisses my cheek before getting into his car. "Happy Christmas, Steph."

"Merry Christmas, Cal." It takes everything I have not to throw my arms around him and kiss him again. I smile at him through the glass window. He holds his phone up and I hear a ping. Looking at my mobile, I tap on the shared playlist without even seeing what songs are on there.

The first song plays. "Oh my goodness." I burst out laughing, listening to the words, 'Touch Too Much' by AC/DC. Typical. He has a cheeky grin on his face and nods along doing air guitar moves in his car like the adorable-bastard he is. I want to get in his car and have him, all of him, right here and now. The thought sends a flutter below as I relive the feel of him inside me. I contemplate getting in his car for a quickie somewhere, but he backs out of his parking space with a nod and pulls off, still smiling as he goes.

I start my car and continue listening to the songs he put together for me. With each song, I'm besotted with this playlist even more. Every song is meaningful and pulls at my heartstrings. 'Let's Make a Night to Remember' by Bryan Adams reminds me of our first time. 'I'm Your Man' and 'Born to be my Baby' by Bon Jovi have me in tears. He really has toned this down for me. Not a Rob Zombie song in sight, although he has slipped in a bit of Mötley Crüe, which makes me smile.

I dry my eyes as I arrive at Claire's house. She greets me with a hug; I hand over her Christmas present, which is wrapped in a sealed gift bag.

"Thank you so much, lovely. You're staying for coffee, aren't you?"

"I could use a coffee right now."

She hands me a gift. "No peeking till tomorrow, okay." She also has presents for my kids too.

"Thank you."

She turns on her Nespresso machine. "So, do you want to talk about it?"

I sit at her kitchen table. "About what?"

"The reason you've been crying."

"Is it that obvious?" I pull out my compact mirror and touch up around my eyes with some pressed powder. "Cal's got a new job. I've just said goodbye to him." I sigh.

She tilts her head. Her eyes are full of empathy. "That's a good thing though, isn't it?"

I nod my head, but my eyes betray me.

She hands me a tissue. "Did something happen between the two of you?"

"No." I dab the moisture away with the tissue and sniffle. I can't tell her the truth. She doesn't need to know how weak I am.

Claire hands me my posh coffee and squeezes my shoulder. "Keep writing everything down if it helps and when you're ready to talk, I'm here for you."

"Thank you. What about you, anyway?" Hopefully, she can take my mind off all this. I live for her dating stories.

"I've been seeing someone. It's nothing serious." The smile on her face reaches her eyes.

"Who? Anyone I know?" I blow the froth on my hot drink.

"He's not from around here. His name is Liam."

I can't help but smile when her eyes twinkle as she talks about her new man. "And what does Liam do?"

"He's a personal trainer, and he's fit. He's good in bed too."

I giggle. "Sounds perfect."

Another coffee later—after Claire has told me all about her sex life—which sounds almost as exciting as mine has lately. I get back into my car with my gifts and drive home. Thinking about Cal, I want to tell him I've listened to the playlist, so I pull over in a lay-by and call him.

"Are you all right? You haven't broken down, have you?"

"My car's fine. I just wanted to tell you I love my playlist. I broke down emotionally though, listening to these songs."

"Which song?"

"'Don't Cry' and 'I Don't Want to Miss a Thing'." I dab the corner of my eyes where the tears gather again.

"Ah yeah, I wondered if I would get you going with those."

"Callum, I think this is the nicest thing you've ever done for me."

"Fuck off, I used to do nice shit for you all the time." I hear a smile in his voice.

Silence lingers for a moment as if time itself has slowed down. "Steph."

"Yes?"

"If you ever need anything, I'll be there." A lump forms in my throat and I sniffle.

"Cal, take care of yourself."

"You too, baby."

I cancel the call before I cry again.

I ARRIVE HOME to find Justin sitting at the kitchen table with his head in his hands. "Everything all right?"

"No." He glares at me.

"What's happened?" The first thing that pops into my head is the children. The house is eerily quiet and my eyes grow wide. "Where are the kids?" My voice is loud and trembling.

"Calm down, the kids are fine."

I let out a breath. "Where are they?"

"Your mother took them while I went to the builders' yard."

The warmth of relief fills me and I relax my shoulders.

"We need to talk," he says in a dark, serious voice that I've never heard from his mouth before and the relief drains away as quickly as it came.

"What do you want to talk about?" My throat tightens as my head fills with the photographs of Cal and me. He knows.

His blue eyes are as dark as a stormy sea. "Who did you go to the cinema with?"

I try to swallow the lump but it won't go down. "I met Callum from work. He brought his kids too."

His knuckles are turning white, gripping his coffee mug. "Callum, who fixed your car?"

"Yes, so?" I can hear my heart pounding in my ears. The blood drains from my face, making me dizzy. I need to sit down.

"The same Callum whose house you stayed at?"

"Yes, but I told you his girlfriend was there too." My hands are sweating. Beads of moisture gather on my forehead as my chest tightens. *Just stay calm.*

He stands, screeching his chair along the parquet floor. A chill shoots through my body. His palms press flat on the table as he leans over; close enough that I can smell the coffee on his breath. "So why didn't he go to the cinema with his chuffin' girlfriend?"

I lean back in my seat. My eyebrows pull together. "He isn't with anyone now."

"Is that because he's sleeping with you?" He spits as he speaks.

My mouth drops, and I struggle to form any words. This can't be happening, not now, not now we've come so far and it's over. Cal has left. Has he said something? He wouldn't. Would he? I stand with my palms flat on the table. "Wha… What on earth are you talking about?"

"Is that whose house you stayed at the night of your Christmas party?"

"No, I told you I stayed at Kelly's." Oh no. Someone must have photographed me walking to his, or leaving his. I knew it was a bad idea. I was just intoxicated by him.

"Prove it."

My shoulders tense. "All right, I'll call her." I hope she covers for me. Why did I say I would call her? What was I thinking? I grab my bag to pull out my mobile.

"Don't bother, she'll only cover for you."

"Justin, why would I? And when would I? I never get a minute's friggin' peace, let alone have the time to have an affair." I don't want to deal with this now. I need to get through Christmas and get my finances in order.

He clenches his fist and slams it against the table, making me jump. The wood splits. "You were seen, Steph," he shouts through his gritted teeth.

I remind myself to breathe as my legs shake and I need to sit back down. My head is light and memories of Callum are swirling on a movie reel. Which time was I seen?

"Seen where? What have I supposed to have done?" I would cry now but I think I'm all cried out from this morning.

"Maxine saw you in Maccy's."

I stare at the split wood on my dining table, then back to Justin. "Who the frig is Maxine?"

"She works at the builder's yard."

"Are you friggin' kidding me? Maxine, who was plastered at your mate's wedding reception?" I let out a sigh of relief that he doesn't actually have any photographic evidence and that nobody has been watching us again, contrary to my overactive imagination.

"Yeah." He folds his arms over his chest.

I lean back in the chair and wave my hand in the air. "If she saw me in Maccy's, she would've seen me sat with the kids."

"She saw him kissing you." His jaw is tense as he chews on his bottom lip.

"Bullshit. He never touched me. For fuck's sake, Justin, the kids were there. You're not seriously going to believe drunk Maxine over your own wife and kids, are you?"

His eyes are now thin slits. But I relax a little, knowing if this is all he has on me, she is definitely lying. I never kissed him that night. *Or did I?* I can't remember. I couldn't have. The kids were with us the whole time.

"She saw the two of you ordering your food and he had his hands all over you and was kissing your neck."

"She was obviously off her friggin' head again, like she was at that wedding. We're just friends. He wouldn't touch me. You can't seriously tell me you're believing this shit."

"Why would she lie?"

"I don't know." I throw my hands in the air. "She probably fancies you. She was all over you at that party." I wipe my brow before my fringe sticks to my forehead.

"Do you know how embarrassing it was to be in the builder's yard, and she comes over talking to me, thinking we've split up because she saw you with some other bloke." His hand runs over his face.

"I think she's misread the situation. She must be confused about what she saw. You have to believe me. Please, Justin. Don't spoil Christmas."

"I think you've already done that, Steph, don't you?" He sits back down. "I should have known something was going on when he drove here to pick you up for London. Why would he drive back on himself and go an hour out of his way?"

I roll my eyes. "I don't know, just being kind, I guess."

"And not to mention how fucking weird it was when he fixed your car."

"Argh. Not this again."

"Yes, Steph, this again. Why did he do that? Was it payment for shagging you?"

I lean over the table and slap him across the face. The palm of my hand burns. I think it hurt me more than him; he didn't even flinch. "How dare you? I'm not a prostitute. How could you say that?"

"Don't think I haven't noticed your new underwear either. Who are you wearing it for, Steph? Cos it sure as heck isn't me. You haven't put out in months."

"Well, if you made me feel sexy, maybe I would be more inclined to sleep with you."

"Is that what he does? He makes you feel sexy when he's fucking your fat arse."

I fall back into my seat and cover my face with my hands. The tears gather in the corners of my eyes. That last comment hit me in the chest, knocking the wind out of me.

The front door handle rattles, followed by a clatter in the hall.

"Hello," Mum shouts from the hallway. "We're back." The kids thunder up the stairs. Mum stops in the kitchen and looks at Justin and me. "Something wrong?"

"You could say that." Justin's lips press into a hard line and his jaw clenches.

"What's going on?" She looks between the two of us, waiting for one of us to elaborate.

"Ask your soddin' daughter."

"Stephanie?" she says as if I'm a naughty child.

"Are you going to tell her about Callum, or shall I?" Justin says through gritted teeth.

"Callum?" Mum tilts her head and furrows her brow.

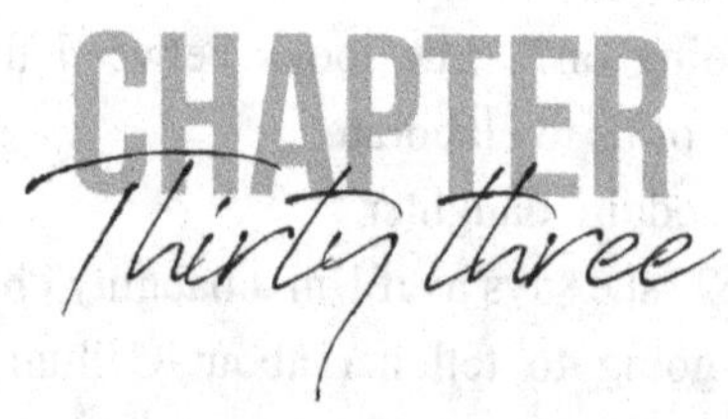

"Justin, there's nothing to tell." My eyes plead with him not to drag my mother into this; I won't hear the end of it.

He slants his eyes, ignoring my silent appeal. "She's been seen with him." He pulls his keys from his pocket, making his way to the hall. "Cook your own damn tea. I'm going out." The front door slams, sending a shudder straight through me. Mum hasn't closed her mouth since she got here and the look on her face is growing more puzzled by the second. She's never witnessed Justin and I argue.

"Who's Callum?" Then her mouth opens wider and her eyeballs almost pop their sockets. "Not that hooligan, Callum?"

I roll my eyes as she takes a seat opposite me, bracing myself, knowing a lecture is coming like I'm fifteen or something.

"Nothing's happened, Mum." I press my fingers into my temple and rub at the pressure building there.

"Something has obviously happened. What does Justin mean, you've been seen?"

I exhale a deep breath, then inhale another. "I went to Maccy's and the cinema with my colleague from work, with the kids," I add. "And someone has told Justin they saw us kiss, which is a complete lie."

"Let me get this right. Callum, your old boyfriend Callum, works with you?"

I don't deny this; I think Mum could tell from my face that it is that Callum.

"Yes, but nothing is going on." I can say this now as nothing is going on anymore.

"How long has he been working there?"

I let out a long breath. "Since before I started."

Mum shakes her head, tutting. "So Justin is mad because you went out with your ex. You can't blame him for that. Of all the stupid things to do, Stephanie. It's bad enough that you work with him."

"He doesn't know he's my ex. I haven't told him."

"Well, this just gets better." She throws her hands up into the air. "Why the big secret if nothing is going on?"

"Because of this. I didn't want him to be paranoid, and you won't tell him either."

"I will not lie."

"You don't have to lie, just don't tell him he was my ex or he really will think something was going on."

"And was it? Is it?"

"No."

"I know you, Stephanie. You were infatuated with him. If you've let him worm his way back into your heart, or worse, your knickers, then you're a fool. After everything he put you through," she huffs.

"Mum, nothing happened. How many times do I have to say it?"

She goes on with her disgust, "I never liked him. I never understood what you saw in him, and then he had the cheek to finish with you. It was like the trash taking itself out."

"Mum, please stop."

"Well, it's true." She has a stiff upper lip and sticks her chin out.

"The only reason you didn't like him is because he was from the poor side of town."

She laughs wildly; she knows it's true. When we were at school, she never thought he would amount to much, but he wasn't a threat when we were just friends. "He was wrong for you, Stephanie, in every way possible. You can't deny it after everything you went through. I was there, Stephanie; I was the one you came crying to. I went through all that pain with you. Forgive me, but I can't stand the boy."

Boy? He's far from the boy she knew. "He's a man now, Mum." My man.

"I don't care what he is. I can't believe you would meet up with him in secret and be so foolish when you've everything you could ever wish for." Cal is everything I ever wished for; him and my kids. Why can't she see that?

"I didn't meet up in secret. I took the kids, for goodness' sake. Justin just doesn't know we dated, and he doesn't need to know that."

"You're going to have to get another job. You can't work alongside him now, not if you want to save your marriage."

"He's left. It was his last day last week."

"Oh."

That's shut her up. "See? If there was anything going on, don't you think he would have stuck around?"

"Well, I'm telling you now, Stephanie, I hope nothing has been going on, because if you've done anything to jeopardise your family, so help me. You have a loving husband and two children. If you go there, especially with him." She shakes her head and pulls a face as if her words leave a bitter taste in her mouth when she mentions him. "Don't come running to me and your father because you won't get any sympathy from us."

"Nothing happened," I shout. "Are you done?"

She stands. "Yes, I'm done. I have to go anyway, but I think you have some explaining to do to poor Justin."

"I've told Justin nothing happened."

"I think you owe him the truth about who Callum is. No good will come of lying, especially to your husband. The truth always comes out in the end, and if he's left work like you say, you've nothing to worry about, do you?"

I know she's right; I should have been honest from the beginning, acted as though we were friends. We were friends. "I can't tell him, Mum. Please, don't say anything. Let this be the end of it."

"Why can't you tell him if you've nothing to hide?"

"Because Cal fixed my car, and I stayed over at his house that night when it snowed."

"Stephanie, you didn't?"

"His girlfriend was there." I quickly add. "I had to stay somewhere. It was no big deal. I think you're forgetting we were best friends before we were lovers, and we can be friends again." Even though Cal's proved to me, we can never be just friends. I get that now.

"Yes, but why would you want to? I wouldn't even talk to him again after what he did."

"He broke up with me, that's all. Yes, he went about it the wrong way, but you're acting as though he beat me up or worse."

"Why are you defending him?" Why am I sticking up for him? I certainly wouldn't have done that this time last year. "He's got to you again, hasn't he? You were always the same, Stephanie. You'd do whatever he said. I don't know what or how he has a hold over you—"

"I won't see him again. He hasn't got to me or got a hold of me, he's gone. I won't be seeing him at work or out of work. Not now, not ever, okay." I scream the words, and the realisation that I really won't be seeing him again hits me like a double-decker bus. I slump into the chair, waiting for Mum to respond with more of her venom. If only I could curl up into a ball and hibernate until the sun comes out again. The sun being him of course with his fiery eyes and his touch like flames licking at my skin.

"I won't say anything." Her voice is softer now. "But I won't lie for you either and if I find out you've lied or you've seen him again, so help me, Steph."

"Mum, please. I'm not stupid." If only that statement was true, I am stupid, and I continue to be stupid, wanting him still. Mum leaves after giving my shoulder a gentle rub, and I go through my phone, checking all my texts, making sure there's nothing incriminating. I'm clearly in the wrong line of work, as I deserve a friggin' Oscar for that performance.

I cook a basic tea for the kids; frozen chips and fish fingers. I'm not hungry, but I polish off some chips that the kids left. More than anything, I'm mad that Justin believes some other woman over his own wife, even if I have told more lies than Pinocchio. It's over. I've ended it with Callum. *He's ended it, you mean.* And there she is, my voice of reason. She never fails to put me in my place. I gulp down the rest of my wine and top the glass up again. *I don't know why you bothered with a glass. We both know you're going to finish the bottle.* She's right again, the smug bitch.

The kids go to bed early. I'm drowning my sorrows, waiting for round two with Justin. The sad thing is that I'm not sure I can be arsed to grovel anymore. The way I'm feeling now—after polishing off a half bottle of red and three-quarters of the way down a rosé—I think stuff it. Perhaps this is it. Is this the push I need to do something for myself; my last chance of real happiness? I gulp down another glass, thinking of my children's happiness, and realise what a selfish mum I am.

"I can't sleep, Mummy." Cassie walks into the living room and cuddles up with me on the sofa. "Why isn't Dad back yet? I need him to tuck me in."

My temple throbs. I wrap my arms around her and squeeze her tight. What was I thinking, splitting my children in two? How can I put them through this misery daily?

"Come on, I'll tuck you in."

"I need Daddy." Her bottom lip quivers.

"He'll be back tomorrow. He's had to sort some work stuff out." I take her back to bed and then return to the sofa. The tears fall down my cheek, but I'm not sure why I'm sobbing, a mixture of everything perhaps, tears for Callum, Justin and the kids, and a single tear for myself. Teddy, our dog, comes and sits on my lap. I stroke his head as he licks my salty face. Another realisation hits me; if we separated, who would get the dog?

I OPEN my eyes to the morning winter sun pouring into the living room. The throb in my temple returns, and I close my eyes again. Teddy scratches at the front door, ready for his early morning walk that Justin always takes him on.

"Mummy." Small hands cling to my arm, tugging on the dress I'm still wearing from yesterday. "Mummy, where's Daddy?"

The empty wine bottles clink as Cairen knocks the coffee table, reminding me of how much I drank last night, and the reason my mouth tastes like a sour grape.

Cairen's pale blue eyes are like a cloudy sky that threatens rain. "When's Daddy coming home?"

"I'm not sure, sweetheart. I'll call him." My arms wrap around his tiny frame and I reach for my phone. The battery is dead. Typical. I slump to the charger and plug it in, tapping my nails against the kitchen worktop as I wait for it to power up. The dog's whining, desperate for his walk. I open the back door and let him into the garden for now. Once my phone comes alive, I tap on Justin's name. It goes straight to voicemail. "Justin, please call me." My lip trembles as I leave the message. He will be home soon. Won't he?

Making myself a large coffee, I take two paracetamol, hoping it will help with my thumping head.

Cassie walks into the kitchen. "Where's Daddy?"

"He's had to go out this morning. He'll be back soon." *Please come back soon.*

She yawns and scratches her knotty hair. "Can I have pancakes for breakfast?"

"No, sweetheart. I'm not cooking pancakes. There's cereal in the cupboard."

"But Daddy always cooks me pancakes." Her blue eyes are like a crystal clear river ready to burst its banks. How can I even think about separating her from her dad? She's always been a daddy's girl. I'm sure if she could choose, she would stay with him over me.

Cairen shouts, "I want pancakes too."

"Okay, I'll do pancakes." I let out a long breath and Google the recipe. How hard can it be? After cracking two eggs in a bowl, I add the flour and milk, and whisk with a fork. A splash of oil into the pan, and I pour in the batter.

Cassie and Cairen sit at the kitchen table, still in their pyjamas. I flip the pancake and cook it on the other side. They look rather nice, if I say so myself. "Who wants the first one?"

"Me," Cassie shouts.

I slide the pancake onto her plate, and she stares at me.

"What's that?"

"A pancake."

She folds her arms in a huff. "That's not how Dad does them."

"I'm sorry, what does Dad do?"

"He does thin ones. That's too thick. I can't eat it."

I take in a deep breath and breathe out slowly through my nostrils, counting to five in my head. "Fine, I'll have that one." I pop it to one side and pour in a small bit of batter, creating a thinner pancake this time. The phone rings and my heart jolts. I run over to the other side of the kitchen where my mobile is plugged in only to see it's my mother. I swipe the screen. "Hello."

"Stephanie. I just thought I'd call to check everything was resolved last night."

I pad into the hall so the kids don't hear me. "He never came home."

"Well, you really have done it now, haven't you?"

"Mum, please. I'll hang up if you're starting another lecture." My delicate head can't take any more. "I'm sure he'll turn up this morning, and we can sort it out."

"I hope you're right."

A loud, piercing beep rings out in the hallway. I turn back to the kitchen to see smoke rising from the pan. "I have to go Mum."

"Call me later."

"Okay." I rush to the hob. The batter is burnt to a crisp. I slide it into the bin and waft a tea towel under the smoke alarm until it stops that deafening noise. Where's Justin? I need him.

Pouring another small amount of mixture into the pan—third time lucky—I forget to add the oil. My shoulders slump. I'm sure it will still cook. After flipping, I slide it onto Cassie's plate. "Is that thin enough for you, Madam?"

"Daddy's doesn't have brown spots on."

"Just eat it." I throw the spatula on the counter and pinch the bridge of my nose.

"Where's mine?" Cairen asks.

"One sec." I pour the remaining batter into the pan and it only makes a small one. I brace myself, knowing he's going to moan that Cassie got a bigger one than him. "Before you say anything, if you want another, I'll make some more mixture."

"It's okay Mum. I don't want a pancake now. I'll just have cereal."

Cassie pushes her plate to the middle of the table. "I'll have cereal too."

I take in a deep breath, counting to ten, while I imagine slapping her around the face with the spatula and pouring cereal over Cairen's head. Justin has spoilt these two rotten. Taking the leftover pancakes that nobody wants, I sprinkle on some sugar and gobble them down; not even tasting or enjoying them. The roiling in my stomach gets faster with each passing minute that Justin doesn't call or come home. Is this really it?

After showering, I look refreshed, but nothing can remove the weariness in my heart. I pull my clothes from the wardrobe and spot the black bin bag on the top shelf that contains Justin's Christmas gift. What if he doesn't come home by Wednesday? What sort of Christmas would the kids have without their dad? He has to fix up Cairen's football net we've bought for the garden, and Cassie's new TV will need fixing to the wall. My chest pounds at the thought of him not being here. I dress and grab my phone to call all our friends, asking if he's there. None have seen him. I call his mum; she hasn't seen him either. Acting like he's just nipped out, I don't want everyone knowing our business.

"When's Dad coming home, Mum?" Cairen's dressed in his football kit and has his goalie gloves on with shin pads and socks.

"I don't know, darling."

"He promised he'd play football with me today." A tear falls down his cheek.

"I'll play with you."

"You can't play football." He storms off, throwing his boots on the floor.

My chest tightens, knowing I've caused all this. No matter how much I love Cal, I should never have betrayed my family. I was so desperate to have children, Justin and I tried for years, and I've turned out to be a terrible mum; putting my own interests before my kids. There's too much at stake here. I call Justin again, desperate to sort things out, but nothing.

Hoping he will be home soon, I make a start on dinner. I roast the chicken and boil the vegetables along with a pan of potatoes.

"Is Dad going to be home for dinner? I thought he'd finished work now for Christmas. It's not fair."

"He should be home soon, darling. Will you set the table?"

I plate up our food, including Justin's, and we sit down to eat.

"Where's Dad?"

I sigh and try his mobile again, but get the voicemail.

"Don't worry, he's just running late." I force a smile. "Eat your dinner."

"This mashed potato isn't like Daddy's," Cassie says.

"Mum, I'm not eating those carrots, they're hard," Cairen says.

I drop my cutlery on my plate, making a clatter. The tears threaten again, and I rush into the bathroom before the kids see me cry. *Ungrateful shits.* Slumping to the floor, I silently cry into my hands. I've done my best today, and it's still not good enough. The tears flow down my cheeks. I pull the toilet paper from the roll and blow my nose. Where is he? My stomach twists. Has something happened to him? A shudder rocks through me. It's not like him to not call. *He went to Dublin on a stag weekend and never called.* That was before we had children, and he said he couldn't get a signal. *Yeah right.* He would call the kids, though. He's a good dad.

After drying my eyes, I come out of the bathroom to find both kids back in the living room, watching TV. They've left most of their dinner, and I can't eat anything either. I put his dinner in the microwave and throw the rest of our meals in the bin.

We all have an early night and the kids fall asleep in my bed, watching a movie. I kiss their foreheads and lie back, staring at the crack on the bedroom ceiling that Justin was going to fix. It seems to have grown these last few months.

THE RADIO ALARM plays 'Driving Home for Christmas', waking me on Christmas Eve. Still no Justin. My eyes squeeze shut. I'm sorry—please be okay and come home— I'm sorry, I'm sorry. I chant in my head, willing everything to be okay and hope he's driving home right now. My stomach roils like it's on a high-speed spin in the washing machine. I have a lot to do today, even more if Justin doesn't show. My brain isn't functioning and my limbs quiver as I picture Justin lying in a ditch somewhere. I shake the thought and make myself a strong coffee. Dad will help with Cairen's football net. I want it setting up tonight, ready for him tomorrow morning.

The door rattles. Justin stomps through the hall, and I cover my mouth with my hands. He steps into the kitchen and I throw my arms around him. The tears build in the corner of my eyes. "I was so worried about you."

He hesitates before placing his hand on my back.

Cassie and Cairen run down the stairs. "Daddy."

He lets go of me and kneels down, scooping them both into his big arms.

"Daddy, I thought you were never coming home," Cairen says.

Justin kisses his forehead and glares at me. "I would never leave you kids. We're a family. I love you too much to just up and leave." His eyebrows pinch together and his lips press into a thin, hard line as his stare burns into my flesh, branding me with a warning.

"Mummy's pancakes are not as good as yours," Cassie says.

"And she almost burnt the house down," Cairen adds.

Trust these kids to dob me in. I shake my head at Justin. "I burnt the pancake a little, that's all."

He pats them on the back. "Get dressed, and I'll make you some.

I stay quiet, sipping my drink.

Once the kids are upstairs, Justin leans against the kitchen cupboard and drags his hand over his face. "You're going to pack that job in." Ugh, he sounds like my mother. His voice seems calmer now though, and less annoying than my mum's. He lets out a long breath. "Even if Maxine is mistaken, I don't want you seeing him."

"You don't have to worry. He's got a new job."

"He's leaving?"

"He left Friday."

"Good, you won't be seeing him again then, will you?"

"No, I won't." My head drops. I stare at the floor, tugging the sleeve of my pyjama top over my hands.

Justin points his finger in my face, and I catch his glare. "I mean it Steph. You'd better start putting this family first."

I nod, knowing he's right. "I will. Are you going to tell that bitch to stop spreading lies or have I got to go down to the builder's yard myself?"

"No, I'll deal with Maxine." He rubs his tired eyes.

"Are we good?" I glance up at him with blurred vision, blinking away the tears.

He nods and pulls out the frying pan.

CHAPTER
Thirty four

"Stephanie, lovely to have you with us this evening," the vicar says, shaking my hand. "We haven't seen you for a while."

"Sorry, I've been busy." The kids grab an orange with a candle in for the Christingle service. Justin points to our parents that are sitting together and the kids run over to them.

"Seb, great to see you, mate." Justin greets my brother, bumping fists as they used to in school. I take Cassie to the choir, then sit on the pew between Justin and my mother.

"She's got nerve, showing her face here." Mum's face looks like she just got a mouthful of antiseptic.

"What are you on about?" I look around and see Julia walk in with her new man. Everyone turns their back to them.

Justin turns to my mum. "I saw Jack in the plumbing centre last week. He's selling the house. I told him he's too soft. If it was me, there's no way I would sell the house. I would make sure I kept the kids and the house. She wouldn't be getting a penny out of me." He stares at me as he says the words, as if warning me. My chest pounds listening to him talk like this.

"It's those boys I feel sorry for." Mum shakes her head.

I huff. "Oh, give it a rest. Let he who is without sin cast the first stone, Mother."

She tuts. My heart breaks as I glance back at the couple sitting at the back of the church.

I get up and make my way over. "Merry Christmas, Julia." I give her a hug, and I feel her choke up in my arms. Her new man strokes her back and hands her a handkerchief. Julia dabs her eyes and I shake his hand. "Nice to meet you, I'm Stephanie."

"And you." He places both hands around mine. "Thank you."

I nod before heading back to my family. Justin frowns, and my mother whisper yells, "What are you doing?"

"It's Christmas, Mum. Season of goodwill and all that."

She tuts again. "Tell that to her boys. I doubt they'll have a merry Christmas this year." I think about what she says and Justin's words ring in my head.

The choir fills the entire church with 'Once in Royal David's City'. My chest feels tighter than ever and I can barely breathe, let alone sing along. I watch my daughter belt out the chorus from the choir loft. Mum's eyes glisten as she watches her granddaughter with pride. The entire family is here, our traditional Christmas Eve gathering.

I look around at the lofty church, so many memories. Most of our friends and family are here. If they knew what I'd done, I doubt any of them would speak to me again. I would be Julia. My heart races at the thought, and I have to take my big coat off before I sweat.

Justin is silently mouthing the words to 'O Little Town of Bethlehem'. At least he's trying to look like he's singing along, unlike Cairen, who's slumped with his hands in his pockets. I thank Callum for being stronger than I am. If he hadn't got another job, I don't think I could stop seeing him. Where would it end? At least now I can move on, I hope.

The large cross above the altar holds my gaze. Callum

was right; I can't have my cake and eat it, and I can't leave my kids. Seeing them half the week or alternate days or whatever arrangement we had wouldn't be enough for me. I like to be the one to tuck them in at night, kiss their poorly's better, read them a story, help with their homework. It has to be this way. Whatever happens, my kids will always come first. I stare at the cross again and thank the Lord for my children.

CHRISTMAS CAME and went and the day has come all too soon when I have to return to work. I was getting used to the late mornings and pyjama days filled with baking and Christmas crafting. But it's nice to see everyone again.

Today is the first day without Callum's handsome face sitting opposite me. Instead, a new bloke has taken his place. He's older and bald, friendly enough, but I miss Cal's warm smile and his brown eyes that sparkle when he looks at me.

"I have a client coming in at two to go over this brochure," Kelly says. "Callum would normally deal with it, but seeing as he isn't here anymore, I thought you could work on the project with me."

I take the booklet from her. "Okay, what brochure is it?"

"We do it every year, it's a bespoke kitchen company. Here's last year's design."

Sarah walks by and sees the brochure in my hand. "Oh, not him again." She giggles. "I'll make sure the sugar's stocked up."

"What do you mean?" I look between her and Kelly.

"He has six sugars in his tea." She giggles again and Kelly is smiling.

"No way?"

"Yes, way."

The client turns up a little early; he knows the team well and Kelly introduces me.

"Isn't Callum here?"

The mention of his name tugs at the emptiness in my heart.

"He left before Christmas, so you'll have to settle for us I'm afraid." Kelly says. He doesn't look like he minds.

Sarah asks, "Would you like a drink?"

"Tea, please, love."

Sarah never fails to put the *tea* in 'team'. "Six sugars, isn't it?" she asks.

I still can't get over it.

"Ah, you remembered," he says.

"Yes." She simpers. *How could anyone forget the six-sugar man?*

"I've actually cut down," he says.

Sarah turns back to him, wide-eyed.

"I had high blood pressure."

"Good for you," I say.

"I bet you feel so much better now," Sarah adds.

"I had to make a few lifestyle changes."

"That's brilliant," Sarah says.

"Thanks, I only have five sugars now."

"All right," Sarah walks away with a huge grin on her face. I daren't look at Kelly; I fear I'll burst out laughing if I see a hint of a smile on her face. Sadness floods my chest as Cal isn't here, and I won't get to share funny moments like this with him again.

"I'M HOME," I shout, stepping into the hall.

"You're home early. I thought tonight was your slimming group?" Justin stands in the kitchen doorway.

"It was, but I'm not going."

"Steph, you shouldn't keep skipping group. It's not good for your weight loss."

"I'm not skipping group. I'm not going anymore."

"If you don't go, you'll pile the weight back on. You know what happened before, you'll end up as big as a house."

"Thanks for the vote of confidence, Justin. Would it really matter how big I am as long as I'm happy?"

"But you won't be happy if you put more weight on."

"I think it's you that won't be happy, not me. I couldn't give a shit."

"Steph, what's got into you?"

"I've never been slim, Justin. You knew what you were marrying."

"You weren't as big as you are now or when you were pregnant."

"No, but I'm happy with how I am. Why can't you be happy too?"

"Fine, if you don't want to go to your slimming group then don't go, but at least use the gym membership I got you. I renewed it for you, it's still valid."

"I'll think about it." I couldn't give a shit what Justin thinks of me. How I feel right now, he can take it or leave it. Talk about double standards. He rarely uses the gym either, and his beer belly grows bigger each year.

"I'll start on tea then, seeing as you're home early."

"Thanks."

"Have you had a bad day or something?"

"No, just the usual. How was your day?"

"Fine."

I slump into the dining room chair, kicking off my shoes.

I could just have a power nap. The first day back at work after the holidays is always the hardest, and today was even harder without Callum.

I read through all my notes in the diary I've been keeping on my laptop since Claire's advice. It's ended up being a novel, full of our life, past and present. I think about sharing it with Callum, although I didn't write this down for anyone but myself, but I owe it to him to at least share what I wrote, seeing as it's all about him. I ponder the thought.

What would I achieve by this? I play out the scenario in my head. I would send him a hard copy of my book and after he'd read it, he would swoop into work, scoop me up like in 'Officer and a Gentleman' and carry me away. *Like that would happen*. Or he would wait for me after work, leaning against his car as he always did. He would demand I get into his Audi, take me to his place and tie me to the bedpost, keeping me prisoner. I smile, thinking about him tying me up. As I read through my diary, I edit it so it reads more like a book, our own love story full of my emotions and feelings for him.

Justin watches the football while I type into my laptop on the couch.

"What are you typing on that thing? I hope they're paying you for all this extra work." I don't correct him. How can I say I'm just writing a love story that's not about you?

"I just have an extensive project that I'm working on at the moment." Once this is edited, I need to send a copy to the printers in thyme for Cal's birthday next week.

———

It's been three weeks since I saw Callum. He doesn't do socials, so I can't stalk him on social media, dammit.

I'll just have to settle with my memories in my book. I thought I would feel closure when he left work, and I could finally concentrate on the task at hand, instead of looking over at him, reliving him inside me. But I still can't get him out of my head.

My book arrives at work; I had it delivered here instead of home. The printers have designed a cover for me and I've titled it 'Forever Yours'. It looks very professional, and I'm proud that I've actually completed it and had it bound into a proper book in time for Callum's birthday.

I open the cover and smell the fresh print before writing on the inside.

For you, Cal.

My best memories are the ones we made together.

I wish I could remember more of our happy times from our teens. I wanted to remember everything this time around, so I wrote it all down for us to share. We will always have our memories until we can be together again.

Forever Yours,
Steph x

I wrap it up with some brown paper from the stationery cupboard and drive to his house after work. My heart races at the thought of seeing him again. I used to believe Cal was my soul mate until he ended our relationship. Now I know he isn't just my soul mate, he's my North Star, my best friend, my lover, my everything. Real love awakens your soul, and I never knew mine was sleeping until I saw him at work that day. Even though we can't be together right now, I hope we can stay in touch, even if it's the odd text at birthdays and Christmas.

His car isn't here when I pull up outside his apartment—I didn't expect it would be—he has a longer commute now. It's his birthday at the weekend, but I wanted to drop this off now before I changed my mind. I post it through his letterbox and hear a thud on the other side of the door. There's no going back now. My chest tightens and I take in a deep breath. What if he hates it? What if it makes him feel worse? What if he's seeing someone? My head goes through a million scenarios, and I wish I hadn't posted it.

My throat tightens. I decide to wait a little longer, hoping he will show. A motorbike pulls up in front of me. The oxygen in the air seems to have disappeared, making me dizzy and nauseous. A man takes off his helmet. The scar is more prominent as he walks over to me with a smirk, making the bile rise from my stomach. The woman takes off her helmet. Her long black hair swishes over the rose on her neck.

"You?" she says with wide eyes. "What are you doing here?"

My muscles grow numb. "I could ask you the same thing." If he's sleeping with her again after what she did, he can fuck off.

She runs her fingers down the edge of her leather jacket. "I'm here to see Callum."

"He isn't in. So you'll have a job finding him." The lump in my throat chokes me. The thought of the two of them together is repulsive.

Scar-face pipes up, "Don't worry, love, I can give you what you came for. Callum's not the only one that likes a buxom woman." He laughs, showing a gob full of manky teeth, and a shiver runs down my spine.

"Piss off." I try to manouevre around the two of them to get to my car. His stale tobacco breath washes over my face. I turn my head and dry retch, but keep my lunch contained.

"Let her pass, Phil, let her run back to her husband. Cal's with me now."

My body reacts to her words before my mind even registers what she's saying, and I swing for her. I want to rip her friggin' head off that skinny body of hers. My fingers claw at her hair but scar-face blocks me. Grabbing both my wrists, he drags me to the side of Cal's house down the dark passage where the dustbins are stored. Squirming from Phil's grip, I try to free myself. He's bigger than me. Though flaccid, with a beefy tyre hanging over his waistband, his strength has me pinned to the wall. Her laugh makes my blood sizzle, and I sneer my nose up and flash her a glare.

"You're a sick bitch. If Callum is with you, he's only using you," I shout.

Her voice echoes down the passageway. "No, love, he was using you."

"Fuck off." I squirm and try my best to knee him in the balls.

Both of them laugh at me as I writhe under his grasp.

"You jealous bitch. You were so jealous you had to take those photos of us. Did you enjoy watching him kiss me?"

She cackles. "Is that what he told you? Dean took those photos for him, he set you up."

"You're lying." She shrugs. "You don't have to believe me. Just know he's with me now. Why do you think he got another job? He got bored with you."

"Don't worry, love, I can make you feel good," he says.

My skin crawls. I wrestle again, breathing heavily as I try to create some space between us. I doubt this swine has ever made anyone feel good. His slimy tongue trails up my face like a slug. "Callum has good taste."

I screw my eyes shut. The salty moisture clings to my lashes as I beg. "Please." My voice is weak. He laughs in my face and his foul breath makes me heave again. My body shakes between him and the wall, and my muffled cries echo around the passage. I don't know what's worse; that I'm being held by this disgusting pig, or that this bitch may be telling the truth.

A shadow forms in the corner of my eye and scar-face is

yanked from me and thrown to the other side of the wall. Callum's fist collides with his nose and blood splatters against the brick. I'm frozen as Phil's face pummels into the wall again.

"I told you to stay the fuck away from her." Cal fists him again.

"I didn't touch your bitch," he shouts, showing his bloodied teeth with a wry smile. Crack. Callum wipes the smirk off the man's face when his fist strikes his jaw.

"Callum," she screams, trying to pull him off her brother. As much as I want to see this sleaze get beaten to a pulp by my man, I worry Cal may do some permanent damage. The pig doesn't stand a chance against Callum's rage.

"If you've hurt her, I'll fucking kill you." He holds the swindler up against the brickwork with the scruff of his t-shirt and Cal's fist threatens another punch.

The pig's head flops to the side and the blood drips from his chin.

"He didn't touch me," I shout, trying to rein in his anger. "I'm okay."

Callum drags the man's sorry ass back to his bike, throwing him against it.

"Fuck off before I *do* kill you." He looks at the girl. "You can fuck off too." Cal stands on a small package that the man had dropped. He picks it up and throws it at him. "And take your shit with you."

I watch the man wipe his bloodied face on his t-shirt.

"I don't want to see you here again, now fuck off."

The bike starts up with a loud revving and they ride off. Cal cups my face in his bloody hands. "Are you all right, baby?" His breath is rugged.

I nod, tears run down my cheeks. My body is violently shaking and my legs are barely holding me. "Are you all right?" My voice trembles. I check Cal's face for cuts, but the blood that's smeared across his skin and splattered on his white shirt isn't his.

"I'm fine. Did he hurt you?"

"No." I rub my wrists that are still sore and burn from his tight grasp, and Cal runs his thumb over the redness there. "He held my wrists in place and licked my face." I shudder at the memory of his rancid tongue on my cheek.

"Come on in." He pulls his keys from his pocket and walks by the post on the floor and straight to the bathroom. He wets a towel with warm water and wipes my face before washing his own, then takes his bloodied shirt off. Taking the towel from him, I wash the blood from his neck.

We walk back to the kitchen. I'm still numb and light-headed. Callum pulls a glass from the cupboard.

"Cal, what was she doing here?" My voice trembles and the sound of my heartbeat pounds in my ears as I wait for his answer.

He runs the tap and fills a glass of water. "What are you doing here?"

"Don't change the subject. Are you sleeping with her again?"

"Fuck, no. Her brother is a drug runner, that's all." He hands me the water.

My hand shakes as I bring the glass to my mouth and take a drink. "Is that what's in the package? Are you on drugs?"

"I'm not on fucking drugs." He folds his arms over his chest.

I wave my hand in the air. "Then why was he here to give you that package?"

"I smoke shit sometimes, that's all." He throws his hands up. "Fuck, it's the only thing I can do to take my mind off you."

"Callum." My chest aches thinking of him suffering as I have been.

He steps closer to me and places his hands on my shoulders. "It's no big deal."

I frown at him. "It is a big deal when your friggin' drug dealer is blackmailing me."

"I told you I sorted that. They haven't sent you anymore pictures, have they?"

"No." Then I remember everything she said about the photos and it all registers. A chill runs down my spine, and I step away from him. "You got your mate to take photos of us. You set me up." Black spots blur my vision. "Oh my goodness, Callum, why would you do that?" My chest is tighter than ever. This hurts more than any physical pain I could ever endure. The tears drip from my swollen lips. I fight with the air, inhaling what I can into my withering lungs.

"Baby." He reaches his arms to me, but I step back again.

"Don't baby me. Why would you do that? It all makes sense now. You told him where we would be to gather evidence to set me up. Is it money you wanted for your drugs?"

He steps closer. "Don't be fucking stupid."

"Cal, are you in trouble? Why? Just tell me why you used me?"

"I never used you."

"I would have gladly given you money if you needed it. You didn't have to do this." I hit his bare chest with both fists clenched. He lets me hit him again and again until he grips my arms, holding them at my side. I don't have the energy to fight him.

"I'm sorry Steph, it's not like that, believe me, please."

"Then tell me, why?"

"I had Dean take those photos. I was going to send them to your husband so he would leave you." He sighs.

"Dean from school?"

"Yeah, it was his idea so we could be together."

"You're sick. You thought if you ruined my marriage I would come running to you?"

"I love you, and you said you wouldn't leave him. I wanted you for myself. The thought of you with another man tore me apart. I told you I was a selfish bastard, but I couldn't go through with it in the end. I love you."

"I fucking hate you, you'll never lay your hands on me again. You'll die a lonely man." I turn towards the hallway, but he pulls me back.

"Steph, please. I'm sorry, I'm fucking sorry. I never meant for the photos to fall into the wrong hands. Dean left his phone at that dirty fucker's place when he was stoned off his head and Liz saw the pictures in his gallery. I swear I deleted every last fucking photo. I promise."

"That's why you were so desperate to get into my pants that day. How could you let someone watch us have sex? The thought of someone watching us makes me sick to my stomach, Cal."

"I only told him to get a picture of us kissing and besides, you wouldn't fuck me that day, remember. You were on your period."

"But you tried. You even tried to get me to suck you off, knowing Dean was going to take photos. You're a sick fucking bastard."

"Steph, please, I love you. I was desperate."

"I loved you, Cal. I loved you with everything I had." My entire body is vibrating. "I even considered moving in with you."

His shoulders curl inwards and he exhales like I've

stabbed him in the chest. "Steph, stay. We can talk about this."

My head shakes. "I knew you'd hurt me again. I just didn't realise how much."

He grips my arms tight. His touch turns my skin to stone. A cold, icy frost creeps over my flesh. Yanking myself away from him, I run to my car. I lock the doors before he can touch me again. He follows, tugging the door handle, still pleading with me. I start the engine and back out of the bay.

With my blurry eyes, I watch him bury his face in his hands in the rear-view mirror as I pull off his estate. A few minutes later, my phone rings. I ignore it, turning on the radio to drown out the vibration and my cries. Mum was right about him. She always is. I pull over when I get near home. Not wanting Justin to see me in this state. I pick up my phone, which is still vibrating, matching my own shaky hand. Cancelling Cal's call, I text Justin.

'Traffic bad, running late.'

Then I make the mistake of pressing Callum's name and go through all his texts.

'I'm sorry, I love you.'

'I never meant to hurt you. Please forgive me.'

'Everything I did was because I wanted you. I know I'm a sick fuck.'

'Don't hate me for loving you too much.'

'I needed you. I didn't know how to let you go when I pulled that shit. You make me do crazy stuff.'

'Please answer your phone.'

'Just answer the phone. Yell, scream, anything, just let me hear your voice again.'

'You've no idea how sick I felt that someone like him had photos of us. I hate myself.'

'Please forgive me, Steph. Don't leave us like this, let's talk.'

Then I remember the book. It's still wrapped up on his hall floor. Oh my goodness. I wish I'd picked it up and taken it back. As fast as I delete each text message, they still keep coming, along with the voicemails. I turn my phone off. How can I trust him again? I always thought I could forgive that boy anything, but not this time. The man I love the most in this world has broken me in two again and there's no going back.

I can't seem to compose myself. The traffic is rushing by, but I don't hear it. I only hear the deafening drumming in my head that's somehow synced to the thumping sensation there. The redness on my wrists is barely visible now, but the ache is still there and the memory of that man's tongue on my face makes me shudder again. I just want to go home and have Justin hug me. I want to tell him how sorry I am and share all my problems with him like any friend would, and I can't even do that or tell him about my ordeal.

I walk in, hoping I can sneak off to the bathroom while Justin is in the kitchen. I scurry upstairs, thankful that he hasn't seen my puffy face and I don't have to concoct any more lies to my ever-growing web of deceit.

Cassie spots me at the top of the stairs. "Mummy, have you been crying?"

"No, I'm fine, honey." I force a smile.

"Your eyes look all puffy."

I wave her off. "I got something in my eye, that's all."

As I run the bath, Justin walks into the room. I really do need to get a lock on this door.

"Steph, what's wrong?"

I don't look at him and pour bath salts into the tub. "Nothing's wrong."

"Cassie said you looked upset."

"I'm fine." My voice quivers.

Justin wraps his big arms around me from behind. I turn around and press my cheek against his chest and he holds me tight.

"You're not fine. Tell me what's wrong, sweetheart."

He hasn't called me that in a long time. His gentle voice and safe arms wrapped around me makes the lump in my throat choke me. His hand strokes my head, and I cry into his chest. My shoulders shudder as I let everything out.

"I'm here. It's okay." His calloused hands hold my face. "Tell me what's upset you."

I always used to share my problems with him. But not this time. "I've just had a bad day at work."

"You don't need that job. You haven't been yourself since you started working there. Jack it in if it's getting you down. We don't need the money. I can support our family."

I hug him and rest my head on his chest and his hand rubs up and down my back. "It's not my job. I just had a bad client today."

"I'm not having a client upset you like this. I'm calling your boss. What's his name again?"

"Please Justin, I'll tell Jerry about it tomorrow. It's probably just me being over sensitive. I'm probably due my period or something. I just want to take a bath."

He kisses my forehead. "Have a bath. I'll run out and pick up your favourite take-away from that Indian restaurant you like, and I'll get your favourite salted caramel ice cream for afterwards."

"Thank you." A hint of a smile plays on my lips.

He holds my chin up. "Was that a smile?" He pecks my swollen lips and the warmth from his mouth comforts me, like a pair of old slippers that you just can't throw out. "I know I don't always show it, but I love you, Steph."

"I love you." The acid coats the lump in my throat and burns as I choke out the words. Him being nice to me makes the pain there more intense. What have I done?

The bath is far too hot, but I welcome it, scrubbing my face and every other part of my body, trying to wash away my sins. I wish I'd never laid eyes on Cal that day at work. My life would be so much simpler. Although, I'm angry with myself the most for getting involved with him again. Annoyingly, I know everything Mum said was true. I let him worm his way back into my heart and knickers, and now I'm paying the price.

Wrapping a towel around my body and making my way to the bedroom to find my fluffy pyjamas, I turn my phone back on. Ping, ping, ping, ping. More text messages and voicemails come through. He is relentless. All saying more of the same shit he was saying before.

'I'm begging you, just let me know you're okay'

'I need to know you made it home. Please, if anything happened to you, I'll never forgive myself.'

'Answer your fucking phone, Steph.'

'Please, just let me know you're safe.'

'I love you so much, you mean everything to me.'

'Is it so much to ask for one text so I know you're all right?'

'If you don't let me know you're safe, I'm coming over.'

No, that's the last thing I want. I've only just stopped the tears, most likely because of the steaming bath dehydrating my body. I text back, 'Piss off and stop calling me. I'm not listening to all your voicemails.'

The phone rings again and I press cancel, then get a text seconds later. 'Are you safe? Just tell me you're all right.'

I don't think I'll ever be all right, but I text back. 'Leave me alone. I don't want to hear from you again. Forget about me, because I'm going to forget about you.'

'Please call me when you've calmed down.'

'I will never call you again. Now piss off and let me live my life with people who actually care about me.'

He doesn't respond and I go through all the messages and repeatedly tap the dustbin icon.

Several weeks go by, and I hear nothing from Callum. I'm glad in a way, but I thought he may have tried to contact me at work after reading my book. Maybe he never got it. Perhaps it's still on the floor, maybe his kids got to it first, or it got lost and slid under the small shoe cabinet. What if someone else picked it up and is reading it? What if he received it and read it and thinks I'm a total idiot? Or worse, a bitch for writing all our personal memories down. I have to focus on the first option; surely he would have replied by now had he read it.

Kelly hands me a coffee. "I saw Callum at the supermarket the other day."

The mention of his name still makes my breath quicken. "How is he?"

She sits down at her desk. "He's doing well in his new job in the city. It's a bigger marketing company than here, but he says he's enjoying the challenge."

I nod along and smile. I'm glad he's doing okay. "Did he ask about me?" I hold my breath.

"He asked if you were happy." Kelly rubs my shoulder and tilts her head, giving me a sympathetic smile.

My voice is flat and quiet. "Did you tell him I am?"

"Yes, but I'm not sure you are." She pulls out a pack of tissues from her bag and hands them to me.

I dab the moisture away from the corners of my eyes before it ruins my makeup and make a mental note that I still need to invest in some waterproof mascara. "Did he say anything else?"

"He said, *'I broke her heart before, and I fucked up a second time.'* What happened between the two of you?"

I sigh. "It doesn't matter now. Did he say anything about a book?"

"What book?"

"Nothing, it doesn't matter."

The tears are running down my cheek. I wish I'd never posted that bloody book. What good can come of this? Other than more suffering for us both. I wanted him to read the book, to know just how much I love him. I never really told him how much I cared, and I wanted to thank him for giving me space and not wanting to ruin my marriage. Well, before I knew the truth, that he was plotting on ruining my marriage all along.

I'm tied to him with an invisible string. I always have been, even for the last twenty years. Wherever he is in the world, my heart is pulled to the memory of him. It swells with love, but the weight crushes my lungs. You never know the value of a moment until it becomes a memory. He has stitched my heart back together, only to create a fresh wound that's raw and tender.

I carry on with my so-called happy marriage and mundane routine, where the most exciting thing that happens in a week is my son scoring a goal at the school's football tournament, or my daughter gets picked for the lead role in the Easter play. I try to forget about everything and move on with my life.

It's spring now and everything seems so much brighter. Each day gets a little easier. Even though I'm no longer working with Cal, he's still on my mind. I often wonder if he still thinks about me. I still care for Justin, and I'm trying to rekindle our relationship. A week in Greece during the Easter break has been a welcome change. The sun, sand, and sex on the odd night the kids actually went to sleep was just what I needed. I think Justin needed it too; we've been distant for so long.

I walk into work Monday morning feeling refreshed. The delicious smell of baked goods fills the air.

I sit at my desk and find a brown package addressed to me. "What's this?" I look at Kelly, who is chewing her morning croissant.

She swallows and wipes her mouth. "Cal dropped it off for you last week while you were on holiday."

My mouth opens and my eyes go wide. "What? He was here?" The smell of pastry now makes my stomach churn.

"He called last Friday. He wanted to leave it for you. I think he was relieved you weren't here, actually."

"How was he?" My heart rate speeds up and there's a dull ache in my chest.

She looks down and lets out her breath. "He looked awful, if I'm honest, Steph. He's obviously suffering as much as you are. I know you put on a smiling face every day, but I can see you're not the same person you were when he was around."

I slump down in my chair and hold the parcel. "Did he ask how I was?"

"Of course he did."

"What did you tell him?" I hug the parcel against my chest, hoping it will make me feel a little closer to him.

"I told him you're fine, and on holiday with your family." If only I was fine, I could perhaps carry on if everything was just fine.

"Is he still working in the city?"

"Yes, but it was odd how he was talking, almost as if he was saying goodbye, like he was going somewhere."

I sit up, broadening my eyes. "You don't think he…" My breathing speeds up. "How bad did he look or seem?"

"He looked tired. What are you thinking?" She pulls her perfectly pruned eyebrows together.

"You don't think he would…" I shake my head. "No, he wouldn't do that, would he? I mean, he has his girls to think about."

"Oh, I don't know. He was acting strange. I just got the impression he was going somewhere." Her eyes change from a sparkling topaz to a dull steel.

I study the package, but I don't want to open it in front of everyone. I know I won't be able to hold back tears, whatever it is. It looks bigger than my book. Is it the rest of our photos? This would be the final blow if he's sent my stuff back. I can't think straight.

Kelly stands. "I'll get you a drink." She brings me over one of my favourite Danish swirly pastries and a strong black coffee.

"Thank you."

"He also asked me to make sure you at least read it before you burn it or throw it away." She giggles.

Has he done me a book? "I won't throw it out." I smile, imagining him saying that, knowing how angry I was with him.

"The meeting's about to start in ten minutes."

I check my emails and prepare myself for the briefing, munching on my pastry. Since I stopped going to my slimming group, my mind is much lighter. The taste of the marmalade reminds me of my first day here, when I looked up to see Cal standing in front of me, the beautiful soul that I'd lost.

I place the package in my drawer along with my bag and head for the meeting. A new project; a holiday company wanting to revamp their image, new vehicle graphics, logo, brochure and website. This sounds like an excellent project to take my mind off everything. At lunchtime, everyone heads out to the pub, but I stay behind to open my package alone.

I pull out the parcel and carefully untie the string wrapped around the brown paper, tearing at the corners where it's taped down. It's his old notebook. I remember the smell of the brown leather cover, now worn and peeling at the corners. Cal was always making notes inside, but he would never show me, not that I asked to look. I assumed it was to do with his work. I open the first page to find a loose, crisp white piece of paper with his handwriting on it.

My Stephanie,

Sorry it's taken me a while to get back to you, baby. I didn't know how to respond and I've spent the last few months trying to move on, but I can't. Forgetting you isn't an option for me. Even if I wanted to, I couldn't.

I went through every emotion possible as I read page after page of your book; even took the day off work, as I stayed up all night reading. I loved reading how you felt about me, back then and even now. It brought me to my knees at how much I hurt you. It was hard to relive it through your eyes, especially knowing I hurt you again. I hope you can forgive me one day.

You should publish your book with a few tweaks here and there. You make me sound hotter than I am, and in ways I don't deserve. I find it hard to believe that you saw me like this, but I see you the same way. You're perfect to me, mind, body, and soul. If I wasn't such a dick, I would have never let you go, not the first time, not now, not ever. I dug out this old journal and read all the things I wrote about you, and I want you to have it. I've added a bit at the back recently, thinking you could add it to your book if you decide to publish it. At least we will have our memories together, even if we're not.

I wish I could express to you in person how sorry I am. If you'd let me, I'd spend the rest of my life making it up to you. You're everything to me. You're my warmth on cold days, my stars on dark nights. The memory of you sustains me. I've relived every memory of ours repeatedly, each one tattooed on my mind. Remember how special you are to me, will you? You were my world back then and you are still today and always. I hope this journal will help you see how much you mean to me. It's the happy memories that will carry us through the challenging times, and remind us that our love was important and worthwhile. Focus on our good times and not the bad, please? Even if you hate me now, I know you loved me once. The love we shared is rare. It doesn't happen with just anybody—it's you and me.

My heart belongs to you, Steph. I miss you. I understand this is where we're meant to be right now—apart—my arms empty, my heart sad. Don't feel guilty; there are no expectations, only love. You don't need to fix me. I'm used to being this way. I've already missed your touch for too long; your full lips that I kiss in my dreams, your warm body pressed against mine, your fingers tracing the tattoos on my stomach, and your smile. Without your smile to brighten my day, everything seems dull, like the world has turned to grey and the only colour are my girls and the memory of you. The luminescent vision of you in my mind, with your shimmering emerald eyes and your dark auburn hair, and you're happy. Be happy, Steph. I can go on knowing you're happy, even if it's not with me.

Know that I love you with every breath and every beat of my heart. I will love you till my dying day and maybe in another life, if we're lucky enough to meet, and I'm not such a fuck-up, we will have it all.

Forever Yours,
Cal

I hold his letter close to my heart and let the tears flow down my puffy cheeks. I'm not even sure how long I've been crying. My throat is scratchy. I pull a tissue from my drawer and wipe my nose. What makes it worse is that I still love him. I hate to love him, but I do all the same. I just don't know if I can forgive him for what he did. My tears drip from my swollen lips. I've learnt that you don't stop loving someone just because you're not together. Just like you don't stop loving your first child because you have a second. The love just keeps coming.

I look back at the journal and study its discoloured cream pages. The first entry starts the year we got together at university.

To be continued...

Enjoyed the book?

The second installment in The Temptation Series,
Forever Mine, is available now.

Would you like to see what their college years were like?
Forever Young is a prequel to The Temptation Series

Want more Cal and Steph? Join my newsletter for
free snippets and Cal's journal
https://sendfox.com/anniecharme

Other Works

When My Ship Comes In
A Naughty Nautical Romance
Join Zac and Lizzie for a cruise around the Hawaiian Islands

www.anniecharme.com

ACKNOWLEDGEMENTS

My husband, you may not have been my first love, but you will always be my last. Thank you for being my Cal and loving me unconditionally, making me feel beautiful regardless of my dress size. Thank you for supporting me with my dream of being an author and listening to all my crazy story ideas. Without your love, support and being a wonderful father to our children, I wouldn't have the time to write.

My wonderful, loving parents, you are always there to offer help and advice. You taught me to believe in myself and gave me the confidence to follow my heart. Thank you for letting me dream.

I am so lucky to have an amazing mother-in-law that shares my passion of books. I am eternally grateful for your love and encouragement.

My friends, your support has been amazing. Even though sometimes you have laughed and joked about my steamy scenes, you always put a smile on my face.

To all the ladies in the After Fandom Facebook group, you

were the ones that set this whole book idea going. You have supported my work and I thank you all for your love. Some of you were my first online readers. Without you pestering me for more chapters, I may never have finished this book. It was your encouragement each week that kept me going, and I thank each one of you for pushing me. I know some of you are still waiting for book 2 and don't worry – it's coming.

To my beta readers, I have made friends for life swapping stories with you, and I want to thank each one of you that read and critiqued my work. Your critique and comments helped shape this story and make it what it is today, as well as your encouragement and knowledge. I've come a long way since I started this dream and hopefully I can show more than tell and I have not made any more comma splices.

To my ARC readers, thank you from the bottom of my heart for taking the time to read my work. I am grateful to all of you that read and reviewed my debut novel.

To my wonderful Yorkshire Lasses… Kat, thank you for paving the way so that we can follow in your footsteps, and for all your help and advice. Without you, this process would have been so much harder. Jo, my number one fan, you are always on hand to boost my confidence and make me smile. Michelle, my other cheerleader, your injection of body positivity was just what myself and my book needed. Between the three of you, your humour makes me laugh out loud each day. Everyone needs a group of friends like you. Special thank you to Michelle Carter and Joanne Nundy for your eyes on this. Not only did you read this book in its early stages, but you took the time to proofread the final version.

My Clitique group—yes, you've read it right—my amazing ladies across the pond. When I first signed up to be part of a romance writer group, I didn't know what to expect, but thought I would give it a whirl. Our video chats brighten my week and I've learned so much from you (in so many ways haha). Without your extensive critique of these chapters, my book wouldn't be half what it is today—literally. Your ideas have helped expand and embellish each scene and hopefully only made this story better. Know there is a little piece of all of you inside this book. Special thanks go to Bonnie and Jennifer for your ideas and support. Brecklyn and Amie for your editing skills. Melissa for your help and advice. And last but not least, Enid for your amazing formatting skills and knowledge on all things publishing, you have helped me in so many ways, I can't thank you enough.

The best part of writing is making new friends along the way. I've found kindred spirits in every one of you and I hope we will still enjoy our chats and each others' work in years to come.

Annie Charme lives in the heart of England with her husband,
two children and a randy dog.
She is a graphic artist by day and author by night.
When she isn't working, you will find her enjoying time with
her family in the English countryside or curled up on the sofa
with a coffee, blanket, dog and a steamy book.

Being an avid reader of romance novels, Annie feels that the
larger woman is not represented enough, and books about
plus size women are very few and far between. This is
something that sparked her passion for writing.

Being plus size, she knows all too well how it feels to grow up
being the funny one and never the sexy one. She wanted to
write a book that would not only pull at your heartstrings but
make the average woman feel good about themselves.
Everyone deserves to be loved regardless of dress size and she
hopes to empower women through her writing, even if it's just
in the bedroom.